Eva Weaver is a writer, art therapist, coach and performance artist. She moved to Britain from Germany in 1995 and lives in Brighton. Like many Germans, she has been haunted by the events of the Second World War, which inspired her to write her first novel, *The Puppet Boy of Warsaw*. It has now been published in thirteen countries.

Eva's second novel, *The Eye of the Reindeer*, was inspired by journeys to Scandinavia, encounters with the Sami people and her work as an art therapist over many years in mental health services in the UK. Alongside her writing, Eva runs her own coaching practice.

www.evaweaver.com

Also by Eva Weaver

The Puppet Boy of Warsaw

THE EYE
of the
REINDEER

Eva Weaver

WEIDENFELD & NICOLSON

A W&N PAPERBACK

First published in Great Britain in 2016
by Weidenfeld & Nicolson
This paperback edition published in 2017
by Weidenfeld & Nicolson
an imprint of the Orion Publishing Group Ltd
Carmelite House, 50 Victoria Embankment
London EC4Y 0DZ
An Hachette UK Company

1 3 5 7 9 10 8 6 4 2

A CIP catalogue record for this book is
available from the British Library.

ISBN (Mass Market Paperback) 978 1 78022 292 9
ISBN (eBook) 978 0 297 86832 3

Printed in Great Britain by Clays Ltd, St Ives plc

www.orionbooks.co.uk

To all those incarcerated in asylums then and now
for the Sami people of Sápmi,
and for my mother Erika Hausladen-Franz, 1931–2014.
May your souls be free and your spirits soar.

'A blue-throat twitters in the spring sun at the life giver, and a Sami future.'

—Nils-Aslak Valkeapää

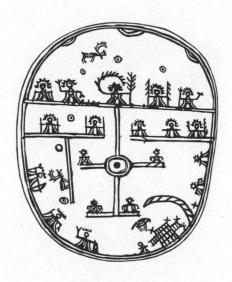

PROLOGUE

This time the men would seize the sacred drum and burn it, Johann could feel it in his bones. He clenched his fists – had the priests not brought their people enough misery? Year after year the churchmen had forced the Sami to abandon their faith, succumb to the bleeding man on the cross and hand over their sacred drums. Many had given in, or at least pretended to, but the disobedient ones were flogged against the courthouse wall, forced to run the gauntlet, or worse, were burnt at the stake together with their drums.

'Open the door!' a voice bellowed. Johann flinched as a heavy hand pounded against the door.

'Stay back, Hilkka,' he commanded his daughter, 'don't say a word, just keep working on the carving.' Johann opened the door of his turf hut, pipe in hand.

'Johann Laiti?' the priest demanded, gripping a wooden cross in front of his chest. He was surrounded by eight grim-faced men. 'We've reason to believe that you are harbouring instruments of the devil in your home. I will ask you one last time to join the Christian faith and hand over those vile objects.' The fierceness of the pastor's anger hit Johann like a blow.

'I harbour nothing but my daughter, Hilkka. As for your faith, I thank you, but I prefer not to belong to any.'

'Liar,' one of the men next to the pastor hissed. 'I heard his drum just a week ago. It's his grandfather's. He must still have it.'

The pastor, towering a head above Johann, stepped so close Johann could smell his stale sweat.

'You're telling me that this honest man from my congregation is lying? He heard your drum, Johann!'

'He might have mistaken the beating of his own heart for the devil's, for all I know.'

'How dare you speak like this about an honest Christian!' the pastor spat, lifting the wooden cross. 'The time of devil worship is over. Give us your drum or we will turn over your hut.'

'Go ahead and search my humble home. I've nothing to hide.'

The men filled the room with their thick presence, sniffing like hungry wolves.

'And who have we here?' the pastor sneered, bending over Hilkka's shoulder.

'You should come to church, rather than spend your time carving knife handles. This is not girl's work.'

Hilkka said nothing. The men stumbled around the hut, examining the fireplace, looking under pots, pulling up reindeer furs and the birch branches that covered the ground.

'That we can't find the drum doesn't mean you are telling the truth, but I am willing to let it go for today.' The pastor's voice had softened. 'It'll be good to see you and Hilkka on Sunday and welcome you into our congregation. I know the grip of the devil is strong and the old gods die slowly, but we can help you.'

Johann looked away and the pastor's face darkened again.

'As you wish, Johann, but rest assured: I will be keeping an eye on you and if I hear another word about the drum, I will not let the matter rest. Satan worship must be punished severely.' He shot Johann a fierce look then gestured to the men.

Johann watched as the group disappeared into the late-summer afternoon until they were no more than dots in the distance . . . He shivered – never before had he come so close to losing his precious drum. He slipped the small oval out from under his cloak.

His heart cramped as he thought of all the sacred drums that had passed from generation to generation, from one *noaidi* shaman to another, only to be destroyed. Even as a child Johann had known that the drums could open a pathway to other worlds and that they were the source of all sacred knowledge, healing and help. Whenever he had caught a glimpse of his grandfather's drum, his heart sang; the mesmerising figures – animals, people, tents, reindeer – drawn with deep red alder sap on the reindeer hide seemed to dance whenever his grandfather beat out a rhythm with his carved little hammer. Sometimes a brass ring was bounced on the drum and they marvelled over the path the ring took across the skin and the spot where it fell once the drumming had stopped.

Johann was eight when the men took his grandfather, the *noaidi* of the *siida* community. The old man had clutched the drum to his chest, but three of them had pushed him to the ground, one ripping the drum from his hands, another tossing it into the blazing fire where it burst with a loud bang. Grandfather had let out a scream and collapsed into the hostile arms of the churchmen who then dragged him away. With the destruction of his drum, his heart had broken too.

When Grandfather finally returned a week later, he was a changed man: grey-faced and drawn, he walked with a limp, hardly talked and drank alcohol whenever he got hold of any. One day he took Johann aside.

'I will tell you a secret, my boy. I've hidden one last drum from the churchmen. I want you to be its keeper.' Johann's heart had pounded as his grandfather entrusted the precious drum to him together with its history, stories and songs. Ever since then, Johann had kept the drum hidden: each time they migrated with the reindeer up the mountains in spring, on the summer pastures and in the *lavvu* tent during the winters spent in the forest. But now the drum was under threat once again.

'The drum is not safe here any more, I need to hide it in the mountains,' Johann said and Hilkka looked up, her eyes large and dark as polished wood.

'Can I come with you?'

Johann saw the same pain in her eyes as he felt in his soul; he placed his large hand on his daughter's shoulder. She would be thirteen in a few weeks.

'Of course you can. We'll beat the drum one more time up on the mountain and I will teach you the sacred *yoik* songs.' He squeezed her shoulder. A smile spread across Hilkka's face and Johann knew he had decided well – his daughter would carry the knowledge of the drum forward for the generations to come.

PART 1

DARK NIGHT OF THE SOUL

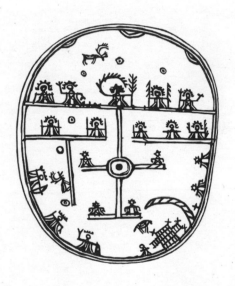

1

Nauvo, southern Finland, summer 1913

The shards of bright June sunlight glistened on the dark waters of the archipelago. Ritva sheltered her eyes as the nurse led her from the carriage down a narrow path towards the shore; after months in hospital, such brilliance hurt and even a short walk left her breathless.

'Where are they taking me, Alma?' Ritva said, grabbing the nurse's hand. The nurse was carrying Ritva's little red suitcase. She had always been kind and her starched white uniform and assured demeanour exuded a calm that Ritva hoped would help keep her rising terror at bay. The nurse bit her lip, but when Ritva looked again, she was smiling.

'To Seili, my dear, or Själö as they call it in Swedish. They can look after you better there. Don't fret, it'll be all right.'

Ritva's heart sank. She had heard Father mention Seili once to the doctor, and in the hospital in Helsinki the island's name had hovered over the patients like a threat. 'They'll send you to Seili if you don't stop blubbering!' her neighbour had hissed more than once. Seili – once a leper colony, now an asylum for hopeless cases; such had been the rumours. She shuddered. To be sent to Seili, the doctors must have declared her not only mad, but incurable . . . Ritva clutched the nurse's arm.

'It's for the best, dear.'

What had she done to deserve this? Suddenly Ritva felt very

cold and alone; the thought of her little sister left behind in the big house, on her own with Father and the housekeeper, choked her, but bromide had sedated her spirit and she craved the sleep it brought. Yet, as she looked ahead, she could not help but be moved by the still, dark waters of the Baltic, and the play of the sun across its luminous surface. She imagined the water stretching westwards for miles, island after small island, all the way to the Åland Islands, then across the gulf to Sweden. She was only two hours from Turku and their village, and had often come to this place on weekends with Mother and Father and little Fredo. How jealous she had been of her younger brother and the attention her mother had paid him. Now nothing seemed as precious as the memory of those sweet days: her family all together under a high summer sun, Mother smiling, Fredo giggling as he ventured his first steps, Father strolling along the shore holding Ritva's hand, telling her the names of flowers, skipping stones across the water . . .

A small boat lay moored at the end of the quay. Ritva noticed the man in charge of it stowing away boxes and sacks of provisions. As he stood up and met her eyes, his face clouded over. Did she look that awful? Maybe he had expected an older woman, not a sixteen-year-old girl? Maybe her hair looked unkempt? She had not seen herself in a mirror for months . . .

By the time she reached the boat, the boatman had covered his expression with a mask of friendliness. On the quay stood another man wearing a similar uniform to the nurse's, only less crisp, its former whiteness turned a shabby grey. He was whistling, staring out at the water as he tapped his foot, a shock of bright blond hair showing under his cap. When the nurse arrived with Ritva, he turned, revealing an angular, sunburnt face and watery grey eyes that held no expression. He did not smile. He acknowledged the nurse, stepped forward and took Ritva's arm, his grip so forceful she gasped. She tried to shake him off, but his hand tightened and he laughed.

'Who've we got here, then? A wild young mare? Ah, we'll see

8

to that. Hush now, young lady, we've got a nice boat ride ahead of us and a fine day for it.'

He nodded at the nurse.

'Thank you for your help, nurse.' The attendant's words were firm and final. The nurse stood rigid, her arms pressed against her skirt.

'I am very happy to accompany Ritva and help her settle in on Seili.'

'That is not necessary, thank you. She'll soon get used to life on our beautiful island.'

'But Dr Heskin asked . . .'

'I said it's fine, nurse,' he cut her off. 'Our doctor will send a report when he has seen her.'

Ritva flinched at the sharpness in his voice. What would he be like once they were alone? Nurse Alma slowly handed the suitcase to the boatman and a thick envelope to the attendant. Then she looked straight at Ritva, trying to smile, but her eyes brimmed with tears and her hand trembled.

'Goodbye dear, God bless you.' She moved as if to embrace Ritva, then, remembering the protocol, she turned away. The attendant ushered Ritva towards the boat.

'A big step now, my lamb,' he said, directing her onto the small vessel. It swayed as she stepped aboard.

'You best sit here.' He pointed to the end of the boat that was bolstered with cushions; it would almost have looked inviting had it not been for everything else. Ritva clambered across boxes and curled-up ropes to the seat. When her eyes found Alma again, the nurse was already walking back towards the carriage. She did not turn around.

The boatman rowed the vessel out onto the glistening water. He had not said a word, and so it would be for the rest of the journey. Maybe he had been told not to talk to her.

Ritva leaned over the side of the boat and let her hand glide though the dark green water. All her senses seemed heightened after being confined for so many months in hospital: the sound of the waves lapping against the boat, the water cooling her wrists, the bright sun caressing her pale skin . . . How she had missed being outside, feeling the sun, touching the world like this. She watched the boatman row with big, strong movements, each stroke taking them further away from the shore. What would it be like in this new hospital? Would she once again be locked inside all the time? Her stomach clenched at the thought.

The attendant lit a pipe. Ritva tried not to cough as smoke drifted into her face and tickled her throat. She did not want anything to do with this brute. She looked for her suitcase, found its red amongst the boxes of provisions stowed in the bow. A stack of freshly cut timber filled the end of the boat, exuding a strong smell of resin that reminded her of outings with Father, hunting for lingonberries and mushrooms in the late-summer forest. She caught the boatman's eye and addressed him directly.

'Are you going to build something on the island with that wood?'

The man's face paled and he looked away.

'Leave him alone, that's none of your business, girl,' the attendant hissed and threw her a cold look. Then his voice softened.

'If you're nice and strong we won't need that wood for a long time, will we?' He winked at the boatman who turned away. 'It all depends on you. Now shut up and enjoy the journey.'

Ritva quivered. What did he mean?

As she sat wondering a loon cut across the sky. The scenery should have been idyllic, but foreboding sat on her chest like an iron weight. If only this were an outing and not a journey taking her further and further away from her home, her freedom . . .

The boatman set the sails and, pushed on by a gentle breeze, the small vessel cut its way through the archipelago, passing islands and small islets, the granite rocks of the shores sprawling along the water's edge like the coloured bellies of sea creatures. Ritva gazed out at the horizon – there were hundreds of islands, stretching as far as she could see.

Suddenly a shimmering shape appeared on the edge of her

vision; a long, silver-grey body, swimming towards a barren islet, then pushing itself up onto a rock. A grey seal. Mother had often told her the tale of Sealskin: a precious skin stolen from a girl, who, without it, had become lost between sea and land. Would the people in the asylum steal her skin too, her freedom, her life? Would she be forever trapped on this island?

'Here it is,' the attendant said and grinned, pointing ahead.

Seili rose out of the water like the back of a giant whale. It looked no different to any of the islands they had passed – soft waves lapped against the grey and pink granite boulders on its shores, washed smooth by time and tide. It seemed impossible that anything could grow here, but a sparse colony of birches and pine trees had taken root further up on elevated ground. Rows of tall golden reeds flanked the small harbour like a golden curtain, contrasting with the brilliant blue water.

Ritva turned and searched for the seal – it was still resting on the islet, a mere dot now. As the boat steered towards the landing, Ritva prayed the lone seal on the barren rock was not some kind of omen for terrible things to come.

The boatman threw the rope ashore and jumped onto the quay, followed by the attendant. He offered Ritva his arm; she hesitated, then took it and stepped off the boat. Standing on the quay she felt herself swaying. A tall man in shabby trousers and a short-sleeved shirt appeared and began to unload the boxes and planks, sweat streaming from his sunburnt face. Ignoring Ritva, he gave the attendant a short nod, then piled the planks onto his shoulders and carried them up a grassy path towards a small workshop.

Ritva searched for her suitcase, the last tangible connection to the world she had left behind. The attendant caught her gaze, pulled the small case out from between a stack of boxes, and handed it to her.

'Here, my poppet.' A brief moment of relief flooded Ritva as she gripped the handle, but then the man seized her arm.

'Let's go, it isn't far.'

11

Ritva looked back at the boatman, but he avoided her gaze. How many women had he ferried to this island, year in, year out? She pinched the skin on her hand between her thumb and finger, a relief she had learned to apply in the long months in hospital. As Ritva peered over the smooth mirror of the Baltic, a large black fish leapt out of the water leaving, just for a moment, a silver arch of glittering pearls in the air. Then it was gone. Ritva's eyes stayed fixed to the spot where the fish had disappeared. Once she had been this free; now she was trapped.

A sandy path led up across some grassland, studded with early summer flowers. Everything was bursting with green: saplings and buds that soon would explode into fireworks of yellow and blue. Ritva ached to walk on the soft grass – how long since her feet had touched the bare earth, not the cold corridors of a hospital? There were few sounds on the island, the silence only disrupted by the wind's soft rustle through the trees and the chatter of birds: blackbirds, thrushes, finches and the occasional seagull. She took a deep breath, letting herself be comforted for a moment by nature's display – maybe there was still hope as long as there were birds, soft grass and sun shining on her face.

Clutching her suitcase, Ritva walked next to the attendant as they made their way up the hill. When she glanced back, the boatman had already set sail for Nauvo. The walk took no more than ten minutes from the small harbour – up a winding path, passing only two landmarks: a rust-red farm building and a grand whitewashed villa surrounded by a large garden.

'The superintendent lives there,' the attendant said. 'It's the perfect spot for keeping an eye on his charges.' Ritva imagined the superintendent sitting at his polished desk, looking through a brass spyglass at his asylum like a captain scanning the sea for bad weather.

'Are you ready?' the attendant said, smirking at Ritva.

'For what?'

He pointed further up the path. As Ritva raised her eyes, the asylum came into view. She stopped in her tracks. Elevated on a slight mound, the imposing building sat large and angular with rows of tiny windows that reflected the afternoon light. Maybe it was the ochre-coloured facade or the size that reminded her of a seminary she had once visited in Turku. The building looked alien, as if the architect had intended it to stand alongside grand town houses but instead it had been whisked away by a giant and dropped here, surrounded only by nature. The impressive facade was surely meant to fool new arrivals, but how could the sun shine through those small, barred windows? Ritva shuddered – it would be cold and dark inside . . .

She gazed back down at the shore – did the island stretch for miles or could one circle it in an hour? A strong impulse to bolt stirred in her, then left her like a tired breath. Trying to flee would be futile: on Seili she would not only be a captive of the hospital, and the superintendent's ever-vigilant eye, but also of the island itself.

As they neared the building, Ritva noticed a group of women behind a white wooden fence. Wearing long skirts with identical striped aprons, heads covered with straw hats or scarves, they attended to small plots, digging and weeding with hoes, spades and trowels. Ritva could make out dark leafy spinach and runner beans, even some yellow flowers growing in the patches. Some women continued to work, as if in a trance, others stopped and looked up at the new arrival. One woman smiled at Ritva, revealing her few remaining teeth – she could not have been older than thirty – another, short and stocky with milky grey eyes, giggled and waved wildly. Ritva looked away. The thought that soon she would be incarcerated amongst those women made her stomach heave.

'Come along now, stop gawking,' the attendant said and ushered her towards the building. Tall white columns flanked the entrance on either side, giving it the appearance of a kind of temple, only less grand. Ritva looked up at a triangular stone relief set above the entrance. Once she stepped across the threshold, life as she knew it would disappear.

One of the women gardening was Martta; she stood taller than the others with long, tanned arms. She had noticed a flash of red from under her straw hat – a small, crimson suitcase and a pale hand, gripping its handle: the new admission, walking next to Petta. Martta sighed – she had witnessed too many such processions, and never once seen a woman being ushered the other way, back to the harbour. The new girl looked as if she had not been outdoors all spring. She was pale with near-colourless lips and there were dark rings under her eyes; only her long, chestnut hair carried some shine. She seemed forlorn, and did not meet Martta's eyes, walking hunched over as if an invisible weight were pressing on her shoulders. Even without fully seeing her face, Martta sensed that the girl had already left her youth behind. Had her childhood crumpled under the burden of responsibility, or had it slipped from her gently like a scarf in the wind? No, Martta was sure that this girl's childhood, like her own, had been stripped from her with one violent gesture.

Martta wiped the sweat from her forehead and continued to rake her vegetable patch. It had been two years since she had been sent to Seili. Nearly as young then as the new arrival but already deemed dangerous, she had been sedated and bundled into a coat, arms crossed at the front, a scarf wrapped around her chest as a makeshift restraint. Propped up between Petta and Nurse Katja, she had stumbled up the path from the harbour, kicking at shins and groins to no avail. Martta tried to still the memories that buzzed around her head like a swarm of mosquitoes – there was nothing she could do for the new girl; she would have to find her own way in this place, just as Martta had done.

2

The attendant took the three steps in one, pulled at the entrance door and held it open for Ritva. She hesitated, then stepped across the threshold.

It was chilly inside and while the warm summer day brought the colours alive outside, in here the whitewashed walls and linoleum floor presented a bleak picture. Where she had expected a cackle of voices and shouting, only deep silence greeted her. The attendant ushered her into a small office. A rotund woman in a white nurse's uniform sat behind a cluttered desk. She looked up at the new arrival, revealing a pale, plain face with a small nose and tight lips. A mole the size of a small fingernail sat at the bottom of her left cheek. For a split second the woman flinched, her eyes wide as if she had seen a ghost; then her mouth morphed into a thin smile. Ritva noticed an enormous bunch of keys of different sizes attached to her right hip. She forced her gaze away from the keys to look at the woman.

'Welcome, my dear. You must be Ritva. I am the matron of this humble place. You'll get plenty of rest here on Seili; it's not luxurious but it is quiet and we are pretty much self-sufficient. We even catch our own fish, don't we?' She laughed, a brief hacking sound, then winked at the attendant.

'And you have met Petta, our only male attendant and the caretaker here. We have female nurses but sometimes it is handy to have a man around. Of course, on matters of administration our superintendent oversees everything. Has your journey been pleasant?' She looked from Ritva to Petta and back.

'She's been quite a lamb, haven't you?' The attendant said before Ritva could answer, pinching her cheek. Ritva shuddered and stepped back – how dare he touch her like that! Petta laughed and handed a thick envelope to the matron.

'These are most of her doctor's notes from Turku and Helsinki. More to follow shortly.'

'Thank you.' The matron placed the envelope on the desk.

Ritva stared at the brown envelope with its neat handwriting, addressing the letter to the doctor of the 'Seili Asylum for Women'. What had they written about her, she wondered. The doctors who had examined her in Helsinki had used strange words when talking to each other: 'dementia praecox, quite possibly,' one had mumbled, forehead frowning. 'Oh, I disagree, it surely is melancholia or even mania,' another judged. Most often 'hysteria' was mentioned, a word that seemed to arouse much excitement in the doctors, but one that no one ever explained to her, except to say that something was wrong with her nerves and her womb.

'Doctor Olafson will have a look at you on his next visit. He comes once a month, but I'm afraid he was just here two days ago. He's a good man; well, maybe a bit too kind . . .'

The matron's grey eyes moved from Ritva's face down to her dress, her shoes, then back.

'I hear you've been a good girl with only a few outbursts in the hospital? That is very favourable, my dear. I hope it stays that way.'

Ritva remembered the first weeks well, the pleading and crying, the kicking even, but soon enough her fighting spirit had been damped down by the bromide.

'Now, let's have a look at your case. You won't have need of much here, we'll provide you with everything.' The matron stretched out her hand to receive Ritva's suitcase. For a moment Ritva gripped it tightly, then released it.

'Good girl.' The matron placed the case on the table and opened the little locks; the lid sprang open with a click.

'So, what have we got here then?'

Ritva tried to peep over the lid into her case – the cornflower-blue summer dress Mother had made for her; the little mirror with shells, a birthday gift from Elke . . . would she be allowed to keep them? She remembered the day Mother had surprised her with the dress; Ritva had woken early to find it spread out on her bed as if it had always belonged to her. It would be a bit tight now, but it lifted her spirits just to see it.

'Ah, you wouldn't want this,' the matron said, holding up the dress. 'There's no need for fancy clothes here. We see that each person has enough but doesn't invite the envy of others.'

'Please, Matron, let me keep it, my mother made it for me.' Ritva's voice was shrill. The matron threw her a fierce look.

'So, you can talk, I see. But I wasn't asking a question. I've told you, you won't need it.' She folded the dress and put it to one side. 'Now this could be helpful,' she said and fished out a brush and comb, 'but this,' she pointed at the little hand mirror, 'will only distract you.' She placed the mirror on top of the blue dress. Ritva's pulse was racing. She wanted to scream at the matron, grab her things and run, but instead she stood rigid, clenching her teeth, sweat gathering in her armpits.

'And this, my dear, is surely most detrimental to your sensitive nerves and your overstretched imagination.' The matron pulled out the thick volume of Andersen tales, and held it out in front of her as if it were a poisonous snake. Seeing the anguish on Ritva's face, her voice softened.

'Don't worry, dear, we'll keep the book for you. And you never know, there might come a time when you're allowed to read it again.'

Why could she not at least keep her treasured book? Mother had read her all the tales when she was young and, when Mother got ill, Ritva had spent many nights poring over the book with its beautiful pictures or reading it aloud to Elke. Ritva held on to the table with both hands as dizziness overcame her. She did not want to faint or weep in front of this woman, but she could feel the panic rising in her.

And then she heard it: a muffled scream as if from far away, yet she was sure it had come from within the building, or maybe another part of the building.

'What was that?' The question tumbled out of her mouth before she could stop it.

'What, my dear? I didn't hear anything.' The matron turned to Petta. 'Did you?'

'No, nothing.'

'But I heard it . . . like someone was . . .'

'Someone was what? Don't fret, dear, let me show you to your room. Your nerves are clearly still on edge.' The matron started to move out from behind the desk.

'But I'm sure I heard something.'

'It's just the wind, dear, it makes queer noises sometimes. Now hurry along, we don't have all day.' She handed Ritva the brush and comb and gestured for her to follow. Ritva didn't dare refuse – her instincts told her that the matron's friendly attitude could turn in seconds to wrath. As she walked down the corridor behind the matron, Ritva noticed heavy wooden doors standing open on both sides, like cells in a prison. She had an eerie sense that the walls were not solid but malleable and could move in on her at any moment. She had arrived on an island of stranded souls and the trap was about to shut.

She clutched her brush and comb as they entered a large day-room filled with murmuring like a beehive. About thirty women sat bent over looms, some at wooden tables, while others stitched and mended pieces from a mountain of tatty garments. Just as they had earlier in the garden, some women looked up and grinned or stared at Ritva, while others ignored her, gripping their needlework and humming to themselves. Despite the bright day outside, the windows were closed and the air reeked of old sweat and musty clothes. Ritva found it hard to breathe. Amongst the women sat two nurses, rotund as the matron, dressed in tidy white uniforms. Ritva noticed how thin and pale most of the women looked compared to these red-cheeked nurses who were chatting between themselves.

'We'll give you an apron like the other women, but otherwise everyone sees to their own clothing,' the matron said. 'We often get parcels from the congregation in Nauvo or even Turku. Now come along this way.'

The thought of wearing other people's clothes, maybe even from her old church community, filled Ritva with dread; what if she came across a neighbour's dress, a school friend's blouse . . . The matron held a door open that led into another long corridor, then approached one of the rooms on the left side with a crooked number 29 written on the heavy door. She pulled out her bunch of keys.

'Let me see.' She tried several keys until the door sprang open. Ritva held her breath. The room was not much bigger than the narrow iron bed that sat against the wall, leaving space only for a small commode and a wooden chair. A window, barred and set so high she would need to stand on a stool to peer out, let in a shaft of pale afternoon light.

'The toilets and the washroom are at the end of the corridor, and during the night you have a pot,' the matron said, grinning, and pointed at a white, chipped enamel pot underneath the bed.

'You lock us in at night?' Ritva felt sweat breaking out all over her body.

'But of course, dear, it's for your own good and safety.'

'What do you mean, my own good?'

'There are women you would not want to meet at night in the corridor, believe me. But you're asking far too many questions, Ritva. Now, come along.'

They moved back along the corridor, through the dayroom and down another corridor to the dining room, a bright space with large windows and rows of benches and chairs set for the next meal.

'Let me give you some towels.' The matron opened a cabinet and took out two grey towels – they might once have been white, but had been worn thin by years of use.

'You must be tired from the journey, why don't you rest and we'll see you later. You'll hear the bell. Make yourself at home.' The matron patted Ritva on her cheek. Ritva flinched but did not pull away.

'I can see you're a good girl. I don't think we'll have any problems, isn't that so, my petal? Anyway, welcome to Seili!' With this the matron left.

Ritva walked back to her cell, her body aching as if she hadn't slept for days – and maybe she hadn't? She couldn't remember. What had she done to deserve being put in such a place?

She pushed the wooden chair against the wall and clambered up onto it. Her window faced another building, painted in the same ochre – was this colour meant to make everyone feel calm, she wondered. Rows of barred windows stretched along the wall opposite and into another wing to the right, which enclosed a small courtyard. A few benches stood on neatly cut grass around an elder bush and a dark-brown fence, so high one could not see beyond it, closed off the yard – but from what? From a meadow, a forest, the sandy path leading back to the harbour?

A handful of women sat on the benches, absorbed in their needlework. One woman crawled on all fours, combing the grass with her fingers, searching for something; another woman wearing a white cap walked sideways like a crab around the yard, her back pressed against the walls, mumbling and giggling to herself. A nurse with round black spectacles and chestnut hair in a neat bun sat on one bench, a book closed in her lap, like a mother hen presiding over her charges. The woman skirting the walls noticed Ritva behind the window and grimaced, exposing a mouthful of crooked teeth; then, within seconds her grin turned into a snarl. When Ritva did not respond, the woman stuck out her tongue. Ritva scrambled down from the chair. Was this her world now: a patch of grass, a square of sky hovering above a group of madwomen, and a cell she could barely turn around in that would be locked at night?

'Make yourself at home,' the matron's words echoed in her head. Home had been Mother brushing her hair before bed, thirty strokes until it shone; chasing butterflies in the garden with little Elke; their summer outings and picnics at the lakes; baking with Mother and making intricate straw stars for Christmas decorations . . . Never had anything felt further from home than this bleak cell. The thought of lying on the old, hard straw mattress repulsed her, but tiredness clawed at her and she curled up in a tight ball and closed her eyes. Despite her exhaustion, her mind was racing: who had lain here before her? Had someone died in this bed? Just how had she ended up here?

Shards of memory darted at her like flies: her bare room at home, the doctor's visit the day before she was taken away, the look on Father's face and before that, the nightmares . . .

When the pounding on the front door woke her, Ritva knew that she'd been having the same recurrent dream again – the nightmare always ended with a pounding, the heavy beating of her own heart. There were always men in her dream, and water, still and dark as oil. She would feel herself drowning, pulled down by weeds and the stems of water lilies, the men's spiteful laughter in her ears. She woke up gasping, and could hear Father's quiet mumbling and then another man's deep voice. She tried to anchor her gaze but nothing steadied her. Her room was as sparse as a monk's cell now that Father had stripped it bare, removing one piece after another when she admitted that everything had started speaking to her. First he took the painting of the ship, then the mirror, the little commode with the washing bowl and finally the small wooden cross. Still, the voices continued. Only the day before the doctor's visit, the wooden eye in the beam above her bed had warned her of things to come, bad things . . . She had tried to ignore the voice just as she had ignored the whisperings of the mirror, but the eye had carried itself forward into her nightmares.

A quiet knock that morning had startled her, then Father's voice: 'Ritva, the doctor has come to examine you, can you put on your robe please.'

She shivered but did as she was asked. The doctor had entered carrying his large brown leather bag like pride itself. He was smiling, but she didn't trust him. Wasn't he the same doctor who had taken her mother away, nearly four years ago? Her head hurt. No, she couldn't be sure it was the same man, but still he unnerved her. He took out a stethoscope from his bag, set it on her back. She gasped; it was cold as ice.

'Take a deep breath, dear.' His voice sounded too sweet and she had wanted to get away, but there was nothing she could do. Tears were spilling from her eyes.

'You see, Doctor, it's been like this for weeks,' Father said. 'She either weeps or talks to herself. She doesn't speak with me any more, just shakes her head or nods.' He gave a sigh. 'And that's on a good day. She only lets her little sister in. But it can't be good for Elke seeing Ritva like this – she's only eight. Ritva has slept better with the powders you gave her, but I still hear her shouting sometimes in the middle of the night. I don't know what to do.' He lowered his voice, but she could still hear every word.

'I think . . . she hears voices. I hear her mumbling and arguing when there's no one there. That's just how it started with her mother.'

The doctor had patted Ritva's shoulder as if she were a dog.

'We'll send you to Helsinki for some observation, my dear. We've a good physician there.' The doctor's voice was firm and Ritva shuddered at the finality of his words. He turned to her father.

'I'll come to collect her tomorrow. Make sure she is ready.'

She swallowed the sedative he gave her and slipped under the sheets, curling up tightly while her father ushered the doctor downstairs. She struggled against the wave of tiredness, scared of more nightmares, but her sleep that night was dreamless and empty.

When she opened her eyes again it was morning and she was looking straight into the face of the doctor. She sat up, clasping her blanket, her heart pounding. What would happen now? When she met her father's eyes for a brief moment, she could read nothing in them. She could hear Elke crying in the bedroom next door; Father must have locked her in.

'I've packed a few things for you in your little suitcase,' he had said, bending over her. 'You won't need much, darling, you'll be back soon. Won't she, Doctor?'

'Oh, certainly. We'll do our very best. But we must get on our way now. Please, Larson, tell the housekeeper to get the girl ready.'

Where were they taking her? Helsinki, the doctor had said, a hospital there. Would she disappear as her mother had done? Ritva slipped her mother's scarf that she kept under her pillow into her undershirt. Berta the housekeeper helped Ritva dress, her eyes brimming with tears.

'You might want to take your Andersen tales, they'll keep you company.' Berta placed the book in the small suitcase. 'Not that you will need it, you've got all those stories in here.' She put a hand on Ritva's heart and Ritva threw herself into the woman's arms, sobbing.

'Please, look after Elke, she's still little, promise me you will.'

'Of course, dear, and if you're good, they'll soon let you come back home. I'll pray for you, Ritva.'

'But I haven't done anything wrong! Why are they doing this to me?' Berta held her for a moment, kissed her forehead, then gently pushed her away.

'The doctor will be back in a minute.'

'I'm not going without saying goodbye to Elke.'

'Come on then, be quick,' Berta said and unlocked the door of Elke's room. The two sisters flew into each other's arms, Elke's words swallowed by their sobbing, until their father appeared and prised Elke's tiny fingers from Ritva's dress one by one. Elke had screamed and kicked, straining after her sister. Then the doctor

23

was there and he ushered Ritva downstairs, out of the house and into the waiting carriage. Ritva had not looked back; instead she had closed her eyes and allowed herself to be swallowed by the semi-darkness of the carriage.

Ritva woke, hearing a knock on the open cell door. For a moment she struggled to remember where she was. Had she fallen asleep or was this a daydream? Every detail she recalled was as vivid as if it had happened yesterday . . . She buried her face in the pillow and tears filled her eyes, loss opening up in her like an abyss.

'Can I come in?' A young woman, no older than twenty, appeared in the door frame. 'I'm Irina. You must be the new arrival?'

Ritva nodded but said nothing, wiping away her tears.

'You look like you've seen a ghost! What's your name, mute girl?' Irina smiled at Ritva with a face that seemed to have nothing to hide. She was slim with bright blonde hair and a healthy complexion and spoke with a strong local accent. Relieved to meet someone closer to her age, Ritva finally smiled too.

'I am Ritva. I . . . I must have fallen asleep.'

'Well then, welcome to Seili. It can be difficult in the beginning, but it's not so bad once you get used to it.'

Ritva stared at her.

'I don't think I will ever get used to this,' Ritva said, looking around the cell.

'We can be friends, if you like,' Irina chirped, her smile exposing two rows of excellent teeth.

'Thank you, I would like that,' Ritva said without conviction. Irina's syrupy voice and her offer of friendship had arrived too quickly – and yet how could she refuse such a gesture? In this godforsaken place, she would need all the friends she could find.

3

Ritva kept close to Irina for the rest of the day. Irina seemed to be on good terms with most of the women and staff – she showed Ritva around the dayroom and the kitchen, introducing her to the cook, a barrel-shaped woman called Alma with rosy cheeks, a white bonnet and a smile as wide as her face.

'She chats with everyone,' Irina whispered. 'And if no one's around she even talks to the soup. I'm not lying, I sneaked into the kitchen once and there she was, standing over the big pot, whispering away like a witch over her cauldron.'

Back when Mother was still around, this was the sort of thing that would have made Ritva giggle – now she couldn't even remember the last time she had laughed.

As the day passed, Ritva grew tired. She hoped that sleep would take her far away from this place. When the high-pitched bell rang at nine o'clock, the signal for all women to retire to their cells, she crouched on her bed, knees pulled up to her chest and listened as the nurses went from cell to cell, locking them with their heavy keys.

'Sweet dreams, dear, you did well today,' the nurse chirped, closing the heavy door and turning the key.

How could she have sweet dreams in a place as cold and inhospitable as the bottom of the sea? Suddenly Ritva panicked.

'Please don't lock me in!' Her throat, tight as a funnel, released only a hoarse whisper. Would she ever escape this place? Would she even wake up again?

Pale light shone in from the corridor beneath the door. Ritva searched for something to distract her, but there were no pictures on the walls, only a small vase stood on the commode, the few wilted flowers casting pale, spindly shadows against the wall. And what was that smell? Musty, like the cellar of her father's house in autumn after weeks of rain. The cell was as chilly and damp as a grave . . . Ritva struggled to calm her breathing, desperate to ward off the thought. But wasn't this what was happening: hadn't she been buried alive within these walls? Someone had thrown away the key, or rather strolled away, with a cheerful whistle on their lips, indifferent to her torment . . . How many unfortunate souls had slept on this mattress, had suffered and hoped to be released? Ritva shuddered as she remembered her neighbour in Helsinki whispering stories about Seili's grim past: the raging lunatics, secured to the bed with heavy iron chains, and before that the lepers, outcast and crippled with festering limbs, left to die on this island without the aid of any doctor. Lying in the semi-darkness, it was easy to conjure up those tormented souls – did they still haunt this place? Ritva had always enjoyed stories as a girl, but now the ghosts and monsters seemed all too real.

With a pang she thought of her mother – had she endured such a place? After the doctor had taken her away, Ritva was never allowed to visit her and no letter had arrived – Mother had disappeared without a trace like a boat taken in a storm. Was she even still alive? Ritva remembered the warmth of her mother's arms, her kind eyes, the stories she used to tell, the joy in her face as she bounced a giggling Fredo in her arms . . .

Little Fredo – a chill ran down Ritva's back. Was it her fault that he had died and Mother had fallen ill? Ritva's thoughts galloped like a spooked horse. But no, it was a fever that had taken her brother. She remembered the long weeks, her parents sitting at Fredo's bedside, his little face swollen and blotchy . . .

For months after Fredo's death Mother had spent hours locked in her bedroom, only joining Ritva and Father for evening meals. Sometimes she had let Ritva sit on her lap, and Ritva had soaked up those moments like the first spring sunshine. Ritva had tried everything to comfort her but her mother had remained absent, as if on the day they had buried Fredo a part of her had leapt into that dark hole after him. Then slowly Mother got better, and a year and a half after Fredo's death little Elke had arrived. All seemed to be well after that, but five years later things went wrong again; Ritva had woken one night to hear a loud argument. She could not make out what they were saying, only her father's hollering and Mother's sobbing, then silence. The next morning Mother had stayed in bed, and did not leave her room all day. Soon she only appeared at dinner, pale and puffy-eyed, picking at her food, staring ahead, her silence interrupted by nightly bursts of arguing.

One day she had called for Ritva, pulled her close and showered her with kisses.

'Promise me you'll look after yourself and your sister,' her hoarse voice had croaked.

'Why, of course I will . . .' Ritva nodded, bewildered, and her mother had sunk back on a pile of cushions.

That night Ritva had jolted awake to hear a mumbling outside her bedroom door, followed by a click, the turning of a key. She had shot out of bed and rattled the door. It was locked.

'Let me out!'

'It's fine, darling, I'm just making sure you and Elke are safe.'

'Mother, please open the door, we're fine.' But Ritva could hear the patter of her mother's feet, then her parents' bedroom door closing. She had lain awake until the morning and when finally the door had swung open, it was her father into whose arms she threw herself.

'Your mother needs rest, Ritva. Please don't worry, she'll be fine. We'll call the doctor tomorrow.'

After the doctor's visit, her mother had never tried to lock Ritva's bedroom door again. Her bedside table was covered with medicine bottles and powders, and four weeks later her mother had stopped eating and talking altogether. Ritva had watched in dismay as her mother wasted away in front of her eyes and one icy November morning in 1909 the doctor had appeared. Father stood on the landing, his face frozen in a mask of anguish, the confident Pastor Larson gone. Mother had floated down the stairs like the ghost she had become, but before the doctor could usher her out into the carriage, she had grabbed Ritva's sleeve.

'You must run away, dear!' she whispered, her hot breath on Ritva's ear. 'It's not safe here for you and Elke. I'm so sorry I can't help you. I love you so!' Then her large green eyes had clouded over and she had collapsed into the doctor's arms. Ritva stood as if she'd been slapped in the face. What did her mother mean that she was not safe? And where could she possibly run away to? Ritva was only twelve and had never even travelled beyond Turku. She had stumbled upstairs and pressed her face against the cold window, watching as the doctor bundled her sweet mother into the carriage. Tears ran down her cheeks as the window steamed up beneath her breath.

The following week her father had employed Berta Janson, a middle-aged widow from the neighbouring village, to run their motherless household. Berta was kind, but to Ritva and Elke she was a poor stand-in. Although she cooked well and did her best in every way, she rarely made them laugh when she read a story, her finger clumsily following each word on the page, and she didn't know a single story about the people of the North, as their mother had. Still, Berta tucked them in at night, kissing them on the forehead after prayers. Father mostly visited members of his congregation or sat hunched over his desk writing sermons, spending little time with his daughters so that the house was quieter than ever. Every few months a doctor's letter arrived, reporting on Mother's progress – the only words that still vouched for her existence. Ritva ached to visit her or at least write to her, but Father had demanded patience.

'She's getting better, my dear, but the doctor says she still needs as much quiet as possible so it's best we do not write to her. God is looking after her.'

Ritva found no solace in her father's words, nor in the Sunday sermons he now delivered with even more fervour. Squeezed between Berta and Elke in the church pew, Ritva raged quietly: what kind of god would let her mother be taken away in the first place? She craved her mother with every fibre of her being. Often, when Father was out, she sneaked into her parents' bedroom, opened her mother's wardrobe and stroked her soft blouses, skirts and her fur-lined winter coat and buried her face in the pelt – it soaked up her tears without a trace. Once, as she pressed one of Mother's scarves to her cheek, she caught a faint whiff of her scent, sweet and spicy with a hint of lilac . . . She had slipped the scarf into her pocket and it was the same scarf that she took with her to Helsinki.

Where was it now? Ritva's hands touched the place where she used to keep it, under her blouse, but it was not there.

Mother's absence had opened the door for many shadows to pass into Ritva's life, as if until then, even with her fragile presence, her mother had kept the wild currents at bay. Ritva shivered. She did not want to think about the murky days that had followed.

As her eyes wandered up the wall of her cell, Ritva was struck by faint marks scratched like simple drawings into the plaster. She kneeled on the bed and traced the shapes with her fingertips. She held her breath – they were butterflies! Five of them in different sizes, their wings outstretched towards the window . . .

Tears stung Ritva's eyes and this time she allowed them to flow. As she sobbed, the vice around her chest loosened and after a time, she remembered happier childhood days, and the memories felt like a warm coat she could wrap herself in against the fear in her heart. Mother sitting at Ritva's bedside, telling stories with her warm, deep voice. She would transport Ritva to strange lands where mysterious creatures reigned, or stir her with Andersen's bittersweet tales about the Snow Queen, Sealskin or the Ugly Duckling. Most of all, though, Ritva loved it when Mother told her about the reindeer people of the North, the 'children of the sun' as she called them. As her mother spoke, Ritva saw in her mind herds of reindeer crossing the tundra, followed by groups of herders on foot or with sledges; she could smell the hearth fires in the tents, feel the warmth of the midnight sun or the crisp autumn air. Ritva had never seen a reindeer, but her mother's description of the beautiful creatures made her long to run her hands through their thick fur and gaze into their large, dark eyes.

'The story goes that the people of the North were created by Big Father Sun and Old Mother Earth and when the people roamed the mountains and the wide tundra, they lived peacefully with all creatures, knowing that they all belonged together.'

'You mean, it wasn't God who made the reindeer people?' Ritva had asked, wide-eyed.

'It's just a story, darling.'

Ritva had seen a shadow pass over Mother's face; she knew that her father did not approve of these tales, nor of his wife telling them to his daughter. Many a Sunday Ritva had heard him preach that people were made by the one almighty God and that man was king and ruler of all creation. Still, Ritva had wanted to know more about the reindeer people, who lived so far up north that in summer the sun never slept and in the long winter months it didn't rise above the horizon.

Eventually Ritva must have fallen asleep, as she woke to the sound of her cell being unlocked in the early morning.

'Breakfast is served, my dear.' The nurse popped her head round the door and smiled. Faint light shone onto Ritva's bed.

'I'm Nurse Erika, by the way, I don't think I've introduced myself properly. I hope you had a pleasant night.'

'Thank you, but I wouldn't call it that.' Ritva did not smile and her voice was hoarse. She gazed around the cell and, although they were paler now in the morning light, she noticed the butterflies again. Who of all the souls that had passed through this asylum had scratched them into the wall? Had they taken flight like the butterflies? Had anyone ever escaped from Seili or been released?

'Up you get.' The nurse slid a grey bundle onto the floor. 'Here are some fresh clothes for you. Leave your old ones in the corner, I'll take them to the laundry later.'

'When will I get them back?'

'Don't you worry about that. Just pick something and then join us for breakfast.'

Ritva's heart sank as she looked at the bundle – would she ever get her own clothes again? Not that they were new or pretty, but they were hers, not some hand-me-downs from goodness knows where. She slipped on a brown skirt she found in the bundle and the black-and-grey-striped apron which all the patients wore over their bodice and skirts. With a stab she thought of little Elke getting ready for school without her, facing the daily chores by herself. The nurse scooped up Ritva's old clothes and hurried away.

Had they not taken enough from her already? Her freedom, her family . . . now they were forcing her to blend in with everyone else, to become an invisible thread in the fabric of the asylum, and should she resist . . . She knew instinctively that the general friendliness only stretched as far as each woman's obedience. Ritva had never been a rebel, but as she tied the apron at her back, a sudden wildness stirred in her like the deep growl of a wolf.

4

Over the next few days Ritva learned about the asylum's routines and met most of the patients and nurses. Mornings began with a breakfast of dry rye bread and a slim spread of butter, thin coffee and lumpy, lukewarm porridge. On the first morning, Ritva looked around the room between spoonfuls of the gruel, surprised that despite the uniform aprons, such variety existed amongst the women. If all these patients were ingredients in a soup, she thought, what an odd taste that would be. It was not a blend she ever wanted to become a part of.

Everyone sat on long benches hunched over plates and bowls; some slurped their porridge with great appetite, others picked at it like sparrows. A table near the window was set aside for the nurses, who shared the latest gossip like a cackle of cheerful magpies, oblivious of their charges. Ritva sat next to Irina, who filled her in on the other patients with great enthusiasm.

There were those, she explained, like Mitria, who had given up a long time ago. Lost in their own world, they made no effort to speak and broke their silence only with occasional wild laughter or a curse, spitting at anyone who dared stroll too close to their imaginary territory. Or Olga, a woman in her forties, who had been on Seili for over twenty years.

'She's been sitting in that same old chair for years – and God forbid anyone should try to take it from her; she nearly blinded a woman who once tried to grab it for a joke. Olga turned into an animal, she kicked and tried to scratch out the woman's eyes. Took three nurses to get her off.' Ritva glanced at Olga. With her frail body and greying hair she looked much older than forty. How could she have so much strength?

Some of the women felt compelled to take off their clothes and scream obscenities, Irina said, flashing their bare breasts at breakfast, or running naked down the corridors, shrieking and dancing. It was never long before they were captured by the nurses, dragged into their cells and put into straitjackets.

'The doctor calls it mania, says the jacket cools their temper. You've got to watch them,' Irina whispered, 'you don't want any of them to pounce on you.'

Ritva shivered.

Then there was Ilka who, thin and pale as a candlestick, seemed to live solely on air. She sat with a nearly empty plate, slowly chewing one tiny morsel after another, tears streaming down her face.

'They force-fed her once,' Irina whispered. 'Pushed a rubber tube down her throat and poured a thick, grey liquid into her stomach. It looked ghastly. Took three of them to hold her down . . . ever since then she's been making an effort to eat.'

As if she had heard Irina, Ilka suddenly looked up. Ritva flinched as Ilka's eyes met hers: they were the darkest she had ever seen, earth-brown with dilated pupils that gave nothing away.

Another woman, Orleana, would suddenly stop whatever she was doing and stand stock-still. She might lift her cup, then lose herself in a universe at the bottom of the cup or stare at the fine cracks across the plaster in the ceiling as if they might open up into another world.

'The nurses sometimes make fun of Orleana,' Irina said, and smirked. 'They ask her to put her hands in the air and she stands there like a tree until all the blood has drained from her hands and her arms are trembling. The nurses don't mean any harm, it's just a little game and they always give her a sweet afterwards and rub her arms until the blood comes back.'

The longer she listened to Irina's stories, the harder Ritva found it to keep eating.

'What about Petta?' Ritva asked. The man gave her the shivers, with his piercing grey eyes and the way he called her 'my dove' whenever he saw her.

'He's an attendant. The nurses call him whenever there's trouble. Nobody likes him much, not even the nurses. And he is a bit of a bully. Rumour has it he found his wife with someone else only a few months after their wedding. He locked her in their bedroom for weeks on end and when he finally let her out she was not the same any more. The doctors sent her here and she died five years ago. Christa was her name – some of the women still remember her. I don't mind him really. In fact, I feel a bit sorry for him.'

Ritva didn't feel like pitying him – if anything, Irina's story confirmed that Petta was to be avoided at all costs.

'Ah, and that one over there is Sophia. She was a seamstress in one of the poorhouses in Turku.' Irina lowered her voice. 'They took her baby boy away and she never got over it, the poor thing, still looks for him everywhere. Walks around with a cushion under her dress, pretending to be pregnant again.'

Ritva dug her fingers into her palm. She wanted to get away from Irina; she felt as if all these stories were clinging to her like a foul smell. She knew she wasn't like these women, so what was she doing here? Were there others like her? And how could Irina know so much about everyone? Irina pointed to a group of seven women sitting around a table in the right-hand corner of the dining room.

'Best to stay away from them,' she whispered. 'They'll slit your throat if you get on the wrong side of them.' She smiled, seeing the terror on Ritva's face. 'Well, it's not that bad, but you don't want to cross a line with that lot. They should be in prison, but instead they ended up here. Thieves and drunkards . . .' Irina moved closer to her.

'You want to mind Katrina especially, the large one. She used to be a prostitute, came over from Russia. They say she killed two men, slit their throats while they were still lying on top of her.'

Now that Irina mentioned it, Ritva thought that there was something different about the group; they were red-cheeked and louder than anyone else, and appeared more animated and confident. Just then, Katrina pounded her fist on the table and broke into coarse laughter and the women around her joined in.

'They like a good drink, and sometimes even manage to get a piece of meat. If you're clever, you can get a lot of things here, even drink. Everything changes hands quickly, you'll soon find out. There are many currencies, and if you have a good body . . .' She held Ritva's gaze; Ritva blushed and looked down at her plate.

'I'm just saying – with a lovely body like yours, you can get a lot of things here. But I can see that thought doesn't appeal to you.'

Ritva had only swallowed a few spoonfuls of porridge and had not touched the bread, yet her stomach ached as if it were filled with stones.

'Forget what I just said, please, I didn't mean it,' Irina said. 'But let me tell you, the nurses will watch you a lot in the first weeks. You might as well be on your best behaviour. So, eat up! It won't do you any harm.'

Ritva took another spoonful of the porridge – it tasted the way it looked, like mashed-up paper mixed with lukewarm water. A thought flitted through her mind and she turned to Irina.

'And what about you, Irina? Why are you here?'

'Oh, me?' Irina's eyes darkened as she looked straight at Ritva. 'I burnt down my father's farm. Went up in flames like a bonfire, all of it: the barn, the house . . . what a blaze! The bastard survived, but he lost all his cattle. Believe me, he deserved it . . . and more. Touching his own flesh and blood . . .' For a second Irina's facade crumbled and her wide green eyes revealed an abyss of hurt and hatred. Then she quickly composed herself, forcing her mouth into a smile.

'It happened a long time ago . . . Now, eat up and be a good girl, the nurses will take note of that.'

Ritva sighed inwardly. Could she really trust this woman? But at that moment she badly needed a friend and she certainly did not want to risk Irina's wrath. And there was something else that had stirred in her when Irina was talking. She pushed the thought away and forced herself to finish the porridge.

That night, Ritva lay on the hard bed, searching for the portal through which a darkness had slipped into her life. Little Fredo's death had plunged them all into deep despair, but once Mother had recovered, everything seemed to settle down again. Had it been the day Father's brother had visited that the true darkness had arrived in their home, the year little Elke was born?

It had been a chilly day in March. Uncle Sebastian had strolled up the grassy path to their house and just as he stepped across the threshold, a cloud had covered the sun and the blackbirds had stopped singing. As he passed Ritva in the entrance, he had stopped and looked her up and down, then smiled, exposing two rows of crooked yellow teeth.

'Well haven't you grown into a beauty!' he said and pulled her close to his chest. 'Why, won't you say hello to your uncle?' His smell of old sweat, alcohol and tobacco made her nauseous and she struggled out of his embrace like a sheep about to be shorn.

'Last time I saw you, you were a squirming baby. Now you're a young lady and still squirming!' He laughed and turned to Ritva's father.

'Johann, you've done well, look at her pretty face!' He clapped his brother on the shoulder, but her father did not smile.

'Yes, she is my treasure, Sebastian.' Ritva did not understand her father's formality, but she sensed a hint of threat in his voice. Pride warmed her – she was her father's treasure and that was that. Then Mother entered the room. Ritva slid behind her and pressed her face into her dress. Comforted by the warm fabric and the safe smell of soap, she peered out again – maybe Uncle was only trying to be friendly?

'Ah, and here's the woman of the house. Lara, good to see you!' As with Ritva, he let his gaze wander from her face to her whole body, lingering a moment on her belly.

'Have you forgotten to tell me something? You're expecting again!'

Her mother blushed. At that moment, a curtain of rain lashed against the window.

Uncle, five years older than Father, stood tall and broad as a crudely timbered wardrobe, his face tanned and creased from working outdoors. An unkempt, bushy beard covered his chin and his eyebrows sat like hairy caterpillars above his piercing grey eyes. When he spoke, Ritva could feel his deep voice resonating through her slim body, even when she was standing on the other side of the room. He too could have become a pastor with that voice, she thought, but instead of a congregation, he tended sheep. Ritva imagined his muscular arms effortlessly slinging a sheep over his shoulders, carrying it for miles, or holding it down to be shorn or slaughtered, a sharp knife slitting its throat. The thought made her feel sick.

And then, shortly after this visit, Uncle's wife had died suddenly from pneumonia. Nine months later, a short letter had arrived for Father, enquiring in barely legible writing about the dilapidated farm next door; could he purchase and rebuild it? And, as he had no female presence to attend to his household, would the pastor, his dear brother, be so kind as to consider . . .

Father had not replied for a long time, yet when two more letters arrived, he eventually sent a favourable response. And so Uncle had finally appeared in September 1906, two years after little Elke was born, with only his flock of sheep, a battered suitcase and a few boxes, set to repair the farm next door and create a new life for himself.

Staring at the butterflies on the wall of her cell, Ritva's thoughts tumbled: had there not been signs from the very beginning of what was to come? Birds stopping their song in the presence of this man; the air itself turning cold around him. Then again, it was such a long time ago and everything was a blur; maybe nothing had happened at all.

It was at dinner on the second day that Ritva noticed Martta. She thought she recognised her as one of the women who had been tending the garden on the day she had arrived, but she was not sure. Martta was taller than most, with lanky arms, broad shoulders and hips as slim as a boy's, yet as she turned, Ritva could make out the shape of her small breasts and a soft mouth in the young woman's angular face. She could not have been older than eighteen. A thin white scar, as long as Ritva's small finger, ran across Martta's right cheek. Her serious face and knitted eyebrows gave the impression of being deeply in thought, yet Ritva sensed she was as alert as a fox.

When Martta's gaze met hers, Ritva was surprised by the fire that shone from the woman's bright green eyes. She did not smile but gave Ritva a quick nod, then sat down at the criminals' table and dunked her spoon into the bowl of soup. Despite the tightness in Ritva's chest and a feeling of dread that had kept her stomach knotted ever since she arrived here, something stirred in Ritva and drew her to this woman who could hold such fire in her eyes even in a place as desolate as this.

'What about that woman over there?' she asked Irina, nodding towards Martta.

'Oh her,' Irina said, 'that's Martta; she threw boiling water at her employer. She is quite unpredictable and, well, she's not quite like us. Arrived two years ago, you should've seen her then, not two days passed without her being dragged to her cell. She was like a wild mare, a right wolf, kicking and spitting at the nurses. She even tried to run away once, but she didn't get very far, they caught her and kept her in seclusion for weeks. I'm not sure whether it's true, but she said they tied her down and kept her in a straitjacket. She's calmed down now but the nurses keep a close eye on her.' Irina lowered her voice. 'If I were you I'd keep my distance. You never know with these Lapps . . . they're different.'

Ritva's heart beat faster. Martta came from the North? Was she one of the reindeer people? Despite her mother's many tales of the North and its people, Ritva had never met anyone who came from anywhere further north than Oulu.

Whatever Irina or any of the other women said made no difference to Ritva. She wanted to get to know the mysterious woman who had tried to escape from this forsaken place, had kicked and bucked like a wild horse, alive and unbroken.

Martta, in turn, was intrigued by the new arrival; there was an innocence about Ritva that moved her, a shyness and something else she could not put her finger on – a darker, hidden side, a wounded spirit, or was it a spark of resistance behind a mask of compliance? Perhaps Ritva could become her ally, a friend even? Martta brushed the thought aside – she knew she could trust no one here.

Martta had experienced the cruelty that lay behind the asylum's pleasant facade from her very first day and had quickly learned the rules of survival: to keep herself to herself and, more importantly, to avoid Nurse Katja, a fervent Protestant in her late twenties who loved preaching about Heaven and Hell and the Path of Obedience and who had managed to persuade the other nurses, and at times even the doctor, that restraints and seclusion were the best tools to cope with Martta's temper.

One of the older patients had warned Martta in her first week about the wiry nurse: 'Watch out. Katja has beady eyes, that's why we call her the hawk. She sees everything and she's in with the matron – you best be on your guard around her.'

But at first Martta had not listened and so it had been the best part of a year before she was finally allowed into the courtyard, and another year before she was allocated a small patch of garden. Even now Katja seized any opportunity to torment Martta, trying to take back her privileges. Had something singled her out to be abused, Martta often wondered. Was it because she was a Sami, or because she had broad shoulders and a strong body?

There wasn't a day that passed when Martta was not gripped by a fierce desire to escape and a longing to see her homeland once more. As she gazed through the barred windows, she strained not only to see beyond the asylum walls, but far beyond Seili, to catch a glimpse of the tundra – a place far up north as large and as wide as the world, where patches of snow speckled the fells and snow-covered peaks rose majestically in the distance. There, the landscape was alive with rivers and grasslands, lakes and soft green hills; elk, foxes, hares and wolves wandered its vast spaces and swans and falcons flew high above. Most of all, Martta's heart ached for the reindeer and her people, a bond so strong, neither despair nor hardship could break it. Memories of those early years were etched into her soul, a refuge for the times when the asylum threatened to break her spirit. She could conjure up scents and colours, images of herself as a toddler in a fur-lined parka carried by a pack-reindeer, the world bobbing up and down; years later sitting astride the same animal, holding its reins, and later still, leading the reindeer up into the mountains during the spring migration with Father . . .

She saw herself kneeling next to her father as he marked the new calves in spring, the way he broke into a *yoik*, the special singing that poured straight from the heart. And the *lavvus*, their cone-shaped tents, dotted across the tundra, where she had listened to stories and laughter while the stew pot boiled over the fire, bread was warmed and coffee brewed. Each night she had slept on thick reindeer furs, the aroma of freshly cut birch branches in her nose, the dogs' warm bodies pushing against her while shadows played across the tent and sparks rose through the smoke holes. How could she have lost all this? If only Mother had stayed in the North; they could have survived, even without Father . . .

Martta shook herself – there was no use in wallowing in the memories of a girl who had been lost a long time ago.

When she looked up, she saw Ritva leaving the dining room with Irina. Irina had wasted no time in grooming the new arrival and the girl had fallen for it, just as she once had. Martta promised herself to watch them both closely.

5

Ritva soon found out about the asylum's hierarchies and how to gain privileges. She was assigned two weeks of observation by the nurses, who noted her every interaction with staff and patients, her intake of food and drink, the movements of her legs, bladder and bowels. Not allowed out even into the courtyard, Ritva was confined to her cell, the corridors, the dining room and the stuffy dayroom with its looms, spinning wheels and tables laden with wool, needlework and embroidery. Having been used to roaming the fields and forests when she was a child, this captivity was suffocating. Ritva pressed her face against the large dayroom window, gazing out at the small patches of earth tended by a group of patients; how she craved fresh air and to feel the sun on her face. She recognised Martta by her height and broad shoulders. Martta was curved over a patch, weeding; she looked up, startled as if she had sensed Ritva's gaze on the back of her neck, then turned round and found Ritva's face behind the window. This time Martta smiled.

'You're doing all right,' Irina whispered, startling Ritva. 'Just bear with it for the next two weeks, then they'll move you up. What you don't want is to end up at the bottom like the violent ones.'

'What do you mean?'

'The ones locked in their cells, tied in straitjackets and strapped down, or . . .' Irina lowered her voice, 'swaddled like babes, arms, legs, everything, all wrapped in sheets, with only their head sticking out. Then there are the ones in the west wing, who have to stay in their cells all day long. When you look into their eyes it's as if the lights went out a long time ago; they don't get up any more and the nurses let them "rest" as they call it. Living ghosts, they are, if you ask me.' Irina shrugged as if to shake off her own words. 'If you want to get yourself out into the courtyard, then take up some needlework or crochet and make yourself busy. Pretend you like it.'

'Thank you,' Ritva said. 'I'll try.' Anything to get her out of this stuffy place. Today even the courtyard seemed like a different country. How must the women feel who only saw the walls of their cells day in, day out?

'I saw you gaping at Martta. You'd best stay away from her – she's different from us, and I don't just mean because she's a Lapp.'

'Irina, stop whispering.' Erika, one of the two nurses overseeing the dayroom threw Irina a stern look. 'Don't pester poor Ritva, she's hardly settled in.' Irina winked at Ritva and left the room. What did Irina mean, Martta was different? She picked up a piece of cotton, needle and thread and sat down on a chair near the window. When she looked outside, Martta was gone.

As the dinner bell rang, Nurse Erika clapped her hands like a cheerful toddler playing pitter patter.

'Dining room, ladies.'

Ritva lifted herself out of the hard chair, only to be seized by a powerful dizziness. The nurse rushed over.

'What's the matter, dear?' Ritva did not trust Erika's sweet voice, but was grateful for the offered arm.

'Come on, dear, I'll take you to the dining room, you must be tired after all the travelling, and of course it's all new for you here, isn't it?' She patted Ritva's arm. They walked along the corridor, Ritva dazed and stiff, the nurse smiling, showing off her patient – the newest addition to the asylum's collection.

'Sophie, this is Ritva, she joined us yesterday. She is very good at needlework, aren't you, dear?' Ritva cringed hearing her name and looked away. Sophie ignored them and continued shuffling along the corridor.

'Ah, Jaana, meet Ritva, maybe you can show her some of your nice embroidery later?' But no one threw more than a glance at Ritva and the nurse. When they finally reached the dining room, Ritva slumped on the first bench and stared at her hands, wanting nothing but to close her eyes and sleep. She sensed someone moving beside her. When she lifted her head, she found herself looking straight into Martta's face.

'She's quite harmless, Nurse Erika,' Martta said, leaning closer. 'A bit clumsy, but good at heart. Katja's the one you need to watch.' She lowered her voice. 'And of course the matron. But I haven't even introduced myself.' She held out her hand. 'I'm Martta.'

Ritva took her hand, surprised by the formal gesture and by the largeness of the young woman's hand; the warmth and strength of her handshake.

'I'm Ritva. I saw you in the garden earlier.'

'Yes, I saw you too. The nurses won't let you out in the first weeks. I've finally been allowed a patch in the garden, but don't ask how long it took.'

'What are you growing?'

'They want me to grow vegetables, but I like flowers. So I grow carrots and whatever flower seeds I can get.'

Ritva felt strangely comforted by Martta's deep, resonant voice. She glanced at her face, her strong jawline, intrigued by the fine white scar on her right cheek.

'You arrived yesterday?'

Ritva nodded.

'I'm sorry, but I can't say "welcome", even if I'd like to. It's not that kind of a place.'

'Watch out, new girl, be careful with Martta. The Lapp might have you for breakfast,' a tall, red-cheeked woman a few seats away called out and broke into crude laughter. Ritva flinched when she recognised the woman as one of the criminals.

'Just ignore her,' Martta said. 'That's Petrushka, from Russia, she doesn't mean any harm.'

Ritva lowered her head and stared at her plate. 'There aren't many young women here, everyone seems so much older. How old are you?'

'I'm eighteen. And you?'

'Sixteen.'

'Yes, most of the women are older, but some of them have been here since they were young. Can you imagine spending a whole life in this foul place?' Martta's voice had grown hard. For a while they sat in silence, Ritva picking at the herring and potatoes. The way the fish eyes stared up at her made her feel nauseous. To be locked up here a whole lifetime . . .

'There's Ilka over there, of course,' Martta continued, 'she doesn't look it, but she's only seventeen.' Ritva followed Martta's eyes across the room and her heart sank. She remembered the ashen-faced woman who had been force-fed by the nurses, according to Irina. Ilka seemed to have fallen out of time with her emaciated body, sunken cheeks and glazed eyes, neither child nor grown woman.

'And there is another girl, called Mira. She's younger than all of us . . .' Martta said, a shadow flitting across her face. 'But we shouldn't talk so much, the nurses don't approve of it and you are under observation.'

As if drawing an invisible curtain across her face, Martta retreated. Ritva's mind was racing. She had so many questions for Martta, about the North and the reindeer people. But Martta sat in silence with the other group, picking at her fish and they did not look at each other again until the end of dinner.

Later that evening in the two hours before lock-in when everyone gathered in the dayroom, Irina sneaked up to Ritva.

'I see you've found yourself a new friend,' she sneered. 'Just watch out for her, she'll swallow you whole.' Ritva said nothing.

What had she done wrong? She badly needed friends in this place. Was there no one here she could trust, no one who would look out for her? Although Father had called her a loner, she had always had friends at school, and of course Elke . . . Her stomach contracted at the thought of her little sister. How much she missed her.

That night, Ritva dreamt of running across a large expanse of ice, all the details etched in blinding white. She was searching for a hole in the ice where something precious had sunk into the water. When she spotted a tiny smudge on the ice she rushed towards it, her lungs stinging, but just as she reached the hole she woke up in the darkness of her cell, gasping for breath.

'I'm sorry about the other night,' Martta said as she passed Ritva in the corridor the next morning. Both of them stopped and looked at each other. Ritva was intrigued by Martta – was there shyness hidden behind her brusque facade? Tenderness even, or grief? Whatever it was – whatever the stories she might tell or others might tell about her – Ritva was sure there was no cruelty hiding there. And what did Martta see when she looked at her? For a brief moment, Ritva had the strange sensation that Martta could see straight into her soul.

'I owe you an explanation. I saw Katja staring at me, giving me that look. That nurse would prefer it if I was dead; she's made it her mission to stick me in seclusion again. But when I thought of little Mira I got so angry – she's only twelve, an epileptic. They keep her in a cell with padded walls most of the time and make her sleep on a mattress on the floor. They say it's so she doesn't hurt herself.'

There was a child here? What other horrid secrets did this place hold? Martta was as tight as a spring, her hands clenched into fists, her shoulders pulled up high.

'Thank you for telling me.'

Ritva felt shy around Martta but was touched by the trust this young woman of few words had placed in her.

'I'm sorry – about the girl and the nurse. Why does she hate you so much?'

'I don't know, I guess I'm just different in some ways.'

'Oi, you two,' a sharp voice from down the corridor rang out, 'stop that chattering! Haven't you got work to do? And you . . .' With a few quick steps Nurse Katja had reached them and pointed a slim, manicured finger at Martta. 'You should know better than to talk to a vulnerable young girl like this. I warn you, keep your dirty fingers off her, or else . . .' She glared at Martta, then her face changed into a mask of sweetness as she addressed Ritva.

'As for you, Ritva, I advise you to seek the company of better folk; you don't want to hang around with such . . .' she dropped her voice, 'Lappish filth, do you? Off you go now. The doctor will be here in three weeks, surely you want me to sing your praises?'

Martta's face was flushed, and there were furrows across her forehead.

'There, you heard her. It's best to stay away from me. She means it and you don't want to get on the wrong side of her, believe me.'

Martta walked off along the corridor, leaving Ritva behind, as if their conversation had never taken place. Why did Katja hate Martta so much? Was it because she came from the North or was there something Ritva did not know? Ritva shuddered when she saw Katja minutes later in the dayroom praising Irina's needlework with a broad smile, exposing her large, white teeth.

One afternoon in her second week on Seili, Ritva was seized by another dizzy spell and was escorted by Nurse Erika to her cell.

'Now tuck yourself in, dear, and sleep, you'll soon be as good as new.' Ritva's head hurt – what if these spells signalled another fever attack like the one she had had as a child, full of strange visions of flying people and a giant drum, big as the sun? Then the nurses would think her mad for sure. But instead of a fever, Ritva fell into a fitful sleep, dreaming that she was walking down a bare, echoing corridor. She started to run, desperate to reach the end, but the corridor seemed to stretch to infinity. She woke suddenly, her heart pounding. The corridor had looked just like the ones in the Helsinki hospital. How long had she been there? Time had held no meaning inside those walls where she was examined, told to rest and then to rest some more. The voices had soon stopped but she had been seized by a profound tiredness, an impenetrable fog that had taken over her mind. There had always been a nurse to guide her to the dining room or back to her bed, to prop her up, wash her hair, hold her hand, until she found it difficult to do anything for herself. Father had visited her every month and had always brought a small bunch of flowers, chocolates and drawings from Elke, but never any favourable news from his meetings with the doctor concerning her discharge; nor any news about her mother.

'I want you to come home too, Ritva, believe me,' he said, 'but the doctors don't think it wise. They don't yet know what is wrong with you.' But even after the doctors seemed satisfied with their diagnosis of 'hysteria', Ritva was met with the same answer: 'Not quite yet, dear.'

Winter had turned to spring and then summer, then one day one of the doctors told her she was going to be sent to a quiet hospital in a beautiful place where they could better look after her.

'Can Father visit me there? And my sister? Surely, if I am better . . .' The doctor had looked away.

'Not for a while, Ritva. I recommend you get as much peace for your nerves as possible. Total rest, and then we'll see.' His voice was friendly, but a shiver had rushed down her spine as if her body had realised something her mind could not yet comprehend.

As she lay in her cell on Seili, Ritva tried to dispel the memory of that fateful day and gradually dropped off to sleep. When she woke, she sensed a presence in the cell. She opened her eyes to see an old woman standing at the foot of her bed, dressed in a grey gown sewn from rough material. Her white hair stood up in all directions and her red-rimmed eyes stared at Ritva with contempt.

'Where have you been?' The woman screeched, her voice as

high-pitched as a boiling kettle. 'How dare you just leave me here!' She lunged at Ritva, shaking her like a rag doll and pulling at her hair. 'Why did you leave me?' For a moment Ritva was unable to move, at the mercy of the raging crone, then the blood rushed back to her heart and she screamed at the top of her lungs.

'Help!'

She hit back at the old woman who was trying to scratch Ritva's face. As they faced each other, Ritva noticed how small the woman was, her head reaching just above Ritva's shoulder. Suddenly tears welled up in the old woman's eyes.

'I missed you so! Don't you know how much I care about you?'

That moment two nurses burst into the cell and seized the woman, one wrenching her arms behind her back, the other restraining her kicking legs.

'I'm sorry for this foul welcome, Ritva,' the nurse said. 'Katarina is one of our old crows, aren't you?' She patted the old woman on the head like a pet, while Katarina struggled to break free. 'She isn't quite with us, I'm afraid. She took you for someone she once knew.' The nurse bent down and whispered in Ritva's ear: 'Poor thing, she gets attached to people so quickly.'

'Come on now, Katarina, be good.' The other nurse tried to usher her out of the cell, but she writhed and spat in her face. Within seconds the nurse released one hand and slapped the old woman across the cheek.

'You know what this means.'

Ritva recoiled at the threat in the nurse's voice, devoid now of any friendliness. The nurses grabbed Katarina's shoulders and walked her out of Ritva's cell. As they retreated down the corridor, Ritva could hear the old woman shouting insults. Where were they taking her?

'She'll calm down quick enough. The jacket works every time.' Out of nowhere Irina had appeared. 'Katarina can be nice, but when she gets upset, there's no stopping her. I feel sorry for her, she's been here such a long time.' Irina looked at Ritva. 'Are you all right?'

'Yes, I guess so.' Ritva stood up. 'This place puts the fear of the devil in you.'

'I'm sorry, I should have tried to catch Katarina earlier and spared you the ordeal. We've got to look out for each other here. Come on, let's apply ourselves to some handiwork.'

Ritva was grateful for Irina's company and followed her to the dayroom. She had enjoyed embroidery in the past and Mother had often praised her neat stitches, but here everything repulsed her: the stale air in the dayroom, the senseless repetition of the loom paddle pressed by a tired foot, hands propelling the wooden shuttle back and forth, the spinning wheel circling round and round in endless rotations. Many of the older women sat hunched over crochet work, straining with arthritic hands to finish tiny squares for a bedspread, or stitching intricate patterns onto cushion covers. Although the women were allowed to make articles for themselves, this was not encouraged, and much of their work ended up with the nurses or the farm folk who lived on the island: decorated handkerchiefs, tablecloths or tiny mittens for babies.

'You can trade your handiwork for chocolate, a late lock-in or even a visit to the Beach of Fools,' Irina whispered. 'There's only so many cushion covers a person can use, anyway.'

'What's the Beach of Fools?'

'Oh, it's a small sandy cove on the east side of Seili. In the old days when they still had men in the asylum, the rich from Turku came out here on Sundays with their boats to observe the lunatics.'

'Is that true?'

'So I heard. It's a nice beach though, I've been there twice – worth trading a bit of handiwork for. Come on now, pick up a needle and thread,' Irina chirped, 'you look like you're good at this.'

Was this her future now, Ritva wondered. Scrabbling over tiny morsels of freedom? Yes, such handiwork could take one's thoughts off their situation for a while, yet she longed to be outdoors, to apply herself to the garden, to feel the wind in her hair, dig with her hands in the crumbly soil and, like Martta, prise beetroots, carrots and potatoes from the ground. What a joy it would be to smell the sea air, the scent of honeysuckle and hawthorn, anything other than the sour stench of the dayroom. Martta would never be found fussing away at needlework or the loom, but spent as much time as she could outside. Ritva gazed though the window at the garden and spotted Martta pruning some plants in her plot. Irina might be of some comfort to her, but she felt drawn to Martta, this quiet woman who carried dirt underneath her fingernails and tended her flower patch with such tenderness and passion, as if her life depended on it.

6

Weeks passed and Ritva still had not been allowed outdoors, nor
had she seen the doctor, whose visit had been delayed. When
she first arrived on Seili, Ritva had been tormented by memories
of her past, missing Elke, Father and her mother, but slowly her
thoughts had lost their sharpness and gaps had begun to appear in
her mind, like the holes in her moth-riddled clothes. Ritva often
gazed at a photograph that hung lopsided in the dayroom above
one of the looms. Taken one summer in the courtyard, it showed a
group of smiling nurses surrounded by their charges; some sat on
the grass with empty faces, others grinned into the camera. Ritva
thought she recognised Katarina and Nurse Katja, but she could
not be sure. The sun had bleached the image, not distinguishing
between patients and staff, each person fading along with the photograph. Would she forget everything she had ever known and
waste away, ravaged by tuberculosis, or end up like the west-wing
women who had stopped eating and lay in their beds week after
week? She could not allow this . . .

One morning as Ritva crossed the dayroom on her way to the
bathroom, she spotted a box on the table, packed with a wild
spray of coloured wool, a gift from the parish women of Nauvo.
Quick as a thief, she slid her hand into the box and moments
later rushed to her cell and stowed a small ball of bright red wool
in a slit inside her mattress. Bright colours were banned in the
asylum, lest they induce excitement or even mania; the corridors
were whitewashed, the cells were magnolia and the floors were

tiled with grey squares; even most of the embroidery yarn was dull. But Ritva craved red – red to remind her of the warmth of glowing embers, of her favourite childhood dress, of Christmas stars, of the blood still flowing through her veins.

That night she was jolted awake by an idea and for the first time in months a smile played on her lips. The next day, Ritva applied herself to her needlework, following the decorative pattern she had started. Suddenly she jumped up, waving her hand as if she'd been stung.

'Ouch!'

'What is it, dear?' Nurse Erika said.

'It's the damn needle. This isn't for me.' Ritva threw the embroidered cloth on the table and rushed out of the room, her fingers curled around the precious object: a short needle, its sharp end stinging her palm.

Ritva still possessed her overcoat, the one personal item of clothing the matron had not taken from her. But as she unfolded it, her heart sank – the silky inside was mud brown and red would not show up well. She pulled out a drawer – whenever a parcel from the local church arrived, the women scrambled for any decent item that fitted and by now Ritva had collected a meagre wardrobe of summer and winter clothes: three blouses, two dresses, underwear, two skirts, a jumper and some woollen stockings for winter. Maybe a white undershirt she could wear next to her skin would do? She tore a piece of wool from the precious red ball, the length of her outstretched arm, divided the yarn into three thin strands and fiddled one through the eye of the needle.

She would need to choose each word carefully. This shirt of memories would take some time, but then time was the one thing she had plenty of here. That and light – abundant, gleaming, late-summer light. Lock-in was at nine and it would not get dark until late.

That night Ritva sat on her bed, the undershirt stretched across her lap, needle and thread between her fingers. She shivered at the thought of how most of the women here were mere shells of their former selves and had forgotten their past; she was determined not to lose herself and her story. But how could she condense her childhood into a few words? Memories of a mother, a father, a sister, a dead brother? Still, her hands began, needle and thread working together, forming a single letter from the tiniest of cross stitches. Everything had begun with this first simple chalk mark on the board of life: I.

I, RITVA. Mother had named her after the slender hanging birch tree; those gentle, elegant trees with soft, flowing branches and smooth white bark that clustered around her childhood home like old friends.

WAS BORN IN A SMALL VILLAGE NEAR TURKU IN 1897. Ritva saw herself running over fields, the wind catching in her long chestnut hair, her arms outstretched, pretending to fly. She adored each season for the special things it brought: the first exuberant green of spring; the golden summer light that gleamed on wildflowers, bees and jubilant birds – starlings, thrushes, blackbirds and larks, hovering high in the cornflower-blue sky; autumn's plump lingonberries that shone red in the forest and winter's many formations of snow and ice, invitations to skate on the village pond, build snow houses or to snuggle up with Mother next to the fireplace.

MY PARENTS CALLED ME A DREAMER. It was true, she had roamed outdoors whenever the weather allowed, had whispered sweet words to butterflies, had whistled back at starlings and chased rabbits and hares. She conversed with trees and the wind, with dogs and sheep and horses, and it came as a great disappointment to her when she realised, at the age of five, that not everyone spoke with the wind and no one seemed to understand the language of the birds.

MY FATHER WAS THE VILLAGE PASTOR. She didn't see much of Father. Dressed summer and winter in his long black robes, a large white collar draped around his neck on Sundays, he cut an impressive figure, delivering his weekly sermon from the pulpit of their small wooden church, like a big crow spreading his cloak over his congregation, feeding his charges not crumbs and worms, but words. How she had adored and feared the passion with which Pastor Larson unleashed his sermons on the small congregation, leaving the eager worshippers who had taken a seat in the front pew not only with heart-stirring tales, but also showered with spittle. No one squirmed; instead they welcomed Father's tirades like a weekly baptism.

MOTHER. How could Ritva remember the one who had been her light, her whole universe, with a single piece of thread and a few stitches? Mother with her beautiful chestnut-brown hair, her dark green eyes, slender hands that never rested and a rare smile that lit up everything around her. Yet there had been so much sadness . . . Mother, who knew all of Andersen's tales by heart and who had told her many more about the reindeer people of the North . . .

I WAS MOTHER'S FIRST AND THEN FREDO CAME. Ritva remembered the resentment at seeing her mother's love being poured over her little brother when he first arrived, this wrinkled, screaming baby, and how she had secretly pinched and poked him as often as she dared. But soon she had realised that Mother would coo even harder over a screaming baby and then all of a sudden she too became besotted with this little being, his podgy arms and legs, his impossibly long eyelashes, the perfectly formed fingers with their tiny half-moon nails. When Fredo smiled and gurgled, all Ritva's rage vanished and it became her most important mission to make him giggle. During the Sunday sermons Ritva sat with Mother and her beloved brother, always in the third row, Fredo changing between his mother's and Ritva's lap, babbling, drawing smiles from everyone. Until, one April day, a violent fever struck. Mother sat flushed and restless at his side, eyes wide with fear as, over the course of three weeks, Fredo shrank and became a creature with glazed eyes who did not recognise anyone. He was prayed and cried over, kissed and hugged, but not even Father's prayers, nor those of the whole congregation, could keep him from slipping away.

FREDO DIED three days before Ritva's sixth birthday, when he was not even three years old. Ritva remembered this saddest of all birthdays well: the fifth of May and Fredo's funeral, Mother kneeling, stroking the wood of his little pine coffin. Father had helped Mother to her feet, propping her up like a rigid doll. Ritva had heard Mother sobbing all through the night before, but in the morning the housekeeper had braided Mother's hair and pinned it neatly to her head, then helped her into a black dress and matching hat, her red-rimmed eyes hidden behind a black veil. Ritva's stockings itched and the dark blue lace dress pinched at the waist. Mother had gripped her hand as they walked up the path towards the little church, but once inside, she had let go. Ritva thought it strange that Father should stand as tall as ever above his congregation that day – wasn't he hit as hard as they were by Fredo's death, his prayers coming to nothing? She saw the strain in his pale face as he towered over his people. She wanted Fredo next to her, longed to hold her brother in her arms, to free him from the small coffin. What if he woke up and found himself locked in that small box deep in the earth? She clenched her jaw but did not allow her tears to spill. She had glanced at the people around her. Everyone was there: the teacher, the baker, their housekeeper, the neighbours and their children, the doctor and his wife, the farmers – yet they looked odd to Ritva that day, as if they had been dunked in black ink. She knew there would be no birthday celebration for her today. Dazed, with flushed cheeks, she walked next to her mother and father behind the small coffin as it left the church. When they gathered at the open grave, some people embraced her, others bent down and whispered: 'I am sorry for your loss', shaking her tiny hand, some forcefully, others limp, with cold, clammy hands, but Ritva only thought about her brother in the box in the cold earth. Summer was yet to come but it never lasted long, and there would be a long winter when the ground froze as hard as bone.

That day no one had wished her a happy birthday and she knew she could never mend the hole in her mother's heart or the emptiness in her father's – she would never be as precious as Fredo.

Ritva could still remember the loneliness that followed Fredo's death, how she had missed his gurgling laughter, Mother telling her stories or their outings as a family to the coast. Grief had settled on the house until one year later, when, on a stormy May day, everything had changed. Mother had been pale and nauseous for weeks, but on the day before Ritva's seventh birthday she had sat her on her lap and announced with a broad smile: 'You're going to have another brother or sister soon, Ritva. Your father and I are having another baby.'

Ritva had jumped off her mother's lap and run to her room – she did not want another brother, or a sister, she wanted Fredo, not some new screaming baby. And couldn't Mother have waited another week and let her have her birthday without more bad news?

From that day on, Father had fussed around Mother, showering her with affection; the dark rings under Mother's eyes disappeared and there came a time when Ritva told herself that a new baby might not be such a bad thing – maybe her little brother would even return to the earth as another tiny baby? Yet, if he had, he arrived in the shape of a girl with bright blonde hair who they named Elke.

ELKE . . . as Ritva stitched the letters of her sister's name into the cloth, grief hit her like a punch to the gut. Like a child that could not understand how it could have spent so long playing with a silly toy, she bundled up the undershirt and hid it under her mattress, determined to ask again for some paper and a pencil. The matron had refused her when she had asked a week before, but the following morning Nurse Erika was more forthcoming and handed her what she needed.

'Just keep it nice and light,' Erika had whispered and winked at her. Ritva settled in a corner of the dayroom and did not look up until she had finished the letter.

Dear Elke,

How are you, my sweet little sister? Are you doing your home-work? Is Berta treating you well? Oh, I can hardly stand how much I miss you, and Father too, of course!

I try to sleep as much as I can to forget my miserable position and each night I hope I will wake up back in my old life, with your sweet face next to me. Some women sleep day in, day out; they do not rise from their bed and hardly eat. The nurses, whose attempts to make them get up seem less than half-hearted, say 'rest calms the mind' and the doctor has ordered this 'rest cure' for many. But no one gets better that way, they only grow quiet and pale. Sleep is never refreshing here, I am always so tired, as if this place thickens my blood and eats away at my soul. I am slowly turning into a ghost, Elke, like the old women who have been here for years that shuffle up and down the corridors. There have been many women before us; I can sense them gliding along the corridor, looking out of the dayroom window towards the sea – those old ghosts that walk side by side with us.

Oh, I am sorry, Elke, I did not intend to be so gloomy. I am trying to be sociable and make friends. There is Irina, who seems to know everything about the hospital, and there is a woman from the North called Martta, who keeps herself to herself, but she intrigues me. I always loved Mama's stories about the rein-deer people of the North – I don't think you'll remember them, you were only little at the time. I hope I can get Martta to tell me some stories.

There is some good news also: the matron has finally changed my room and now I have one at the front of the building, not overlooking the courtyard; not that I can see anything but a stretch of sky, the windows are too high, but when I stand on a chair I can see the garden and even a slither of the sea ... The shore is so close, but we are not allowed there. We do occasionally pass by it on the way to church, which is a short walk away, but that has happened only once so far.

I must be grateful, I am allowed to work in the dayroom, while others are kept in their cells for weeks, even months. Some have never left the courtyard, but others are trusted to work in the kitchen, the bakery or even to help out on the farms. Those are the obedient ones, the 'yes-Matron-thank-you-Nurse' ones. Oh, I shouldn't talk like this, but I doubt I will ever be asked to help out anywhere, although I try to be good.

I hope to see the doctor soon and that he will tell me I am fit to come home. Wish me luck, dear sister. I love you so much! Please write to me and say hello to Papa from me.

Your sister, Ritva

She folded the letter and for a moment let her hand linger on the paper, wishing Elke could receive her caress.

7

Whenever the news spread of the doctor's impending visit, the nurses set up a surgery in the dining room. Leaving his busy practice as the general doctor in Nauvo for the day, Niels Olafson arrived on one of the fishermen's boats around eleven and left in the late afternoon on the post boat.

A tall man in his fifties with a shock of silver hair, a broad forehead and large hands that never seemed to rest, Doctor Olafson cut an impressive figure and naturally exuded authority. He had taken a personal interest in the mentally afflicted after his niece had walked into the Baltic during a spell of deep sadness, her pockets bulging with stones. He blamed himself for failing the girl – if only he had spotted the signs, given her a sedative that day . . . When, four years ago, the opportunity had arisen to look after the women of Seili, he had accepted the post as penitence, hoping to prevent further loss of life and with a fierce ambition to bring relief to these women who were fated to spend the rest of their wretched lives on the island.

Unlike other physicians, he thought it important to build trust with a woman before performing a thorough physical examination. He was also intrigued about the 'talking cure' advocated by a Viennese doctor he had read about, which promised to alleviate the symptoms of hysteria. Although he did not understand how it might be possible to cure a woman from melancholia, hysteria and a wandering womb through talking, he liked the idea of learning about each patient's past, about her family, dreams and nightmares. If only there had not been so many women in his charge. He made himself available from the moment he passed through the garden, and, as if he were a flowering bush, the women flocked to him like butterflies, pulling on the sleeve of his coat, calling after him, fighting for his attention.

'Doctor, look, my cushion cover is finished!'

'Can you examine the rash on my back, please, it's itching so much it's making me crazy.'

'Doctor, I haven't slept for days; please give me some of that powder again.'

He replied to each one with a smile, a nod or some praise, dreading only the one question he could never answer favourably, yet which was asked most of all.

'When can I go home, Doctor? I'm well now, please let me go!'

'Not quite yet, dear, but I can see you're getting better, that's for sure,' he would say, patting an arm or a shoulder, before moving on to the next patient. The sad truth was he didn't have the power to release any of the women from Seili – only to tend to their illnesses.

With rumours that he was a widower in search of a new wife, the nurses created their own flirtatious dance around the doctor, putting on dazzling smiles when offering coffee and biscuits or lengthy commentaries about their allocated patients: 'If you ask my humble opinion, Doctor, I would prescribe a few days in seclusion for this one,' Katja would whisper in his ear, then hold his gaze for as long as he allowed. 'Oh, I wish you'd come more often, the patients ask for you all the time.'

By three o'clock Doctor Olafson's patience had worn thin and his replies grew shorter. Defeated by a rising sense of powerlessness, he was acutely aware of his limited tools: an exhausted listening ear, a variety of sedatives, recommendations for needlework, weaving or gardening, and of course a dose of kindness; yet all of that was nothing more than a flimsy bandage on a gushing wound. Nothing would cure these women or assure their release.

*

Doctor Olafson met Ritva for the first time on a drizzly grey afternoon.

'This is Ritva, a pastor's daughter from a small village outside Turku,' Erika chirped. 'Hysteria, with delusions, possibly, but good as gold, aren't you, dear?' She patted Ritva's cheek.

Ritva was one of his last patients for the day. Despite his weariness, something intrigued him about this girl – maybe it was her long shining chestnut hair, an exception in a place where everything had lost its lustre and shine; or was it the fact that she was the same tender age as his niece had been when she killed herself? Yet there was something else too, a familiarity he could not place.

'Hello, Ritva. How are you settling in?'

'Fine, thank you. When can I go home, Doctor?'

'Ah, not so quick, my dear. We want to make sure you're completely well first.'

'But I feel well. The only thing I've got is a headache from being inside all the time.'

'Well, that can be easily solved.' He turned to the nurse.

'She seems quite ready for some time in the yard, wouldn't you say so, Nurse?'

'Oh yes. Isn't that wonderful, Ritva?'

'I don't just want to wander around the courtyard with the crazy crones, I want to see the water or at least do some gardening. I'm suffocating inside these walls. We're on an island and I haven't even been down to the sea.'

'All in its time, dear, small steps will get you there,' Olafson said. 'If you get better and behave well you might even get your own patch of garden, isn't that so, Erika?'

'I've told her that already, Doctor.'

'You could also try your hand at more needlework; it calms the turbulent mind, I've been told.'

Ritva glared at them both.

Despite the young woman's apparent obedience, Olafson sensed a rebellious fire lying just beneath the surface and there was something else he could not put his finger on. He took a deep breath.

'So, it's all settled then. You can enjoy the courtyard as much as you like and busy yourself in the dayroom, and I look forward to hearing about your progress when I see you again. We can have a longer chat the next time, if you like.' Ritva stood, saying nothing. The doctor scribbled some notes in Ritva's file and leafed through the pages; when he looked up again he was pale.

'Goodbye for now.'

'Goodbye, Doctor Olafson,' Nurse Erika said and ushered Ritva out of the room. 'Now that went very well, wouldn't you say?'

Ritva only stared ahead – what had the doctor seen in her notes that made him turn so white?

Although Ritva was grateful for the fresh air, the courtyard seemed almost as claustrophobic as her cell; at least from the dayroom she could see trees and a strip of sea, but here the bright blue autumn sky mocked her, and even if she craned her neck or stood on a bench, she could not see beyond the brown fence. For some women this small patch of grass was the first natural thing they had seen after months in seclusion; for others, like Sofia who endlessly skirted the yard in a crab-like fashion babbling to herself, the courtyard was the most freedom they would ever enjoy.

Would Doctor Olafson allow her into the garden soon? He seemed kind enough, but could he be trusted? Ritva began to apply herself to her needlework – compliance, she decided, would be the quickest way to succeed in getting her own garden patch.

That month, the women saw more of the doctor than usual. One of the women had seriously injured her leg so he came out once a week to check on the wound and to tend to the dressing. Because of the frequency of his visits, the nurses allocated him a private room, a disused cell. During these visits, he always made sure to check up on the most recent arrival, Ritva.

During their conversations, he asked Ritva about her village, her father and sister, whether she had enjoyed school and what life was like as a pastor's daughter. He spoke with a calm, low voice and slowly Ritva began to trust this quiet man and even found some comfort in their conversation. If he could see just how well she was now, surely he would find her fit to leave soon? Then one day he started to ask her about her dreams.

'I don't remember my dreams,' she lied. Although she knew that everyone dreamt, surely her dreams were too tumultuous and odd and it would be better to show a more rational side to the doctor. He did not push her further.

'Would you mind if I performed a full examination on you today?' Doctor Olafson asked after a few weeks. 'I want to make sure all my charges are cared for in the best possible way. Not only that their minds get rest, but that their bodies grow strong too.'

Ritva was puzzled that he should ask her permission – none of the doctors in Helsinki had ever asked, but Doctor Olafson chatted away as if to spare her as much of the procedure's embarrassment as possible. He had listened to her back and chest with the stethoscope before, but now he asked her to undress, lie on her back and prop up her legs. He continued to talk as he examined her, then all of a sudden he grew quiet.

'Ritva, has anyone ever . . . touched you . . . down there before?' He coughed and took a noisy breath. Ritva sat up and stared at him.

'What do you mean?'

'I mean, you . . . it looks like you are not . . .' He blushed and looked away, then gathered himself. 'You are not a virgin any more.'

What was he saying? She had overheard some of the women talk about such things: men forcing themselves onto them against their will, but she, a pastor's daughter? Her stomach cramped and she felt nauseous.

'You're just trying to put thoughts into my head,' she shouted. She grabbed her underwear and skirt and started to dress – she needed to get away from this man and what he was trying to make her believe.

'Ritva, I . . .' But Ritva had already stomped out of the room, leaving the heavy door wide open.

That evening, Nurse Erika approached Ritva.

'I've a sleeping powder for you. The doctor recommended it.'

'I don't want it, I'm fine.' Ritva snapped. She could not forget the doctor's words and needed to think clearly.

'But, dear, it's for your own good. I'm to tell the matron if you refuse.'

What choice did she have? As she lay on her bed, struggling against the force of the sedative, sparks of memory illuminated her mind for brief moments, like the beam of a lighthouse flashing across the sea . . .

It had all started four months after the doctor took Mother away. She woke one night with the smell of alcohol and bad breath on her face, the back of a hairy hand stroking her cheek like a creeping spider. Her heart hammered. Was she dreaming? Only a week ago, on her thirteenth birthday, Father had offered her and her sister separate rooms. What would she have given in that moment to feel her little sister next to her. She was drowsy and her head hurt.

'There's nothing to fear, my treasure.'

She did not recognise the hoarse voice, but in the small sliver of moonlight that fell into the room, she saw the man's profile – a broad forehead, pronounced nose and unkempt beard. She held her breath and hit out at him, but his hand dug into her arm, his weight pressing on her.

'Shhh, don't struggle.' His other hand found her cheeks, touched her neck, the skin over her collarbone, her breasts. She felt the man's quickening breath against her neck and soon he moaned as if in pain. She tried to scream but her mouth felt like it had been filled with earth and no sound escaped; she lay rigid, a girl turned to marble, the man's fleshy hand moving over her body. Suddenly she felt herself being lifted, taken higher and higher into the air, floating weightlessly, her arms wrapped around a bird's neck, the sound of whooshing wings filling her ears, warm feathers engulfing her . . .

When she found herself back in her bed, the man was gone. Only a whiff of alcohol and sweat lingered in the air.

Every night after that, Ritva had locked her little sister into her room and kept the key safe. Father had hidden the key to Ritva's room after Mother had locked her in, and Ritva did not dare ask for it.

She dreaded each night – would she wake again with the man's weight on her, Uncle's clammy hand reaching under her nightdress while her body sank under a leaden drowsiness? Uncle . . . she was sure it was him though she had only heard him whisper, his face shadowy in the dark; the beard, the stench of alcohol . . . Was it Uncle Mother had tried to warn her about before she left?

When he joined their small family for lunch after church each Sunday, Ritva could not look at him nor bring herself to make conversation with the brute. If only Mother were still here. Finally one evening she gathered her courage and told the housekeeper about the nightly visits. Berta frowned, then tucked Ritva in tightly and placed a hand on her forehead.

'Oh, your head is quite hot. My dear child, this is surely one of those dreaded fevers your father has told me to watch out for. Look, there is no man roaming the house at night. I know you've a vivid imagination, and a fever will bring it out even more.'

Maybe Berta was right and her memories were like quicksand, not to be trusted? She recalled her first fever attack well, six months after her brother died. Fredo's death had left a gaping hole in all of their hearts and Mother had taken to her darkened room for weeks, leaving Ritva to spend most of her time on her own, roaming the fields and forests. Her favourite place to sit was under an old poplar tree. More than ever before, all of nature seemed to be communicating with her and she felt the mighty tree strengthen and comfort her as she leaned into the trunk. But then the fever had come on, furious and sudden as a raging winter storm. One night Ritva was sitting at the dinner table, chewing a piece of rye bread that wouldn't soften. As she gazed at the fireplace, the flames seemed to crawl across the room towards her and heat rose from her belly, rushing up to her head and making her ears ring.

'I'm not feeling well, Father, I need to . . .' she whispered before she slid from her chair. For the first time, Ritva experienced a sensation of complete weightlessness, as if the ground beneath her had opened up and she had slipped into a dark vortex, a deep night.

Over the next days, Ritva moved in and out of consciousness, dreaming of places so strange and otherworldly that she thought she had died. A bird as large as a tree swooped down, grabbed her and threw her high up into the air. She landed on the bird's dark-feathered back and grabbed hold of its neck. As they flew further up into the sky it grew hotter and hotter and, as if the sun had turned into a giant drum, Ritva heard a deep beat; she saw reindeer and wolves, foxes, bears, birds, people, ladders and tents floating on its surface like a drawing, and yet they looked so real, all swirling, tumbling . . . the beat pounding like never before, quickening and slowing and quickening again, an ever-changing rhythm.

'Not you as well!' Ritva heard her father cry through the fever daze. And indeed he told her later that he had been sitting at her bedside for days, wringing his hands and praying as he saw her being tossed around by the same visions of a devil world that had taken her brother. But as quickly as it had started, the fever vanished, and one morning Ritva's eyes shone clear again. And yet, having glimpsed a universe so immense and filled with wonder changed everything – Ritva's ordinary world seemed dull and she ached to understand the strange images she had seen and her flight to the sun.

'I don't want to hear about it,' her father snapped when she tried to tell him. 'You've been tempted by the devil and whatever you saw you must forget. I don't want to hear another word, d'you understand? And you must pray for forgiveness.'

Had Father been right? Had those visions opened the door to all the anguish that had followed? Perhaps she was indeed sinful and had been punished? Ritva's head spun as she lay now in her cell, besieged by the past. She rummaged under the mattress for the undershirt she had started to embroider with the red yarn. All that she had so carefully stitched into the shirt, was that not real either? She sat in the twilight clutching the shirt to her chest, tears dripping onto the fabric – was she mad after all? She had tried so hard to do as Father said, had prayed to his God and asked for forgiveness, but there had been only silence. Only when she had sat amid nature and communed with the birds and trees had she felt something bigger than herself, a benevolent power – but this was very different from the God of wrath and punishment that Father preached about. She was so tired; if she could only reach back to the very beginning . . . Maybe the doctor could help her untangle the mess and find the truth.

8

On the next occasion they met, Doctor Olafson greeted Ritva with a warm smile.

'Look, Ritva, I am happy to suggest to the matron that you be given a plot in the garden, I think you're quite ready. Would you like that?'

Ritva nodded. She had dreaded meeting the doctor again, but now a sense of relief flooded through her – finally she would be able to put her hands in the earth and nurture some seeds. But was there a price to pay?

'I just want to help you,' Doctor Olafson said as if he could read her mind. 'I am sorry I was so direct last time.'

'And you made me take a sleeping powder too. I don't want that again,' Ritva said.

'Fine. But should we talk some more? Maybe you . . . have remembered some things?'

Ritva went pale. How did he know? Would it be safe to talk to him? She longed to place her trust in someone. Maybe this man could shed some light on all the turmoil in her heart?

'I . . . I used to have these dreams. And sometimes I'm not sure whether things really happened to me or I dreamt them.'

Doctor Olafson nodded but said nothing. Ritva took a deep breath and continued. She told him about the first night the man had come into her room, reeking of alcohol, and what he had done to her; how the housekeeper had dismissed her words; how she missed Mother and Elke, and Father too. He listened without interrupting as the torrent of words tumbled out of her mouth. After some time he leaned forward and lightly touched Ritva's arm. She flinched.

'I am sorry, Ritva, but we have to finish for today. I'm so glad you could trust me with all this and I do want to hear more another time.' She stared at him. That was all he had to say? Maybe it had been a terrible mistake to trust him.

As Ritva lay awake that night, more memories pushed their way to the surface . . . One evening after supper with Father, Uncle and Elke, Ritva's head had started to pound and a leaden tiredness overcame her. She dragged herself upstairs and dropped off to sleep. Hours later she woke, a large hand pressing over her mouth, hot breath brushing her ear.

'Shhh now, be a good girl,' the man whispered, his other hand reaching under her nightdress, touching her where she had been told never to touch herself. He pushed himself onto her, heavy, like a sack of flour. She tried to scream but the fleshy hand muffled her voice. She pushed with her whole body against the crushing weight, trying to wriggle free, hitting the man's back, but he didn't even seem to notice.

'Keep still,' he hissed. She gasped for air, choking, suffocating. Suddenly, a sharp blinding pain ripped her insides; then everything went dark . . .

When she came to, her heart was still hammering. She held her breath. The man was gone, but she sensed a presence in the room and a smell of violets hung in the air. She bolted upright but could see nothing. No one but her mother had worn this distinct scent . . . She reached for the dull, pulsing pain between her legs, recoiled at her wet hand. Only twice before had blood flowed from her body; she had rushed to Berta who had handed her cotton bandages and advised her how to use them.

'You'll be a woman soon,' the housekeeper had whispered, patting Ritva's back. Was this what being a woman meant, having blood dripping from between her legs?

'Mama?' Ritva had called out that night, but there was only

deep silence. She clutched her pillow and sobbed as her nightdress stuck cold and wet to her body.

The man never returned after that night, but Ritva felt no relief – something inside her had broken. She attended school, read books and did her homework, but even within innocent fairy tales and botanical volumes she now sensed sinister and unpredictable forces. She ate little and lay awake at night, observing the shadows on the floor, hoping for the bird of her visions to come and take her away. And sometimes it did; then she felt herself being lifted from her bed and carried to strange and beautiful places, only to return to her room and the memories of those terrible nights. She excused herself on Sundays after church and never again attended the dreaded lunches with Uncle. Slowly she lost interest in everything around her. If she could only sleep forever . . . Her fourteenth birthday passed quietly, her hopes of receiving a letter from her mother dashed once more.

Two days after the doctor's visit, the matron allocated her a small patch of garden. Ritva felt her heart lift – and the plot was close to Martta's! Both patches bordered the fence and could be seen from the kitchen window. Ritva smiled – there would be more opportunities to get to know Martta and maybe Martta would share stories about the North with her and they could become friends.

When Ritva first started to weed her overgrown plot, she let her hands dig deep into the damp earth. Tears streamed down her face – how she missed her childhood garden, the beautiful flowers she had grown there; how she longed for Elke and Father. Why had they not sent a single letter or a parcel during the three long months since her arrival here? Soon winter would come and no post boat would be able to make it through the ice from Nauvo.

Despite the soothing moments the gardening work brought her, fragments of dark memories still invaded Ritva when she least expected them. One afternoon as she stood over the sink in the washroom, scrubbing her earth-covered hands, Ritva froze – in

71

the mornings after Uncle had come to her room, she had scrubbed her skin with a rough brush until it nearly bled, yet she had never felt clean. She had only combed her hair when the housekeeper chided her and wore three layers of nightclothes. When Father saw this he told her off.

'You need to get some air around your body at night; it's not healthy to cover yourself up like this.' If only he had known . . . What if she had told him about Uncle? Would he have believed her? Why was there still no word from him?

Ritva took every opportunity she could find to be in the garden; the earth would not give her vegetables freely but demanded much attention: stones had to be prised out, the earth nourished with ash and ground fish bone, the beds weeded, seeds protected from birds with improvised scarecrows. And even then, with the short summers and strong winds, their efforts could easily come to nothing, could be destroyed in a summer hailstorm or a late frost. Still, Ritva found comfort in the challenge. The asylum aspired to be independent from the mainland; they owned four cows and a handful of sheep that provided milk and the women tended the vegetable gardens. Mostly though, the women were fed potatoes the superintendent bought from the few farmers who had settled on the island, and there was always herring.

'One day I'll turn into a seal and just swim away, you'll see,' Ritva said to Martta as they worked next to each other one afternoon. 'All that fish they feed us, I swear my skin already smells like it. Do you know the story of Sealskin?'

'No, please tell me.'

'Well, in a land far to the north lived a lonely fisherman. He had heard stories about seals that once were human and whenever a seal came near him, he was deeply moved by their wise and loving eyes. One night he was on his way home and the moon was rising when he spotted a group of naked women dancing on a large rock. He hid behind a boulder and watched them, dazzled by their beauty. As he turned to leave, he noticed a sealskin lying in a heap near his boat – he scooped it up without a thought and

72

stuffed it under his coat. Soon the maidens began to slip back into their sealskins and the water, except for one; she searched everywhere for her skin but could not find it. The man stepped out from behind the rock and appealed to her. "Will you be my wife?" he said. "I promise to return your sealskin in seven summers, then you can decide whether to stay or go."

'The maiden knew she had no choice and agreed with a heavy heart. The fisherman took her to his hut and after some time they had a son. She shared stories of the creatures of her world with the boy, of whales and seals, walruses and salmon, but as time passed, she became weak and her flesh began to dry out; her skin flaked and cracked and her hair began to fall out. She even started to limp and her eyes became more and more dull until she was nearly blind.'

'That sounds just like us here,' Martta said with a bitter tone. 'They've stolen our skins and we're losing all our strength. But sorry, please go on.'

'After seven winters she confronted the man – she had fulfilled her side of the promise and wanted her sealskin back. But the man refused, worried that she would abandon him and the child. Later that night the boy woke to hear the voice of the wind, calling him. He followed the sound to a cliff where a large, old seal lay sprawled out on a rock – it was Grandfather Seal who had summoned him. The boy scrambled down the cliff and at the base he tripped over a bundle – it was a sealskin and it smelled just like his mother! As he hugged her sealskin, the love of his mother filled him with joy and pain as her soul passed through him. He ran back and gave his mother her sealskin; she quickly slipped into it, scooped up her boy and ran towards the sea. She breathed air into his lungs and together they swam to the underwater coves of the seals. After seven days and seven nights the lustre came back to the seal woman's hair and eyes. Her body was restored and she no longer limped. At the end of the seventh day she returned her son to the world above the water where he belonged and assured him that he would always feel her presence and love, whenever he touched anything that reminded him of her.'

'I like that story,' Martta said, looking out towards the sea. 'I swear, one day I'll make it back into my real skin too, even if I have to lose my life over it.' She gripped the hoe so hard her knuckles went white, and her green eyes flashed as she looked at Ritva. Ritva's heart beat hard – there was such determination and strength in Martta.

A moment later they heard a loud swooshing of wings. As they looked up, two large geese flew low above their heads; Ritva could see each feather in the birds' outstretched wings shimmering in the afternoon light. They stood and followed the flight of the geese until they disappeared, seeds of hope stirring in both their hearts.

It was nearly the end of September, and Ritva and Martta were sitting in a corner of the dayroom, Ritva busy with her needlework, Martta flicking through an illustrated tome on botany, one of the few books they were allowed besides the catechism and hymn books. The short summer had given way to sweeping autumn winds and the rainy morning did not allow for gardening. Ritva enjoyed Martta's presence and she sought her out whenever she could, but today her head hurt. At first it had only been a dull pressure, but soon it spread across the whole left side of her head and face, the pain coming and going in violent waves.

'It's a boredom headache,' Martta said when Ritva mentioned it. 'I've a headache pretty much all of the time – it feels as if my brain is being eaten alive from the inside. It's hungry but there's nothing to do. At least in prison you can do proper work and they let you out once you've done your time. I wish they had sent me there instead.' She gazed out of the window and fell into a brooding silence. After a while she asked in a more cheerful voice: 'So, tell me, what kind of things did you like doing back home?'

'Well, I loved school and roaming in the forest, chasing after woodpeckers, building dens and snow houses,' Ritva said. 'Oh, and drawing and playing with my sister and my collection of carved animals. And stories, I've always loved stories.'

The animals were a bittersweet memory from the time before it had all turned bad. Uncle had carved them out of small pieces of pine and over time he had created a whole collection for her. Later she had tried to throw them all into the fire, but despite everything he had done, she adored the little creations – they might still be standing on the mantelpiece now: a sheep, cows, a pig, a dog and a cat.

'What about you?' Ritva asked. 'What did you like doing?'

'I've never had a lot of time for play, but when I was young everything felt like playing . . . feeding the dogs, running after the reindeer, trying to catch the calves with a lasso, collecting firewood. My mother taught me how to weave bowls from tiny birch roots and other crafts, but . . .' She put her right hand into the seam of her skirt and pulled out what looked like a simple piece of wood, 'what I loved most was to carve. Not from wood, but from bone and antlers. Girls don't usually do that kind of thing but I begged my parents and finally Father taught me.' She handed Ritva the piece; it felt smooth and warm in her hand. Little animals and strange patterns were carved into the side. Something stirred in Ritva like music – she had seen these images before, but where?

'It's made from reindeer antler. It takes a long time to carve, but it feels nice. And,' Martta looked around to see whether anyone could overhear them, 'it makes me feel closer to my people.'

'You mean your family?'

'My parents came from the very north, from Lapland or Sápmi, as we call our homeland.'

'You don't look like a real Lapp,' Ritva said. 'I've seen pictures. Aren't Lapps usually small in height?'

Martta's face went pale, then bright red.

'Please don't call me a Lapp, Ritva. It's like calling you a dirty pastor's daughter.'

Ritva's heart plummeted. 'I'm sorry.'

'They call us Lapps down here as if we're dirty rags, but I am a Sami, a woman from the North.'

'But you don't look different. Well, except, you are strong . . . and you have large hands.' Ritva blushed.

'There's not just one look to the Sami. We can have dark or very fair hair, blue eyes, green or brown; either way they hate us and our old customs and many of us have been sent to boarding school so we will forget our language and what we once knew, to learn their ways, to become one of them.'

'Who are they?'

'The church people, settlers, farmers, people from the South. It started a long time ago when the Christians came with their bibles. They called us heathens, burnt our ancestors' drums and killed those who wouldn't follow their faith, until my people bowed down and accepted their god. The farmers took many of our grazing lands and the government charged us huge taxes. It became harder and harder for us.' Martta snapped the botany book shut. 'And with the bibles they brought alcohol, and like so many my father got hooked on it. After he died, Mother thought we'd have a better life in the South, but I couldn't get used to the city and kept asking her where the reindeer were, and our tents. I hated living in a house – there was no fireplace in the attic where we slept and the straw mattress was filthy. I missed the smell of fresh birch twigs and seeing the stars through the smoke hole. Whenever I could, I sneaked out to the edge of the town and poured my heart out to the trees and the birds.'

'You did?' Ritva burst out. 'So did I!'

'And why shouldn't we talk to the creatures that live all around us?' Martta said. 'But most people have forgotten how, even my mother nearly did . . .' She fell quiet. 'She was a good soul. What about yours?'

'She became ill and then the doctor took her away, just like me. I don't know where she is now. My father told me she was getting better, but we never received a single letter from her. For all I know she could be . . .' Ritva broke off.

'I am sorry,' Martta said.

'It's not your fault.' Tears fell on Ritva's needlework.

'I wish I could show you the North,' Martta whispered. 'I dream every night of returning to the land of my ancestors, the mountains and reindeer. But I'm not even sure I will survive another year here.'

'What do you mean? Are you ill?'

'You can't see it from the outside but my soul is dying. They are destroying the strength of our souls and bodies here, at the end of the world, while everyone who has ever known us has forgotten us.' Martta stared ahead.

'Do you think, maybe . . . you could tell me one of the stories of your people?' Ritva broke the silence. Maybe this time she could prevent Martta from retreating. 'My mother used to tell me stories about the people of the North.'

'She did?'

'Yes. It angered my father, but I loved them.'

'Well, there is a story about how the whole world was made from a reindeer doe. Do you want to hear it?'

'Oh, yes, please,' Ritva said, moving closer. Martta took a deep breath, dropped her voice and began.

'In a time long before our time, the God Jubmel created the world from a beautiful young reindeer doe called Vaja. First he took a tiny bone from her body and built with it a bridge between the light world and the lower world; from the rest of the bones he made rocks and boulders, peaks and mountain ridges. The reindeer's flesh became the earth and her blood the flowing rivers. From her fur he made the forests and her skull came to be the wide sky that shields the earth from the blazing brightness of the heavens. The reindeer doe had deep sad eyes and Jubmel decided they should become the morning and the evening star, to guide dreamers and parted lovers. But the doe's beating heart he hid in the middle of the earth. And now, whenever you put your ear to the ground and listen with your heart you can hear it beating far below. It's the heartbeat of the earth.'

'Oh, that's beautiful!' Ritva said.

'When peace and love reign, the doe's heart beats with joy, but when hatred and greed disrupt the earth's harmony, Vaja's heart convulses with pain and tremors shake the earth. This is why when the *noaidi* beats the drum, he reminds people to listen for Vaja's joyful throbbing heartbeat.'

'What's a *noaidi*?'

'The *noaidi* is a healer and protector of the people, a wise Sami who can travel to the spirit world and converse with them. When he beats his sacred drum he can find out where the reindeer are, where the best feeding grounds are or what a sick person needs in order to heal.'

'The spirits? Does this mean you don't believe in God?' Ritva remembered Father warning her of people who believed in such heathen things.

'Well, I believe that what you call God wears many skins and guises – he might come in a storm, live in the golden light of the midnight sun or wear the fur of a bear.'

'I see,' Ritva said, goosebumps rising on her arms. Deep down, all this made sense to her, much more so than the vengeful angry God Father preached about in his sermons, or the God that the pastor from Nauvo evoked on the rare Sundays and special holidays when the women were allowed to visit the church on Seili. Ritva no longer found solace in the ritual and thought it entirely possible that God could appear in all those many forms; hadn't she felt closest to God when she had leaned against the poplar tree near her house, the tree's strength supporting her as she watched the clouds through its branches?

'Please go on.' She wanted to hear more about the drum.

'The beat of the sacred drum is an echo of Vaja's heart and people say that, as long as we can hear the doe's heart beating, there is a future for the Sami.'

'That is so beautiful, Martta.' Martta looked at her, holding her gaze.

'It is also true.' Martta's green eyes had a wild glimmer. 'But the priests took away the drums, forbade our language and *yoiks*, our beautiful songs, and told the people that the *noaidi*'s work was devil worship. My grandfather was a *noaidi*, though he never called himself one. These days few Sami will talk about their sacred drums and fewer still keep a drum hidden in the mountains or at home. The fear of the old days still sits deep in our bones. Grandfather often told me stories about the old times, and once he even showed me his drum – it was just a bit bigger than his hands, but beautifully carved. I don't know what happened to it, he died when I was only six, and when I asked Mother, she didn't want to talk about it.'

When Martta spoke of the drum, Ritva's neck tingled and memories stirred in her of puzzling images and a drumbeat, strong as a pounding heart. Maybe Martta could help her solve the mystery of her visions?

9

As the first autumn storms raged over Seili, Ritva dreaded what winter would do to them all in this place. The older women bragged like war veterans sharing battlefield stories, describing how they made it through winter after winter in barely heated cells with only a thin blanket and the occasional warm brick handed out by the nurses.

'The thermometer plummets to minus thirty,' Katarina told Ritva one day in late October, fixing her watery grey eyes on her. The old woman had gifted Ritva a cushion cover to make amends for the day she had attacked her, and Ritva had accepted it.

'That's when the pipes freeze and there's no running water. We have to heat up snow – it takes forever to make a cup of tea. Sometimes it's so cold, even the birds drop out of the sky.' Katarina was kneading her hands in her lap. 'The worst thing is that you never know whether you will wake up in the morning. You try all night to sleep – first you lie shivering, then your body goes stiff and achy and you tremble all over. I'm sure if they left the light on you'd see your feet turning blue. You want nothing but sleep, but when you finally drift off you're terrified you might never wake up. After weeks of this, you don't care any more.'

'And you hear the TBs coughing all night,' Olga said, joining the conversation. 'I could kill them after a while.'

Ritva shivered. How could she prepare herself for such cold? She could tell by her arms and belly that she had grown thinner in the five months she had been here, although there were no mirrors anywhere. Still, she liked the feeling of her ribs sticking out; the sharp contours gave her edges in a place that felt as if it was suffocating her.

'You better try and put some fat on your ribs,' Katarina said as if she had heard Ritva's thoughts. 'The thin ones don't do so well in winter. Last year two didn't make it, poor souls.'

'And don't rely on Doctor Olafson,' Olga said, 'he only appears at the beginning and the end of winter, when the steam boat can plough through the ice; in the depths of winter we're alone.'

Ritva would miss Doctor Olafson – although she didn't see him as often now as the demands on him were crushing, their conversations had helped her untangle some of the confusion in her heart. He had never pushed her to speak about her childhood, but bit by bit she had shared what Uncle had done to her. Olafson said little and mostly listened, but one day she saw tears in his eyes, and it was this silent recognition that made her accept that what had happened to her had not been a figment of her imagination or a fever vision, but the terrible truth.

'They should at least give us more blankets,' Ritva told Olafson when she saw him next. 'Surely one thin blanket to get through the winter is a cruel joke.'

'You still have only one blanket?' Doctor Olafson gasped.

'Yes, and it's not very warm either.'

His features hardened.

'I will speak to the matron and investigate this. I was assured months ago that more blankets would be purchased. Especially after last winter . . .'

But two days after his visit the temperature plummeted and with the thickening ice cutting off Seili weeks earlier than expected, Doctor Olafson was unable to return. Whether or not he had confronted the matron, no new blankets appeared.

As it happened, nothing could have prepared Ritva for the brutal cold. Although a wood-fired heating system had been installed to heat the cells, it was hardly enough to take the edge off the cold as it warmed only one wall. Ritva shivered in her sleep and by the first snow at the end of November she found herself cowering each night in her bed, wrapped in her thin blanket, knees hugged to her chest, wearing all her clothes. She flapped her arms like a bird, hitting her shoulder blades, trying to fight the growing numbness; she breathed into her hands and rubbed them until she grew tired, but it made no difference: her teeth chattered and she couldn't stop trembling. The corridors echoed from the coughing and whimpering of those plagued by bronchitis, bedsores and arthritic limbs. What if she didn't wake up? On such icy nights at home, she and Elke had often cuddled together for warmth, holding each other tight. Ritva sorely missed her sister – why did Elke never write to her?

One evening shortly before lock-in a knock at her door startled Ritva. It was Petta, a crooked grin on his face.

'Surely you could do with another blanket or a hot-water bottle, my dove?' His syrupy voice made her hair stand on end. Although she managed to keep a distance from him most of the time, he often threw her a wink or glanced up and down her body.

'Thank you, I am quite fine.' She hugged a cushion tight to her stomach.

'As you wish, my dove, but my offer stands.' He smiled, exposing his yellowed teeth. She would rather suffer than take anything from this thug.

'I'm sure I can find some other takers. Although . . .' he looked at her directly,' I really hoped you would want to make it easier for yourself in this cold. I know we didn't have a good start the day I accompanied you here, but I meant well.' Ritva shuddered, thinking about what he might claim as payment should anyone accept his offer. She turned away and he left the cell.

The cold continued for weeks and Ritva grew raw with sleeplessness. Each morning she shuffled out of her cell and huddled around the one wood stove in the dayroom with her fellow inmates. Hunched together like crows, they rubbed their aching limbs, coughing and cursing under their breath. Ritva felt more like a woman of seventy than her seventeen years.

'God, if it goes on like this, the cold will snap my bones,' Ritva whispered in Martta's ear – her voice had grown hoarse in the night. She was glad Martta looked out for her each morning, but even if her body survived, she feared it wouldn't be long before the cold shattered her spirit. She wished they could hold and warm each other, but Ritva knew Katja's fierce eye was always on Martta, and indeed on any affectionate gesture she saw shared between the women. Martta tried to distract Ritva with stories of the childhood winters she had spent in the far north – of reindeer races, how they had chased each other on skis, rolled around with the sledge dogs, the nights they sat around the tent fire, listening to tales of Stallo, the giant . . .

'You're probably made for this cold,' Ritva said with a small smile.

'I don't know, I'm cold too,' Martta said. 'We might have better clothes but still some winters were very bad.' She looked away.

'I've no idea what it's like up there,' Ritva said. 'It must be even colder?'

'Oh, it is, and not everyone makes it through. One winter we lost nearly all of our reindeer. They couldn't dig through the ice to the lichen and they starved.' Martta fell silent again.

'I'm sorry,' Ritva said and placed her hand on Martta's shoulder.

'Thank you.' Martta lingered there for a moment, aware of the warmth and sweet weight of Ritva's hand, then moved away.

One morning as Ritva entered the dayroom, she sensed great excitement.

'Irina has gone,' Martta whispered. 'She must've left last night before lock-in. Her cell was empty this morning.'

Ritva stared at her.

'In this cold?' How far could Irina possibly make it before she froze to death? Ritva had kept her distance from Irina as her former friend kept telling her to stay away from Martta; recently she had been argumentative and moody, bickering with everyone over minor things. Yet all this time she had been plotting to get away . . .

'Yes, but at least she can walk across the ice and they have still to organise a sledge and dogs to chase her,' Martta said.

'They'll bring dogs?'

'Yes, I'm sure.'

'Where do you think she is headed?'

'It depends. If she wants to get somewhere quick and then hide, she'll head east to Nauvo or Turku. But if she has courage and stamina, she'll go west towards Åland and Sweden.'

Ritva gasped.

'Sweden? But that's impossible, she'll never make it.'

Martta frowned.

'It's the only way to be free, Ritva.'

Ritva shuddered at the thought of Irina stumbling over the ice, wherever she was headed. And how would she know in which direction to go?

A moment later the superintendent stomped with heavy boots along the corridor towards the matron's office, ignoring everyone in his path. Ritva had never seen him before now, but he looked just as she had imagined him: tall and grey-haired with a full beard and bushy eyebrows. He could have been a ship's captain with the right uniform, while his sharp angular nose and piercing blue eyes gave him the appearance of a hawk. The nurses ushered everyone into the dayroom, but Martta asked for permission to go to the bathroom. A while later she returned and took Ritva to one side.

'The superintendent has offered a hefty reward to whoever catches her.'

'You eavesdropped?'

'Yes. He was raging – a missing girl reflects badly on the asylum's reputation. And guess who volunteered? Petta. That bastard . . . wherever he can smell money or power. And of course Katja; at least that will get her off my back for a while.'

Late that morning a team lead by Petta set out onto the ice, but returned without Irina at dusk. Ritva imagined Irina out on the wide expanse of the archipelago, hiding on small islands, cautiously crossing the ice. So early in winter the ice was still treacherous and there were dangerous currents . . . What if Irina fell through?

The next day the requested sledge from Nauvo arrived, drawn by six barking dogs. That night, the women watched silently as Petta and Nurse Katja escorted Irina along the corridor. Like a rag doll, Irina hung pale and expressionless between them. Her boots were undone and she could hardly shuffle along. She did not look up as she passed the women, nor as she was ushered into the seclusion sector of the west wing. Ritva pinched the skin between her fingers, suppressing her tears.

Irina was kept in seclusion over Christmas and New Year and when she was released in the first week of January, she looked like a broken toy. Ritva's heart cramped seeing her like this, but whenever she tried to talk to her, Irina only stared blankly through her.

No one else tried to escape, and the cold only began to ease at the end of April. Ritva's body had never fully felt warm and she ached all over, but besides a hacking cough she had made it through that first winter. Not everyone was as lucky – Cara, a frail, elderly woman died from pneumonia and one February morning Erika found Ilka stiff and frozen in her cell. Ilka had never managed to put more weight on her emaciated body and one night she had simply fallen asleep and never woken up.

The February earth was frozen like granite so the dead were wrapped in sheets and left in a makeshift morgue, an external store room adjacent to the laundry. When in April the earth finally thawed, the two women were buried in the small cemetery behind the church, their graves adorned with simple wooden crosses, sharing the ground with the bones of the many unfortunate souls who had died on Seili before them. The funeral was the first time after the long winter that Ritva spotted Doctor Olafson again. During the ceremony, Ritva saw him glaring at the matron and a week later everyone was handed a second blanket. A surge of rage rushed through Ritva as she wrapped herself in the scratchy blanket – it was too little and too late for Ilka and Cara.

The day after the burial, Ritva woke with an overwhelming urge to write to her father and Elke again. She had written to Elke in the summer, and other women had also sent letters to their loved ones, but the post boat hardly delivered any letters in return. She asked one of the nurses for a pencil and paper and settled into a quiet spot in the dayroom.

15 April 1914

Dear Father, my sweet Elke,

I have been here for many months now and still no word from you. I miss you so! Did you receive my letter?

I wish it would stop raining. After the snow, it is all so grey and everything is damp. I have survived one winter here but I am not sure I can bear another.

Many of us have a cough from the relentless cold and the lack of fresh air. Some are even coughing up blood – those unfortunate souls who suffer from tuberculosis. The nurses have put them in the cells at the end of the west wing, away from the rest of us, but we can still hear their muffled coughing. There is no cure and each day they waste away a little more. I have not been out in weeks and I fear this rain will take my health – and if it is not the rain, then it will be the snow when it returns. My soul is withering away.

Why did you let the doctor take me here, Father? What have I done to deserve this? This wretched place looks so calm and orderly when you first approach it, but our souls are in torment here, all tangled up in one big ache like a messed-up ball of wool the cat has left in tatters.

The nurses in their neat uniforms talk gently to us, as if we were unpredictable animals or small children, but sometimes they shout in our faces and then everyone is afraid. We have no say in anything here.

I am as lonely as the windmill on the hill where the lepers used to live. I stand on the bed and look out of the window at the stars, but I cannot see them clearly behind the thick, smeared glass. Sometimes on the way to church I can sense the lepers as they come out of the woods and stretch their bandaged stumps towards me, begging for food. I can even smell their foul wounds that never heal. I feel them in the church too, crouched on crudely carved seats in their pens, separated from us by a wooden screen. The church is like an upside-down boat where we are meant to feel safe as we sail the ocean of our troubled lives. The lepers all died long ago, of course, and all I know is that I am still here. Are you praying for me, Father? I hope so!

To be separated from you both makes me ache so badly I want to scratch my face, but I wouldn't do it – the nurses would lock me in my cell for days and my only comfort is to see the trees and smell the sea.

How is the garden? Are my little carved animals still sitting on the mantelpiece waiting for me? And Elke, are you doing well at school? Please write to me soon and, Father, please talk to the doctor so I can come home, I beg you!

Always,

your Ritva

Ritva stuck the letter in an envelope, wrote the address and kissed it.

'Please, can you make sure it gets there?' she said and handed the letter to Erika.

'But of course, dear, why wouldn't it?'

'I still haven't heard back from my father and sister.'

'Don't you worry, I'm sure you'll hear from them soon.'

The nurse put the letter in her pocket and, minutes later, delivered it to the matron's office.

10

That night Ritva dreamt of the small carved animals lined up on the mantelpiece in the old house. As she touched them, they grew bigger and hopped down onto the floor. They marched off into her father's bedroom and jumped up onto his bed. 'Wake up, Larson,' they whispered in his ear, 'fetch your daughter, bring her home.' After a while her father stirred, but at that moment the dream began to fade and Ritva awoke. Early-morning light fell in narrow beams onto her mattress. Why had Father sent her to this desolate place? And why . . . why was there never a letter? She stared at the bare walls, loss opening inside her like a dark well.

At breakfast as she sat over her porridge, crumbling bread between her fingers, an idea struck her – a ripple of excitement flowed through her and she slipped two slices under her blouse.

That night after lock-in, Ritva pulled out a slice and chewed the bread into a soft pulp. She played with the dough and let her hands work without forcing any shape. For some time the chewy mass stuck to her hands, resisting any form, until Ritva thought of the two geese she had seen the day she had shared the story of Sealskin with Martta. Slowly the body of a bird formed under her fingers: a head and beak, a body and wings. The pulp was too moist to finish the details and Ritva hid the little figure under her bed to return to it later. Then she curled up and fell asleep.

She woke to hear a strange pecking sound: a large white bird was tapping its beak on the window – a goose. It was as though the bird was inviting her to come with it. Was she dreaming?

Suddenly, her hands touched feathers and she found herself sitting on the goose's back. She wrapped her arms around the bird's neck and, with a flapping of its large wings, the goose took off. As it flew higher and higher into the sky, the asylum grew smaller until Seili was just a tiny speck amongst hundreds of small dots, the many islands of the archipelago. Finally, the land below was so distant she could see the giant horseshoe it formed around the waters of the Baltic, all the countries of the North . . . And still they flew higher. Ritva's ears were ringing as the goose shot near-vertically upwards and she realised they were headed straight for the flaming furnace of the sun. Her skin tingled as they approached the giant fireball; she held her breath as, with a few powerful strokes, the goose flew straight into the sun. Ritva lost all sense of time and space; inside it was silent as if she had arrived at the heart of all things.

She looked around but the goose had disappeared. She stumbled through a labyrinth of caves and tunnels, following a strange grumbling sound, and suddenly around a corner she found a giant golden dragon. He roared, spitting fire and clouds of smoke, but Ritva stood firm, fearing nothing. She looked down at herself and to her amazement, her whole body shimmered gold from head to toe. Standing in the presence of the dragon, she suddenly understood deep in her soul that to fulfil her destiny she had to learn about the secrets of the North and listen to the dragon: he was Grandfather Sun, ancient as the beginning of the world and at the same time the spirit of her own heart. Filled with wonder, she breathed deeply until out of nowhere the goose appeared, inviting her onto its back once more. The bird pierced the membrane of the sun and darted back through the universe towards the earth. Soon they were circling above Seili and Ritva could make out the asylum's roof; the goose tilted and with a somersault Ritva slid off its back and found herself on the hard straw mattress, wide awake. When she looked down at herself, all the gold had disappeared.

It was still dark outside and she heard the night nurse's feet shuffling outside her door. Despair gripped her – there was no goose, no shining dragon, only a cold cell and a little bread figure of a bird that would soon crumble.

Ritva must have fallen asleep again because when she woke she heard the rattling of keys unlocking her door. Her head hurt and she staggered towards the washroom. What hope was there of ever getting out of here? Irina had not made it and there was no bird to take her away, no flight to the sun, only her bruised heart.

She didn't speak with anyone that morning as she sat slurping the thin coffee. When someone squeezed in next to her on the bench she shrank away.

'Did a mouse keep you awake last night?' Martta asked, appearing beside her, a smile on her lips.

'No, I just slept badly and had strange dreams.' She was not even in the mood to talk with Martta.

'Here, maybe this'll cheer you up. I found it in the garden this morning.' Martta pulled a large white feather from under her cardigan. 'I'm not sure which bird it's from, maybe a goose or a swan, but it made me think of the geese we saw a while ago. Maybe it's a sign.'

Ritva's back tingled.

'Thank you.' She took the feather and hid it under her blouse. Ritva burned to tell Martta about her dream, but would she think her mad? And what if the feather was indeed a sign and not just a cruel joke, seducing her heart into thinking the unthinkable: that hope and freedom might indeed be close?

Ritva kept the feather and sat up many nights, shaping animals from the grey, sticky dough: little sheep, a dog, a bear, a fox. One evening she finished modelling a wolf, and that night she dreamt of just such a creature coming to her: a large male with silvery-grey fur and glittering yellow eyes. He dropped his large head into her lap and licked her hand, softly, so softly. She didn't know how he communicated with her but, as with the goose, she knew instinctively that he was inviting her onto his back. She put her hand into his thick fur and pulled herself up. As he grew larger under her, his agile body moved swiftly, lifting her up into the sky, his paws galloping through the air above the tops of the trees, carrying her away from the island, higher and higher into the night sky. That moment she knew in her heart that the wolf was taking her to the vast forests of the North.

And then she heard it, a deep pounding, beating in unison with the heartbeat of the universe. As the beat quickened, she saw the stars shifting position in an intricate dance; some moved to form a large oval shape, others gathered in constellations of human figures, of animals, ladders and a sun, all held inside the oval as if it were a huge picture frame. Her heart hammered, about to burst as the beat grew quicker and louder until it drowned out everything else. Then, all of a sudden, it stopped. In the total silence she fell from the sky like a stone, yet as weightless as a feather.

She woke in her cell, filled with a strong, sweet energy. She crawled under her bed and in the first light drew her vision with a piece of charcoal on the cold ground – the oval shape, the people, the animals and the strange signs she did not understand. She placed her bread creatures around the oval shape, the little wolf in the middle. Had she heard one of the sacred drums that Martta had told her about? This dream was so similar to the fever vision she had had as a child.

When she told Martta the next day, Martta stared at her.

'Yes, what you are describing is just such a drum! Perhaps it is calling you.'

'Calling *me*? If the drum is calling anyone, it will be you; I don't know anything about the North or about your people.'

'That might be so, but I think it's a *noaidi* drum you've seen. Maybe we ought to find it.'

'Martta, we're stuck in an asylum! How could we take off and search for a drum?' The more she spoke the angrier Ritva became; she punched her thigh.

'It's only a dream, Martta, a crazy, stupid dream. Wake up!' She was crying now – what were these dreams of drums, of wolves and geese carrying her on their backs, more signs that she had lost her mind? Perhaps she really was mad after all? Perhaps her father had been right to leave her here?

Ritva tried to forget the dreams and their conversation and Martta did not press her, but although Ritva was relieved to be able to work in the garden again, over the following weeks she fell into a deep sadness. When the ice had finally melted, the post boat had returned with Doctor Olafson, but there were no letters for her. Had Elke and Father given up on her?

'Just have patience, dear!' Erika said. 'You've not even been here a year.'

One year! Ritva swallowed her anger. She would keep writing until she received an answer.

9 May 1914

Dearest Elke,

The post boat came yesterday, but still no letter from you. Today I can report some good news! I was told I would receive another plot in the garden soon, so it will be a decent size. If I could only stop comparing it to our garden back home, with its many colours and butterflies. Maybe I could coax some here? But why should such beautiful creatures come to this wretched place? There is so little colour here in the long winter, only ice-white and shades of brown, blue, black and a bit of ochre, but I am craving red. We are not encouraged to wear red here – the nurses say it evokes anger and makes us take off our clothes. But I feel like I am being suffocated by magnolia!

This Sunday we were allowed to go to church and on the short walk I heard a woodpecker's frantic pecking. I bolted off the path, the nurses shouting after me, but I kept running. I couldn't see it, but I followed its sound. And then I saw it high up in a pine, its red belly like a flicker of joy and hope. The nurses were not happy but I, for once, had seen some colour. When I was little, I always ran after woodpeckers and never stopped until I found them, even if the bird fluttered from tree to tree.

It is May now but there are no flowers and the branches are still as naked as they were in November, although the days have grown longer. How can the sun betray us so? Such piercing, sharp light – you would think it could melt everything, but the icy air still carries the breath of Siberia and hardly warms my hands.

Oh, I am sorry, Elke, I did not mean to burden you with my misery. There is some beauty here too. The dry reeds stretch along the shore like a band of gold and yesterday I saw a couple of cranes flying across the water.

I am keeping busy and I have started to make little figures from bread dough, I think you would find them quite lovely. The doctor says I am doing well, so I hope and pray that I will be with you again soon.

I love you dearly, Elke, please write to me soon!

Your sister Ritva

Ritva's visits to Doctor Olafson continued and one day he surprised her with a volume of Andersen tales. She had told him how upset she was when the matron had taken her beloved book from her, and although Olafson's wasn't as pretty and well illustrated as her own, she cherished the doctor's gift and kept it hidden under her pillow.

Ritva never showed her bread animals to anyone except Martta, but one day as she pulled out a handkerchief from her pocket, a small figure fell onto the stone floor – the wolf. She bent down but Katarina was quicker and held up the creature which had lost a leg in the fall.

'Oh, we've a sculptor here, now look everyone, isn't our Ritva clever?' The old woman's mocking voice aroused little interest in anyone but Martta, who looked up from her plate when she heard Ritva's name.

'Give it back,' Ritva said, glaring at Katarina. The creatures were her secret.

'But it's so sweet, can you make me one too?' Katarina's voice was softer now and any hint of mockery had disappeared. 'I would love a little dog like this.'

Ritva bit her tongue but did not correct her. Now a few other women had gathered around her. Ritva stretched out her hand to take the wolf back.

'Have you got others like this? Can you do faces too?' Olga asked.

'I . . . I don't know, I'm just playing around.'

'Looks pretty clever to me,' Olga insisted.

'First I want to repair this one. Katarina, hand it over,' Ritva said. The old woman stretched out her bony hand and placed the three-legged wolf on Ritva's hand.

'I had a dog just like that when I was growing up,' Katarina said. 'A brown mongrel. A fox bit him and they had to cut off his leg.' Her face clouded over; she slouched into a chair, grabbed her needlework and disappeared into her world.

After that day Ritva allowed some of the women into her secret and soon Irina asked Ritva to make her a dog too. Since her failed escape, it was rare that Irina spoke with anyone; she had lost a great deal of weight and now that she had developed TB she was confined mainly to the west wing. Ritva was glad she could give Irina something that might bring her some joy.

For Martta she modelled a horse and surprised her one day in the garden.

'For the wild mare that you are,' she said, laughing.

'Thank you, Ritva, that is beautiful.' Martta held it in her palm. Others wanted cats or dogs or even a baby. Ritva asked for the women's own bread and over time more and more little creatures appeared in the cells. Ritva had found her own currency to attain privileges, swapping her bread creatures for pieces of chocolate, soap, and once even for a small glass of vodka-soaked cherries. Ritva hoped in her heart that her figures were not just coarsely sculpted bread animals, but secret helpers that might bring strength and hope. And often in the mornings a woman would seek Ritva out, flushed and excited, whispering tales of strange nightly visitations, dreams so vivid they could have been true, of wolves that had licked hands, a bear who put his paw on a chest, relieving a pain that had lingered there for months . . . And as odd as those experiences might have been, they brought a flicker of hope to many of the women's hearts.

11

Months merged into one another, flowing like a sluggish stream, throwing up little excitement except for the occasional outburst, the doctor's visits, a spell of fever, the sermons in the wooden church, a piece of cake on one's birthday and a parcel for a few fortunates – but there was never anything for Ritva. How long had she been here now? Months of boredom and despair had stripped away more and more of her old life. Somehow she had survived another winter on Seili and spring had come around once more. It seemed as if this was her life now; how different from the dreams she had had when she was a little girl and Mother was still around. She had hoped to be a teacher when she grew up or even a writer of great stories; now she felt as if her thoughts had dried up and she could hardly remember her sister's sweet face. But despite this, she did not stop writing to Elke.

21 June 1915

Dear Elke!

How are you, dear? Still no word from you or Father. It is summer again, but the only comfort I take is from my garden plot. Nature is the prettiest thing here and sometimes, on a bright summer's day, it brings me brief moments of joy. Maybe it is the song of a thrush or a blackbird, a flock of geese flying over our heads or a tern falling out of the sky like a stone to catch a fish. Even the sad cry of a loon is more comforting than the suffocating silence inside these walls. Here we walk in twilight, while outside the sun glistens during the long summer evenings and long shadows stretch across the garden down to the sea. My soul cries when they lock us in at night and the long summer nights are the worst. Today is the longest day of the year but there is no celebration. Do you remember how we used to dance on midsummer's night at the village fair and then go down to swim in the river? And the long evenings we spent in the garden, picking flowers and chasing butterflies, Mother bringing us lemonade and, later, hot cocoa? How I miss doing all those things with you!

Well, last week something unusual occurred. Nurse Erika took me and three others to the 'Beach of Fools', a small sandy cove on the east side of the island. They say that in the old days rich people from Turku took a boat to Seili to watch the lunatics on the beach. Is this what I am to you now, a mad person? Oh, I don't know what to think of the fact that you and Father are not writing to me. Why? I miss you so and love you dearly.

All my love to you and Father,

Ritva

Sometimes Ritva stole away from the garden and leapt over the low fence into the nearby forest to a secret refuge she had found – a lichen-covered rocky area with a small mossy boulder on which she could sit, surrounded by dripping green with soft light falling through the trees. In this special place something in her relaxed and she became one with the forest. More than once she took diary scribblings and short poems she had written, rolled them into a scroll and stuffed them into empty ink bottles. She hid them in small rock crevices, covering the hole with pebbles and moss. Even if her letters to Elke and Father never reached them, or if they had abandoned her in the asylum, at least here in this hidden place she could keep her thoughts safe. And maybe, like messages in a bottle tossed out to sea, one day someone might find them . . .

Ritva survived the third harsh winter, but in the spring of 1916, after nearly three years on Seili, her body stopped fighting and she collapsed one morning over her porridge bowl. She hung limp in the nurses' arms as they carried her to her cell and for days she burned with a high fever, mumbling unrecognisable words, thrashing her arms about as if she were fighting an invisible enemy. Dark dreams plagued her: Uncle holding her down and another shadow-like figure standing over her . . .

As the fever continued into the second week, her nightmares dissolved and animals began to appear in her dreams: first Wolf, then Goose and, at last, Bear. Ritva sensed their powerful presence surrounding her, Wolf licking her hand, Bear placing his large paw on her heart. And one day she heard the drum again, beckoning to her. She saw the markings on the oval drum more clearly than ever, the drum's figures moving and dancing, its vibrating skin illuminated. How she ached to join this dance, to understand its meaning.

As Ritva lay there half-waking, half-sleeping, she was vaguely aware of Martta beside her. What she didn't know was that when the nurses had refused to let Martta in, Martta had smashed a window in the dining room and endured two days in a straitjacket in her cell; yet the moment she was released, Martta had returned to sit outside Ritva's cell. Luckily for Martta, Nurse Katja was scheduled for home leave that week and on Doctor Olafson's recommendation, the matron gave in.

'But don't think we won't be keeping a close eye on you,' the matron hissed in Martta's ear so the doctor could not hear.

As Martta sat by Ritva's bedside she told her stories about her own past – not just the Sami stories handed down to her by her mother, but the story of her life, her family's misfortune and how she had ended up on Seili. She hardly slept, but whenever she nodded off, she, like Ritva, fought the demons of her past. And through the fever haze Ritva heard Martta's story . . .

'Come here, you dirty Lapp, scrub the floor again!' The master's voice rang in Martta's ears. At first she had been grateful that the master had allowed her to stay on as a maid in the large house in Turku, even if he gave her the hardest jobs – boiling linen in the laundry, fetching coal and tending the many fireplaces. The meagre meals barely kept her alive and she was always cold, but she worked without complaining, morning to night. When Mother was still alive the master had not said a bad word to her, but now, as if she exuded a smell the master despised, he started to taunt her with cruel jokes and encouraged his boisterous twin sons to join in.

'Hey, ugly Lapp,' he sneered, 'you haven't finished cleaning the fireplace. It shouldn't be hard for you – where you come from, you should be well used to filth!' Martta avoided his gaze and bit her lip.

But soon the beatings started. In public the master dealt her only the occasional slap, but behind locked doors, cornering Martta in the cellar or pushing her over a chair in his sitting room, he used his cane and belt. He hit her with such force that often she passed out and more than once, her skin broke and she bled. The mistress never interfered, only looked at Martta with watery eyes and once slipped her a piece of chocolate as Martta staggered out of the master's room, blood trickling down her legs.

All through the five years she worked for the family, Martta clenched her teeth and not once did she let the master see her tears; but late at night, aching in the freezing attic with red, swollen welts all across her legs and back, she sobbed into her pillow.

Then one chilly April morning everything changed.

Martta could not say what had been different that day, but when the master came up behind her in the laundry and shouted in her ear, something in her had snapped; she dunked the large ladle into the boiling soapy water, turned and aimed it at his face. Her ears were ringing and everything merged into a blur: the master's screams as he covered his face, the twins rushing in, the mistress's cries . . . All the while, Martta stood rooted to the spot, ladle in hand, staring at the spectacle. She did not fully grasp what she had done, until two constables wrenched her arms behind her back and led her away. The charges were serious; having blinded the master in one eye and burnt the left side of his face, Martta was deemed vicious and dangerous, with no prospect for recovery. The judge crashed down his hammer and sentenced her: a violent Lapp who would need to be watched closely forever, and what better place for this than with the incurable womenfolk of the Seili asylum?

'It's been nearly five years now,' Martta whispered. 'Please Ritva, you must get better, you're my only hope . . .' Watching Ritva fight the fever, Martta told her about her most precious dream that had come to her the night before Ritva had collapsed. Lying in her cell she had suddenly felt a warm weight on her legs – a white reindeer had laid its head in her lap and gazed at her with shiny black eyes. When Martta looked deep into the animal's pupils she could make out Grandfather smiling at her, fine wrinkles surrounding his eyes, his small silver pipe in his mouth, puffing perfectly formed smoke rings towards her. In the reflection of the reindeer's eye, dark as a black mirror, Martta had seen him reach into his tunic, pull out a small oval drum and the little drum hammer. 'Remember the drum, Martta!' Then he had vanished, together with the drum and the white reindeer. Not since her childhood had her grandfather come to her in a dream . . .

When Ritva opened her eyes on the ninth day of the fever, Martta was sitting next to the bed, looking straight at her.

'I saw the drum again . . .' Ritva's voice was hoarse and when she sat up the world began to spin.

'Shhh, just rest. You can tell me another time.'

Later, Martta fed her spoonfuls of a thick stew the cook had delivered especially for Ritva on Doctor Olafson's orders. When Ritva fully came to, she looked at her friend for a long time; Martta had lost not only weight but also the colour in her cheeks. Ritva reached for Martta's hand – it lay cool and heavy in hers. How many days and nights had Martta sat with her like a guardian?

'Thank you for looking out for me,' Ritva said, her voice thick with emotion. She glanced at her blanket – many of the women had left small gifts for her: scribbled notes, biscuits, drawings, a scarf, and Katarina had even tried her hand at modelling a small bread figure. As word of Ritva's recovery spread, the women flocked to her cell, chatting and cooing over her. Ritva's heart was warmed by the thought that even here in this dark place she had found kindness and support amongst women the world had declared mad. And, above all, Martta who had been so loyal and sweet to her.

Slowly Ritva began to feel better; but in the same way that the fever dreams of her childhood had shaken her, she felt changed, and as her body grew stronger, she became restless – the drum of her dreams was calling to her and she needed to follow its summons, even if she did not understand it.

A few days later, when Martta looked in on her, she sat up.

'Martta, I keep dreaming about this drum, covered with strange drawings and symbols, animals and people dancing and travelling to different worlds. And I can hear its beat. You were right, it feels as if the drum is calling me.'

Martta said nothing for a long time.

'Ritva, I'm sure what you have seen in your dreams is one of the old sacred Sami drums of the North. When the Christians came they took our old drums and burnt them, but some of my ancestors hid their drums in the mountains.' She looked out of the small barred window, then picked up her heavy skirt, searched around the seams and then tore the stitching open with her teeth. A small angular object slid into her hand.

'This is a drum hammer. It's the only thing I have left from my mother. She gave it to me just before she died. The sacred drums were played with it. She told me it was my grandfather's and that it doesn't really belong to me but to the sacred drum and my people.' She put the hammer in Ritva's hands – it felt cool and

101

smooth; beautiful patterns and two reindeer were carved into it.

'You know that my people are reindeer herders from the North and when you spoke about the drum, my heart ached.' She lowered her voice. 'We need to find that drum, Ritva.'

'Look under the bed,' Ritva whispered, her neck tingling. Martta kneeled next to the bed for a long time. When she brought her head up again, her face was flushed.

'It looks just like a drawing of a drum my grandfather once showed me when I was a girl. How can you know this?'

'I don't know, Martta, it just came to me in my dreams.'

'I don't understand this, Ritva, but I'm certain that we're not meant to die here.'

'But what can we do?'

'Shhh now, you need to rest.'

Ritva's heart beat fast. There was such fire in Martta's eyes – could they really escape from this place?

'Sleep, first you need to regain your strength,' Martta said and lightly brushed her cheek. Hope and fear stirred in Ritva. She could still feel the warmth of Martta's touch as her body relaxed and her eyelids grew heavy.

12

The thought that they might find a way to escape from Seili for-
tified Ritva more than the ghastly cod-liver oil Doctor Olafson
had prescribed. Soon she was up and she found she bumped into
Martta everywhere, as if they were drawn together by a magnet.
Yet Martta behaved as if Ritva were a stranger; she hardly looked
at her and seemed to be avoiding talking to her.

After two days of this, Ritva sneaked up behind Martta in the
garden and tapped her on the shoulder. Martta turned as if stung.

'What's the matter, Martta? Have I offended you?'

'Don't talk to me, please!' Martta was pale.

'What is it? Has something happened?'

'No. I'm sorry, you don't understand.'

'What do you mean, I don't understand? I thought you were
my friend. You sat at my bedside for days, you told me about
your people and the sacred drum and you said we should escape
together. But now you won't even talk to me?'

'Please, Ritva, someone might see us.'

'I don't care who sees us.'

'Believe me, you will,' Martta said, her face clouding over; she
turned and continued to dig her patch. Ritva could see that her
back was as tense as a spring.

Had Martta suddenly become a coward? Did she regret telling
Ritva so much about herself? Ritva stomped back towards the
building, swallowing her tears.

'Finished already?' The new nurse, Anna, said frowning.

Although young, she already seemed stern and suspicious.

'Yes, thank you!' Ritva snapped. The nurse unlocked the door and let her inside. Ritva headed for the dayroom and approached Erika.

'Can you show me how to use the loom?' She might as well learn to weave, keep herself busy.

'But of course, my dear,' Erika said, 'I thought you'd never ask.'

Ritva was spending more hours than ever in the dayroom. But a week later, as they passed each other in the garden, Martta reached for Ritva's hand and pulled her towards her.

'I'm sorry about the other day, Ritva. Please, let's meet behind the west wing. None of the nurses will be able to see us there.'

Looking into Martta's warm eyes, Ritva's pride and anger dissolved; she nodded and waited a few minutes after Martta disappeared before following her round the corner.

'I got scared, Ritva,' Martta said, leaning against the wall. 'When Katja heard I had been sitting at your bedside while you were ill, she was furious. She warned me to leave you alone and I'm afraid she's just waiting to trip me up.'

Despite her anxious words, Martta had the solidity and strength of a large tree. Ritva sighed – she needed Martta to be strong and to be her friend; she recalled the poplar of her childhood and how it had been her refuge. As if Martta had sensed her thoughts, she briefly pulled Ritva into an embrace. Ritva could feel Martta's heart beating against her own, the soft skin of Martta's neck against her temple. How long had it been since she had been wrapped in an embrace, felt the warmth of another person like this? Ritva breathed deeply as if to fill her lungs with the preciousness of this moment, then Martta pushed her away.

'We need to go. Wait here a while so the nurses won't see us coming back together,' Martta said, then slipped along the wall of the west wing and disappeared around the corner.

*

A while later, still in the garden, Ritva heard a loud commotion coming from inside the building: nurses shouting, swearing and a scream. She froze – it was Martta.

'So, you're back from your adventure then, are you?' Anna sneered. Ritva had not heard the nurse approach.

'You both disappeared for at least ten minutes, if not more. Then Martta appears, asking to be allowed inside and I see you sneaking out from behind the west wing. It doesn't take much figuring out, does it?' Ritva looked at her blankly. 'And don't blame me. It was Katja who saw you as she came back from the superintendent's house.'

'Please let me inside.' Ritva's heart pounded. The nurse unlocked the front door. As Ritva peered along the dim corridor, she felt sick: she could see Martta kicking and screaming, her arms twisted behind her back as Petta and Katja pushed her towards the west wing. They passed the matron's office and Ritva could hear the matron's syrupy voice: 'It's for your own good, Martta. Remember, the more you struggle the more it hurts. You should know this by now.'

Everything in Ritva longed to run after Martta, but instead she slid down the wall and collapsed in a heap. The large iron door separating the seclusion wing from the rest of the building shut with a loud clang. When, half an hour later, Katja and Petta escorted Ritva to the same wing, she did not resist.

The night that followed would etch itself deep into Ritva's memory.

'Come along, now,' Katja said, 'the less you struggle the easier it'll be. A night in the jacket will do you no harm.'

Ritva had seen the grey straitjackets before, sewn from strong, rough cotton with buttons at the back and sleeves three times the length of a normal jacket. To be trapped in one of these . . . She stumbled between Petta and Katja like a beaten dog and did not resist as they slipped on the jacket and buttoned it up at the back. But as Katja crossed Ritva's arms over her chest and yanked the sleeves into a knot behind Ritva's back, panic gripped her.

'Please, don't do this to me. I haven't done anything!'

'Now, now, my petal,' Katja purred, 'it's nothing to be afraid of. It will help cool your queer desires and emotions. In other places they use ice baths but we prefer the jackets. Well, sometimes a bath might also help . . .'

'Please, Nurse.'

Katja threw her a cold look.

'You can say please all you like, but it won't help you here.'

'I will look in on you later, to make sure you're comfortable,' Petta said, a grin spreading across his face. He stroked her cheek with the back of his hand. Ritva squirmed, trying to pull away.

'Don't make it hard for us,' Katja hissed. 'Now then – you can choose between the sheets or restraints. Which would you prefer?'

A wave of nausea swept through Ritva.

'I beg you!'

'Well, then, we'll choose for you.' Katja sighed. 'I can see you're a decent, Christian girl and I believe that this is all Martta's fault, she's gone sweet on you. You just need some thinking time. I think we should use the sheets.' She spread a large sheet across the bed.

'Now lie down and be a good girl.'

Ritva, arms tied across her chest, sat on the bed, struggling to maintain her balance. Katja pushed her down and with a few quick moves she and Petta wrapped Ritva's whole body up in the sheets until she was swaddled like a baby with only her head sticking out.

'Please, I can't move,' Ritva pleaded, trying to free herself.

'Well, that is the point, my dear. Don't worry, it won't do you any harm. But the more you struggle, the worse it will feel. I'll be back in the morning with breakfast. And Petta here will look in on you later.'

'Please!' Ritva's voice was hoarse. 'What have I done?'

'You won't scream, will you?' Petta held up a rag and a bandage. 'Of course we can always put this in your pretty mouth. Shall we?'

'No . . .'

'All right then. I knew you'd be a good girl,' Katja said. 'Now go to sleep. Sweet dreams.'

As they left, the room went dark and Ritva heard the key turn in the lock; then, except for a soft moan from one of the cells at the end of the west wing, it was quiet.

Where was Martta? Had they restrained and gagged her? Was she lying in the cell right next to hers? Ritva could no longer control herself and started to sob.

'Martta!' Her voice came out as a whisper. 'Are you there?' Nothing. Ritva gasped for air, unable to turn on her side, a fly caught in a spider's web, stuck in a sticky cocoon. Her back and neck itched but when she tried to wriggle, the sheets fastened even tighter around her.

'Help!' She could not hold back her cry. Moments later, Petta entered. He closed the door behind him and locked it.

'What is it, my dove? Can't you sleep?' Her heart almost stopped at the sound of his sickly voice.

'I'm sorry, I'm itchy and I can't breathe.'

'Ah, you poor thing, let me help you blow your nose.' He took out a rag and held it over her nose.

'Now blow!' She obeyed.

'So, you have an itch, do you?' he whispered; she could feel his hot breath near her ear. She stiffened.

'Let me relieve you of that itch then.'

His tongue entered her ear, then trailed across her cheek and neck and tried to enter her mouth. She pressed her lips together, closed her eyes and willed herself to be far away. The next moment, she felt herself being lifted from her body. Sensing nothing but her soul in flight and warm feathers engulfing her, she knew she was safe – at least for a while.

Ritva did not know how much time had passed, but when she woke, dawn had broken and Petta was gone. She tensed when she heard the bunch of keys clanking outside the cell. She glanced down at herself. The sheets were still wrapped tightly around her

– at least Petta would not have been able to touch more than her face. She shuddered as she remembered him leaning over her, his hot breath on her. She recalled him saying he would be back. Would she ever be safe from him now?

'I hope you had a pleasant night,' Katja said cheerily as she entered the room and placed a tray on a chair next to the bed. 'I brought you breakfast. The question is, are you ready to join us again?'

Ritva nodded.

'Have you lost your voice?'

'No, Nurse, but I am ready.'

'Well, that is surely for me to decide. Do you regret what you did?'

Ritva closed her eyes. What had she done? She would never regret a second she had spent with Martta, yet the thought of another day swaddled in sheets, at the mercy of Petta, made her feel sick. Why couldn't she be friends with Martta?

'So?' Katja raised her eyebrows.

'But I . . . did nothing,' Ritva whispered.

Katja's pupils grew small. 'So you don't regret it?'

Ritva's throat tightened as she pushed back the tears, the taste of betrayal like bile in her mouth.

'Yes, yes, I do regret it.' She knew what some women said about Martta, that she didn't like men, that she was different . . . But it wasn't like that between them. Surely it couldn't be that?

'Well, all right then, there's a good girl. Let me get you out of here.' With a few swift moves, Katja untucked the sheets and unwrapped Ritva.

'Now sit up while I undo the jacket.' Freed from the contraption, Ritva suddenly felt naked; she pulled up her legs and wrapped her arms around her knees.

'Have your breakfast, and there's a pot under the bed for your business. I'll be back in an hour to collect you.'

Once Katja had left, Ritva put her ear to the wall. Nothing. Her heart ached thinking of Martta – would the nurses release her today as well? She prayed that Martta, just as she had done, would say what they wanted to hear.

Ritva was greeted by Erika and a cackle of women in the dayroom but she could not see Martta. She spent the next few days spinning, welcoming the monotony of the endlessly rotating wheel, the coarse wool gliding though her fingers until they were raw, while she observed the iron door of the west wing, hoping that Martta would appear. When the matron finally released Martta a week later, Ritva hardly recognised her friend: slumped over, ash-pale and propped up by two nurses, Martta shuffled along the corridor to her cell, avoiding Ritva's gaze, her skirt hanging loose from her sagging frame. Ritva turned away. What had they done to her? Had they not given her any food?

In the following weeks neither Ritva nor Martta spoke about what had happened to them in seclusion and it was months before they both regained the privilege of working in the garden. They kept their distance, yet the notes they secretly slipped to each other spoke of a bond that had only grown stronger.

That spring passed quickly and turned into a wet summer. After three years on Seili, time was losing all meaning for Ritva, and although she told herself she should no longer expect a letter from Father or Elke, she still missed them badly. She pined for Elke, their silly games and sisterly hugs, and she worried what might have happened to her. Would Father protect Elke from Uncle? It was only her connection with Martta and the other women that gave Ritva a sense of not being completely alone in the world.

Ritva also became aware that, ever since that night in seclusion, Petta was watching her more closely than ever. Sometimes he sneaked up behind her in the garden, sliding his hand along her arm, his hot breath against her ear, whispering 'my dove'. Each time a new patient arrived, she hoped he might turn his attention elsewhere and leave her alone, but he always seemed to be near her, watching her. She shuddered at the thought of another winter ahead. She was only nineteen, but her back ached and her joints were swollen – how much longer could she withstand the cruelty of this place before her body gave up?

Sometimes Ritva and Martta managed to meet at her secret place in the forest, sharing poems she had written or thinking up stories together, but fear had lodged itself in both their hearts and after their time in seclusion, neither of them talked any more about escape, or the vision of the drum.

Then, like a sudden fierce thunderstorm, one day in August everything changed.

13

It was the day Doctor Olafson came on his monthly visit, and as usual he was surrounded by a swarm of patients, fighting like dogs over scraps for his attention. Ritva still met with him occasionally, but these days she felt resigned, knowing he had never managed to have anyone released from the asylum. In the late afternoon he called her to his office.

'Ritva, I want you to listen to me very carefully . . .' He looked pale and his eyebrows were drawn. 'There's nothing much I can do to better your situation, or in fact that of any of the women here, but once a year, in April, I can apply to the Board of Trustees for one case to be reviewed in depth. I've decided this should be you, Ritva. I will ask them to consider your release.'

Ritva gasped.

'Release? But why me, Doctor?'

'Because you're smart and young, Ritva, and you have your whole life ahead of you.' He looked out of the window towards the shore.

'But there are other young patients here too: Irina, Martta, Klara.'

'Yes, but I believe that you, more than any of the others, have recovered well and deserve to leave. You've faced your memories and this has made you strong. I wish I could ask now, but the Board only meets to review such cases at Easter.'

Easter was still a whole winter away; why was he even telling her this now? To bolster her spirits? Ritva's skin tingled, sensing that

111

there was another reason; that he was not telling her everything. Then a sudden insight struck her.

'Did you know my mother?' she blurted out. He avoided her gaze.

'You knew her, didn't you? ' Ritva's heart was thumping.

'No, Ritva.'

'You're lying, I can feel it.'

'I didn't *know* her. Not really, not well anyway . . .'

Ritva's eyes widened.

'Ritva, your mother was already very ill when I took up my position here. She had developed tuberculosis, and there was nothing I could do for her. She died in December 1912. It was a terrible winter and I couldn't get to Seili until early March . . .' His voice trailed off.

'No, my mother was sent somewhere else and you don't want to tell me where.' Ritva felt breathless and dizzy.

'No, Ritva. I'm so sorry. We buried your mother in March 1913, right here, in the small cemetery behind the church.'

Ritva pinched the skin between her fingers. She had once walked through the cemetery and had studied every name on the simple wooden crosses.

'You're lying! There is no cross with my mother's name on it.'

'The matron had it taken down when she heard that you were being sent here. Not many people know that Lara was your mother. You mustn't tell her . . .'

Lara – her mother's name cut her to the bone. Ritva shot up and stumbled out of the office; she had to get to the cemetery. She composed herself and asked Nurse Erika to be allowed out into the garden. Outside, she pulled up some weeds from her patch and waited for an opportunity to jump over the fence. It was never designed to keep the women in; there was no need, the whole island was their prison.

'Finish off your work, dear, it'll be dinner time soon,' Nurse Anna called to her. As soon as the nurse went inside, Ritva climbed over the fence and bolted downhill, choosing the quickest route to the church, across the meadow and a small birch forest.

As always, the wooden building surprised her as she stood breathless in front of its rust-coloured facade, a rosebush sprawling next to the entrance. She shuddered as she recalled the Easter and Christmas sermons, the church filled with nurses and other island folk, farming families with their children squeezed next to one another on the hard benches – from the eldest down to the youngest, like the pipes in the church organ – the asylum women seated in the back pews.

Did these people have to flaunt their children in front of those who would never kiss the head of a newborn? What cruelty, to expect smiles and gratitude from those who had been deprived of everything. Ritva still remembered the clammy shame and bitterness she experienced after those mornings in church, her face flushed as if she had been slapped by the children's stares and whispers. The most daring children poked their tongues out at the women. And yet she had been so keen to see them, and even more so, be seen by them. Once, she had flashed a smile at a little boy, but he had turned away and buried his head in his sister's hair.

Ritva shook herself and walked to the left of the church where a small white gate stood open. The cemetery was a fenced-in area at the back of the church, surrounded by pines and birch. A handful of wooden crosses stuck out from the grass at various angles and stages of decay: one leaning to the side, white paint peeling from the wood, another bolt upright with a name spelled out in neat black letters; others had fallen or were overgrown with moss.

As Ritva walked amongst the crosses, she realised that even in death the ones deemed mad had been separated from those who proclaimed themselves to be sane: the asylum women's graves were marked with wooden crosses that barely lasted two winters, and were separated by a stretch of grass from a row of metal crosses that signalled the graves of the asylum's previous superintendents and their families. Although rusty, their names had been cast in iron so they would be remembered for generations to come.

Ritva stumbled between the crosses, searching for her mother's name, her fingers picking away at moss and lichen: Ida Vilhelmina, Sarah Englund, Anna, Else, Maria . . . but no Lara. She gazed at the bright green grass bursting from the ground. Was her mother really buried here? With no cross, how could she ever know? Hundreds of crosses had crumbled here, leaving no trace of the deceased women of the asylum; and before that, the men and the lepers – women, men, whole families, cast out and buried in the same sandy earth, their bones tangled, indistinguishable . . .

Ritva's eyes fell on an overgrown patch behind the church. A tug in her stomach pulled her towards the spot and she stared down into the green mess of nettles. And there they were: half-broken crosses, names almost extinguished by rain and snow. Her heart pounded. Without regard for her skin, she plunged into the nettles and pulled out piece after piece. Rosa, Jaana, Olga . . . Her hands were covered in nettle stings, but there – finally she held a board in her shaking hands: LARA LARSON *Born 1875. Died on Seili 20th of December 1912*. Blind with tears, Ritva tossed the piece of wood back into the nettles.

'And what are you doing here?' A voice she knew all too well startled her. Petta stood at the entrance to the graveyard, grinning.

'You're looking for your mother? She was just as stubborn as you are. Didn't want my help with the extra blanket, and look where that got her.' Ritva stared at him. 'Well, I shouldn't waste this rare opportunity – meeting you out here, all alone.'

'What do you want?'

'Oh, you know what I want!'

In seconds he had reached her. He grabbed her arm, pulled her towards him and then pinned her wrists against the church wall.

'I want you, Ritva, and you know I'm used to getting what I want.' His hoarse voice filled her ear. She tried to break free, but he only pushed harder. For a moment his voice softened.

'You're different to the others . . . you've done something to me . . .'

'Leave me alone, you brute,' Ritva snapped. He slapped her cheek.

'Let me go, you're hurting me,' Ritva hissed. Her wrists hurt – what if he forced himself on her? Ritva realised she needed to be smart.

'If I give you a kiss, will you let go of me?'

Petta blinked and loosened his grip a fraction. Ritva pulled away with all her strength and punched her right fist into Petta's stomach. He doubled over, clutching his gut. Ritva bolted off, stumbling through the forest.

'I'll get you, witch!' His raging voice rang in her ears.

'Never, never . . .' she muttered under her breath, pounding up the hill towards the asylum, her skirt catching on branches, ripping. If she could just throw herself into the doctor's arms, tell him about Petta . . . maybe the matron would listen to him? Suddenly, a deep hooting sound cut through the silence: the steam boat. Her heart sank – Doctor Olafson was already on his way back to Nauvo and he wouldn't return for a month. She reached the entrance to the asylum with stinging lungs. She smoothed her hair and clothes then rang the bell. When Nurse Erika opened the door, Ritva mumbled an excuse and rushed to her cell. Lock-in would be a relief today; keeping herself safe from Petta her only goal.

Ritva tossed and turned all night; chills ran down her spine whenever she thought of Petta, and as her panic faded, grief about her mother's death washed over her. And what about Father – for Mother to have been brought here, surely he must have signed the papers, declaring her incurably insane? He had lied and betrayed them both. All her life she had respected him and yes, had also feared his temper, but she had always harboured a fierce love for him. She stifled her furious sobs with the pillow. And now that she had hurt Petta's pride, he would find some foul reason to put her in seclusion again and take what he wanted. Her stomach heaved; if she didn't escape she would die in this place, just like her mother had. Doctor Olafson's pathetic attempt to have her released was useless – by next spring it would be too late.

Finally sleep overcame her, and in her exhausted state she sensed her mother standing by her bedside, a smell of violets lingering in the air.

14

Ritva awoke to the clinking of the keys. Her stomach cramped as everything came flooding back to her – Petta's threat, her mother's death, the graveyard – and it took all of her strength not to rush straight to Martta. Instead, she waited until that afternoon, when they were both working in the garden.

'Martta, my mother died here on Seili! This place is going to kill us all.'

'Slow down, Ritva, what do you mean your mother died here?'

'They sent her here a few years before me. I never knew where they had taken her, we never received any letters. Martta, I'll die if I stay here a moment longer. Look at us, this place is eating us alive! And yesterday Petta cornered me in the cemetery and tried to force himself on me. I don't know how much longer I can keep him away.'

'In the cemetery?'

'Yes. I was looking for a sign that my mother had been buried there. Doctor Olafson told me—' Ritva was crying now. 'And I found it, Martta. They hid her cross so I wouldn't see it. She died only six months before I came here!'

Martta's face went pale, then turned scarlet.

'Those bastards,' she muttered under her breath. She looked at Ritva.

'Ritva, I've been thinking about little else other than how we can escape; and even more so since they stuck us in seclusion.

117

Do you remember those wooden planks on the boat when they brought you here?' Ritva nodded.

'Do you think they use them to build houses with? No, they're for us, Ritva. It's the timber for our coffins! There are too few trees here, so they send us with the wood for our coffins, just as they did with the lepers before us. We're not expected to return home. Ever. Why they even bother with coffins, I don't know; there'll certainly be no gravestone for any of us.'

Ritva recalled how she had asked the boatman about the planks that first fateful day; then her gaze wandered to the west wing where Irina was fighting her last battle. Bed-bound for weeks now, illness had ravaged her body and there were rumours that she had only days to live.

'In the old days before the Christians came, my people buried our dead on small islands. No one was to visit them there, it was their special resting place. We're not even dead yet, and they have abandoned us on this island and buried us alive. Ritva, we've got nothing to lose.' Martta's green eyes were alight with a fierceness and determination Ritva had never seen in her before.

'This is our only chance,' Martta whispered. 'If we get ill this winter, we'll never make it. And with Irina dying . . .'

Ritva breathed in sharply; Martta was right.

'Yes! Let's leave before Petta can get to me.'

'But we need more provisions,' Martta said. 'Food, tools, blankets, matches . . . and a plan.'

'You tried it before, didn't you? Running away, I mean.'

Martta looked towards the shore. Finally she spoke.

'Yes. I just bolted off without a plan, like a spooked horse. But this time it'll be different. There will be two of us.' She put her hand on Ritva's arm. 'Trust me, I couldn't bear to be caught again. And we won't be. The days are still too long now, but September will be ideal. Let's leave then.'

They stood for a moment, facing each other. Everything is changing already, Ritva thought. *There will be two of us*, Martta had said. Ritva's heart pounded like the sacred drum of her dreams. Maybe escape was possible after all?

That evening at dinner, the matron informed everyone that a bereavement had occurred in Petta's family in Oulu and he would be away for some time. Ritva swallowed hard – was this true or had the matron got wind of Petta's behaviour and suspended him? If so, she could imagine Petta plotting his revenge from afar. She didn't trust him – there was no time to lose. However, they still needed a plan.

'I must see my sister, Martta. God knows what kind of danger she's in,' Ritva said when they met in the garden the following day. 'My uncle is not to be trusted, nor is my father, really. I do worry about her so much.'

'I understand, Ritva, but we cannot go to Turku. That's the first place they would look. We need to go west.'

'West? You mean across the archipelago?' Ritva's eyes widened. There were more than a hundred miles of water to cross, a maze of islands and tiny islets and then a deep gulf between the Åland Islands and Sweden – it was impossible.

'Yes, it's our only chance, Ritva. Once we're in Sweden and some time has passed we can work out what to do about your sister. Maybe we can send a letter, or . . .'

'Sweden?'

'Yes. If we're lucky the whole gulf will freeze over and then we can cross over to Sweden and head northwards.'

Ritva gasped – Martta really had lost her mind.

'Trust me, Ritva. Yes, it will take us months and we'll have to be cunning and careful, but it is possible. The only thing we can be certain of is that if we stay here, we'll die.'

Ritva knew that Martta was right; and if death was certain, she would rather face it under an open sky and be free.

Two days later Martta showed Ritva a small piece of folded paper she had hidden under her blouse. She smoothed the neatly drawn map over her knee.

'I know there're nearly as many islands in the archipelago as there're stars above and this is only a simple map, but I think it'll do.'

'How did you get this?' Ritva whispered.

'Arianna drew it. She used to pass as a man and went fishing with the fishermen all over the archipelago. She filled in as much detail as she could remember.' A chill ran down Ritva's back. Had Martta shared their plan with Arianna? Was she trustworthy? And what price had she paid? Nothing was free on Seili; had it been food, alcohol, a kiss, more? Ritva had always kept her distance from the stocky, red-faced woman. 'Killed a man with her bare hands,' Irina had once told her. But who was she to judge? So many women lived with a darkness they never talked about.

'And together with your map, I trust we'll find the way.'

'My map?'

'Yes, the drawing of the drum you made. It's a kind of map, too, I think. My grandfather told me that in the old days our sacred drums could be used when you were lost or needed to find the reindeer herd . . .'

Ritva frowned – they would need a great deal of luck if Martta's hand-drawn map and the faint images that had come to her in a dream were all they had to go by.

Two weeks later, Petta was back. Ritva stayed out of his way but observed him and the nurses closely. Petta kept his matches, tobacco and a small pipe in his jacket, which hung on a hook in the nurses' office. He guarded his tobacco fiercely and sometimes traded it for sweets.

'We need a distraction, some sort of fight that everyone will get drawn into,' Ritva whispered, pulling Martta to the side one morning. 'Then one of us can sneak into the office and steal his matches. Maybe we can use Katarina?' She felt guilty about involving the old woman, but no one shrieked louder than Katarina, as Ritva had found out on her first day.

'How about we get Olga to start something?' Martta replied.

'She won't be able to resist the bacon I kept back from yesterday.' Olga hated fish, and they both knew she would pounce on the offer.

That evening, Ritva pulled Olga aside and showed her the bacon under the table that Martta had wrapped in a handkerchief.

'Tomorrow, after dinner, I need you to poke Katarina, get her to make a racket. I don't mind how you do it; I'll give you half of the bacon now if you say yes, the rest tomorrow night.' Olga glanced at the glistening piece of meat and frowned. She's thinking about the jacket and seclusion, weighing it all up, Ritva thought.

'I'll do it,' Olga hissed, 'just give me the bacon.'

Ritva opened the handkerchief and took out one of the two rashers. The sliver disappeared into Olga's mouth in seconds, leaving a fatty stain on her chin. She walked away without another word.

That evening Ritva and Martta finished dinner early and were walking towards the dayroom when they heard something crash to the floor, followed by Katarina's high-pitched squeal: 'You devil!' Within minutes three nurses had rushed into the dining room together with many of the women who were eager to watch the unfolding spectacle.

Ritva ran in the opposite direction. The office was empty and, as she had hoped, in their haste the nurses had left the door unlocked. She made straight for Petta's jacket. Her hand slid into the right pocket – nothing. Blood was pounding in her ears – if they found her here, all their plans would be ruined. Her hands shook as she reached into the other pocket. There! The small box between her fingers felt more precious than a nugget of gold. She hid it under her blouse, slipped out of the office and ran down the corridor. She could still hear Katarina screaming insults at the nurses and slowed down to catch her breath before entering the dining room. Martta was trying to calm the old woman, but as so often, once enraged, Katarina could not stop and was screaming at the top of her lungs, lashing out at everyone around her. Ritva felt a lump in her throat as the nurses carried her off to her cell. Olga stood in a corner, commanding Ritva with her watery eyes to settle the bill and hand over the bacon.

'First step accomplished,' Ritva whispered as she passed Martta, pointing to the invisible box of matches hidden under her blouse.

'When is Doctor Olafson coming next?' Ritva asked Nurse Erika the next morning. She was anxious to find out more about her mother before their escape.

'Oh, I don't think he'll be coming back, dear. I heard he's got another position in Turku. It'll be better for him. You lot did tire him out, you know.' She laughed. 'Besides,' she lowered her voice, 'the matron thought he was too soft, said you all had him wrapped around your little fingers.' The nurse's words hit Ritva like a bullet.

'He was a good man,' was all she managed to say – no doubt the matron had got rid of him because of his complaints about the treatment of the women. Had she also heard that he wanted to put Ritva forward for a review?

'Oh yes, and I'm sure his replacement will be just as competent. Although, of course, he might not be so soft.'

'He was kind, Nurse Erika, not soft,' Ritva said and moved away.

With the doctor's departure, Petta seemed to feel his power growing and two days later he cornered Ritva in an alcove.

'You think you can get rid of me that easily?' he snarled.

Ritva broke into a sweat – Petta was pale, there were dark rings under his eyes and he had lost weight. His breath smelled of alcohol and had his voice not carried such threat, she would have thought him pathetic.

'I was going to be gentle, but now you can have it your way.'

Ritva's eyes darted around – none of the other women or nurses was nearby.

'I'll get what I want, Ritva. You'll never escape me.' He groped her breast. With all her force Ritva pushed him off and ran down the corridor, his laughter making her hair stand on end.

'We've got to leave,' Ritva panted when she found Martta in the garden. 'Petta won't stop until he's had me!'

'God, what happened?'

Ritva told her about the encounter and Martta agreed – there was no time to lose. Later that afternoon when none of the nurses was around, they climbed over the fence. The workshop could be seen from the dining room window so they had to take a detour across a small forest. Once they reached the workshop, Ritva kept lookout, while Martta wedged a small garden shovel into the door frame – the lock sprang open with a clang. A strong smell of pine and varnish wafted towards them. In the dusty twilight, amongst piles of wood on a simple bench sat a large wooden box – a newly finished coffin. Ritva swallowed hard. How efficient the asylum was when death was approaching: now that Irina's condition had worsened and she was expected to die, the superintendent had wasted no time and had already instructed the island carpenter to build her coffin. Ritva looked around the dim room and with a pang she saw a bunch of neatly stacked boards in the corner, just like the timbers that had been shipped with her to Seili. Ritva's eyes met Martta's.

'You were right, they sent us here with the wood for our own coffins! What a perfect plan – make us do the chores, grow our own food and sell our handicraft. Then on top of all that, we even come equipped with the wood for our own coffins.' Ritva spat the words out like a foul apple.

'I promise you they'll never bury us in these coffins,' Martta said and placed a hand on Ritva's shoulder. 'I'll do everything I can to get us out of here.'

She picked up two wooden staffs, a few thin boards, a hammer, an axe and a saw that hung neatly on the wall and threw them into the coffin on the bench together with a box of nails.

'Let's go.'

The coffin was heavier than Ritva had imagined. Martta lifted it up, reaching behind her with her back facing the bench, while Ritva took the other end. It only just fitted through the door.

'We've got to be quick or they will miss us at dinner,' Martta whispered although no one could overhear them here. They carried the coffin down towards the shore, staying in the shadows of the trees, then headed along the water's edge towards the eastern part of the island. Despite the evening chill, sweat poured from their faces. The light pine gave off a pale shine, but Martta assured Ritva that no one could see them in the twilight. They hid the coffin near the shore, close to one of the biggest trees on the island, and started to cover it with branches and earth. It would only take them ten minutes on foot to get there from the asylum, just enough time for a swift escape.

'But will it hold us?' Ritva frowned. The coffin looked smaller than she had thought it would be, but then Irina had shrunk to a mere shadow over the last few weeks.

'It's all we have,' Martta said. She took the hammer out of the coffin and nailed a board to the end of each staff. 'That should do – our oars. We'll only get one chance at this, Ritva – it has to work! Let's hope Irina survives another night.'

The plan was for Martta to stay in the garden the following evening. It would be suspicious if they were both absent from dinner, but sometimes Martta stayed out longer than the others. 'Try to grab some more things in the chaos,' Martta urged, 'food, blankets, water bottles, anything. We'll wear all our clothes in layers. I'll meet you here. You can see the tree from up there.'

'What if they lock all the doors and I can't get out?' Ritva cringed at the thought.

'They'll want to save the workshop, believe me, and that'll be your chance.'

'I can't bear the thought that I won't get to you in time.' Ritva's voice trembled.

'You'll make it, Ritva. You will, and you must! Women are dying like flies here – I don't want us to be next.' Martta brushed a strand of hair from Ritva's forehead and stroked her left cheek with her hand. Warmth spread through Ritva like a swarm of butterflies.

'There will be a new life for us out there, Ritva. Somewhere no one knows about us or where we came from.' Ritva leaned against Martta's shoulder, then pulled out the box of matches and pressed it into Martta's hand.

'Here, please keep yourself safe. I'll see you on the shore.'

Martta closed her fingers around the box. They stood for a long moment, gazing out at a cluster of small islands rising out of the water in the distance.

'Please be here,' Martta whispered.

'I will. I promise.'

15

The next afternoon, Martta stayed in the garden until the other women and the last nurse had returned inside. She gripped the small matchbox in her cardigan pocket and smiled, holding the accomplice to their freedom in her palm. She was wearing all her clothes: two undershirts, two blouses, a jumper and a cardigan, stockings and two longs skirts, and although the afternoon had begun to cool, her face was flushed and a trickle of sweat ran down her back. She had hidden a blanket and a bundle of food under a bush in the far corner of the garden. She took a swig from her water bottle, careful not to waste a drop; she would not be going back inside – ever.

'I think you've done enough for today.' Martta jumped; she had not heard Anna approach, her mind occupied with thoughts of Ritva, their provisions . . .

'Oh, I won't be long, I just want to finish up here.'

'You look tired and you're drenched in sweat. Are you feeling well?'

'Yes, I'm fine, thank you.' Martta steadied her voice. Usually the nurses left her alone when she worked in the garden each afternoon and Martta would knock at the main entrance just before dinner to be let back in. What if Anna insisted that she return inside now? An image flashed through her mind: Anna bloodied, dragged by her wrists into a bush . . . If she had to, Martta would hit her over the head with the spade – nothing would stop her plans now. The nurse frowned and looked at Martta, holding her gaze for a long moment, then she sighed.

'Very well, then, but don't linger.' She turned and made her way inside. Martta took a deep breath; it wouldn't be long now . . . .

The shadows stretched and soon the sun would set. Martta walked to the vegetable beds that lay closest to the fence; the carrots and beetroot were not fully grown but she could no longer wait. With her back to the asylum's windows she prised some beetroot and carrots from the bed, shook off the earth and slipped the precious cargo into her pockets, then smoothed the earth as if it had never been disturbed. She could be seen from most of the asylum's windows and the kitchen, but shortly before dinner the cook was always too busy to peep outside. Pretending to do some more weeding, Martta kneeled in front of the bush that hid her belongings, gathered them into a bundle and stuffed everything under her cardigan. Then, armed with a small shovel, she made her way over to the flowerbeds at the westernmost corner of the garden.

She had often returned inside with a bunch of flowers for the dining room table and the nurses had praised her about how much calmer she was these days. Martta shivered – she would not be taking them flowers again. She looked up and smiled; the sun had lit the sky with blazing shades of orange and red. As luck would have it, she did not have to climb the fence, but found three loose boards and managed to squeeze through the gap. Once out of sight, she gathered speed, running across meadows and through the birch forest so that she could arrive at the workshop unseen. By now the fiery sky had cooled to soft pink. Dusk would be their ally, the blue hour between day and night when the wind died down and the first creatures of the night began to emerge.

She hid her bundle behind a tree, approached the workshop and opened the door. The work bench lay empty just as they had left it, yet she could still see the coffin in her mind's eye. Now it waited for them on the other side of the island, covered with branches and earth. They had taken a great risk, but Irina had made it through the night and the carpenter had not returned to the workshop.

Martta looked around. Next to a simple wood burner stood an iron bucket full of kindling and wood shavings. She placed the shavings on the table in a neat heap, stacked the kindling around it, then added larger pieces of wood, constructing a bonfire. She dragged some of the timber planks from the corner and stacked them around the workbench. There would be no more coffins made here – at least not for a long time. She heard the dinner bell chime five times. From this distance, it sounded thin and eerie, like the bell the superintendent rang whenever one of the women was buried. Everyone would be sitting down to their meal now, but soon someone would lift their head, look out of the dining room window and let out a scream . . .

Martta admired her neat pile of wood; the timber was dry and air could flow freely from all sides to fan the flames. The whole workshop smelled of nothing but dry wood – it would burn like tinder.

Ritva stole to her cell just before dinner to gather her things. The previous day she had drawn the charcoal image of the drum on a piece of paper, rolled it up and hidden it under her pillow; now she slid it into her bundle. Her heart fluttered at the thought of what Martta was doing – had she already broken into the workshop? With Martta at her side everything seemed possible. Ritva was collecting her remaining bread creatures from under the bed when a shadow fell across the doorway. For a moment she did not recognise the figure standing in the entrance.

'What are you doing, crawling around under your bed like a bug?' It was Katarina. 'You've got something sweet hidden there?' Ritva had grown fond of the old woman who had been locked up on Seili for more than half a century. She had been brought here as a young woman and no one knew exactly how old she really was. Now, despite her occasional outbursts, she was very frail, her spirit faded. Ritva shuddered – a whole life lost in the shadow of the asylum. If she and Martta were caught, this would be their fate.

'I'm just looking after my little friends, you know, the animals,' Ritva said, picking up a four-legged creature that resembled a sheep, holding it close to Katarina's face. The old woman grabbed it.

'Baaaahhh, baaahhh,' Katarina mimicked a sheep. 'You have a baby sheep too?'

Ritva reached underneath her bed and pulled out a small figure, a lamb.

'Here, you can keep them both if you like.' She wouldn't need them any more.

'You're leaving, aren't you?' Katarina's face clouded over, her voice as shrill as fingernails scratching down a blackboard. 'You're leaving me to rot here with all the others. You only have eyes for that Lapp woman. What do you care?' She spat on the floor.

'Shush, is that how you want to thank me for everything I've done for you?' Ritva gasped; what if the old woman started a fight? But as quickly as rage had gripped Katarina it dissolved into nothing and her eyes filled with tears.

'You're still young, why wouldn't you try? I can smell it on you, you're leaving.' She stepped closer and fixed her red-rimmed eyes on Ritva.

'Don't be silly, Katarina, no one ever escapes from this place. Remember how Irina tried? It got her nowhere and now she is dying. Please, go now before I tell the nurses. I'll see you at dinner.'

Katarina stared at Ritva – then she put first the sheep, then the lamb into her mouth. She chewed loudly, and swallowed hard. Ritva looked away, sick to her stomach. Katarina turned around, a look of triumph on her face, and left.

Martta looked down at the matchbox. How could such a small object hold so much power? She slid the box open, took out a match and struck it. The flame caught the wood shavings, then the kindling. Martta stood back and let the fire take; it greedily lapped up the kindling and small pieces of wood, then spread to the planks, catching everything in its path, growing within minutes into a fierce bonfire. Martta's heart beat hard as she watched the fire blacken the workbench, licking along its sides until it engulfed it completely. The fire crackled and roared as it caught the wooden boards around the bench, the heat so intense that Martta could smell her hair beginning to singe. Her eyes were transfixed by the flames, their elemental power. As she watched, she could see images in the flames: the comforting *lavvu* fires of her childhood and, long before that, the burning of the sacred drums, her ancestors' turf huts torched to the ground; then a bird rising with shimmering wings from the ashes . . . She coughed and the vision vanished.

Dizzy from the smoke and heat, Martta realised she had to get out; it wouldn't be long before someone noticed the fire. The flames had already reached the door, almost cutting her off from the exit. She lifted her heavy skirts, pulled her cardigan over her face and the sleeves over her hands, then leapt across the burning timber towards the door. She grabbed the handle, pushed the door open and threw herself outside. At that moment the roof and walls caught fire and now the whole workshop was ablaze. Martta backed away, her face stinging, holding her right hand which had grabbed the door handle. She would need to bandage it – but not now. She could hear a cacophony of voices coming from the direction of the asylum: 'Help, the workshop's on fire!' and moments later, the fire bell.

She scrambled to retrieve her bundle and bolted through the bushes towards the shore. The nurses would not be able to douse the fire, the workshop stood too far from the water's edge and there were no hoses. Even if they arrived with buckets, the fire would soon leave nothing but soot and ash. Martta thought she could make out hysterical laughter coming from some of the women. Maybe someone else would seize the opportunity, if not to escape, at least to steal something amid the chaos; perhaps the fire would remind them of their own fierceness that lay hidden beneath the despair and resignation . . .

Martta stumbled across a meadow and a small patch of woodland, branches tugging at her, scratching her face and hands. Finally she reached the shore and moved along its edge towards the silhouette of the tall pine. When she reached the tree she leaned against the rough bark and scanned the shore and fields for Ritva. Had she made it out of the building? Martta ripped a piece of fabric from her blouse and bandaged her hand.

It would be a moonless night and it was almost dark now. The spot was not far from the asylum, but in the darkness the tree would be hard to see. Martta uncovered the coffin from its hiding place and for a moment she thought of Irina – how would they bury her now? Would they cocoon her in a sheet and put her straight into the earth? Despite everything that had occurred between them, Martta had never wished Irina any harm; no one deserved to die the way she would, racked by TB, abandoned in the west wing.

Martta clenched her fists. There was no time to lose; soon the nurses would realise who was missing and they would never have another chance like this again. She remembered the rough hands that had grabbed her the first time she had escaped; they had pushed her down into the bushes, kicked her, then dragged her into a cell in the seclusion wing, gagged her and tied her down with leather straps. Petta had only taken the dirty rag out of her mouth to spoon-feed her, then put it back; when he touched her under her skirts, his face had distorted into an ugly grimace. Somehow she had survived those three weeks, but this time she knew it would break her.

She could hear men's voices near the workshop. Her heart cramped – would Ritva make it? Suddenly Martta was startled by the sound of breaking twigs behind her; and there was Ritva, panting, chest heaving.

'They nearly got me, Martta, I was so scared! They know it's us!' Ritva lunged at Martta and hugged her.

'I'm so glad to see you,' Martta said. 'Let's get out of here. I know we can make it but we need to leave right now. Help me get the coffin.'

They dragged the pale coffin down towards the shore.

'You get in first,' Martta whispered. 'I'll give it a push and climb in after you.' She took Ritva's hand.

'Here, take my bundle and don't hurt yourself on the tools.' A saw, hammer and axe lay stowed at one end. The coffin slid into the water and Ritva stepped in, steadying herself on Martta's arm. The vessel rocked precariously so she sat down immediately; she pulled her knees up and held their bundles between her legs, her spine pressed against the back of the coffin. She grabbed the sides with both hands. How could they hope to escape in such a ridiculous craft?

'Here, hold this too,' Martta said, handing Ritva one of the makeshift oars. Then she gave the coffin a push and a moment later Martta climbed in. A gush of water spilled over the side, splashing their skirts – now that it held their combined weight, the coffin floated only a handspan above the water.

'God help us,' Ritva gasped and gripped the wood. Water seeped through her shoes and skirt.

'Just put your oar in the water and row gently,' Martta said, plunging hers into the dark sea. Ritva followed suit, trying to keep her body as still as possible. The coffin spun around in circles until they found a shared rhythm and steered the vessel towards a shadowy shape ahead.

Looking back, they could see the orange glow of the burning workshop. Muffled voices carried across the water like broken notes, but no one seemed to have spotted them. In the morning a search party would comb Seili then take the boats and cover the islands close by, or even bring in a bigger boat from Nauvo. But not yet – this moonless night would shelter them like a mother, letting them hide underneath her dark sky.

*

They did not speak but steered their vessel towards the small island ahead, trying not to let the coffin flood. The wind turned out to be favourable, blowing softly in the right direction. Suddenly, with a thump the coffin struck a rock, then glided towards the nearly invisible shore. A whooshing of wings and a seagull's scream greeted them as they reached the islet, which seemed to be inhabited only by birds. Martta lifted her skirt, stepped out of the coffin onto the shore and pulled the vessel up the stony slope.

'We can rest for a short while here but they'll soon realise we aren't hiding on Seili. We've got to go further south, to Svartholm; it's smaller than Seili with meadows and trees but no houses. We can hide there for a day or two. We'll have to navigate between three other islands so it's best we wait until dawn.'

They pulled the coffin up the shore then leaned their tired backs against it. In the far distance the dim orange light of the fire still gleamed.

'There, it's done. No more timber for coffins,' Martta murmured.

'I hope they still bury Irina properly,' Ritva whispered.

Despite their escape, Ritva had thought a great deal about the dying woman who had been a friend to her in the first confusing weeks in the asylum, and whose coffin would now carry them across the archipelago.

At that moment they heard a deep grunt and caught a glimpse of movement nearby – a heavy body slipping into the water with a splash. It was a large seal. Ritva's heart pounded. Had Irina died tonight?

'Maybe Irina found her sealskin again,' Ritva said. Irina's passing and the appearance of the seal had opened a place in her heart that she had tried to harden in the days before their escape; now she let her tears run.

'She is free now.'

'Yes, she is,' Martta whispered, 'and so are we.'

16

Martta stayed awake through the night, Ritva leaning against her shoulder, asleep. When the faintest light of dawn broke through, Martta woke her.

'We need to reach Svartholm before they get out on the boats.'

The two women stretched their sore limbs and with few words they launched the coffin back into the water, steering towards Vaetjan, an island with little vegetation except for a small number of trees. By the time they reached the shore, the sun had risen above the horizon. They could see Seili from their position but could not make out any activity. A wide stretch of sea still separated them from Svartholm.

'What shall we do now?' Ritva said. 'If they catch up with us when we're in the channel between the islands, we're finished.'

'We could row to the other side of this island and look for shelter there,' Martta suggested. 'They're bound to think we've escaped to one of the bigger islands, so why don't we hide out here instead, right under their noses?'

This seemed as good a plan as any, Ritva thought, exhaustion gripping her. They went round the island, keeping close to the shore, then pulled the coffin out of the water and went into the small copse of trees.

'How about we dig a hole, turn the coffin upside down over it and cover all of it with earth and leaves?' Martta suggested. 'If we see anyone approaching the island we can crawl into the den and hide. If we cover the entrance with branches it'll look just like a small mound of earth.'

The idea sounded crazy to Ritva, but then, wasn't their whole plan to escape slightly mad? Martta grabbed the small shovel and handed Ritva the axe. They found a place with just enough space to accommodate the length and breadth of the coffin.

'Whoever decided women should wear long skirts?' Martta said, looking down at the soaked, dirty fabric that kept getting in the way. 'Completely foolish things for scrambling around in nature.'

'You're right, let's hitch them up and get rid of these terrible aprons.'

They slipped off the asylum aprons, lifted their ankle-length skirts and tucked them in at the waist. They returned to the shore and pushed the coffin uphill into the shelter of the trees, then worked feverishly as the sun rose higher and higher, hacking away at earth and roots. When they had dug down about three feet, Martta's shovel struck rock.

'That's it, we can't go any deeper than that. Let's try it.' They turned the coffin upside down and pulled it over the hole, then dug a small entrance. Ritva crawled first in first, but came back out immediately, pale and panting.

'Oh God, it's like being in your own grave. I can't do this, Martta, I can't breathe in there.'

'Let me try.' Martta squeezed herself into the tunnel but soon she too clambered out.

'We need to make it bigger,' she said, brushing dirt from her knees. For hours they dug, widening their underground den, glancing over their shoulder through the trees for any sign of a boat. By the afternoon they had broadened out the floor enough for both of them to be able to squeeze in next to each other. The coffin would prevent earth falling on their heads and they spread birch branches and moss on the rocky floor for warmth – it would not get more comfortable than this. They shovelled earth on top of the coffin, then covered the mound with moss and leaves.

'I don't want to go in, but it looks all right,' Ritva said.

'Why don't we stay on the island until the moon is fuller again? Then we can travel during the night,' Martta suggested. 'After a week they might even give up searching for us.'

Ritva gave a small smile at the thought of some rest.

'Yes, but how much water do we have?' They had three canteens, but as far as they could see there was no fresh water on this island.

'We need to be cautious with the water,' Martta said, 'and eat as many berries as we can find.'

They had eaten little since the day before and the moment their thoughts turned to food, both their stomachs rumbled.

'Let's see what we have.' They opened their bundles, laid blankets on the mossy ground and sat under the late-afternoon sun, nibbling on leftovers and carrots from the garden, forgetting for a moment that they were fugitives. In the commotion after Martta had set the fire, Ritva had grabbed whatever she could from the dinner tables: slices of bread, vegetables and smoked herring. Ritva searched for an apple she had hidden in her bag, but instead pulled out a bunch of envelopes.

'What's that?' Martta asked.

'Oh, after I took the food I ran to my cell to get my things. Then I saw a nurse rushing out of the office and I could tell she hadn't locked the door. I went inside to look for anything we could use – bandages, disinfectant, paper, pencils – there was this stack of letters in a corner. There were so many, I just grabbed a pile.' One by one Ritva picked up the envelopes, running her fingertip over the addresses written in delicate or untidy handwriting. Her heart cramped as she recognised a letter written in her own hand.

'None of them has a stamp, Martta – the matron never sent them!' All those letters had never reached their destinations . . . If Father had never told Elke, her sister would not even know where Ritva was.

'I am so sorry,' Martta said, gently taking the letters out of Ritva's hands and putting her arm around Ritva's shoulders.

Ritva stayed in the same spot all afternoon, staring blindly ahead of her. Only with the soft light of evening did she finally allow the tears to come.

When night fell they crawled into the den. Smelling the damp earth and fresh pine wood, Ritva's chest tightened – Mother must have been buried in a coffin like this. Would the earth cave in, would their coffin boat turn into their grave? Lying so close to Martta she could feel her warmth, smell her strong scent – she thought of the day they had sneaked behind the west wing and Martta, just for a moment, had pulled her into her arms. Ritva longed to be comforted by her friend, to feel safe, to be held. Yet suddenly she felt shy – what had Irina meant when she said that Martta was different from other women? She had never asked . . .

Ritva shivered, her body tense.

'Hush,' Martta whispered, 'it'll be fine, Ritva.' Martta's warm, resonant voice cut through Ritva's thoughts and she let her head lean on Martta's shoulder.

'Try to sleep, Ritva,' Martta whispered and for a moment stroked her cheek, light as a feather, then she withdrew her hand.

Ritva must have fallen asleep, because when she woke, a pale light crept through the entrance into the den. Ritva was alone. She crawled outside, leaves and moss in her hair. Martta was sitting on a rock, sawing at her skirt with a small knife.

'What are you doing?'

'Did you bring some needles and thread?' Martta said and smiled.

'Yes. What do you want to sew?'

'I'm tired of these skirts. If I cut the skirt down through the middle, remove a bit of fabric and sew both sides together, I could make trousers. What do you think?' Despite her heavy heart, Ritva laughed. She rummaged through her bundle and pulled out a tiny cushion spiked with needles and two spools of black thread.

'Here, seamstress, or should I say tailor?' Ritva said, watching as Martta cut the fabric. Despite her large, calloused hands, Martta sewed quickly.

'Did someone teach you how to do this?'

'Not with fabric, but with hides, yes. When you grow up around reindeer you learn to work with everything the animals give you.'

Within two hours Martta's skirt had been transformed into a pair of trousers, with wide legs like swinging bells. Martta posed with one foot on top of a rock as if she'd just conquered a mountain.

'That'll be much more practical. Do you want me to help you with yours?'

'Yes, please.'

That afternoon they found a small pond on the other side of the island and filled their canteens. They had just started on the way back when Martta suddenly grabbed Ritva's arm and pointed out to sea. Through the trees Ritva could make out a small boat heading their way in the channel between the two islands. Three figures on the boat were scanning the horizon.

'Do you think they can see us from there?' Ritva whispered, her heart thumping. She'd rather die than be dragged back to Seili.

'I don't think so, but they might search the island. We've got to hide in the den and cover the entrance.'

They raced back and pushed their bundles into the hole. Ritva climbed in first. Martta checked the mound from all sides, gathered some moss and branches and then plunged into the dark den, plugging the entrance with more moss and branches.

'I can't breathe!' Ritva panted. The boat would have landed by now, the search party spreading out.

'Try to breathe slowly, that'll help,' Martta muttered. 'Remember, last night after a while you were fine.' She put her arm around Ritva and indeed, after a few minutes the panic subsided and Ritva's breathing steadied. Soon she could hear nothing but her own heartbeat and she surrendered herself to the dark mustiness of the den. Suddenly a slight vibration and the cracking of twigs above startled her. If the men spotted anything unusual, all would be lost.

'They can't have gone far.' It was Petta's voice. The den turned into a cold grave in Ritva's mind. She held her breath and clung on to Martta, biting her own hand so she would not scream.

Ritva could not recall how long they had stayed like that or if she had passed out, but eventually she felt Martta patting her arm.

'I think they've gone.'

When they finally clambered out, the light had faded.

'We've got to leave tonight,' Martta said. They could not risk staying any longer. And so it was that that night their journey across the archipelago truly began, navigating from island to island in their tiny coffin boat. The water would remain free of ice for about a month before winter broke. Then, if they made it to Åland, the last group of small islands in the archipelago, the ice would become their road to freedom.

It was completely dark as they set off, with the sparkling band of the Milky Way stretched high above them, the giant backbone of the universe.

PART 2

TOWARDS THE MIDNIGHT SUN

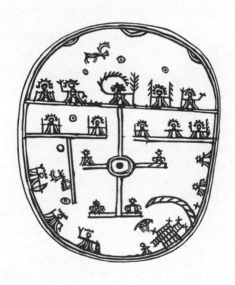

17

Ritva and Martta had been paddling for two weeks, scratching a mark into a piece of birch bark each day to keep track of the time. Stopping at small islands to rest, they replenished with fresh water from streams and ponds, living on a meagre diet of mushrooms, berries and fish they caught with makeshift rods, always watching out for Petta and the search parties. Some islands offered the shelter of trees and soft ground, while others were barren with granite rocks that rose from the water like sea creatures.

One afternoon as they rested on such a rock, Ritva stood up, stretched out her arms and turned a full circle, her eyes filled with water and sky. To the west, islet after islet rose from the smooth water like mole hills. They had spotted cabins on some of the bigger islands, but no one seemed to inhabit these small granite worlds. It was so peaceful here. With a stab she thought of Elke – if only she could share this beauty with her and know that she was safe. Martta beckoned to her and together they climbed across the slippery rocks to the other side of the islet where they found a sheltered bay; it would have been an excellent place to swim, but summer had passed and when Ritva dipped her toe into the water, it was icy. They sat in the vanishing light as the smooth granite rocks changed from grey to purple, then a shimmering ink-blue, as if readying themselves to slip into the night water like seals. The moon rose full and orange above the horizon.

'We've been gone two weeks now,' Martta said. 'It was a new moon when we left, *moon's eye* as we call it in Sami. Whoever chased us had no luck.' She threw a flat pebble at the water – it skipped across the surface in nine smooth leaps. 'And they never will.'

But despite Martta's optimism, fear stirred in Ritva. Surely they were kidding themselves? Petta's threat still echoed in her head – she had wounded his pride and he hated her with a passion. Besides, the superintendent would have offered a hefty reward for them both. They could not afford to let down their guard – Petta would not give up easily. Ritva shivered as a gust of chilly air rose from the water – a warning of the hardships of winter to come.

One week later the weather turned, as if the sun had suddenly lost all its strength. Steam rose from their nostrils each morning – it would not be long before the first frost. Most days they paddled in silence, holding a steady rhythm, but by the first week of October they had eaten all their supplies and after days of strong winds and heavy rain, they were soaked and exhausted. One afternoon, Martta spotted a small cabin on an island ahead, nestled between a cluster of birch trees that glowed golden like torches in their autumn mantle.

'Look!'

Ritva sighed; they had passed other summer houses and fishing huts, but had never dared to stop. Even if they looked abandoned, the owner might suddenly appear to do repairs or stock up. But what she wouldn't give for just one night in a proper bed! Her head felt seething hot and she had been shivering all day. There would be provisions in the cabin and with winter approaching fast, surely . . . Martta turned round and met her eye – and with only a glance passing between them, they changed course and headed towards the island.

They hid their vessel in a small pine forest close to the cabin. It was quiet on the island but for a loon's piercing cry. Martta broke the lock on the cabin door with a few axe blows; the door sprang open, releasing a waft of cool, musty air. Ritva could make out the outline of a table and chairs; as she opened the shutters, beams of glistening afternoon light pierced the dirt-streaked windows. As if Ritva and Martta had been possessed by a wild force, they raided the cupboards, delving into every drawer and corner.

'Six tins of mackerel,' Martta called and piled her findings on the table, 'two tins of herring, four jars of lingonberry jam.'

'I've got matches, a packet of candles and a nice sharp knife,' Ritva called.

'Ground coffee, sugar lumps, oats, a pouch of tobacco, salt and . . .' Martta held up a bottle, 'vodka. Oh, and some dried mushrooms. We shall have a feast tonight!'

'Four pairs of socks, binoculars and a fishing rod! You'll never have to use my red yarn again.'

'Oh, but I like your red yarn,' Martta said and smiled. Both spotted the bed at the same time. It was built into a corner of the cabin, and had been made up, though the blankets were covered in dust. Ritva jumped onto it and Martta followed, both elated at the thought of finally being able to sleep in a proper bed, sheltered from the elements with no nurse breathing down their necks.

'Even if we get caught, I'll never regret running away with you,' Ritva said.

'Neither will I, Ritva, neither will I.' A shadow fell across Martta's face; it lasted only a moment, but Ritva's heart contracted. What was this sadness she glimpsed in Martta? Did Martta really believe they would be caught? Ritva shrugged off the thought and let her head rest against Martta's chest; Martta lay very still beside her, but Ritva could feel her heart beating hard – if she could only stay like this, close to Martta, safe, wrapped up in her warmth.

When Ritva woke, Martta was sitting at the table.

'Look at the beauty I found.' Martta smiled and held up a small brass object that shimmered in the candlelight.

'A compass!'

Finding the compass seemed like a good omen to Ritva and that evening, after a feast of mackerel, mushrooms and coffee accompanied by shots of vodka, she dreamt of holding the compass in her hands. As she watched it, the needle swung wildly around: first eastwards towards Turku, then west towards Sweden, until it quivered, pointed north and remained there.

Ritva's heart skipped a beat when she woke – she knew that despite her yearning for her sister the dream was true; they needed to travel to Sweden first, then northwards to the land of the Sami and Martta's community. Only there would they be safe. And maybe somewhere there was a drum, lying hidden, calling to them . . .

'Look, Ritva, another godsend!' Martta said when Ritva joined her at the table that morning.

Ritva gasped, staring at the object.

'A rifle? Does it work?'

'I haven't tried it yet. I found a box of ammunition, but I didn't want to scare you.'

Ritva looked at the pile of provisions.

'Don't you think the owners will come after us if we steal all this?'

'Maybe. But this will be very useful,' Martta stroked the rifle as if it were a cherished pet. 'We can hunt with it, and think about it: two women alone on the ice, two fugitives . . .'

In truth, the gun scared Ritva; maybe it was superstition, but wouldn't a weapon draw even more danger towards them?

'I just feel bad about stealing all this.'

'But it's a godsend, Ritva, it might just help us make it through the winter. God knows we deserve it.'

'I just wish we could pay for it somehow.'

Martta's face darkened. 'We'd better not pay for it with our freedom,' she mumbled and stomped outside. How could Ritva care more about other people's belongings than their own safety? Martta sat down on a tree stump and gazed across the water. Frost and a fine layer of snow had covered the ground overnight – winter was sharpening its claws. They could paddle for another week or two, but soon the first sea ice would set in, too brittle to walk on, yet difficult to navigate through. Would it be better to hide out here until the ice was strong enough?

It was tempting – although she had tried to hide it from Ritva, the wound on Martta's palm was infected and it hurt badly – the blisters had burst and they oozed a sticky liquid underneath the bandage. While Ritva was asleep, she had poured vodka over the throbbing wound; the searing pain had been worse than when she had grabbed the door handle in the blazing workshop. Yet this pain was nothing compared to the emotion that gripped her heart whenever Ritva sat close to her, leaned her head on her shoulder or brushed against her by accident: a sticky shame and a wild longing that she had driven deep down inside herself for so long. She tried to shake off these thoughts; out here, an infected wound was far more important than matters of the heart. She needed to save her hand and rein in her heart as Father had shown her how to tame a wild reindeer. When she stepped back inside the cabin, Martta had decided.

'It's best we leave tomorrow and keep moving until the hard frost sets in.'

Without waiting for Ritva's answer Martta loaded the rifle, stepped outside again and aimed at the sky. The force of the shot knocked her backwards. This beauty was fierce, but it would be a helpful companion.

'We need to keep the rifle, Ritva,' Martta said, putting the gun on the table.

Ritva knew it was pointless to argue when Martta had made up her mind, but she did not speak for the rest of the day. The next morning they packed their provisions.

'Let's take the bed sheets, they'll make good sails,' Martta said.

'Sails?'

'Yes, you'll see, one day we'll turn our little coffin into a dinghy.'

Ritva couldn't help but smile – at times Martta was truly impossible, and certainly strong-willed, but maybe this quality was what she admired most in her.

They closed the shutters and collected the coffin. Ritva sat at the back while Martta handed her the things they wanted to take, but as the coffin filled, it sank deeper and deeper.

'It'll sink if I get in,' Martta said, her brow furrowed. 'We can do without coffee and the extra tins; let's just take our bundles, the sheets, the fishing rod, the binoculars, and this.' She slung the rifle over her shoulder and stepped in. Moments later they set out, paddling cautiously, holding themselves rigid so as not to upset the precarious balance of their boat.

Progress was slow. Some mornings, a thin layer of ice covered the water and they had to wear every item of clothing they owned and cover themselves with the blankets. Although Martta lit a fire each evening, they often couldn't stop trembling for hours. Exhausted, they no longer dug dens, but simply propped up the coffin and crawled underneath it for shelter.

'I'm so tired, Martta,' Ritva whispered one night in early November, her voice hoarse from the cold. 'I don't know if I can make it much further.' Her teeth chattered and her cheeks were ablaze. Martta touched Ritva's forehead, feeling the warmth even through her gloves.

'We can make it, Ritva, please don't give up now! We'll find another cabin and stay there until the ice can carry us. Then we'll trek to Åland and hide there until February when the ice is thickest. After that, it's only a few kilometres to Sweden.'

Ritva soaked up Martta's words, but her body felt as if it did not belong to her any more; hunger gnawed at her and she felt dizzy most of the time. Also Petta's shadow loomed larger than ever in her mind – he would be well equipped for the winter and she still felt sure that he wouldn't stop until he'd hunted them down.

That night the first winter storm raged across the archipelago. Luckily, they had indeed found another cabin to shelter in.

'Do you think someone is watching over us?' Ritva said, feeding wood into the burner. 'If we'd been out there in this weather . . .'

'Yes, I'm sure the ancestors are looking out for us. My mother told me a story about one winter when she was ten and she got lost in thick fog. She stumbled around in the snow for hours, calling out for her mother or anyone from her *siida*, but to no avail. Night fell and she thought she would die, but suddenly she felt a warm presence next to her and she heard the familiar voice of her grandmother telling her to dig a shelter in the snow. She did as she was told and curled up in the snow den. By morning, the fog had lifted and she could see the tents of her *siida* through the trees. She rushed back and when she reached them, her mother sobbed and squeezed her hard. "I thought I lost you both!" This is how my mother learned that her grandmother had died that very night in her sleep . . .'

Ritva's neck tingled. She had never thought of her own ancestors in that way – her grandfather lay buried in the small village cemetery and Mother had told her that her own parents were both long dead. Father would never approve of the idea of the dead helping out the living – wasn't that reserved for God? But out here, Ritva decided, they would need all the help they could get.

18

They stayed in the cabin for over two weeks, waiting for the ice to harden, fishing for herring, trout and pike through ice holes in the Baltic. Finally, in the first week of December, Martta tested the ice.

'Be careful,' Ritva said, holding her mittened fists to her mouth as she watched Martta inch out onto the glistening surface. At first Martta stepped delicately, like a crane, but soon she stamped her feet hard.

'It's all right,' Martta shouted, 'we can set off tomorrow.' It would be a relief to be on the move again, thought Martta – weeks cramped in the tiny cabin with Ritva had tested her every strength. Suddenly, as she gave another hard stomp, a thin crack appeared. Martta's heart faltered and she sped back towards the shore, the crack widening behind her, an eerie drawn-out sound following her like a ghost. Suddenly her left foot broke through the ice, the biting cold gripping her leg like a vice. She tried to free herself, but within seconds the crack had turned into a dark hole and her entire body crashed through the ice.

'Martta!' Ritva screamed and threw off her coat. Martta, submerged to her shoulders, gripped the edge of the ice with both hands. The icy water burnt like fire; she wouldn't have long.

'Don't run, get the oar!' Martta shouted. Within moments Ritva stepped out onto the ice. 'No, get down and wriggle on your belly.'

Ritva obeyed, moving like a seal, pushing the oar out in front of her. When she drew near, Martta grabbed the oar and inch by inch she heaved herself up and out of the water, while Ritva slithered backwards, pulling her closer to the shore where the ice was thicker. Propping up Martta, Ritva felt sick at the thought of what could have happened – Martta drowning right there, in front of her eyes . . . The morning had given them a stark warning – if they were to fall through the ice out on the archipelago, they would be dead within minutes.

It was almost Christmas before they tried the ice again – this time it held. It might also have bought them some time because while the sea was frozen, it would be difficult for anyone to follow them in a boat – although of course the superintendent could have sent a search party with dogs and sledges.

They set out in the midwinter twilight, the coffin now a cumbersome sledge, loaded with all their belongings and as much firewood as they could gather, together with a pair of skis they had found in the last cabin, which they had nailed to the bottom of the coffin. Although they had suffered much during their winters in the asylum, nothing could have prepared them for the brutal December cold on the archipelago. Bent over like gnarled trees, ropes wrapped tightly around their bodies, they pulled the heavy vessel across the bumpy ice, fighting every step of the way through the short daylight hours – winter had turned them into tired, numb pack animals.

During the daylight hours, the sun's reflection on the ice was so blinding they had to bind pieces of birch bark with tiny eye-slits around their faces. On grey days, the horizon merged with the frozen ground, the only landmarks small ice-locked islets of barren rock, spiked with the occasional tree.

As they trudged across the ice, a fierce north wind sliced through their clothing as if it were newspaper. How could they have thought these flimsy layers could protect them in such conditions? Their shoes and gloves had not kept them warm in the asylum; out here they were useless. They sacrificed a blanket, cut it into strips and wrapped the pieces around their shoes and gloves. Their eyelashes froze in the cold and small icicles grew under their noses. They were always thirsty – thawing snow into water cost time and lots of firewood and during the day they simply sucked on pieces of snow for some relief.

The fear of being caught had long since been replaced by other terrors: would they starve or freeze to death in this cruel landscape, or simply die of exhaustion? Frozen stiff, with aching bones and swollen ankles, they hardly talked any more. Martta tried to take most of the coffin's weight and always moved one step ahead of Ritva, to allow her to walk in her wind-shadow. Yet the ice could also be beautiful as it shimmered and sparkled, and sometimes from a distance an island with its ice-encrusted trees and rocks made Ritva think of the wondrous palace of a snow queen.

In the afternoons, when the sun dropped close to the horizon, they would steer towards a nearby island and if they were lucky they might find shelter in a cabin or at least in a forest where they could dig a burrow in the snow and warm themselves by a small fire. Other days, they had to camp out on the ice, huddled together under the propped-up coffin, their only shelter from the howling wind.

Every few days, Martta picked up the axe and hacked a hole in the thick ice so they could fish.

One morning, when it was Ritva's turn to fish, something pulled with such force that the rod slipped out of her hand and nearly disappeared into the hole. Ritva screamed, dug her heels into the snow and snatched at the rod. Martta slid across the ice and grabbed Ritva's waist. Sweat poured from their foreheads as they struggled not to lose the precious rod or be pulled into the hole. Slowly Ritva regained control and bit by bit they heaved the creature onto the ice: it was a huge pike, flapping its shimmering tail, straining to return to the water.

'God, look at that beauty!' Martta said and laughed; she plunged her small knife into the fish's gills and with one clean cut separated the head from the body. The pike still flapped as they dragged its body across the ice into the forest. There, they lit a fire and prepared their feast. That night even the wind seemed to give them a break and they rested well, wrapped in blankets with full bellies, their spirits lifted.

The weather was not their ally for long, however, and one afternoon they watched in horror as a spiralling tornado danced across the ice, picking up snow, branches and debris on its way. They turned the coffin over and cowered underneath it, holding onto each other until the roaring storm passed. When it did, the temperature plummeted still further and although they tried to protect every part of their bodies, their eyes were sore, lips cut and swollen.

'I can't feel my right foot,' Ritva whispered the next night as they sat around a smouldering fire. She unwrapped the strips of blanket and pulled off her shoes. Martta frowned as she examined Ritva's feet.

'You've got the first stages of frostbite. We need to get you some better shoes.'

'Maybe we'll stumble across a shop tomorrow and buy a new pair.' Ritva tried to sound light-hearted, but with the relentless cold her mood was bleaker by the day.

'I mean it, it's dangerous, Ritva, you could lose your foot. We need to find another cabin, or . . .' She rummaged through the sledge and pulled out the rifle. 'Why didn't I think of this earlier? If I shoot a seal I can try to make you a pair of boots.'

They had often seen seals sunning themselves on granite rocks or out on the ice; once a seal had even pushed its head through their fishing hole. Ritva had stood transfixed, gazing into the animal's dark, inquisitive eyes until it disappeared back into the black water.

'No, we can't do that.'

'Oh yes, believe me, I won't let you lose your foot, Ritva. It's all right – in times like these, we can kill such a creature.' Martta took Ritva's foot in both hands and rubbed it until some sensation returned.

They made little progress the following day; now that the numbness had disappeared, Ritva's foot throbbed and she could only shuffle. With the last light of afternoon, they spotted a small fishing hut behind a row of birch trees. It was not much bigger than one of the asylum's cells, but it held a bed, a cupboard and a small wood burner. Ritva burst into tears and fell onto the bed.

'Let's rest here and tomorrow I'll see what I can find,' Martta said. As she stowed their bundles under the bed she found half a bottle of vodka; she rubbed Ritva's foot with the alcohol and poured a large dose into their mugs. They knocked back the drinks and Ritva fell asleep within minutes.

The sound of a single shot woke her. Stumbling outside, Ritva searched the white expanse and there, far out on the ice, stood Martta, rifle slung across her shoulder, bent over a dark shape. Ritva's heart sank as she watched Martta drag a dark carcass across the ice, leaving a bright red trail behind her. When Martta reached the shore, Ritva glared at her.

'How could you do that? I told you I didn't want you to!' Tears stung her eyes. Did Martta not remember the story of Sealskin? Seals were such magnificent creatures.

'I did it for us, Ritva, please don't be angry.'

'We could've made shoes from . . . oh, I don't know—'

'Ritva, we're suffering. You might lose your toes, your whole foot even. I can make boots and mittens from the skin and the meat will feed us for weeks. Nothing will be wasted, I promise you. The seal's a godsend – why do you think it just appeared here?'

Ritva stared at Martta then at the animal.

'Besides, it gave me permission.'

'What? Permission to be shot?' Ritva's voice was shrill.

'I know it's difficult to understand, but whenever my people go on a hunt, they always ask the animal before they kill it. Out there on the ice when I saw the seal, I suddenly remembered this. So I asked it in my thoughts – I prayed, if you like – and suddenly I felt it . . . agree. I don't know how to explain it.'

'You felt it agree?' Ritva was shaking her head.

'Yes,' Martta whispered and reached out her hand, but Ritva pulled away and stomped back into the hut.

Martta spent the rest of the daylight hours skinning and cutting up the large grey seal. It had been years since she had helped her father with the autumn slaughter of the reindeer bulls – that had been the last precious year her family had been together. Before Father started to drink heavily and everything fell apart. Martta had not minded the bloody work; indeed she was keen to learn as much as she could, as if she had sensed their time together would soon end. She had loved her father fiercely, but when the alcohol had taken hold of him there was no end to the family's misfortune. First he had traded more and more reindeer for drink and then one spring little Uma, Martta's three-year-old sister, had fallen through the ice while they were crossing a river. Father, too drunk to react quickly, had not been able to rescue her. A wave of helplessness, rage and sorrow rushed through Martta as she remembered that fateful day; if she had just been quicker, had slid on her belly instead of running over the ice . . . Mother never forgave Father and the next winter the family's luck had completely run out: the herd could not dig through the frozen snow to reach the lichen and all but four animals starved to death.

Martta stared at her hands now, willing herself back to the present. The seal was quite different from a reindeer and yet she knew exactly what to do. Working quickly, she peeled off the precious skin in one large piece, cutting away the blubber, then separated the meat from the bones. She would freeze the meat in small chunks – it would stay fresh for months. Then she had to deal with the bones and make sure she collected them all. In the fading light, Martta scraped the flesh off the seal's fur – the hide had to be completely clean and dry before she could make the boots, but would Ritva tolerate the smell in the hut? She ached for the seal and the distress she had caused Ritva, yet how could they make it through this brutal winter without meat and warm boots? Martta's heart was in her throat as she readied herself to join Ritva in the cabin, but it was Ritva who spoke first.

'I'm sorry, maybe you're right,' she said, a shy smile playing on her lips. 'I know you did it for me.'

'It pains me, too, to kill such a beautiful creature, but I promise you, this seal won't have died in vain. Tomorrow I'll clean the rest of the hide.'

They kept a fire going day and night and the fur dried quickly but still Ritva retched from the smell of the sealskin, and worse, from the cooked meat and blubber.

Martta had often watched her mother's skilled fingers sewing pair after pair of boots for the family; Martta's boots had always been made from the softest reindeer fur and her feet had never once got cold or wet. Compared to such boots, the footwear in the towns of the South failed with the first bad weather, and yet were hailed as superior. When the master had seen Martta's boots, he had ripped them off her feet and thrown them into the fire. Out here, fur boots would save their feet and maybe their lives.

As the winter storms raged around the small hut and the ice grew thicker by the day, Martta spun sinew into thread and cut patterns out of the precious sealskin. Back in her *siida*, whenever the women gathered in one of the *lavvu* tents to share news and smoke their pipes, they spun reindeer sinew into fine thread, chewing and separating it into finer strands until it was tough and soft and would hold together boots, gloves, trousers and coats.

'You're amazing,' Ritva said, leaning over Martta's shoulder. 'You've never done this before and here you are, making boots.'

'It feels as if my mother is right behind me, guiding my hands.'

'What was she like, your mother?'

'Oh, she was beautiful. And very kind,' Martta said. 'But when we lost my sister and nearly all our reindeer, Mother left Father, sent me to a boarding school and went to work as a farmhand in the valley. I was nine. I hated that school, I had to speak Finnish and the children called me a "lazy Lapp". I missed my people so badly.'

'That's awful. Did you stay there long?'

'No. One morning Mother appeared with our pack-reindeer and told me that Father was dead. He had fallen over during a blizzard and frozen to death. She did not mention the drink, but I knew. She had always hidden her silver spoons and jewellery from Father and now she was determined to turn her back on reindeer herding and start a new life in the South. At first it seemed like an adventure – we walked from Inari to Rovaniemi, then Oulo. Each place was different, and Mother told me stories while we were hiking. It was only much later that I understood just how many risks she had taken for us. But she could not settle; I knew she missed the North and our people, but instead of returning home she pushed on south. When she finally found work with a wealthy family in Turku as their housekeeper, and they allowed her to keep me there, she was so happy. But a few months later her health deteriorated and she died within the space of a few weeks, from pneumonia. I was only eleven. That's when I began to work for the master . . .'

That night, as she sewed, Martta told Ritva about the cruel master and how she came to be taken to Seili. Ritva listened without interrupting, tears brimming in her eyes.

A few days later, Martta finished two pairs of boots and some new mittens for Ritva. Despite her bleeding fingers, she wore a proud smile as she presented Ritva with her pair.

'I can't wait to try them,' Ritva said, lacing them up with a piece of rope and then slipping out onto the ice.

'Oh Martta, they're beautiful, and so warm!' Ritva beamed, whirling across the ice like a five-year-old girl.

'Thank you, Martta!'

Martta's heart soared. From now on she would ask for nothing but to make Ritva happy.

Two days later, on a sunny January morning, they packed up the sledge and set out towards the Åland Islands.

19

For three days they did not come across another island and were forced to camp out on the ice, sleeping underneath the propped-up coffin with only blankets to protect them from the cold. On the fourth morning, Ritva woke up sweating and shivering. She clenched her teeth and fastened the ropes to her waist so they could pull the sledge as they did every day – she couldn't give up now, not when they were so close to Sweden. She trudged behind Martta in a daze, one heavy step after another, but an hour into their trek, her heart started to race and dizziness seized her. She swayed and grabbed hold of the sledge, a beating sound in her ears like the rushing of wings. Was it the bird of her visions taking her away? Would she die in this forsaken wilderness after all? Before she could steady herself a blinding flash exploded behind her eyes; for a moment she saw the oval drum, its fast rhythm matching the beating of her heart, then everything was plunged into darkness and she collapsed on the ice.

Martta felt a sudden tug on the harness.

'Ritva!' Seeing her companion sprawled on the ice, Martta rushed to untie herself from the ropes and lifted Ritva's limp body. Ritva's skin was clammy and her pulse raced. Martta balled her fists and breathed hard – no, they would not die out here! She put Ritva down, emptied out the coffin and then laid Ritva inside. Martta's heart lurched at the sight of Ritva, so pale and lifeless in the wooden box.

'Please hang on, my sweet,' she whispered in Ritva's ear,

tucking every single blanket they had around her. She stuffed the scattered tools and food into her bundle, heaved it onto her back and wrapped the rope around her waist, then threw her whole weight forward. Fighting against the icy wind, she took step after slow step, her lungs stinging, the rope cutting deep into her flesh despite her many layers of clothes. Whenever she stopped to catch her breath she glanced back; Ritva lay unmoving, her eyes shut, her face near translucent except for the scarlet-red fever in her cheeks.

Beaivi, mother of all humankind, please lend me strength, Martta prayed as she edged forward, invoking every spirit, god and ancestor she had ever known: *Mano, God of the moon, Biegkegaellies, God of the winter winds, Jabbmeaakka, Goddess of death, please spare us . . .*

But with each hour the weight of the coffin seemed heavier and heavier and still an endless expanse of blinding nothingness stretched before her. Suddenly her boot caught on a piece of ice and she crumpled to her knees. A sharp pain shot through her leg and she let out a scream. *Why? Why now, when they were so close?* She pounded her fists against the ice, sobbing. When she lifted her head again – moments or hours later – she noticed the silhouette of a little girl in the twilight, only a few metres ahead. Had she too caught a fever? The girl looked at her, nodded and gestured for her to get up and follow. Martta's heart skipped a beat – the girl was wearing the same clothes little Uma had worn the day she drowned and her face was so like that of Martta's little sister . . .

Martta heaved herself up and scrambled, coffin in tow, after the girl as if she were a single, faint flame guiding the way. Hours later in the fading light, she glimpsed a strip of land ahead – the first of the Åland Islands. She turned to Ritva.

'We've made it, Ritva! We'll get help for you here.' But Ritva did not stir and when Martta looked ahead again, the girl was gone. Tears stung her eyes.

'Thank you, thank you,' she whispered, warmth spreading across her chest. Of course they weren't totally safe yet. If she approached a stranger on the island, there was the risk they might tell the authorities. And would they even understand Finnish here? Still, she had no choice, Ritva would die if they spent another night on the ice.

On the edge of a small village Martta knocked at the door of the first hut, a small rust-coloured dwelling with white window frames, tied down with metal ropes against the winter storms. No one opened the door, but Martta thought she saw a shadow flit across the window. Bent low, she approached the second hut and knocked quietly; this time an old woman opened the door a crack.

'Come in,' the woman croaked after Martta had delivered her plea in short sentences of Finnish mixed with some Swedish. The woman was dressed entirely in black, lively green eyes glinted in her weathered face and her thin lips curled into a warm smile.

'Fetch your friend and hide that strange sledge of yours behind the house. I'll put the kettle on the fire.' Relief flooded Martta and minutes later, she carried Ritva across the threshold.

'I've got something that will wake this beautiful soul,' the old woman said and pulled a small blue bottle from a dusty shelf. 'It's bitter, but it could wake the dead – strong herbs soaked in vodka for two years and a few other things besides.' She winked. 'Spells, wishes . . . here, give your friend a few spoonfuls.'

Who was this old woman who lived alone at the end of the world, brewing strange concoctions, Martta wondered. But she did as ordered and soon Ritva gave a loud cough.

'Where am I?' Ritva's bloodshot eyes opened wide.

'We're safe, Ritva, we've made it to the Åland Islands. You collapsed on the ice.'

'I remember . . . there was a bright flash and for a moment I saw the drum again . . .'

'Shhh dear, rest now.' Martta stroked Ritva's forehead until Ritva fell asleep once more.

The old woman sat down next to Martta.

'I had a daughter once, your friend reminds me of her.'

'Is she . . . dead, your daughter?'

The woman looked away. When she faced Martta again her eyes brimmed with tears.

'She wasn't quite right, or so they said . . . and one day they took her away.' She shook her head. 'I don't want to think about it, it was a long time ago. But what is your story? Why are you out on the ice?'

Martta bit her bottom lip – why should she trust this woman? The story about her daughter could be a trap. But then, those tears . . .

'You don't have to tell me, it's fine.' The woman put her hand on Martta's. 'I quite understand.'

In the dim light the woman's face looked ancient, as if she were the keeper of a lifetime of secrets. Maybe her daughter had been taken to Seili too? At the thought of the asylum, Martta felt the months of tension overwhelm her – if only she could put this burden down, even for one night, and curl up in another person's loving presence . . . She decided to trust her instincts and tell the old woman about their past.

'Oh, dear girl, no one should have to suffer as you two did,' the woman said after some time, stroking Martta's arm. 'Rest assured, I'll be as silent as the bottom of the Baltic – your secret is safe with me.' She drew the curtains, ordered Martta to stay where she was, and disappeared into the kitchen to prepare some soup.

Over the next two weeks, Ritva slowly recovered from the fever and regained her strength, nourished by sleep, soup, potent herbal potions and the kindness of the stranger who introduced herself as Gerta Englund, a widow who was not only an excellent cook but also an avid storyteller. They sat together in the evenings listening to Gerta's fantastic tales of sea monsters, mermaids and the Goddess Jurate, who lived in an amber palace at the bottom of the Baltic Sea.

'She fell in love with a fisherman and when she brought him back to live with her,' Gerta said, clicking her knitting needles, 'her father, the thunder God, Pekunas, was so furious that she had entered into a relationship with a mere mortal, that he destroyed her beautiful amber palace with a huge lightning bolt. The only thing that remains of Jurate's palace today are the pieces of yellow amber that sometimes wash up along the beaches of the Baltic Sea.'

With a pang Ritva remembered a necklace with a tear-shaped piece of amber that her mother had often worn – a long, long time ago. That night, in her dreams, she found herself searching for her mother in Jurate's lost palace.

Towards the end of January, Ritva woke one morning to find Gerta's calloused hands brushing her cheek.

'Wake up, dear!'

'What is it?' Ritva sat up, heavy with sleep. When she saw the serious look on Gerta's face she shook Martta.

'Quick, you must leave,' Gerta whispered. 'Someone's seen you – I overheard my neighbour talking to the grocer and she gave me a dirty look. I think she saw you slipping into my house that first day. Now there's a poster at the grocer's, asking people to telegraph the asylum if there's any sighting of "two dangerous young women, escaped from the Seili lunatic asylum". Someone might already have informed on you – you're no longer safe here.'

'But is the ice strong enough?' Martta asked. Åland was a cluster of islands and even if they made it across those, there would still be a long stretch of open ice between the last island and Sweden.

'The ice is as strong as it will get,' Gerta said. 'It's a harsher winter than last year, but yes, in some places it's still thin. You've got to watch the currents – look for *teräsjää*, the clear steel ice, and stay away from the porous stuff. My brother Jacob lives on Eckerö, the last island before the gulf. You can stay with him for a short while – and from there it's only twenty-seven kilometres to Sweden. You can do that last bit in a day or two if you hurry.'

Ritva and Martta immediately started packing their bundles, while Gerta rummaged through a drawer. She handed Ritva a silver spoon embossed with her initials.

'Here, give this to Jacob with a note from me. He'll feed you.' Ritva noticed that Gerta looked tearful.

'And . . . take this.' Gerta unrolled a large grey pelt. Ritva and Martta looked at each other – it was the complete skin of a grey seal.

'It's beautiful!' Ritva cried, thinking of the seal that had saved their lives out on the ice.

'It's quite old and there are a few moth holes, but it'll keep you warm when you're on the ice. My husband shot the seal a long time ago in a harsh winter just like this.' She patted the skin then bundled it up.

'Good luck, girls, and God bless you!'

And just like that, their time of respite came to an end and they were on their way once more, with Gerta's blessing in their hearts, the sledge packed with two more woollen blankets, the seal pelt and generous provisions. Gerta did not wave, but as she watched them pull the sledge onto the ice, her hand curled around the small object Ritva had secretly slipped into her pocket – a little wolf, made from hardened bread.

A fierce westerly wind blasted stinging hail into their faces and only the vague view of Sweden right across the gulf kept them moving. Often the sledge got stuck on the bumpy ice and they had to strain every muscle to haul it across the many obstacles. Yet they had to keep going – now they knew for certain that they were being followed; each hut they had raided on the way left a clue and Petta would be following their tracks.

They navigated around the southern Åland Islands, watching the ice for the flow of currents, their bodies rigid with tension – one false move and they would break through the ice. They stayed for four days and nights out on the icy expanse.

'At least the sealskin is protecting us from the cold when we lie down, and our feet are warm,' Ritva said, stroking the pelt. She offered Martta a piece of dried fish.

'You know, the day Petta brought me to Seili, just before the boat docked, I saw a large grey seal – I thought it was a bad omen, but now I feel as if something is protecting us.'

Ritva gazed out at the ice. The stern God of her father's sermons had no reach in this place where everything, seal, fish, wind, hail and sun, was infused with a spirit that spoke to her – not in a language she could grasp with words, but something more like an inner knowing, a whisper in her heart. Spirits, ancestors, God, did it matter what they called it? Ritva fell silent, praying in the only way she now knew: *may whatever has protected us this far, keep watch over us still . . .*

After five days they reached Eckerö and following Gerta's description they found her brother's hut. Jacob's cabin was even smaller than his sister's, and cluttered with junk. His likeness to his sister showed not only in his features but also in his cooking skills and his kindness. They rested well for two nights and on the fifteenth of February, with the first pale morning light, they embarked on the last stretch across the frozen gulf.

The westerly wind had eased and as the last lighthouse disappeared behind their backs, Ritva's thoughts turned to Petta. If there was a poster on Åland, where else? Would they be safe even when they reached Sweden? Maybe the superintendent had put a large reward on their heads? She shuddered – Petta was out there, somewhere, looking for them . . . would they ever get away from him? She forced herself not to look over her shoulder and instead focused her eyes ahead.

Finally, after two gruelling days, Ritva noticed a small island rising out of the ice like a mirage.

'Sweden,' she said, her voice hoarse. Could it really be? They picked up speed and reached the island within an hour. Hidden behind clusters of birch that stood like rows of skeletons with their white trunks and bare branches, they spotted a hut.

'We've made it,' Martta cried, entering the hut and throwing off her bundle. But no triumph stirred in Ritva, only deep exhaustion. She fell onto the narrow bed and was asleep in minutes.

The next morning, Ritva was woken by a cry – Martta's face was distorted with pain.

'I can't move.'

'What is it?'

'My back. God, it hurts!'

After months of effort, Martta's body had collapsed under the strain and, unable to move her back, she was forced to let Ritva take care of her.

'You're a terrible patient,' Ritva scolded as she caught Martta once again trying to get out of bed. 'You helped me all the way across the archipelago, you even pulled me along in that coffin, so why won't you let me help you for a change?'

'If you put it that way,' Martta said, 'I'll try to be a good patient.'

But a dark mood had settled over Martta; she only spoke when necessary and when Ritva pleaded with her to tell her what was bothering her, Martta simply shook her head and looked away. Now that she was immobile, what had been stirring in her for months became even harder to fight. It was not right to feel for another woman what she felt, especially for someone as innocent as Ritva, who relied on her almost as if Martta were a parent. Ritva needed her as a friend, nothing else. Martta was sure that if Ritva could see the tangle in her heart, she would be disgusted and turn against her, just like Irina had. Martta cringed at the thought of Irina's betrayal – first she had pleaded for a kiss from Martta and even more after that, then she had lied to Katja and spread rumours amongst the women – lies for which Martta had paid dearly.

Maybe one day she would find a place where she could be the person she was inside; but it wasn't here – for now, she had to bury her desire just as she had buried the bones of the seal on the island: every single last piece.

20

Spring arrived slowly and with it came danger. By the third week of March the ice had started to thaw; too weak to carry much weight yet refusing to melt fully, they were left marooned on the little island. For weeks Ritva had swallowed the hurt she felt at Martta's withdrawal and had thrown herself into her daily chores: patching their clothes, keeping a fire going all day, hacking holes into the ice and preparing each catch of fish. Slowly Martta's back recovered and with the first thaw it was as if something in her mood had lifted also.

'*Kelirikko* – that's a nice word for the mess we're in,' she said and looked out of the window towards Åland. 'Ice too thick to get a boat through but too weak to walk on.'

'At least no one can chase after us for the moment,' Ritva said, relieved to see Martta up and in better spirits. 'Do you think they'll still come after us?'

'Yes, we've only just set foot in Sweden.'

'But why would they keep searching after all this time?' Ritva asked, although deep down she already knew the answer.

'I'm sure the superintendent has offered a reward for our capture,' Martta said. 'Remember when Irina disappeared, he was furious. He can't afford to have the reputation of the asylum undermined in any way.'

Ritva knew Martta was right; this cabin was no place to hide for long, and it wasn't a safe place where she could bring her sister. On a clear day they could still see the last Finnish lighthouse across the gulf and at night its beam shone through the window. On many nights Ritva lay awake worrying: should she have fled to Turku instead? She knew the superintendent would have sent someone to her home, but maybe she could have hidden . . .? If Elke was in danger, how could she ever forgive herself for not going there first?

One sleepless night Ritva stepped outside and gazed up into the night sky. *Please God, Sun, Moon, Goose and Seal, sacred drum and dear Mother, if you can hear me, keep little Elke safe.* She pulled her coat tight around her, listening to the night, but only the wind answered her. Just as she was about to return to the cabin her eyes were drawn to the shimmering Milky Way. She felt a pulse moving through her body, a throbbing behind her temples and in her heart. She blinked and when she looked again, the whole sky had arranged itself into shapes and constellations of figures, animals and tents, the band of the Milky Way contained in an oval like the shape of the drum. And as she heard the drum resounding in her heart, she knew that before she could fetch Elke, she needed to head north – to escape Petta once and for all, to find Martta's relatives and to solve the mystery that moved her so much: the sacred drum and why it was calling her. Even if their escape from Seili ended here, their journey to the land of the midnight sun was just beginning.

Slowly the days grew longer and one morning in the first week of April, Ritva became aware of a strange creaking sound.

'The ice is singing, listen!' Ritva said, nudging Martta. They put on their boots and stepped outside – everywhere the ice was cracking, breaking up into large sheets that floated on the water.

'We'll be on our way soon,' Martta said and smiled. She pulled the crumpled map that Arianna had drawn for her from her pocket.

'Ritva, I think we should build a raft.' Martta looked out over the ice floes that nudged against each other.

'This vessel has served us well, but it's as tired as an old reindeer and it'll leak through the timbers now. We don't want to drown in a coffin after everything we've been through, do we?'

'No, but how can we possibly build a raft?'

'My back is as good as new, there are plenty of trees here, we've got a saw and an axe and we can make rope from birch bark. If we put up a mast, we can even sail – all the way north up the Gulf of Bothnia.'

Ritva glanced at their battered vessel.

'What about our coffin boat?'

'Oh, we'll turn it over and use it as our captain's seat.'

They found a spot close to the water with some trees nearby and Martta started to hack into the smooth birch bark, peeling it off in long strips. She beat it with a flat stone until the fibres softened and twisted the strands into a rope. Then she cut down some smaller trees and laid the trunks next to each other, guiding the rope over and under the wood as if weaving on a giant loom. She repeated the process and placed the second layer on top, securing it with bark rope. They worked all day, Martta taking charge, Ritva helping wherever she could. Martta built a small storage area for their provisions, then lit a large fire with fir and pine and collected the sticky black liquid that oozed from the wood. Ritva held her nose.

'It's just tar,' Martta laughed. 'It'll keep everything dry.' They smeared the sticky substance underneath the raft, on the ropes, then turned the coffin over and secured it to the raft with rope. Their vessel was just large enough to hold them and their provisions. They would keep the simple oars they already had and chose one long staff to help them navigate the waters closer to shore.

'Isn't she beautiful?' Martta said. 'Simple, but fine. I think she'll serve us well; let's call her *Freedom*.'

'What's that in your language?' Ritva asked.

'*Friddjavuohta*.'

'*Friddjavuohta*,' Ritva repeated slowly.

'You see, you're a natural,' Martta said, flashing a smile. Ritva's stomach fluttered. It was so good to see Martta laugh, as if the warmth of spring had revived her. If only she could understand Martta better and, for that matter, understand herself – she felt so many things, but those feelings escaped her grasp whenever she wanted to name them. Leaving Martta by the shore, she walked into a small area of forest – she needed to gather her thoughts. The grass here had been flattened by snow and was tinged with the subdued winter palette of browns and ochres. Suddenly her eye caught a speck of bright yellow on the ground – a single perfectly formed butterfly wing. It was too early for butterflies, but here it lay nevertheless, like a sign, a promise . . . She picked it up and ran back to the shore.

'What happened?' Martta asked. 'You just vanished.'

'Open your hand.' Ritva placed the fragile wing on Martta's palm. 'It's for you.'

'It's so delicate. Thank you.' Martta smiled but then for a second, Ritva saw a flicker of sadness or pain in her eyes and her heart sank. What was it that Martta was hiding?

The following week, they closed up the cabin and pulled the raft into the near-iceless water. The *Freedom* swayed but it floated. Giddy with relief and a sense of possibility, they broke into song. They had made it across the archipelago, spring was melting the last of the ice and they were heading towards the midnight sun, following the call of the sacred drum.

'We need sails,' Martta suggested later that afternoon. They had pulled the raft onto the next island and their arms were aching. Together they sewed a large sail using the bulky sheets they had taken from one of the cabins, drawing needle and coarse sinew thread through the cotton until their calloused fingers bled. Martta then felled a slim, sturdy spruce to serve as a mast, set the trunk in the middle of the raft and wedged smaller pieces of wood around it until it stood firm. They secured the makeshift sail to it with ropes and pulled it up the mast – they set out and the wind caught the sail with a smack and the raft gathered speed, slicing through the rippled surface of the water. They clung on to the mast, laughing.

'We did it – she is racing!' Ritva shouted, exhilarated by the speed, their mouths spewing giggles. Neither had sailed before, and for the first hours, their raft seemed to steer itself without much control. Later, when the wind changed direction, they were guided by their bodies' intuitive knowledge, shifting their weight, moving about the raft, turning the sail to this side and that.

They sailed northwards for weeks, living on herring, pike and the occasional egg raided from nests hidden on the many islets: eider duck, gull, red shank, loon. They collected tender green birch leaves, stalks of angelica and sorrel and cut small incisions into birch trunks to collect the clear sap.

'Here, try this.' Martta held out a little bowl, put it to Ritva's lips and poured a small sip into her mouth; it tasted sweet and delicious, like nothing Ritva had ever tried. She closed her eyes. Martta was strong and yet there was such care and tenderness in her also.

One evening, after four weeks on the ice-free water, they spotted a sailing boat to the south. They had passed many vessels at a distance over those weeks and at first glance there seemed to be nothing alarming about this one, but as it came closer, Ritva recognised a Finnish flag fluttering on its mast.

'I don't have a good feeling about this,' Martta mumbled.

'Do you think . . .?' Ritva held her breath.

'I don't know, but something isn't right. I think I saw this boat a few days ago, but then it was in front of us.'

Martta focused the binoculars on the boat. A man dropped the anchor over one side, then lowered a small dinghy into the water and started to row towards the beach.

'He's searching the shore . . . He would know we couldn't just stay on the water all the time. Look.'

'Martta, I don't think this has anything to do with us,' Ritva said, pressing the binoculars to her eyes. But then an icy shiver rushed down her back as she spotted a shock of bright blond hair sticking out from under the man's cap.

'Oh God, you're right.'

'Quick, we need to turn the sails!' Martta cried, grabbing hold of the ropes. There was no time to lose.

21

They left not a minute too soon. In the rush, Ritva got the ropes in a tangle and by the time they finally turned the sails, the man was clambering across the stony shore shaking his fist. He shouted then stopped and aimed a rifle.

'Get down!' Martta pulled Ritva to the floor. A shot whistled past and hit the water, then another, missing them by inches. They lay flat, bellies pressed against the wood, hearts pounding; when they peered back, the man was pacing along the shore, taking aim again. They heard another shot and the raft jolted – a bullet had lodged in the mast. Alive or dead – how they were caught must not matter to Petta any more. Martta pulled at the sail. With a slap it caught a sharp gust of wind; the raft gathered speed and they sailed further out to sea.

'That miserable rat,' Martta spat. 'I knew it was him.' She reached for the rifle and aimed at the man, but they were too far away now.

'You think it's Petta still chasing after us?' Ritva did not want to believe what her gut told her to be true. Martta had been right – if someone had spotted them on Åland and informed the asylum, the superintendent would have sent Petta out again as soon as the ice thawed. And Petta would have grabbed at the opportunity, whether through revenge or greed.

'We poked his goddamn pride when we escaped,' Martta hissed. 'I swear the swine is never going to stop. He'll kill us and earn himself a fat prize. He'll probably make it look like an accident.'

Ritva shivered at her words – Petta had been obsessed with her and she had rejected him, but would he really try and kill them? Petta's small figure was now boarding his dinghy. They needed to get out of sight quickly.

'I don't think he'll stop at anything to catch us,' Martta said. 'Damn it, I wish I'd been able to shoot him out there.' Dusk was settling as they sailed further out to sea, lost in thought for a while.

'What if we tricked him?' Ritva said. 'We could trick him into thinking we were dead.'

'Dead?' Martta frowned. 'Go on, explain. I don't follow.'

'Maybe a wild animal attacked us? A wolf ripped us to pieces?' Ritva bared her teeth and growled.

'You should write books, with your imagination,' Martta said and laughed.

'Do you think it's such a crazy idea?'

'It sounds far-fetched, but I suppose there are wild animals out here . . . Maybe it's not so crazy after all.'

They would need to make sacrifices: one piece of clothing each, an undershirt maybe, a sock, the leftover pieces of their skirts. Hair, a few strands, and of course fresh blood, lots of it.

'If we could hunt down a rabbit? But we're out at sea and I don't really want to land just yet . . .'

Suddenly a thought pierced Ritva: a seal – this beautiful creature that had saved their lives more than once, whose pelt had warmed their feet and hands through the winter, its flesh filling their shrivelled stomachs so they could make it across the last stretch of the archipelago. But could they ask for yet another sacrifice?

'What are you thinking?' Martta asked.

'About the seal you killed out on the ice. It was beautiful, wasn't it?' Her eyes filled with tears.

'Yes, it was a magnificent creature.'

Ritva tried to make out Martta's face, but only her dark silhouette showed in the dusky light. They sat in silence, the raft swaying gently. Then without a word an agreement formed between them

174

– they would ask one more time for a seal's sacrifice to save their lives.

Martta attached her knife to the top of the staff and a length of rope to the bottom, crafting a simple harpoon. It would be difficult to hunt a seal at night; on warm days the animals sunned themselves lazily on the flat rocks around the islands, but at night they glided underwater, surfacing only to breathe. Martta's heart sank at the thought of killing yet another innocent creature; she felt a deep kinship with these mysterious mammals that lived between the water and the land – how could she ever repay such a debt?

A pale half-moon cast its flickering light on the dark sea; a quiet splash broke the surface, then another . . . a fish leaping. Martta listened with her whole body, the harpoon pointed towards the water.

Ritva closed her eyes and pulled deep inside herself. Without a sound she called the spirit of the seal and prayed for its forgiveness. And then she saw it in front of her inner eye, resting, gliding through the water . . . Suddenly Martta's harpoon whistled into the sea and landed with a splash.

'I thought I saw one,' Martta mumbled, pulling the line back in. Ritva opened her eyes, trying to make out a shape on the surface – nothing. Many times that night Martta threw her harpoon only to pull it back without a catch. Ritva fell into a restless sleep, dreaming of diving into the dark, cold water, becoming entangled in seaweed, struggling for air . . .

She was woken by a piercing sound that cut right through her heart: the high-pitched squeal of an injured animal. By the time Martta pulled the creature close to the raft, its cries had stopped. Together they heaved the dead body on board. Martta's harpoon had speared the seal at the back of its head – it wouldn't have suffered for long. Blood oozed from the wound, dark like oil, staining the shimmering pelt. They did not speak but Ritva saw Martta wiping her eyes with the back of her hand before she took the harpoon apart and used the knife to skin the animal, swiftly as if she had done it a thousand times. The seal would give them all they needed; more blood than they could use to drench their clothes and enough meat for the next part of the journey. Ritva said a quiet prayer and watched Martta work.

With the first light of dawn, Ritva searched the horizon for Petta's boat but could not see it. They steered the raft onto a small island where a few gnarled trees clung precariously to the rocks. They could not be seen from the coast here and could prepare.

'Let's do it tomorrow,' Martta said, unrolling their blankets. 'We'll row to the coast at night, pull the raft up on shore and scatter our bloody bundles at the edge of the forest. The moon should give us just enough light. However long Petta takes, at some point he'll stumble across our mess – it'll look as if something has made a meal of us.'

'We could lay a whole bloody trail . . .' Ritva said. They had gathered some of the seal's blood in a jar.

'Yes, and we need strands of hair, scraps of clothes and a few more things from our bags.'

That afternoon, steadying her gaze at a rock far out at sea, Ritva pulled a large chunk of hair from her scalp. She clenched her jaw, willing herself not to scream as hot pain surged through her body. Maybe the pain would repay some of their debt? Martta also pulled out some hair with the same stubborn refusal to express the pain. They tore undershirts and bits of material to shreds and drenched the scraps in blood, then later that night, they rowed ashore to lay their trail, praying for the trickery to work so they could shake off Petta once and for all. Where was he now? They had not spotted his boat since the previous day. Was he still trekking along the coast?

'How will we know that he has been here and seen all this?' Ritva asked.

'We'll hide on another island, then come back in a few days. If he's found it, he's bound to take something with him for evidence. How about we leave some of the letters?'

Ritva was not convinced, but it would be too risky to watch the spot directly from any nearer.

They surveyed the blood-soaked shreds of material, the hair and a few of the crumpled letters Ritva had salvaged from the asylum.

'It looks grim,' Ritva said.

'Yes, two fugitives attacked by a pack of wolves, dragged into the forest and ripped to pieces . . . it's perfect. Let him report us dead to the asylum – we're already dead to the rest of the world.'

Ritva said nothing. Surely Elke would still hold her in her heart? And Father, despite everything?

'Now we'll need all the luck we can get,' Martta said as they sailed towards a small island further out at sea. 'It's a long shot but if it works, we're free.'

They hid for four days without lighting a fire, living off strips of seal meat and berries. During the day Martta scanned the horizon for Petta and the boat, but saw nothing.

When they returned on the fifth day to the spot on the shore they had left behind, all traces of the scene they had prepared had vanished. Had it not been for a small scrap of bloodied fabric Ritva found lodged between two rocks, she would have doubted it was the same place.

'It worked!' Martta cried. 'I can feel it – he's given up.'

Ritva took a deep breath; she so wanted to trust Martta's instinct, but how could she be so sure? What if a wild animal had been attracted by the smell of blood and had taken everything? As she walked along the shore a flash of red caught her eye. She bent down – it was a matchbox just like the one she had stolen from Petta's jacket. She picked it up with trembling hands. Let Petta deliver the bloodied clothes and his false tale to the superintendent; let him write a letter to her father. She was tired to her core of being frightened. Maybe it was good to be dead to the world after all.

22

For weeks the raft sailed at a steady pace northwards along the coast, pushed on by a gentle breeze, but as spring gave way to summer, a lull set in that settled on the coast like a suffocating blanket. The world seemed to stop breathing, the surface of the sea reflecting the harsh light like a giant blue mirror. Early one morning, Ritva slipped off her clothes and slid into the cool water. She swam, breathing deeply, slicing the smooth surface with each stroke. The glistening sun opened a silvery path before her and, at one with the water and sun, she swam far out into the sea. With the island behind her, she let her body float for a while then took a deep breath and dived beneath the surface. A silent, murky world she could not penetrate with her eyes engulfed her. For a moment her chest tightened, then she let go, enjoying the weightless dissolving – feeling free of her worries and her human form.

A memory flashed through her mind of a summer long ago: as a girl of eight, she had been roaming the birch forest close to her home, everything had smelled so strongly of earth and sun that when she had reached a clearing, she had taken off her dress and lain on the ground, pressing her naked belly into the earth, drawing in the beautiful scent, feeling a deep pulsing – her blood's or the earth's? At one with the trees and the birds, everything had melted away until Father's voice shattered the magic . . .

Ritva surfaced and froze – a large grey seal was staring straight at her with its deep, black eyes. Her heart leapt, and she was acutely aware of her naked body, so vulnerable and so close to the creature. Sealskin, soulskin . . . The story rushed back to her and as she looked into the animal's eyes, she felt an energy emanating from it, a wisdom and kindness and something her heart recognised as love. Tears stung as she thought of the two seals Martta had killed to keep them alive.

'Please, forgive us,' she whispered.

The seal kept its eyes on her, droplets of water dripping from its whiskers. Despite her aching heart, Ritva couldn't help but think just how much the seal resembled a dog without ears; she gave a sudden laugh and, as if her laughter had broken the spell, the seal started to move its head rhythmically back and forth. Ritva mirrored its movements and for a while there was nothing but a playful dance between them. Then, without warning, the seal dipped beneath the surface and disappeared. Ritva dived also, but when she opened her eyes underwater she could not see a thing. Then the creature nudged her foot and circled around her. She came up for air and so did the seal; it swam in circles around her, dived again and brushed against her leg. A wave of happiness flooded through her as she marvelled over the creature's beauty, the way it glided through the water so effortlessly and with such pure joy. She turned onto her back; a blue-grey cloud hung low in the sky like a nasty bruise, and the air crackled in anticipation of a storm.

'I need to swim back,' she said aloud, looking at the seal. She swam away fast and when she glanced over her shoulder, the seal had disappeared. Her heart ached as if she had left part of herself behind in the encounter. As she drew closer to the island, lightning flashed across the horizon in a wild zigzag, followed by a deep growl of thunder. Martta stood at the shore, waving her arms.

'Quick, get out of the water! The storm will be here any minute.'

Ritva stumbled ashore, steadying herself against Martta's shoulder, suddenly feeling clumsy on land. Large, heavy raindrops fell like ripe plums and soon blinding sheets of water thrashed down, stinging their arms and faces, whisking the clear surface of the water into a boiling foam. They cowered under the raft; Martta wrapped Ritva's clothes around her shivering body and held her tight; Ritva leaned into her, trembling, overcome with a sense of longing she had no words for.

That night when the rain had finally stopped and they were drying off beside a small fire, Ritva told Martta about her encounter with the seal, how it had touched a place in her that was hard to describe, but that was wild and free and so much larger than the timid girl Martta had met in the asylum. Martta listened without a word, an expression on her face that Ritva could not read.

The storm had broken the calm and for the next few weeks a steady wind took them further north. How long would it be until they reached their destination, Ritva asked Martta every so often; but Martta was vague – if they were lucky they would make it before winter set in . . .

Slowly the long days of summer passed and by August it was high time to stock up on provisions once more; after the golden cloudberries, the blueberries ripened and one morning they went ashore to forage in the woods. Soft morning light fell through the birches, turning the glistening leaves near fluorescent. Ritva could see the waterline shimmering though the trees, her guide back to the shore. The mossy ground put a spring in her step as she combed through the thicket of birch and spruce. She stopped in front of an old lichen-covered tree and took a deep breath of the spicy air. It was easy to imagine fairies and trolls here, and she was aware she was only a visitor in this place that belonged to the forest spirits. It was better to tread lightly here in case a small being might pinch her legs.

Instead, she stumbled over a large brown mushroom, a type not only edible but delicious. She stroked the soft cap, broke it off its stem and inhaled its scent. The first mushroom was always a special gift. She thought of Father by her side, praising her for finding the first mushroom of the season . . . How had it all gone so terribly wrong? Father, signing the papers, sending her and

Mother away? As her thoughts returned to Seili, a shadow fell over Ritva's heart; she remembered the days when she had stolen away into the small wood, stuffed her scribblings into cracks in the rock. How desperate she had been! It wouldn't have been long before her mind had finally cracked under the boredom, the cold and despair . . .

She gazed back over her shoulder but couldn't see Martta. She leaned against a large boulder to rest, stroking its surface, tracing with her fingertips the lines and shapes cut into the rock. Suddenly goosebumps rose all over her arms and with a jolt she understood: these were the outlines of boats, of people and animals, a bear and a moose with its calf. Someone had taken great care to carve these images into the rock, a very long time ago.

Ritva shouted for Martta to come but instead of a reply she heard a strange yapping, then a drawn-out howl. A dog in this forest? She listened hard but the howling had stopped. She looked up through the trees to locate the sun; the sound must be coming from the west. She strode further into the forest, following what now sounded like whimpering. She had been around dogs all her life and had once even heard wolves in the depths of winter, but this? Then her nose picked up a strong scent: a waft of wild animal and something else . . . the smell of blood.

Ritva's eyes strained to penetrate the thicket and she moved swiftly, a light-footed animal herself, following the scent. And then she saw it: a small grey creature, crouched and shivering, caught in a snare, trying to pull its thin, bleeding leg from the metal vice. She had seen traps like this, used by shepherds to catch wolves. The snare cut deep into the animal's flesh and fresh blood trickled from its front leg onto a dirty pelt that was already caked with dried blood. The animal lifted its head, winced and strained to get away, but the iron wire only cut deeper into its flesh. Ritva's heart ached. She had heard such desperate cries before: a dog she had rescued from a pond near their house; a chicken carried between a fox's teeth; and later, on Seili, the women locked in the west wing, their anguished voices calling from behind cell doors.

181

As she stooped down beside the trapped creature her fear dissolved: the wolf was no larger than the size of a three-month-old puppy and had been trapped in the vice for a while; it was wild with pain and thirst. It yapped again and snapped at her hand. Ritva ripped a piece of fabric from her trousers, held the wolfling's head and wrapped the fabric around its nose in a tight bandage. Unable to snap, the wolf growled, its eyes flashing with fear and rage.

'Hush, I won't harm you. Let me see your leg,' Although Ritva spoke softly, the wolf's little body cringed. A wave of nausea rose in Ritva as she examined the wound. She tried to prise the metal from the wolf's tender flesh but it barely moved and caused the animal to yelp in pain. Ritva looked over her shoulder for Martta but could see nothing beyond the green thicket. She needed a knife to force the snare open; maybe Martta had one on her, but Ritva didn't want to leave the wolfling. There must be a way – whoever had laid that snare could also open it. An icy shiver rushed down her spine – she had thought only of the animal, but snares were laid by humans . . . She stroked the animal's matted fur, feeling its frantic heartbeat, then examined the trap again, trying to understand its cruel mechanism.

'I'll give it one more go. Keep still, little one.' She wedged a piece of hard wood between the wire and the wolf's foot, moving it gently back and forth. When it loosened slightly, she inserted her finger, attempting to widen the noose.

'I'll get you out of here.' With another finger she pulled the wire looser still, then, holding the wolf with her right arm close to her chest, she dislodged the wire and pulled it off the creature's leg until the wolf lay limp and bleeding in her lap. It whimpered as she touched it lightly.

'Hush now, we've got to see to this.' Close up the young male wolf looked just like the neighbour's puppy she had adored as a child, and she had to remind herself that this was an unpredictable, wild creature. She tore another strip from her trousers and wrapped it around the wolf's leg, then backtracked through the forest, clutching the wolf to her chest, its eyes following hers, raw with fear.

Where was Martta? Ritva peered through the trees, trying to find the shoreline, but she could see only a thick curtain of vegetation. She pushed onwards then stopped to catch her breath – there was still no sign of the shore or Martta. She looked up through the trees and froze – clouds had covered the sun and there was no way to tell in which direction she should head. What if she got lost and ran into the hunter who had laid the snares? Sweat broke out across her body – what he could do to her, out here alone in the woods . . .

'I'm lost, little one,' she whispered into the wolf's ear, her face touching its fur. She tried to recognise any landmark, a tree she had passed, a stone or a path, but everything looked the same.

'I just wanted to help you . . .' The wolf lifted its head and pricked up its ears, then started to sniff. Ritva could hear nothing but the light breeze playing in the trees.

'Can you guide me back?' She felt silly the moment she whispered her plea into the wolf's ear – he was just an injured, frightened animal that would die in her arms if she didn't find her way back soon; yet she observed him closely as he squirmed and turned his head, sniffing and listening at the same time. There, to the left, he must have noticed something.

Ritva clutched her precious bundle even tighter and moved in the direction its head and nose indicated, taking small steps, avoiding branches, becoming a stalker herself, an instinctual being, nostrils flared, sniffing for a whiff of human scent, eyes wide, the hair on her neck standing on end . . . She picked up the smell of water before she could see it: a stretch of dark grey, a perfect line sitting beneath the light grey of the sky. She stumbled through the forest, her side burning from a stitch. When she reached their raft, she rummaged through their storage box for a blanket and a canteen, then poured some water into a bowl and unwrapped the bandage around the wolf's mouth. This time he did not snap at her but lapped up the water in seconds. Ritva refilled the bowl, then pulled out a piece of dried fish from their provisions, soaked it and fed him small morsels. He gulped everything down without chewing, then coughed.

'Slow down, my friend.' Ritva spoke calmly but the wolf swallowed anything offered in one bite. When he was fed, Ritva bound his nose again, carried him to the shore and gently washed his blood-encrusted fur. The snare had cut deep into his flesh and he winced at the touch of the cold water, all the while keeping his eyes on her face. Suddenly his ears pricked up and he growled. Ritva heard a cracking in the undergrowth. Martta stumbled out of the woods, holding a dead rabbit by its hind legs. At the sight of the wolf she froze.

'What on earth . . .?'

'I found him, Martta, he's badly hurt.' But Martta did not smile. She knew that Sami herders could not afford sympathy for their animal's worst enemy and would hunt or chase away any wolves that came near their herd.

'Please, Martta, I want to keep him until he recovers.'

'You want to keep a . . . *wolf*?' The way Martta spoke made Ritva doubt her actions – could she really save this wild creature? What if he attacked them once he regained his strength? She glanced at the wolf in her arms, meeting his gaze. There was no fear in his eyes now, only surrender and pain.

'He was caught in a nasty snare. Please, we've got to help him!'

'He's a wolf, Ritva!' The wolf lifted his head and eyed the rabbit. 'I bet you would like my rabbit. I found it in a trap. It was already dead but we need to get out of here before the trapper finds us. He'll not be amused at finding his snares emptied.' She looked at the wolf's leg. 'The wound's quite bad, he might not make it.' Martta gazed out to sea and sighed. 'But I guess we've all escaped from somewhere.'

'You mean we can keep him?'

'Let's see what we can do with this rascal. But I tell you, if he ever gets near any reindeer . . . My father shot more than one of these greylegs – they can do a great deal of damage to a herd.'

'Thank you, Martta.' Martta did not answer but walked back into the forest. Ritva continued to wash the wolf's wound, humming a song.

'Let's give you a name then. How about "Grey Beauty"?' The wolf looked at her with dull eyes.

'What about "the one who got away"?' Martta said, stepping out of the woods with a bundle of dark leaves. 'Or "Grey Heart"?'

'I like Greyheart,' Ritva said. 'He looks like he's got a good heart – well, as far as wolves go. Not that I know much about them, but maybe this one can grow up to be a "Greatheart"?'

'You do know he's not a dog, don't you? Now let me take a look at his leg.'

Martta carefully moved the wolf's injured limb. He flinched and might have bitten her had his mouth not been bound.

'Shhh, hold still, I'm going to put some leaves around your leg, they'll help fight the infection.' She wrapped the dark green leaves around his leg, then removed the cloth around his mouth and used it as a bandage. The wolf did not stir but surrendered under her confident touch. Martta wrapped him in a blanket and placed the bundle on the ground.

'Let's get the raft and be off.'

They pulled their vessel into the water.

'You hold the wolf and I'll push you both off from the shore,' Martta said.

Ritva lifted the bundle and stepped onto the raft. The wolf, alarmed by the rocking, curled into an even smaller ball.

'Go to sleep,' Ritva whispered in his ear. With one big push Martta sent their raft out into the water, then jumped aboard. Greyheart lay curled on a blanket, lifting his head only to drink and eat the morsels of fish Ritva fed him. Despite much patting and assurance, he seemed wary of the raft and human company. Ritva prayed that he would make it through and accept their companionship – but could she really expect such a wild creature to trust her?

185

23

It had been nearly a year since their escape from Seili, and despite having got Petta off their trail they were wary as they passed the towns of Umeå and Skellefteå along the coast. Over the weeks, Greyheart's wound had started to heal, but he still watched Ritva's and Martta's every move and occasionally snapped at them. Like her encounter with the seal, the proximity of this wild creature stirred something in Ritva, yet she wondered if it had been a mistake to bring him with them. Wouldn't he miss roaming the forests, hunting for prey and, surely, his pack? Looking into his fierce eyes she thought of the asylum, what it had done to their spirits and what it was still doing to the women held captive there . . .

'But he would have died in that snare,' Martta said when Ritva shared her concerns.

This was true, and as if to soothe her doubts, slowly Greyheart began to allow her to approach him and eventually even to stroke his fur. Martta kept her distance – her reindeer herder's soul did not allow her to bond with the wolf, yet Greyheart tried to win her heart: tilting his head, he watched her manoeuvre the sails, yapping as if to applaud her.

'He's trying to charm you,' Ritva said one day in September as they sailed along.

'It takes more than a cute face to charm a reindeer herder. I've seen too many calves taken by greylegs. You can never trust a wolf.' Still, as she looked at the young wolf, Martta's features softened. 'Maybe if I pretend you're a dog . . .'

As if to answer her, Greyheart walked over and licked Martta's hand and she ruffled his pelt. That evening they lit a generous fire against the September chill and settled early to bed.

'Psst, did you hear that?' Martta pulled Ritva's sleeve.

'What?'

'It might be a moose – or a wolf?'

'I hope it's not the mother of our grey bundle here,' Ritva whispered, her instincts alert. Suddenly Martta scrambled to her feet, pounced forward and wrestled a small, squealing shape to the ground.

'You little devil!' Martta's fists rained down on the dark heap.

'Please, don't hurt me!' the shape whimpered. Not an animal's growl then, but a child's voice, pleading. As Ritva's eyes adjusted to the twilight, she saw that Martta was holding a boy, no older than eleven, a dirty feral being with ripped clothes and a flushed face. He squirmed and kicked, trying to wriggle out of Martta's grip.

'Not so fast, my boy. What are you doing here?' Martta stared at him, then at the axe he was clutching in his right hand.

'What on earth . . . were you trying to steal our axe?' Martta wrenched the tool from his small fist. 'A boy your age should be in bed at this hour of the night, not out in the woods, stealing.' Slowly she loosened her grip. The boy looked at Martta then Ritva, his eyes wide with fear.

'Please don't hurt me! I'm sorry.' His voice was hoarse, as if he had not used it in a long while.

'What is he saying?' Martta asked, unable to understand his rough Swedish.

'He's sorry he tried to steal from us,' Ritva replied.

'He'd better be. Ask him what he's doing in the woods on his own.'

Ritva spoke slowly and deliberately, just as she had done with Greyheart, trying to call on all the Swedish she remembered.

'He lives here, in the forest.'

'Here? Where are his parents?'

When Ritva asked the boy, he shrugged and looked away. Surely he was hiding something?

'Where are you heading?' Ritva crouched next to him.

'I want to go to the place where the sun doesn't sleep.'

'Ah, the midnight sun. We're also heading there – all the way up north.' She smiled at him. Martta threw Ritva a puzzled look and released the boy. He remained on the ground, alert and tense.

'Maybe we should ask him to come with us? There are still berries and mushrooms around now, but come winter, what's he going to do? He's too young to fend for himself.'

'Ritva, we're only just surviving ourselves. First you want to bring a wolf with us, now a child?'

The boy looked from Martta to Ritva and back. Ritva's throat tightened; maybe this boy reminded her of Elke, but all she wanted to do was hug him and keep him safe . . .

'What about his parents?' Martta said, her eyes boring into the boy, trying to read him like snow tracks. 'He's clearly run away – surely they'll come looking for him?'

The boy stared at his feet.

'Don't you have parents?' Ritva asked again, but he only shook his head and looked away. 'How can we leave this child on his own, Martta? Maybe he's run away from something terrible, like we did.'

'I can't even talk to him,' Martta scowled.

'Maybe he can teach you some Swedish.'

At that moment Greyheart stirred and yawned. The boy's eyes widened at the sight of the wolf.

'This is Greyheart,' Ritva said. 'A little wolf who was wounded and is recovering with us. And what's your name?'

'Arvid,' the boy whispered, transfixed at the sight of the wolf gnawing away at his bandage.

'And how old are you?'

'Twelve.'

'If someone is looking for the boy we'll have them after us as well,' Martta said. 'Besides, he'll slow us down.' Ritva said nothing – how could Martta be like this after all they had been through?

The night was fading now; pink light replaced the twilight and the birds had started their morning song; the forest filled with light and music like a holy place.

'Fine,' Martta said. 'Tell him he can come.'

'You're sure?'

Martta only nodded.

'Would you like to join us?' Ritva asked. 'We're heading north on our raft. We called it *Freedom*.' The boy looked from Ritva to Martta and back.

'What about her? Does she want me to come?'

'She is called Martta and she says yes, you can come. But she wants to know about your parents – and so do I.' Pain flitted across the boy's face. 'Won't they come searching for you?'

He shook his head and crossed his arms over his chest. After a long silence Martta turned to the boy.

'Well, I guess we can feed another mouth – but no more stealing, understood?'

Ritva translated and Arvid smiled, revealing two rows of straight teeth, with a large gap where two front teeth were missing.

Relenting at last, Martta placed her hand on the boy's head and ruffled his hair. He ran back into the woods and returned with his knapsack. He poured the contents onto the ground: a few candle stubs, a box of matches, some dried mushrooms, two blankets and a water bottle.

'And what have you got there?' Ritva asked, pointing at his right arm which was hidden behind his back. He pulled out a small knife. Martta's face darkened and she stretched out her arm.

'Why don't you give us that for now? We'll keep it safe for you,' Ritva said softly. Arvid stood unmoving, clutching his knife. 'Please, Arvid.'

He looked at Martta, who glared at him, then handed the knife to Ritva.

'Thank you,' Ritva said. 'You can have it back in a while.'

Slowly the boy began to trust Ritva and relaxed, particularly in the presence of the injured creature. He would gaze at Greyheart in awe, run his fingers through the animal's thick pelt and let him sniff his hand, but he always kept a vigilant eye on Martta. She clearly did not like him and hardly spoke any Swedish.

Ritva showed Arvid how to bind up Greyheart's mouth with a bandage and take it off to feed him morsels of fish or dried rabbit. With the help of medicinal leaves the wound had nearly closed, but its itchiness irritated the wolf and he kept trying to gnaw off the bandage.

'Stop, don't do that, little one,' Arvid whispered into Greyheart's ear. 'It'll get better, I promise.' He patted Greyheart's fur as if he were a dog.

One evening three weeks later, they were woken by a piercing scream. Arvid lay curled up, gasping for air, trapped deep in a nightmare. Ritva pulled him into her lap and whispered in his ear.

'Shhh, Arvid,' she said, stroking his damp hair. 'You're safe here, you're with us.' Martta joined them, embracing both. A moment later Arvid woke, a wild gaze in his eyes. He struggled to speak.

'They couldn't get out,' he panted. 'The fire . . . there was a fire . . . I tried to . . . I ran for help, but it was too late—'

'Shhh, it's only a bad dream,' Ritva whispered, but he pulled away, wide awake.

'You don't understand! I remember now.' He turned his face away, his whole body shaking. 'They all burned in that fire, my parents and Mia.' He was shouting, and when Ritva and Martta tried to calm him, he lashed out at them with his arms, pushing them away.

'I should've got Mia out first, but Father said to run for help—'

Martta wrapped her strong arms around him and pulled him close; he struggled but Martta held tight. After a while Arvid collapsed, his body still trembling but no longer fighting her. They stayed like this throughout the night – a tangle of embraces trying to hold back a terrible flood. With the first light of dawn, Arvid fell asleep and did not wake until the afternoon. He found himself next to Greyheart, who had not moved from his side, the thick fur of his belly warming Arvid's body. Slowly, like drawing buckets of water from a deep well, Arvid retrieved piece after piece of his nightmare and shared it with Ritva and Martta: how he had seen the sinister light flicker above the forest, and stumbled through the woods towards the blazing farm, blinded by smoke, a terrible smell in his nose.

'Mama, Papa!'

He had raced towards the burning front door but his neighbour's strong hands had grabbed him.

'Stay back, Arvid!' The neighbour's voice was hoarse, a grown man sobbing. 'There's nothing anyone can do!' Arvid had kicked, his whole body straining towards the blaze. He bit the man's hand, pulled free and rushed towards the inferno, but a wall of heat pushed him back. He screamed then bolted into the woods, a panicked animal, lungs stinging, until he tripped and crashed to the ground, hitting his head on a rock. When he awoke, darkness had fallen and he was alone.

Arvid was very quiet once he had told Ritva and Martta about the loss of his family. For the next few days he lay curled up next to Greyheart, his fingers in the wolf's pelt, whispering into the wolf's ear, and Ritva and Martta let him be. Then one morning he got up and asked to help out with the sails. Greyheart stretched and sniffed the breeze.

'God, look at us, we're quite the ship of fools!' Ritva said and laughed, relieved to see Arvid more animated again. 'Two women, a boy, a wolf and a battered raft!'

'You should be careful with that word,' Martta cautioned.

'What word?'

'Fools,' Martta spat. 'Haven't we been called fools long enough?

Remember the "Beach of Fools" on Seili? They might as well have called it the "Beach of Lunatics".'

'I didn't mean anything bad,' Ritva said. 'It's just that we've become quite a little family – an odd one, yes, but we love each other and sometimes what we're doing must seem a little mad . . .'

'You are mad people?' Arvid said, his eyes wide.

'Oh, Arvid, of course not,' Ritva said and put her hand on his shoulder. 'We were just . . . unlucky.' Silence stretched between them all. Suddenly Greyheart yapped and jumped, trying to catch a seagull that was flying low over the raft.

'Anyway, now,' Ritva continued, 'we're lucky, especially since we met you and Greyheart. This is a ship of wanderers and dreamers and, most of all, adventurers.'

A smile flitted across Arvid's face. Martta placed her arm around his shoulder and they stood looking out over the water.

That night, after they had set up camp on a rocky beach, Ritva fell into a fitful sleep. She dreamt of her father spitting condemnation from the pulpit: 'Beware the Ship of Fools, packed with sinners and lunatics! Beware the weak flesh, gluttony, envy, lust. Confess your sins, my sheep, and jump off that ship before it's too late!'

Ritva woke sweating. She listened to the waves lapping against the shore and Martta's and Arvid's steady breathing. The dream reminded her of what her heart was still trying to forget – not only had her father been self-righteous, he had also been downright cruel – how could he have condemned Mother and her to a life on Seili? Had he known that they were sent there with the planks for their own coffins? With a pang of guilt she thought about Elke, left so far behind, fending for herself . . .

About a week later, Martta pulled out the map and searched the horizon. The sky was granite grey, and black clouds were gathering in the distance like a flock of crows.

'I think we should leave the Baltic and head into the forest. We don't want to get caught in the autumn storms. We're not far from Luleå.'

Ritva agreed – it would be good to feel solid ground beneath her feet and walk again. They navigated through a maze of small islands towards the coast and in the evening, ashore, they roasted their daily catch on sticks over a fire.

'What shall we do with our magnificent *Freedom*?' Ritva said between bites of tender fish.

'We could leave her here for another wanderer?' Martta suggested.

Ritva threw a glance at their vessel. 'Yes, that would be kind. And what about . . . the box?' They had never told Arvid about their coffin boat.

'I think the fire is getting a little low,' Martta said and got up. Arvid watched wide-eyed as Martta pounded the axe into the wooden seat until it splintered. Soon flames licked the pine boards, the coffin wood fuelling a crackling fire. As Ritva gazed into the flames, images appeared, blurry at first, then clearer: Seili during the winter, locked in by ice and snow; an old man, hunched over and wrapped in a heavy coat, pulling a sleigh piled high with mattresses, sheets, broken chairs, pots and crockery, even an iron bed. As he walked, a suitcase broke open, spilling a jumble of clothes and tangled-up straitjackets onto the ice. The man stopped, then stacked everything into a large heap and poured liquid from a canister over the lot. The moment he struck a match the wind picked up and sheets, clothes and straitjackets caught fire, a furnace devouring the remnants of asylum life.

As the images dissolved, Ritva found herself back on the shore. She shuddered.

'You look like you've seen a ghost,' Arvid said, 'are you all right?'

'Yes, I'm fine,' Ritva said, but her knees were weak – if only her vision were a premonition that the asylum would soon be closed for ever . . .

*

The next day they turned away from the sea and headed inland. September had made nature come alive with the most vibrant colours – birch leaves had turned into glistening gold, lichen burnt orange on rocks, and berries glowed in brilliant shades of red amongst moss and blueberry bushes. The cooler winds also brought relief from the swarms of mosquitoes and blackflies that had plagued them all summer. Despite the women lighting fires to ward the insects off whenever possible, the tiny flies had crawled into their ears and eyes and many mornings they had woken with swollen faces from all the bites.

They trekked for days, peering at the compass, forging paths through the forest. One morning Martta showed them tufts of sedge grass near a creek.

'That's *suoidni*, the grass we need for our shoes and it's even the right time to harvest it, a waxing moon.'

They cut the long grass, bound it into thick strands and once it had dried they filled their boots with it. After months on the raft they were all enjoying walking on land, especially with the new soft grass in their shoes that kept their feet dry and warm, better than any socks.

In the evenings they set up camp and Martta tied the sail between trees to serve as a windbreak. One evening Martta stared at Greyheart in the firelight.

'He can't live on dried fish alone, he needs to hunt.'

As Ritva patted his fur she felt each rib.

'You're right, but I guess we don't look much better.' They were fast running out of food.

'In bad times my people made bark bread from pine,' Martta said, 'at least it fills the stomach; I'll show you.'

In the morning they spotted a large gnarly pine. Martta cut through the outer bark and peeled it back, then sliced away a large strip of the grey mass inside.

'You can eat that?' Arvid said, curling up his nose.

'Not like this, silly,' Martta said and laughed. 'It has to be dried first, then ground and baked over a hot stone.' She draped the bark sheet over a branch.

'No one is chasing us now, so let's stay here for a few days, bake some bread and hunt – we might catch something if we're lucky.'

That afternoon Martta built their first *lavvu* tent.

'We'll need eight or nine hearthstones for the fireplace and some long thin poles,' she said and sent Arvid off to look for the stones. Martta cut down some birch trees, Ritva sliced the branches off with the knife and together they leaned the poles against each other to form the tent's structure.

'Now our former sail will become a tent cloth,' Martta said. She knotted the sheet to a long stick and draped the fabric around the poles. Within minutes they entered the tent and carried the hearth stones inside.

'In come the mattresses,' Martta said, pulling large birch branches into the *lavvu* and placing them in thick layers over each other.

'Now we only need some reindeer hides – but at least we've got the seal fur and our blankets.' She showed Greyheart his place next to the entrance, rolled out their sleeping blankets and lit a fire; soon the tent was filled with the spicy aroma of birch.

'This is so cosy,' Arvid said and snuggled up to Martta.

'Yes, it is. My people have lived like this for thousands of years.'

'A thousand years?'

'Yes, my dear, and longer. We've lived with half-wild reindeer since the beginning of time, following their migration up into the mountains and into the tundra, sleeping in *lavvus* just like this one.'

Ritva smiled. The closer they got to the North, the more Martta seemed to change into how Ritva had imagined a Sami woman to be, full of knowledge and skills, not only about how to survive in the wilderness, but also how to live comfortably and with pride. Martta had been born in a *lavvu* and was at home in such simple housing, but could Ritva ever get used to this way of living? For a moment she saw herself in her childhood room, her soft bed, the crisp sheets . . . and yet that bed had turned into a terrible trap. It was here with Martta, Arvid and Greyheart that she felt safe – safer than she had felt for many years. The only thing that pained her was Elke's absence – if only she could reach high into the night sky, stretch her arms across the Baltic, scoop up her little sister and bring her here . . .

24

They slept for three nights in the *lavvu*. They hunted for food and baked flat round bark bread over hot stones, eating it as quickly as it was prepared. On the morning of the fourth day, Ritva found Martta studying the map once more.

'We're in the land of the Lule Sami, but I only speak North Sami. Besides, I want to show you the tundra and the mountains. Let's trek westwards along the Lule river, past Jokkmokk, then head north-west.'

Her finger traced a route along the crumpled map. Jokkmokk – Ritva rolled the name around in her mouth; it felt good to be heading towards a place with a name after so long in the wilderness.

They kept close to the river, casting fishing lines in the afternoons and being rewarded most days with a catch of shimmering river salmon or rainbow trout. One morning as they entered a denser part of the forest, Greyheart put his nose to the ground, sniffed around for a moment, then tensed, ears alert.

'What's the matter?' Martta said, watching the wolf.

'Shhh!' Ritva signalled for Martta and Arvid to stop and pointed straight ahead. Behind a curtain of leaves, a large brown creature grazed the forest floor, its wide head crowned with massive velvety brown antlers. Ritva's heart leapt; a god in brown fur, a mighty moose stood large and proud and underneath its belly, a suckling calf. The moose raised its head and peered through the foliage – would it pick up their scent and charge them? Ritva gestured to Martta to hold Greyheart back, but at that moment the wolf gave a loud yap and the moose plunged deeper into the forest, the stunned calf stumbling behind it.

The next evening they set up camp in a clearing next to a granite boulder. Ritva quickly fell asleep, but a few hours later Martta woke her.

'What is it?' A brilliant arc of dazzling stars stretched across the sky above the clearing.

'We can't stay here,' Martta whispered.

'Why, what's wrong?' Ritva was still half asleep, a taste of earth in her mouth.

'It's the *uldas*; they don't want us here. We must have stopped right above their dwelling place and woken them when we arrived. They're angry and won't let me sleep.'

'*Uldas*? Who are they?' Arvid said, bolting up and staring at Martta.

'The *uldas* are beings just like us, but they live underground,' Martta said. 'They're awake at night and sleep during the day. I had a feeling when we stopped here that it might not be the best place, especially next to the boulder.'

'You believe all those old tales?' Ritva asked. She remembered Mother telling her about such beings, though she had called them a different name. One night, Father had stormed into her bedroom and shouted at Mother, 'I won't have you spoiling Ritva with your tales. They are the work of the devil, do you hear me?' Mother had looked as if she had been slapped and for a long time there were no more stories.

'It's not something I believe, Ritva, it's something I've experienced,' Martta said. 'I know the *uldas* exist. Believe me, we're better off leaving; at the very least we won't be able to sleep, and it could be much worse . . .'

Just then Ritva recalled that her fitful sleep had been filled with strange dreams – of tinkling bells and voices whispering in a language she could not understand.

'Fine,' she said, 'but can't we wait until it gets lighter?' Yet Arvid had already packed his things. As they left the clearing, guided only by a pale half-moon that cast a silvery light through the trees, Ritva thought she could hear faint laughter behind their backs and the sound of silver bells.

They passed Jokkmokk in the last week of September. The further north they got, the more restless Martta became; the mountains and fells were calling to her. Sometimes now the dense forests opened out, allowing glimpses of large lakes, the snow-covered Kebnekaise and the Norge mountains to the far west. And somewhere, not too far away, reindeer herds were heading from the high plateaux of the summer pastures to lower ground for the winter. Martta's heart ached at the thought of the animals. One morning she climbed up on a large rock and gazed towards the mountains. She opened her mouth and let a song rush through her. The chant rose and fell as she threw her head back, the notes like a flock of wild birds, spiralling to lofty heights, then plunging low and rising again; simple words travelling on melodies, while her eyes remained fixed on the mountain range, the place from which the herd would come.

When she clambered down from the boulder, she was calm.

'What a beautiful song, Martta,' Ritva said. 'Were you singing about the mountains?'

'Yes, but when I sing like this, it's as if I *am* the mountain, as if I'm a part of it.' Martta smiled. 'It's what we call *yoiking*. I've *yoiked* from when I was little. My grandfather taught me many of the old songs, I was even given a *lulohti*, my very own song, when I was born. But then the church people forbade us our songs and said *yoiking* was a form of devil worship. Even my mother chided me sometimes, but I can't help it – when my heart is full, the *yoik* just fills me and I can't do anything but open my throat and let it out.'

Ritva's skin prickled. How could this beautiful chant that touched her to the core be the work of the devil? And although she had no name for it, she too knew this need to let her mouth fall open and release the sounds that wanted to fly out of her, that made her feel at one with the land, the lakes and the birds . . . Father had never liked her singing that way and had told her to save her voice for the Sunday hymns, but singing in church had always paled in comparison to this.

That night as they slept in the open, huddled around a smouldering fire, Ritva was again woken by Martta's hand on her shoulder.

'What is it?' Ritva's voice was thick with sleep. In her dreams, she was still trying to escape Petta's shadowy figure, which was chasing her over the ice. 'More *uldas*?'

'No, the Northern Lights! Look, the spirits are dancing.'

Ritva opened her eyes and sat up. Arvid was still fast asleep next to her, swaddled up to his nose in blankets. The aurora borealis – Mother had often told Ritva about the magical Northern Lights, but she had only ever seen a hint of green. Now, the sky was ablaze with colour, eerie shades of blue and green, aglow in turquoise and even red, alive and flickering like cold fire.

'Did you know that we call this *revontuli* in Finnish – Fox's Fire? There's a story that a fox ran across the night sky, sweeping the heavens with its bushy tail, leaving a bright glow for all of us to see,' Martta whispered. 'But my grandmother told me another story when I was little. She said it's best to avert your gaze, especially if you're a girl or a woman. She said you should even put something on your head to protect you from the lights. She told me they are spirits moving across the heavens, running, dancing and playing, and sometimes they are restless, the spirits of those who died violently, their souls still battling it out up there in the sky. Sometimes their fighting goes on all night. Grandmother said you mustn't whistle or talk loudly or they might attack you. I was scared as a child and hid under my mother's coat, but I still couldn't resist peeping out.'

They sat for a long time, mesmerised by the night's spectacle: pale green flames racing across the sky, fizzling out only to return in stronger colours, like dancers, whirling around each other against the backdrop of the magnificent star-studded sky.

'This is so beautiful,' Ritva whispered.

'Yes, and I'm sure those warriors up there would be on our side.' The thought of support from the fierce spirits of the heavens calmed the last ripples of Ritva's nightmare; she leaned her head against Martta's chest, feeling the beat of her heart, quick as a hare's.

After a few days they reached the tundra, soft undulating fells that stretched underneath a wide sky for hundreds of miles in countless shades of green and red, against a distant backdrop of the snow-covered mountains of Norway. The ground was soft and springy and after weeks of walking through dense forest, the openness of the land felt like a breath of fresh air to Ritva, and more than that: a promise. Any day now they might come across reindeer . . .

As it happened, the first reindeer they saw came in the shape of scattered bones. Greyheart had picked up a scent and, sniffing for prey, he raced away from their group. When they caught up, they found him yapping over a pile of bones. Ritva gasped at the white bones strewn across the autumnal ground; she could make out a ribcage and some long bones that might have belonged to the animal's legs, but what took her breath away was the neat column of the animal's spine, spilling from the skull like an elaborate necklace. She picked up part of a jawbone, complete with a neat row of teeth – its shape reminded her of a boat, the teeth a group of people rowing in close formation.

'It was a young female reindeer,' Martta said, pointing at the skull that had only stubs instead of antlers. 'Maybe it was injured and a wolf took it.'

She threw Greyheart a glance; he turned away as if ashamed, then grabbed one of the larger bones and started to gnaw on it, but soon gave up. The reindeer must have died many seasons ago – its bones, bleached by rain and sun, had not an ounce of flesh on them.

Ritva watched as Martta carefully stalked the area, looking for any other bones that might have belonged to the animal, then began to place them in a pattern, starting with the skull.

'What are you doing?' Arvid asked.

'It's important that we collect all the bones and lay them out in the right order. If any are missing, the reindeer cannot be reborn.'

Arvid frowned. 'But how can a heap of bones come alive again?'

'Well, you see, it won't be a heap of bones any more, once we've put them all in the right place, and about the rest, we don't need to worry.'

Arvid looked at his feet, then pulled a small bone from his trouser pocket and handed it to Martta.

'Thank you, Arvid. It's part of the leg. It might be only a little bone, but without it, the reindeer would have no spring in its step.'

Ritva was moved by this gesture. She remembered how careful Martta had been with the seal bones too; she had scraped the flesh from all the bones and collected them in a bundle, then disappeared off. Ritva had not asked, but Martta had returned some time later, her hands still bloody, but the torment on her face gone.

'Our ancestors have done this for thousands of years,' Martta continued. 'Especially when we killed a bear. It's so important that all the bones are arranged in the right order and buried just so.'

'You killed bears?' Arvid's mouth gaped open. Martta laughed.

'Not me, Arvid, but yes, my ancestors did. Bears have always been the most sacred animals to us but we needed them to survive the long winters. There were many things we had to do when we killed a bear because it is so sacred. If a bear gave its life we had to treat it well and make sure it could be born again. So, when a hunter killed a bear with his special spear, he would leave the bear where it died for a day so that its soul could settle back into its body and its spirit wouldn't wander about. And when the hunting party brought the bear to the village, the women would pour red alder bark juice over them to honour Leaibeolmmai, the God of hunting. Then all the meat was cooked and eaten and the bones collected and buried in the right order.'

As Martta talked, Ritva's mind was filled with wonder at this ancient, beautiful land and its people who cared so deeply that they made sure not even a single bone would be lost.

'Please tell me more about the *noaidi*,' Arvid pleaded, grabbing Martta's hand. He was beginning to trail behind and they could tell he was tired from walking; maybe Martta's stories would take his mind off his sore feet.

'Well, the *noaidi* were mainly men,' Martta began, 'but sometimes a woman could be a *noaidi* too. Real *noaidi* have immense powers and they are respected and feared amongst the people, although there are also charlatans. There is a tale of a false *noaidi* who challenged an old, powerful *noaidi* to a competition. The true *noaidi* said: "If you are a *noaidi*, that is good. But I don't see why we should compete. I ask you kindly to leave me alone." But the false *noaidi* wouldn't leave the old man in peace. So the true *noaidi* put his hands into the fire, pushed the burning logs aside and grabbed a handful of glowing embers. He thrust them into his mouth and chewed them so that flames shot from his mouth. The false *noaidi* looked on in horror, ran out of the *lavvu* and was never seen again.'

'Really? He chewed burning coals?' Arvid stared at Martta.

'Yes, so the story goes. I told you, *noaidi* are powerful, they just don't always show it, like the way they don't always show off their sacred drums. I remember my grandfather telling me the story of how a man once stole a beautifully decorated knife from him. The man denied it but Grandfather knew he had taken it. So when the man went outside to harness his reindeer, he suddenly couldn't move. He stood there in the cold for hours, freezing, his reindeer sniffing and circling around him. All day and all evening he stood frozen to the spot, shaking with cold and fear. Finally, my grandfather went out to see him.

'"So, do you have something that does not belong to you?"

'"Yes, yes, I am sorry," the man cried, "I lied, I took your knife, please let me go, I will give it back to you along with two of my reindeer." Grandfather agreed and lifted the spell. So you see, Arvid, *noaidi* are great healers, but they can also be fierce.'

Arvid listened, frowning. A quiet pride rose in Martta; it was only in telling Arvid that she remembered her grandfather's powers. She breathed deeply, feeling his strength righting her back. Just then another memory stirred: when Grandfather had shown her his small drum he had pointed to some marks. 'Each mark stands for one hunted bear,' he had said, and there had been many . . . When her mother lay ill in the master's home, she had entrusted Grandfather's drum hammer to Martta, but what happened to his drum? Had he hidden it in the mountains? And was there any connection between his drum and Ritva's visions?

25

The next morning Ritva was up early and lit a fire to ward off the frosty autumn chill. It was Greyheart who sensed them first – his ears suddenly pricked, his nose quivering. He jumped up and paced back and forth.

'What is it, my friend?' Ritva tried to pat his fur, but he pulled away and growled.

Martta picked up the binoculars and searched the hills, her back rigid with tension. And then they heard it: a faint grumbling, a tremor that seemed to rise from the centre of the earth, the drumming of thousands of hearts, thousands of hooves.

'The herd!' Martta shouted. She pressed the binoculars into Arvid's hands, hunted around for a piece of rope, twisted it into a loop, slung it over Greyheart's neck, then pulled him close to her side.

Reindeer after reindeer poured over the hills, a river of grey, a great wave of galloping bodies, legs, antlers and stubby white tails bobbing up and down; hundreds of animals, maybe even a thousand . . .

Ritva's heart thumped – such force and beauty! Martta's face broke into the broadest smile, then she let out a bright laugh.

'What's that sound?' Arvid asked. Ritva could hear it too: a strange clicking beneath the grunting of the animals and the stomping of their hooves.

'It's the tendons in the reindeers' knees,' Martta said, still laughing. 'Nothing to worry about. Aren't they beautiful?' Ritva had never seen Martta so happy and yes, the animals were magnificent. Greyheart growled and strained against the rope.

'Steady, boy,' Martta said, grabbing his coat.

The herd settled nearby to graze; Ritva and Martta found it difficult to attend to any chores that day as, more than anything, they wanted to watch the reindeer.

In the evening, their hearts and minds filled with the presence of the herd, they lit a fire and Martta told the story of Jubmel and Vaja, the reindeer doe. Ritva remembered how Martta had shared this tale with her during those early weeks in the asylum, how it had moved her.

'Did you know that the whole world was made from a reindeer?' Martta said, smiling at Arvid. He shook his head. Martta took a deep breath, stoked the fire and began to tell the tale in her deep melodic voice. When she came to the part about the *noaidi*, the shaman of the *siida*, Arvid looked puzzled.

'Like your grandfather?'

'Yes.'

Suddenly his eyes widened. 'Then you are a Lapp, too? But you don't look like a real Lapp, you aren't wearing the right clothes.' Arvid stared her up and down. 'I've seen pictures, they wear colourful costumes and funny caps.' Ritva's heart contracted as she recognised her own former ignorance in the boy's words.

'Please don't call me a Lapp, Arvid. It's like calling you a dirty boy. We are Sami, the people of the midnight sun, the reindeer people.'

Arvid blushed and looked away. 'I'm sorry,' he whispered. 'And I loved the story – I love all your stories.'

'It's not just our clothes that make us Sami, or the fact that we herd reindeer, nor is it our language or the *yoiking*. It's something else, deep inside our souls: it's when we see the full moon through the smoke hole of the *lavvu* and know that we are home; it's the way we hold the reindeer in our hearts even if they are grazing in the hills and we are in the valley; and how the sun above the mountains wakes us and then a *yoik* comes . . .' Martta was becoming more and more animated.

'The herders and the reindeer have such a close bond. When the herd grazes high up in the mountains, our hearts and thoughts are with them and we're overcome with joy when we see the new calves for the first time. But if the reindeer suffer, we suffer too; if they starve because they cannot get to the lichen under the snow, the herders can hardly eat, and when the reindeer die, part of us dies too. Our bond is as old as time and the land and the reindeer are sacred to us.'

Ritva and Arvid listened without interrupting, awed by Martta's passion.

But when Martta crawled under the blankets that night, she could not sleep; seeing the reindeer and talking about her people had stirred something deep within her. A big part of her heart had always stayed with the reindeer, but now, even if she remembered how to round up the reindeer in the corral and mark the calves, even if she found a *siida* that would take them in, or if she tried to return to her own *siida*, how could she live there with Ritva and Arvid? If Ritva learned of her desires, she would surely despise her – and even if Ritva felt the same way about her, could she put up with the gossip? Martta remembered the rumours in her *siida* when two unmarried women had shared a *lavvu*. And even without such rumours, once they had spent the winter with a *siida*, would Ritva still care about her or would she start thinking about courting a young man? Martta's heart ached at the thought. No, she could not risk revealing herself. She tossed and turned throughout the night and when Ritva's hand searched for hers, she pulled away.

The next day in the early afternoon they spotted the first Sami *siida* at the edge of a lake – a group of six *lavvus*, dotted across the open landscape, coils of smoke curling up from their cone-shaped tents. Arvid grabbed the binoculars and climbed onto a rock.

'Can we go and meet them? Surely they'll give us meat and let us sleep in their tents?' He looked at Ritva, then Martta, his face flushed.

'Maybe,' Martta said. 'I'm sure they're on their way to the corral. Let's decide tomorrow.'

Arvid could not keep his eyes off the tents; he sat next to Greyheart and watched the *siida*'s comings and goings for hours through the binoculars. At night the tents glowed like little volcanoes, orange sparks flying out of the smoke holes into the starry sky. But when they woke late the next morning, the *lavvus* had disappeared. Arvid stamped his feet in disappointment and Ritva's heart sank – why hadn't she insisted on meeting the people? Why had Martta been so hesitant?

'Don't worry,' Martta said, 'they won't have gone far, we'll soon catch up.' But they did not come across the *siida* that day or the next, and soon Ritva began to wonder whether the glowing tents had been nothing but a dream.

After that first sighting of the reindeer and the *siida*, Martta became broody and remained silent for hours and whenever Ritva approached her, she brushed her aside with a short comment. Ritva swallowed her hurt and said nothing. Then, like a spell of bad weather that had suddenly turned, Martta became her old self again, telling stories of her ancestors as they sat around the fire and insisting that Ritva and Arvid should learn the language of the North Sami.

'But there's no rush,' Ritva said, 'you can speak for us, and we'll pick it up gradually.'

'It would be good if you could speak a little for yourself,' Martta said, her voice determined.

'*Eallu lea buaatán* – the herd has come!' Arvid pronounced slowly. He enjoyed the challenge of putting small sentences together and savoured the way the new words tasted in his mouth.

'That's very good Arvid, yes, *eallu lea buaatán* – the herd has come,' Martta said and smiled. However, moments later, Ritva saw a shadow fall over her face. What was she hiding?

That evening Ritva collected firewood then stopped at a small pond to wash herself. She had just put on her old embroidered vest that she usually hid underneath her blouse, when Martta surprised her.

'Oh, what's this?' Martta asked, pointing at the vest. 'I thought you didn't like embroidery?' Ritva blushed, but Martta laughed with only tenderness in her eyes.

'There was a time in the asylum when I worried that I would forget everything about my family. One day I found some red yarn, stole it and started to embroider some of my memories into the vest.'

As Ritva spoke, Martta's heart fluttered, remembering one of her mother's tales.

'Ah, the red thread . . . you know, my people believe that in the place we live before we're born – the spirit world – each of us has a soulmate, a connection with another being that is stronger than anything else, and that we're bound, toe to little toe, to that special soul with a red thread. When the time comes to make our journey into this life, the red thread is cut and we are born. Then we spend most of our time on this earth searching for this special companion. And when we recognise each other . . .' Martta held Ritva's gaze; they stood in silence for a long time, then Ritva looked away, put on her blouse and headed back to the camp.

Martta stayed behind, pacing around the edge of the pond. She knew that Ritva was her soulmate: she was bound to her by a mysterious connection – call it fate, destiny, love or desire. A torrent of emotion had rushed between them as they gazed at each other, but then Ritva had left without another word . . . All of a sudden the tight ring around Martta's heart burst and she began to sob – how could she go on like this? To hold herself back every single day, to avert her gaze, withdraw her hand that so desperately wanted to explore and caress; to not look at Ritva's lips, her breasts, the nape of her neck, to not want Ritva with every inch of her being? Many nights she had crawled out of the sleeping blankets, buried her face in the forest's cool moss and returned at dawn, empty and washed out, but today not even nature brought solace. Had Ritva no idea of the pain eating away at her heart? She dried her tears and gathered herself – no, she had to be strong. For Ritva, for Arvid and for herself.

'Please, let me go and check the snares,' Arvid begged Ritva a few days later as they set up camp. Ritva knew he was still hoping to spot the *siida* again. She didn't need to worry about him getting lost; Martta had taught him to memorise landmarks so he would always be able to find his way back.

'Fine, but don't be too long.'

It was a cold, bright October afternoon – they could have snow any day now. Ritva knelt at the fireplace and blew into the ashes, rekindling the fire in minutes. She looked at Martta who was sitting on a boulder, repairing her boots. What would happen to their little pack once they met the Sami people? Would Martta go off with the herders to tend the reindeer? And what would be expected of her? Martta had been so withdrawn and moody since they spotted the first Sami tents; if only she would open up her heart to Ritva, if they could talk about what was bothering her . . .

She didn't hear Martta approach, only felt her hot, dry hand touching her cheek, light as a butterfly. Ritva let her cheek rest in Martta's hand and for a brief moment, leaned against her. Martta's heart pounded hard against her back. Then Ritva turned to face her.

'Ritva, I . . .'

Ritva's heart sank as she saw the haunted look on Martta's face, grey as their tent cloth, her eyes filled with a deep sadness she had never seen in Martta.

'What is it? You're scaring me.'

'I . . .' Martta's voice broke; she placed her hands on Ritva's shoulders, pulled her up onto her feet, then cupped her face in both hands. Ritva could smell Martta's sweat, strong and pungent. The kiss hit Ritva like a force of nature. She gasped and pushed Martta away.

'What are you doing?'

'Ritva, please, I . . .' As Martta leaned forward, as if to kiss her again, Ritva slapped her across the face. She glared at her.

'What's got into you?' Ritva shouted. Martta stood rigid, her face even paler except for a scarlet patch that rose on her cheek like an ugly mark.

'I'm sorry, Ritva. I'm so sorry.'

Martta turned and stumbled away towards a group of bushes. Ritva stood rooted to the spot, shaking. But even if her mind had emptied itself of all thought, her hot stinging hand bore witness to the moment that had just shattered her world.

By the time Arvid arrived back an hour later, a rabbit slung over his shoulder, Martta was brewing coffee and Ritva was sitting on a tree stump pretending to sew, struggling to keep her hands from trembling. She tried not to look at Martta or Arvid. She was undone, her heart cracked wide open, her mind unravelled. She glanced at Martta, who had taken the rabbit from Arvid and started to skin it.

An onslaught of feelings hit her like a hailstorm and she felt nauseous. They had not spoken a word since Martta had stumbled away and with Arvid around they could not talk.

'Aren't you hungry?' Arvid asked Ritva later as she picked at the roasted meat.

'No, I'm sorry.' She could not swallow a morsel.

What would happen now? Martta had just stood there, looking down at her hands, mumbled that she was sorry and then run off. Ritva had seen the turmoil in her face and knew that words were difficult for Martta, but couldn't she at least have tried to explain?

When later that night Ritva reached for Martta across their sleeping blankets, she felt her friend's strong back and shoulders tense under her hand. Martta did not turn, and when Ritva touched her cheek, it was wet.

26

The next morning frost had covered everything with a sparkling crust and the air was crisp. Ritva did not know what had woken her, but when she opened her eyes, Martta was gone. Arvid lay curled up, fast asleep, but Greyheart's blanket was empty like an abandoned nest. Ritva looked around their camp – there was no trace of Martta or the wolf. She searched the horizon for any *lavvus*, but there were none. Her heart cramped as her gaze fell on a folded piece of paper and a small bundle next to her blanket, weighted down with a rock. She unwrapped the bundle – inside were Martta's drum hammer and the small brass compass together with the map. She unfolded the note. Martta's handwriting was small, trailing off at the end of each line – she must have written by the last firelight.

My dearest Ritva,

When you read this, I will be gone. There is no excuse for what I have done – you must think me disgusting and no better than Petta, but please believe me, I never meant you any harm. I care about you deeply and I ask your forgiveness, although I don't know whether you will ever be able to grant me that. My heart is breaking as I write this. I could not bear to look into your eyes and find disgust there, or to watch you turn your back on me – because surely you will have turned away from me now. Maybe I am a coward, but I cannot stand the thought of being with you every day and watching you fall in love with someone else once we join a siida. *I don't know if there is a place for someone like me in this world, but I know that winter is approaching and you and Arvid need to find shelter – and you will, I am sure of it; the* siida *won't be far away. It will also be easier for you without Greyheart – the Sami need good dogs, not a wolf, and they would not trust you with him. Nor would they necessarily trust me – I fear that even if you did feel the same way as I feel for you, we would not easily be accepted there.*

You have learned so many skills by now, and Arvid has too. This makes my heart glad.

I am entrusting my drum hammer to you – it belongs to this land and its people and it is also a token of my love for you. Please keep a place in your heart for me, if you can, and do not worry about me, my beautiful Ritva. If the heavens are kind, we will meet again. This is my hope, although perhaps you may not want to see me again.

Arvid, you are a bright light that I will keep in my heart always, and your light, Ritva, will warm me through the lonely winters to come.

Please forgive me. You have my heart always, should you still want it.

Martta

'Where is Martta?' Arvid asked, rubbing his eyes.

Ritva crumpled up the note and hid the drum hammer under her blanket.

'Where's Greyheart?'

When Ritva did not respond, Arvid jumped to his feet, pulled on his boots and ran around, shouting for Martta and the wolf. He returned, out of breath, holding his side.

'Where *are* they?'

Ritva stood frozen, her nails digging into her palms, staring at the boy. He pounded his fists against her thighs.

213

'Say something! They've gone, haven't they? But why? Why?'

His voice echoed in her head. Yes, why? Ritva clenched her jaw and kicked her foot against a stone. What a pathetic letter! Martta could handle a rifle, build a raft and drag a coffin over the ice, but when it came to people, she was as dumb as a rock. Yes, she had slapped Martta, but didn't Martta *know* how fond she was of her? If Martta had dared to look into Ritva's eyes afterwards, she would have seen questions, yes, but never disgust. Why had Martta thrown everything away as if none of it mattered: their journey, their vision, their friendship . . .? How could she just abandon them? Would Ritva's friendship not have been enough? And was it really only friendship that she, Ritva, craved? Whatever had happened, how could Martta not have *known* that she always held a special place in Ritva's heart?

Ritva's head was spinning, and for the next few days she hardly ate or spoke. Her soul had been scorched and it was only because of Arvid that she continued to drag herself across the tundra. He walked beside her, mute and sullen, sometimes slipping his small hand into hers; she let it rest there, but her whole body felt limp, like a wilted flower. She saw loss in everything – a buzzard's cry echoed her despair and when she lay at night listening to the wind, its howling became her lament. Whenever they lit a fire and huddled around its precious warmth, Ritva saw images in the flames: snow-covered mountains, the dancing figures of the sacred drum, little Greyheart in the snare, Arvid's gleaming face in the firelight of the *lavvu*, and always Martta – steering the boat, cutting wood, placing her hand on Arvid's head, smiling, gazing at her. Then images of that fateful afternoon, Martta's haunted expression, the kiss . . . Pushing Martta away had been a reflex; the kiss had shaken Ritva to the core, spooked her like a young horse that had been approached suddenly, and yet there had been something else too . . .

The images dissolved into flames. But, as Ritva kept gazing into the embers it was as if the fire itself began to speak to her, telling her of its many ways, raging as it burnt down forests and fields, warming hearts and bodies at the hearth – and yet its essence always remained the same. Tears streamed down Ritva's face. What more had she ever wanted other than to belong somewhere? And more than anyone or anything, Martta had been her home, her true north. How could a place ever become home without her? Ritva pressed her hand around the drum hammer until it hurt.

Arvid had not cried since Martta left but had marched on next to Ritva, pale and with clenched teeth. She had told him what Martta had written in her letter about him, and only that, but he had trudged on without a word. She could sense how he had hardened since Martta's departure and saw the hurt and confusion in his eyes: had Martta ever even liked him? Maybe it was his fault that she had left. He had trusted her and she had taken his precious Greyheart and turned her back on their little pack. It pained Ritva to see Arvid like this – would he ever trust another soul? And would she?

Slowly, like embers losing their heat, Ritva's rage calmed, leaving only a gaping emptiness.

The next morning the tundra lay covered with a first layer of snow. They trekked through the dim daylight hours, hoping to find the *siida* and a community that would take them in.

'Slow down, Arvid, please, I can't keep up with you.' How could he keep going with only morsels of dried rabbit meat in his stomach? Ritva ached all over and had it not been for Arvid, she would have stayed in the grubby cocoon of her sleeping blanket.

'Come on, lean on me, we can make it,' Arvid said, pulling her arm around his shoulders.

Too tired to argue, Ritva let him take her arm, feeling his bony shoulder under the jacket.

The next day, a blizzard hit the tundra, wiping out the last scraps of autumn colour and any sense of the direction in which they were headed. They were lost.

27

Ritva did not remember how the Sami people came to take her and Arvid in. She recalled trudging through the faintest twilight of the winter darkness, snow and wind whipping at her face, Arvid's little mittened hand lying in hers as he pulled her along, pleading with her to keep moving until he too went silent. Frozen to the core, she fought an overwhelming desire to lie down in the soft, deep snow and go to sleep for ever. But then it had been Arvid who had fallen and not got up. She had scooped him into her arms and stumbled on through the impenetrable white until her legs had buckled. She dug a den in the snow, pulled the boy close and folded herself around him, sheltering him as best as she could. A sense of relief had flowed through her: it was all over. As she lay there, images of Martta played through her mind: Martta's broad smile as she swung the axe, felling a birch tree; all of them on the raft, laughing, splashing each other with water, sun on their faces; swimming in the cool water of the Baltic; Martta feeding Greyheart little morsels of fish, ruffling Arvid's hair . . .

When she woke, Ritva found that she was wrapped in thick blankets and furs next to a warm fire, the smell of coffee and birch filling the air. Someone poured a swig of bitter liquid into her mouth; her throat burned and she gasped. People around her giggled and whispered to each other. Ritva could make out a young woman nursing a baby and three old women sucking on small silver pipes. One of the women stretched a hand out towards Ritva and smiled, exposing a large gap between her front teeth. Ritva knew from the simple dwelling and colourful tunics that the women were North Sami. Had she finally found the *siida* they had spotted before the blizzard? And where was Arvid? She threw off the blankets and sat up. One of the women pointed to the other side of the tent, and there, lying on reindeer furs and wrapped in blankets, was Arvid, fast asleep, snoring gently. They were safe, the journey over, at least for now. Ritva surrendered to her exhaustion and fell asleep again in moments.

'Martta, please, stop!' The dream threw her back into the endless expanse of ice, her voice swallowed by the snow as she stumbled on, but as hard as she tried she could not get closer to the fleeing shape. Suddenly, sharp claws dug into her coat and with a rushing of wings a mighty bird lifted her off the ground. Gazing up, she recognised the brown feathery belly of a majestic eagle. The bird carried her across the tundra, the boundless white emptiness disrupted only by a few dark specks: a bush or boulders, an animal in flight, a herd of galloping reindeer . . .

Ritva woke in the tent's twilight to a strong aroma: a bowl of soup was being offered to her by a woman whose wrinkly skin shone like polished leather in the firelight. The woman smiled and bent forward to feed Ritva the spicy broth, and as if she were a child, Ritva let herself be nourished by the woman's kindness, soaking it up like the first rays of spring. As she slurped the liquid from the smooth wooden spoon, she recalled the eagle in her dream, its flight and strength. A wave of warmth flowed through her and she felt the creature's power pouring into her, filling her heart and limbs like liquid gold.

'Good soup,' Ritva said and smiled. She gently took the spoon from the old woman's hand and ate the rest of the broth by herself. The woman, who introduced herself as Sunna, smiled and pointed at Arvid, who sat with glowing cheeks over a bowl of the same steaming soup. When he raised his head, his eyes lit up.

'Ritva!' He peeled himself from the blankets, crawled over to her and threw his arms around her. 'I thought we'd die out there.' Suddenly he sobbed. Ritva held him close, burying her face in his soft hair.

'We're safe now, Arvid.' She would do anything to protect him. And yet, wasn't it Arvid who had protected her in the days before they were found? She pulled him even closer and they stayed like that for a long time.

Ritva was unsure how many days had passed while they recovered in the warmth of the *lavvu* tent. Whenever she and Arvid finally ventured outside, no one was in a hurry to see them leave. The *siida* was on migration, following the reindeer to the lower grounds, and several times Ritva and Arvid found themselves bundled in reindeer furs on a sledge speeding across bogs and hills, pulled by a string of reindeer. Sometimes Ritva couldn't make out the horizon. In the winter darkness, earth and sky merged, the snow only faintly illuminated. But every evening she found herself next to the fire again. And, staring into the flames, she couldn't help but think of Martta . . . Martta out there alone in the ice and snow; she pulled out the little drum hammer, brushed her thumb across the finely etched carvings. If only she could reach Martta, know that she was safe. How could it all have gone so wrong?

Over and over she replayed the moment when Martta kissed her. The kiss had confused and scared her, but there had been something else too – a stirring in her body and heart that she had not known before. Or maybe she had known it, but ignored it, brushed it aside, for how could a pastor's daughter feel such a thing, and for a woman? Father had always warned against the 'desires of the flesh' in his sermons and spoken of 'unnatural tendencies', but hadn't she learned over the last year that her father's beliefs no longer matched her own? Ritva shook herself – what did it matter now? She might never see Martta again. She curled up next to the fire, staring into the dying embers, fingers gripping the drum hammer.

*

Slowly, over the weeks that followed, Ritva met the people of the *siida*. Sunna, who had fed her on that first day, was one of the oldest women in the community. She often sat with folded legs next to the tent's kitchen area, sucking on her small pipe. With her tanned skin she looked as old as the earth and her dark, lively eyes shone in the firelight. In the evenings she kept everyone entertained with stories of the *uldas* and Stallo, the giant.

Besides old Sunna, Ritva and Arvid shared the tent with Jutta – a warm-hearted, practical woman in her thirties – her husband, Martin, their baby and their twins, Anni and Lars. Jutta was a quiet soul and Ritva admired how content she was at being a mother, always finding time to ruffle Lars's hair, or tell a story to the twins in between her many chores. Jutta kept the tent immaculate – everything had its place. Opposite the entrance was the kitchen area where a blackened, bashed coffee pot sat on the fire, and behind it, hanging from a chain, was a large stew pot. Their dog slept by the entrance and the sleeping furs were placed around the side. Their staple diet was simple – reindeer stew, bread and lots of coffee drunk from cups or saucers.

Ritva had only picked up a few words of North Sami and her meagre vocabulary was a fragile bridge between her and the people of the *siida*. She tried to make herself as helpful as she could, but she was a novice at many tasks: how to prepare reindeer skins, cook stew, spin sinews into thread or help sew the many boots and mittens that were needed. She often pricked her finger on the thick needles and the women who had come together to spin laughed as she fumbled with the unfamiliar tools. Yet, as if they sensed Ritva's need for tenderness, they also showered her with smiles and gentle taps on her back, especially Jutta, who had taken Ritva under her wing and was teaching her the practical tasks required for life in the *siida*.

One morning Ritva noticed a young man who had stayed behind after the other herders had left. Short, with coal-black hair, he walked with a slight limp. She smiled and nodded at him – he looked back at her and blushed, then flashed her a smile.

'My name is Piers,' he said slowly.

'I am Ritva.' They shook hands. He was shy and did not pursue the conversation, but from then on, whenever he saw Ritva he enquired about her well-being and slowly she got to know him better. He spoke some Swedish and was very proud of his skill at carving – he showed her knives with beautiful antler handles that he had decorated with delicate patterns, and *guksis*, carved wooden cups made from birch burls.

'I might have a limp and I can't always go out with the herders, but I am good with my hands,' he said and winked at Ritva. He also turned out to be an excellent *yoiker* and storyteller and Ritva enjoyed learning new words and expanding her vocabulary when he patiently translated for her. She liked his humble nature and quiet strength and, although he could not run as fast as the other men, he had an uncanny ability to sense changes in the weather, his leg telling him with a sharp pain when a storm was on its way.

Arvid had also befriended a boy his age, Mitta, and the two became inseparable, feeding the dogs together, helping the herders drive the reindeer into the corral and practising with lassos. Everyone admired Arvid's courage and commanding attitude with the dogs, but to him they were simply friends, just as Greyheart had been.

Although life was harsh so far north and the Sami owned only what they could carry, the *siida* shared everything with Ritva and Arvid, offering them sleeping blankets, the same portion of stew from the pot and the closest place by the fire. Ritva was deeply grateful for the hospitality, yet she wondered why the *siida* had allowed them to stay on, now that they had recovered. Was it because of the cold or because of Arvid? He had quickly won the hearts of the Sami and especially of Antje, a young woman who had lost her son to influenza a few months earlier.

Or maybe the Sami's continued hospitality had something to do with the drum hammer. One night when the herders returned, a lively group had gathered around the fire in the neighbouring *lavvu*. Ritva had reached into her coat, pulled out the small hammer and showed it to one of the old men. His eyes lit up as he took the small object and looked at it from all sides, then handed it on. As Martta's hammer was passed around the tent, Ritva saw delight but also fear and disapproval in people's faces. Piers held it for a long time, tracing the carving with his fingertips. However, one of the older women kept hissing a word over and over. Arvid nudged Ritva.

'I think it's the word for the devil,' he whispered, 'if Martta taught me right, that is.'

The old man patted Ritva's shoulder, handed her the drum hammer and one of the women gestured for her to hide it in her pocket. Ritva remembered Martta's words about the burning of the drums, how fear was still lodged deep in people's hearts. She slipped the hammer into her coat – maybe it was best not to show it again. But ever since that night people seemed to look at her differently; some with suspicion, others with curiosity and respect.

As the weeks went on, it grew colder. The tents groaned and shook in the winter storms like vessels lost at sea, the tent cloth thrashing against the poles. The frozen kettle creaked and it took a long time in the mornings to prepare the first coffee.

One dark morning as Ritva put her lips to the saucer, she noticed specks of light reflected in the liquid – stars shining through the smoke hole. *I am drinking in the stars*, she thought as a moment of grace flowed through her.

In February when the sun finally peered over the horizon again, Ritva marvelled at the bright orange glow that illuminated the snow-laden trees with its otherworldly light; the *lavvus* sat like glittering cones amongst the trees, surrounded by reindeer who were digging beneath the snow crust for lichen and moss. Ritva loved being close to the reindeer – and having spent most of her life almost alone, she was starting to enjoy being part of a group. *A herd of animals, a herd of people*, she thought, watching the reindeer, their gentle presence touching her.

Despite the bitter cold of the long winter months, Ritva let herself be carried along by the many chores, and with Jutta's encouragement she learned how to sew mittens and simple trousers. Jutta and some of the other women complimented her on her needlework and it warmed her heart that she had been given a particular place in the *lavvu* – each time the tent was set up, she, like everyone else in the family, knew where her place was and yet, seeing the tight bond between the families, Ritva's heart ached. She thought of her own lost family – Elke and Father seemed as far off as the Milky Way. Would she ever be strong enough to make the long journey back south?

And often, lying awake at night, Ritva thought of Martta. Had she frozen to death? Had Greyheart turned against her in this unforgiving wilderness? On such nights her hands clawed at the blankets and she quietly cried herself to sleep.

28

It was spring now. The ice on the rivers had broken and water gushed everywhere; the first green shoots were pushing through the earth and one bright day in June, Ritva heard a swell of sudden cries.

'*Eallu lea buaatán!* The herd has come!' Sofia, a young woman, clapped Ritva on the back as she ran past, Piers stumbling after her.

'Quick, you don't want to miss this!' Piers said, laughing. Sofia had a lasso slung over her shoulder and her eyes sparkled. Everybody gathered in the nearby corral – the reindeer had come down from the mountains and the earmarking of the new calves would soon begin. The Sami's joy was infectious and Ritva's heart sang as hundreds of reindeer thundered counterclockwise around the corral: males with magnificent antlers; grunting cows in all shades of brown, grey and even white with their moulting winter fur, followed by their bleating calves. And amongst this melee, the herders. Elated as they spotted their new calves, they hurled their lassos through the air to catch them, each herder marking the tiny ears with their particular pattern.

'How can you possibly make out which reindeer belongs to you?' Ritva asked Sofia that evening.

'Oh, you learn it from when you're little. You just look really hard at the patterns cut into their ears.' Ritva was stunned – all she had seen was a stream of grey bodies galloping past. Surely one had to be born a Sami to learn this . . .

After the day in the corral, Ritva started to befriend Sofia. Everything about the young woman was large: her hands, her dark brown eyes, her stature and a smile that revealed big white teeth, but particularly her heart. Unmarried and Ritva's age, she knew little shyness and happily taught Ritva everything she could about healing plants and *duodji*, the beautiful Sami handicrafts. Spending time with Sofia reminded Ritva sorely of her days with Elke, and as the weather grew warmer, Ritva often got out the map, wondering how she could make it back south. Although she had grown stronger since the winter, the years in the asylum and the long journey had taken their toll. Maybe if she rested another few months she would be strong enough.

Soon it was time for the *siida* to migrate to the summer camp up in the cooler mountains where reindeer and people found respite from the swarms of mosquitoes. Ritva adored the dwellings the *siida* stayed in, small turf huts one could mistake for grass mounds were it not for the windows and the fine coils of smoke rising from iron chimneys. Seeing the mountains so close, Ritva felt as if a deep longing had been answered and under the midnight sun, which painted everything with its brilliant golden light, for the first time since Martta had left, she relaxed.

It was during this carefree summer that she spent more time with Piers. Something in this shy young man moved her and she soaked up his gentle kindness as he showed her more of his craft. But mostly, he taught her mountain *yoiks* and told her Sami stories. Some of the younger girls giggled and whispered behind Ritva's back, passing her messages that they pretended had come from Piers, but Ritva laughed off their attempts at matchmaking – Piers did not stir her passion, but rather he touched her like the young injured wolf had done, or the way she imagined a brother might. Inside she was beginning to heal and her heart, closed for so long amid the cold of the asylum, was starting to open again. She had survived the long journey and a fierce winter, and whatever lay ahead, she was determined she would embrace it.

After the grace of summer and the migration back to lower grounds, Ritva observed the autumn slaughter, noting each part of the reindeer's inner geography as Piers and Sofia pointed it out: heart, liver, kidneys, sinew. Reindeer meat was the Sami's staple diet – smoked, dried or cooked with grease for dripping, she had eaten it every day, but seeing the bloody carcass, Ritva's stomach heaved, and stark images flashed before her mind: Martta with scarlet hands, slaughtering the seal, quickly and skilfully, just like the herders. She rushed away, grief washing over her, sudden and sharp. That night she couldn't stop thinking about Martta, stumbling across the snow-covered tundra, fighting against ice and wind. Would she have made it to her *siida* in Finland? Had Martta even survived?

'Don't you ever want to stay in one place and build a home?' Ritva asked Sofia the next day as they gathered firewood. 'You're always on the move.' By now Ritva had picked up many more words in North Sami and Sofia, like Piers, spoke some Swedish.

'Ah, but the *lavvu* is our home,' Sofia said and laughed, 'we don't need four walls to feel secure. Wherever we go, we set up the *lavvu* and everything is in exactly the same place – the fire is lit, the kettle is put on and we're home. But "a tent without heat is a death tent", my grandmother used to say – we live with snow for nine months of the year, so the fire is the heart of the *lavvu* and draws us all together.'

Ritva nodded; all this made sense to her. She had grown increasingly curious about the herding life – ever since she had seen the herd gallop around the corral, she had wanted to learn more about the graceful animals.

'It's important to imagine the world through their eyes and observe them closely,' Sofia said, 'then you'll know where they want to go, whether a predator is making them skittish or the weather is changing. Have you ever looked deep into the eye of a reindeer?'

'No, why?'

'It's like a magic mirror. First you glimpse the tundra and everything the reindeer sees, but when you look deeper, you can see so much more – some people even see omens. It changes you, looking into a reindeer's eye.'

What would she see if she gazed into a reindeer's eye, Ritva wondered? Mother stroking her hair? Uncle, forcing himself on her? Martta and her in the coffin boat out on the archipelago? So many things she had not spoken about . . .

'You know, Arvid and I aren't siblings,' she began.

'I never thought you were. I mean, look at you two, you're as different as day and night. You don't even speak good Swedish like he does.' Sofia laughed and held Ritva's gaze for a long moment. 'Why don't you start at the beginning and tell me about yourself?'

And so that afternoon Ritva told Sofia about her home and her mother, the time in the asylum and her escape. She said little about Martta and did not mention the drum, yet she felt as if a huge weight had been lifted.

Autumn with its feast of vivid colours was brief in Sápmi, and when in early October the first snow fell, Sofia introduced Ritva to the many Sami words for snow: virgin snow, new snow on top of old snow, falling rain mixed with snow, powdery snow, hard rugged-crust snow, blizzard snow . . .

Would she ever be able to learn what was needed in order to belong to the *siida*, Ritva wondered? And was this what she wanted? With a pang she realised it had been a whole year since Martta had left her and now a long winter lay ahead of them once more. Another year with poor Elke wondering what had happened to her. Guilt weighed heavy on her, and one night she had a vivid dream: Father in his black gown, preaching to his congregation from the pulpit, a bible in his right hand, gripping the banister with his left. Suddenly his words became jumbled and he gasped for air, trying to tear off his gown. Then from nowhere, snakes appeared: black-scaled and glistening, they slithered up from the bottom of the pulpit, across his chest and throat, into his greying hair, licking at his ear with tiny purple tongues. 'Forgive me, Ritva, please!' he shouted, stretching his arms towards her, his eyes wide in terror. When the snakes disappeared the pulpit filled with dark water, spilling over into the church. Her father lost his grip and the water swallowed him . . .

The dream visited her many times. Each night Ritva woke with a pounding heart. Was Father dying? What was it he wanted to tell her? She shuddered at the thought of Elke still living in that big house with him. Wasn't the most important thing to be united with Elke again, to save her from Uncle and from the fate Ritva and her mother had endured? Surely it was safe to return now; Petta and the superintendent believed her dead and she had grown stronger throughout the summer. Maybe soon, after the snow melted, in late spring, she could leave . . .

One day in March as she prepared firewood after another restless night, a voice startled her.

'Ritva!' It was Piers. In his large dark brown eyes was something Ritva could not read.

'Close your eyes and stretch out your hands.' She did as he asked and felt a cool weight across her palms. It was a knife, crafted from antler and birch wood, elaborately decorated.

'Oh, it's beautiful, Piers!'

'How can you live with us and not have a knife? I thought it was time you had one of your own.' It was true, even children wore small knives on their belts and though Jutta had lent her one, to have her own would be different.

'Thank you, Piers!' She hugged him, but his body stiffened. He looked tense and slowly dangled a necklace in front of her as if he were offering a sweet to a child. It was a simple white pebble framed by silver wire, attached to a braided leather strap.

'Please, accept this gift too, I made it for you. I want you to stay with our *siida*, Ritva, and . . .' he blushed, 'be my wife.'

Ritva gasped; had she not sensed that he was deeply sincere, she would have giggled, but knowing he was speaking from the

227

heart, his words crushed her. When she said nothing, Piers laid the necklace in front of her and rushed away. She stood frozen, her stomach a sack of stones. Slowly she bent down and picked up the necklace, the weight of Piers's love in her palm.

That night, Ritva tossed and turned in her blankets. She had come to like Piers as a dear, trusted friend: he was kind and a joy to be around and when he told her stories he conjured places and people like no one else. But he did not stir her with the passion she hoped to feel at the thought of becoming someone's wife . . . Never had she even wanted to kiss him, nor had her heart fluttered when she was sitting beside him – how could she possibly marry him, share a sleeping fur with him, bear his children?

She threw back her blankets and stole out of the *lavvu*. The full moon lit her way as she set out towards the closest mountain. She climbed a narrow path, quiet as a lynx, and a few hours later, reached a plateau. She took off her cap and let her hair down, then reached for the drum hammer and held it firmly in her hand. She planted her feet on the granite ground and stretched her arms towards the sky, sounds pouring from her mouth; a gentle melody at first, it soon built into a fierce song. She swayed and whirled, her hair spinning out in all directions, her feet stomping the ground like reindeer hooves pounding across the tundra. She surrendered her grief and confusion to the wind, aching to be swept clean by the elements – maybe then grace could flow back into her life, love . . . When she heard a scream, her eyes searched the sky for a bird of prey, but there was none; the scream was her own. As she stood and let her tears flow, the grey sky opened and large raindrops fell on her face.

She did not know how much time had passed, but when she descended, the moon had travelled a long way towards the horizon and she had made up her mind: it would be a long journey, but she had to take the risk. She could not settle here before she had seen Father and Elke and brought her sister back with her if she could. Too much time had passed already, and Elke was no longer a small girl.

It was still dark when she returned to the *siida*, but soon everyone would be awake. She took her knapsack with the compass and the map, filled it with bread and dried reindeer meat and left a note for Arvid, together with the drum hammer. It was the most precious token, to show him she would return. She hoped he would forgive her. She stroked the smooth stone of Piers's necklace; maybe she could come to love Piers, even marry him . . . but not without making this journey first. She was starting to write a note for Piers when Jutta stirred. Her throat closed – if she didn't leave now, she might never get away.

She slipped out of the *lavvu*, saddled up one of the pack-reindeer and with the palest light of dawn, headed east – towards Finland, her old home . . . towards the unknown.

PART 3

THE RECKONING

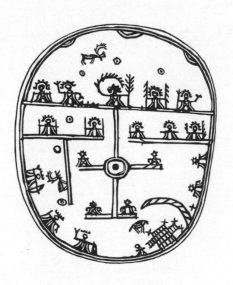

29

Turku, August 1919

Ritva approached the house in the twilight. In the seven years she had been gone, the large garden had turned wild except for a small patch where late-summer flowers – asters, dahlias and gladioli – bloomed in a multitude of colours. Elke had always adored flowers and looked after them like cherished pets.

Now that she had finally arrived, Ritva felt her legs weaken; the gruelling journey through a country ravaged by civil war had left her shaken and exhausted. While her *siida* had migrated into the mountains in the spring of 1918, the people of Turku and Tampere had taken up arms against each other over dubious politics, about which Ritva understood nothing. Although the war had lasted only five months, thousands had been killed on both sides, Red Guards and White Troops alike. Neighbour had fought against neighbour, brother against brother and even women had taken up arms until in the end the White government troops had won against the working-class Socialists. Now, over a year on, chaos and famine still gripped the country. Ritva shook herself; she had come for her own resolution and needed every ounce of strength and focus.

She tiptoed towards one of the illuminated windows, her heart racing. An ordinary domestic scene greeted her: the large wooden dining table was laid with plates and soup-filled bowls, Father at the head, Elke to his left, her back turned towards the window.

There was no sign of Uncle. Relief flooded through Ritva, then a sudden icy fear: what if Uncle was late and he caught her out here, watching through the window? No, they were not expecting anyone else; there was no third place laid out. How Elke had grown! A girl of nine when the doctor had taken Ritva away, here she sat, slender and upright, her hair knotted in a braided bun. Even from the back Ritva could see how Elke had developed into a young woman, but the way her shoulders were drawn up showed a tension she had not possessed as a child. She and Father were not talking. Where was Berta, the housekeeper? Had Father dismissed her? By now she should have served the main course . . .

Father had aged too: his hair was streaked with white and he had grown a full beard. For a second the image of Uncle flashed before her – although Father's beard was shorter and neatly trimmed with sideburns, she had never before noticed the extent of the resemblance between the two brothers. All of a sudden something unnerved her – what if Father trapped her? Uncle and Father could so easily overpower her and send her back to Seili. And even without Uncle, what if Father never wanted to see her again? Her thoughts raced, cold sweat gathering on her forehead.

At that moment Elke got up from the table, faced the window and went out to the kitchen. She was as pale as candle wax and there were dark rings under her eyes, her face distorted in a grimace of pain or rage. In that fleeting second, Ritva recognised the same fierce determination in Elke that she had felt as she prepared to flee the asylum. Guilt filled her like a swell of dark water – how could she have left it so long before coming back here? She should have come last summer . . . Elke returned a few minutes later with a platter of fish, her emotions hidden underneath a mask of calm. She stood next to Father, placing pieces of fish on his plate before sitting down again. Ritva stepped away from the window, merging into the darkness. Would Elke even recognise her? Ritva looked down at her dirty dress, her cracked hands. Still, she could not back out now.

Early the next morning she scribbled a note, put it on her sister's windowsill and weighed it down with a stone.

My darling sister,

Don't be frightened, I am well, and more importantly, I am here, so very close to you!

I will wait for you today – that is, Friday – by the little bridge, at five in the afternoon.

We used to play there when we were young, do you remember?

I can't wait to see you and wrap my arms around you. Please come!

Your loving sister, Ritva

She hid behind an elder bush at the edge of the garden and threw a small pebble at the window. A moment later, Elke's face appeared, her hair a brown mess around her sleepy face; she glanced into the garden, then turned away. When Ritva threw a second stone, Elke opened the window. She saw the note and grabbed it, silently mouthing each word as she read it, then looked out at the garden, trying to glimpse Ritva. Ritva ached for her sister but did not give herself away. Soon, soon they would meet . . .

Ritva slipped out of the garden and headed towards the village, sneaking through the streets like a skittish stray cat. She had not eaten since the day before and her stomach was rumbling. She dreaded being recognised and yet she longed to enter the little shops she had known as a child, to receive a smile or an apple, a kind word . . . but those days were long gone now, although nothing much appeared to have changed in the village. She saw the baker, the butcher, the grocer, all the same familiar shop signs, only a little faded, yet when she peered through the windows she froze – where once there had been nicely laid-out displays, there were only empty shelves. She stopped in front of the grocer's and entered. The young woman behind the counter smiled.

'I'd like three apples, some cheese if you have any, and a loaf of bread – it can be yesterday's. I don't mind.' Ritva had not heard herself speak for weeks and her voice was hoarse.

'Are you all right, dear?'

'Yes, why? I'm fine,' Ritva's voice quivered. Only then did she look straight at the woman in the apron. She flinched – it was Ulla, a girl she had gone to school with a lifetime ago, when she still belonged here, before she was tainted by Uncle's dirty hands and carted away as a lunatic. Their gazes locked for a moment.

'Ritva? Is that you?' Ulla whispered. 'Oh my God, I thought they'd never let you out. But you look so . . . different!'

Ritva stood rigid as a caught thief. She managed to put a finger to her lips.

'Shhh! Please, Ulla, don't say a word, pretend you don't know me.'

'But are you all right?' Ulla asked, looking Ritva up and down. 'You look like a ghost. Did they not treat you well in that hospital?'

Ritva bit her lip. You try a winter on Seili, she thought, let's see how you'd look. How could people believe a place like Seili would show its patients care or kindness? She took a deep breath, trying to swallow her anger.

'Please, just forget you ever saw me, maybe I am a ghost after all,' Ritva said. She handed Ulla a few coins across the counter, but Ulla pushed them back and reached for Ritva's hand.

'No, wait, I want to give you something.'

Ulla rushed to the back of the store and returned a few moments later with a bundle of food: a corner of cheese, some nuts, apples and a piece of pastry. As she handed it all to Ritva, she said, 'Everything is scarce these days but Father still manages to keep some provisions in the shop, even after this damn war.' Her face darkened.

'You have a brother, don't you?' Ritva whispered.

'Here's some apple juice, I made it only last week,' Ulla said, tying the bundle. 'I wish we could speak more, but you must go now.'

'Is he all right, your brother?'

Ulla stared at her.

'I am surrounded by ghosts, Ritva. Good luck to you, my friend, and take care.' For a second she put her hand on Ritva's arm. Ritva smiled, certain that her old friend would not give her away.

'Thank you, this'll go a long way to helping me. Maybe one day we will meet again and then I can repay you.'

She stuffed the food into her knapsack and slipped out of the shop.

30

Ritva walked across a meadow and settled under a tree near the river. She bit off large pieces of Ulla's bread and cheese, then washed her face in the cool water and smoothed down her clothes. Her appearance did not matter to her any more, and yet she did not want to frighten Elke. She looked at her hands – once they had been encased in white gloves holding a hymn book – now they were calloused and cracked, telling a story of bitter winters and an epic journey north. They had made fires, skinned rabbits, chopped wood and freed a wolf from a snare. Maybe they were no longer pretty, but they had grown strong – as strong as Martta's.

Martta . . . How she still missed her, her determination and strength, the way she laughed, the way she had looked at her. Ritva took the clips out of her hair, then combed it through with rough strokes and braided it anew. Thinking of Martta was pointless – she might never see her again.

In the afternoon, Ritva searched for a hiding place. She crouched behind a boulder near the bridge, her stomach in knots – what if Elke didn't come at all, or what if she brought someone with her? A memory flashed before her: Elke, clinging to her, thrashing her arms and legs about, her face blotchy from sobbing, Father prising Elke's little hands from Ritva . . . Ritva had not allowed herself to think about that day – when something inside her had broken. And yet she had survived and was here now. She would persuade Elke to come with her to the North, to the land of the midnight sun and the reindeer people.

She did not hear Elke, but saw her approaching from the corner of her eye. Elke was alone and just as Ritva had done, she had found a hiding place behind a row of bushes. Ritva smiled as the two sisters lay in wait for each other. After a while, Ritva couldn't bear it any longer.

'Elke!' she hissed and threw a small pebble onto the path.

'Ritva?' Elke whispered, crawling out from her hiding place. 'Where are you?'

Seeing her sister's pale and anxious face, Ritva's caution dissolved and she showed herself. The two sisters flew at each other, shrieking and hugging, whirling around like the children they once were.

'Is it really you, Elke?' Ritva marvelled at just how much her sister had grown. She was a young woman now, taller than Ritva herself. But despite her blemish-free skin and slender body, Elke's beauty did not shine. Her eyes, large and green as river water, were dull and filled with sadness.

'Oh, Ritva, I've missed you so much!'

'Me too, Elke, I've missed you so!' Ritva pulled her sister close. Elke's eyes spilled first, then Ritva's, and soon they sobbed in each other's arms.

'Did they finally let you go? I never heard from you, not a single letter, nothing. The matron wrote every six months saying you were getting better but that you were still too unwell to see anyone. She said that it was in your best interests not to hear from us and that you would write when you were well enough – but you never did.'

Ritva breathed in sharply. So it was true, the asylum had not passed on a single one of her letters and possibly not even informed Father and Elke of her escape.

'I thought you'd forgotten me. I wrote to you at first, despite the matron, and when I didn't hear back I scribbled notes to you in a diary – it kept me alive. But then the war came and there was no more post. God, it was so horrible, Ritva! So many people died, and we had so little food. I'm lucky to be alive.' Elke pulled out a small notebook from underneath her cardigan. 'Here, that's just the first one. I want you to have it.'

'Oh, Elke, I'd never have forgotten you!' Ritva's voice quivered. 'I've thought about you every day since they took me to that godforsaken place. And I did write to you, but the nurses lied and never sent my letters. Seili is a place for the damned – they never had any plans to let me go.'

'Oh God!' Elke's hand flew to her mouth. 'And all this time I thought that you were getting better, and they were looking after you.'

'It doesn't matter any more, Elke, I'm here now. I ran away.'

'You ran away?' Elke stared at her.

'Yes, it's a long story. Please believe me, Elke, I really wanted to come straight back here and take you with me, but it was too dangerous, they would have looked for me here. I escaped across the ice to Sweden and then travelled all the way up north, but I got lost and nearly died and when I was found by the Sami people I needed time to recover my strength.' Hearing her own breathless voice, her throat tightened. How could Elke ever forgive her? Elke stood still, not saying a word, but Ritva saw the anxious look on her face.

'I'm so sorry, Elke, truly.' She took the diary from Elke's outstretched hand.

'And thank you for this.' They stood in silence for a long time, then Ritva looked straight at Elke.

'Did he touch you, Elke?' She had not wanted it to come out so bluntly, but she couldn't hold back any longer – not knowing had weighed on her for too long. The colour drained from Elke's face.

'How . . . how did you know?'

Ritva saw the feelings play across Elke's face that she knew so well: panic, rage and then shame.

'Oh, Elke, I'm so sorry I couldn't protect you from him. Not a day went past when I didn't fear for you, and pray that he would leave you alone.' Elke stood biting her lip. Finally she spoke.

'No, I . . . maybe I could've pushed him away.'

'It's not your fault, Elke. He's a big man and so much stronger than you. There was nothing you could do! I couldn't push him off me either.' Ritva gently put her hand on Elke's shoulder, but Elke shrugged it off.

'You too?'

'Yes. But we're together again now, this is all that counts. Please, come away with me, Elke. We can live up north with the reindeer people, far away from all this. The land is beautiful there and the Sami people are so welcoming. It's a good place, Elke, a place where we can forget.'

'You're too late.' Elke's voice was cold and she took a step back. 'I can't just run away, I'm dirty, stained, ripped beyond repair; no one will ever want me now. And besides, he would come after us.'

'Don't say that, Elke, you're beautiful and you've got your whole life ahead of you. And anyway, hasn't the bastard left? I didn't see him last night when I peered through the window. Did Father throw him out?'

Ritva could not read Elke's expression – a deep frown, then Elke's eyes widened and her skin turned grey.

'Who are you talking about?' Elke mumbled the words.

'Uncle, of course – that rancid old drunk who couldn't keep his hands to himself. I feel sick just thinking of him, the way he reeked of drink . . .' Ritva could picture him as clear as if it had been yesterday. Elke opened her mouth but then said nothing.

'What? What is it, Elke?'

'Don't you know?'

'Know what?'

'It was Father!'

'What do you mean, Father?'

'Uncle left nearly seven years ago, Ritva. Six months after they took you away. One evening he and Father had a big row and the next morning he was gone. A few months later Father dismissed Berta and ever since then it's only been me and him in the house . . .' Elke's voice trailed off. 'It's easier for him that way, to do what he likes with me.'

'How could you say such a thing?' Ritva's clenched fists flew to her ears, trying to block out Elke's words. 'Yes, Father was cruel and he sent me away to that awful place, but he's a good Christian, dedicated to his congregation, and he was devastated when Mama got ill. He sat by her bedside for days . . .'

'He probably just sat there so that Mother couldn't run away or tell anyone.' There was such bitterness in Elke's voice, Ritva baulked.

'Tell anyone what?' Then a memory pierced Ritva's mind: Mother, struggling to sit up, gazing at Ritva with wild eyes. Her speech had been slurred from the strong drugs, belladonna – Ritva remembered the exotic name on the medicine bottle.

'Be careful, my dear, he'll come after you too,' Mother had whispered into Ritva's ear. And he had, he had shattered her world. But it had been Uncle, not Father. She clearly remembered the smell of alcohol, his wiry beard.

'You've no idea, Ritva!' Elke's harsh voice brought Ritva back. 'I wish to God Uncle had stayed. I know he was rough on the outside, but he has a good heart.'

'A good heart? He did things to me I can't even talk about! Maybe he managed to convince you . . .' Ritva turned her back, scrambled the few metres down to the river and marched along the muddy bank.

'You don't believe me?' Elke ran after her, grabbing at Ritva's dress. 'I knew it, I knew nobody would believe me. That's why I've told no one all these years. The pastor of Turku molesting his own daughter, who would believe such a thing?' Ritva started to run but Elke kept up.

'He told me he would put me in a hospital if I said anything. Sometimes I thought that would be better than staying in that damned house with him, but he said he'd make sure I was sent to a different place to you and that I would never see you again.' Elke's chest heaved as she spat out the words. 'So I stayed. I waited for you, Ritva, in case they let you go.'

Ritva stopped and looked at her sister whose eyes were red with tears.

'Didn't he do the same to you before he started with me? Sometimes he calls out your name. Answer me!'

Ritva's ears were ringing as if she were about to faint and she remembered the dream: Father drowning in the pulpit, his arms reaching out to her . . .

Elke grabbed Ritva by the shoulders and shook her, but Ritva pushed her away.

'It was Uncle who touched me, Elke. He came in the middle of the night. I was always so tired and drowsy, I could hardly move . . .'

'Maybe it wasn't Uncle, but Father!'

Ritva didn't want to believe her sister's words but deep down a sickening thought stirred – it was Father who had sent her to Seili, Father who had never written to her . . . Could he really be capable of such a thing?

'Please, Elke, I need to be alone.' She prised Elke's hand from her dress and rushed off along the river. This time Elke did not follow her and when Ritva looked back, her sister was gone.

Ritva's stomach heaved. She scrambled down the riverbank but threw up before she reached the water. She washed out her mouth and cooled her face. Her head was throbbing, Elke's words echoing through her mind. How could it be? She dug her nails into her palms and hit the ground hard, sobbing until she felt empty. And then she knew what to do: she would wait for Father and confront him. She rummaged through her knapsack until her hands found the knife Piers had given her – a sharp blade, its handle made from antler; she remembered each of the tiny carvings even before she felt them in her hand. She gripped it hard and slowly grew calm – she would find out the truth. As she put the knife into her jacket pocket, her fingers brushed Elke's notebook. For a moment she stroked the cover as if it were Elke's cheek. She dreaded what she would find in those pages, but she owed it to her sister to read them. Ritva sat on a tree stump and opened the notebook, the late-afternoon light illuminating Elke's neat writing.

Turku, 15 December 1914

Ritva, my dearest sister,

I miss you so! Father says you are getting better but we are still not allowed to write to you, the matron forbids it. So I am writing to you in my notebook instead and maybe one day you will read these pages when we are together again.

I have thought long and hard about where to hide this diary – I can't bear to think what Father would do to me if he found it! I've hidden it beneath the floorboards under my bed. I think it will be quite safe there – safer than I will be, in any case. It's only paper after all.

Ritva, I don't know what has happened to Father but he started ed behaving strangely around me some months after they took you away. Recently he told me to put on one of Mother's dresses although they are far too big for me, then he sat me on his lap and whispered into my ear. He looked all red and flustered and then he put his tongue in my ear. It was horrible, Ritva. And then he wanted to kiss me, he said he was lonely with Mother and you gone, and that I was his big girl now . . .

Ritva forced herself to continue, her heart growing heavier with each page. And this was only Elke's first diary . . . She wanted to run after her, wrap her arms around her, plead for forgiveness – how could she not have believed her sister? Father's betrayal tasted like bile in her mouth, and thoughts of revenge filled her. But how could she confront him? He was much taller and stronger than she was. For a moment her determination wavered, then her hands clenched into fists. She had survived the hell of the asylum, nearly frozen to death on the archipelago, lived on bark bread and berries; Martta had left her, and still she had lived. Life might nearly have crushed her, but now she was creating her own destiny; she was no longer a little girl, no longer a victim. A surge of energy rushed through her; she clutched her knapsack and hurried back to the house. If she had to, she would bind him to a chair, hold the knife to his throat and make him confess.

The house sat quietly like a benevolent creature amid the neglected garden, and nothing hinted at the horror it had harboured. Once more, Ritva peered through the window at the spectacle of Elke serving dinner, Father sitting stiff and mute at the table. How could Elke bear it? Ritva knew the routine: after dinner Father would retire to his armchair in the living room and smoke a pipe, then sit at his desk to work on the sermon for the coming Sunday. She shuddered at the thought of him preaching to his congregation, feeding lies to people who trusted and respected him . . . Once Elke had gone up to her room she would sneak inside and surprise him. She edged along the walls of the house towards the sitting room. The window stood ajar to let in the late-summer breeze; Pastor Larson did not expect thieves, or anyone else, to violate his property. Ritva turned over an empty water barrel, pushed it underneath the window and clambered on top; her knife was hidden in the folds of her dress, the rope firmly wrapped around her waist.

The room lay empty and in semi-darkness, the petroleum lamps had not yet been lit. This was her moment – it wouldn't be long before Father entered. She could hide behind the thick curtains . . . Ritva's heart raced and her hands were sweating. All of a sudden she froze outside the window – wouldn't it be safer to get to him while he was asleep? But what if he came to Elke's room again that night? She flicked her arm, trying to rid herself of the inertia. Then suddenly it was too late – her father appeared, candle in hand, and started to light the lamps. She had missed her moment. As quietly as possible she crept from her spot, cursing herself. She slipped out of the garden and ran towards the river, tears streaming down her face.

That night, she lay under a large birch, trying to still her heart.

Father would have finished his sermon by now and might be making his way to Elke's room . . . She clenched her jaw, turning over and over on the hard ground, only falling asleep in the early hours of the morning.

She knew him first by his smell – unmistakable and wild as the northern forest in which she had found him. She felt his thick fur, sensed him brushing against her back: Greyheart, not a playful puppy any more, but a big, proud male. Even in her dream, her heart ached for him and she knew he had come to help her. As she touched him, his strength became her courage and she found herself morphing into his shape: her limbs growing longer, her sides leaner, her mouth becoming his. She bared her teeth, opened her throat and howled . . .

When Ritva awoke, dawn had not yet broken and her blanket was damp from dew and sweat. She shivered as a new sense of strength flowed through her – it did not matter that she had missed her moment yesterday; there would be another, and soon.

31

That evening Ritva was a secret spectator at the dining room window for a third time. Elke sat hunched over her soup, then left the room and returned with a plate of cold meat; as she passed her father, he slapped her bottom and laughed. She flinched and threw him a furious look. Ritva had to stop herself from breaking the window; instead she skirted around the house and climbed onto the water barrel. She pushed the living room window open, lifted her legs across the ledge and let herself into the dark room, then wrapped herself in the heavy curtain that reached all the way to the ground – in this position she was only two steps away from the back of Father's armchair.

He entered a few minutes later. Ritva's stomach heaved. She could not see anything from behind the musty curtain and forced herself to suppress a cough. How would she know when was the right moment? She heard him strike a match; he never smoked when he was working on his sermon – he must have settled in his armchair.

Ritva slowly pulled the knife from her dress; it felt cool and strong in her hand. She slid from behind the curtain. Although the room was dim, she could not linger long, Father might sense her presence, notice her shadow against the wall. With two light steps she slipped behind the chair and pushed the knife's cold edge against his throat.

'Don't move,' she hissed, dropping her voice. He must not recognise her – not yet. A choked sound escaped his mouth.

'Not a word or I'll cut your throat.'

'Anything, just don't cut me! What do you want? I'm a pastor, I have no riches.' His voice quivered.

'Shhh!' She pressed the knife harder against his throat, dizzy with fear and elation. 'It has come to my attention that you don't treat your daughter well. That you keep her like a maid during the day and a whore at night.' She tried to remain calm yet a blinding rage rose inside her. 'What do you have to say for yourself?'

'But that is not true! I love my daughter more than anyone, she's my life. I would never do anything to harm her. Don't you know I have already lost my wife and my other daughter, Ritva? Elke is all I have now.'

Hearing her own name, Ritva cringed.

'I have indeed heard about your wife and your other daughter. Are you saying I am a liar?' For a moment Ritva did not disguise her voice. He straightened up.

'Ritva?'

Within seconds he had grabbed her wrist, twisted her arm and forced her out in front of him. He stared at her.

'What . . . are you crazy?'

Ritva writhed and pulled the knife back towards herself. As she did so, the blade nicked the side of her father's hand.

'Ah, you've cut me!'

Ritva wriggled free from his grip, jumped back behind the arm-chair and pressed the blade back against his throat.

'Don't move an inch or I really will cut you.' But Larson suddenly leapt out of the chair and punched Ritva's arm with such force, she dropped the knife. He leaned over the chair and gripped her by the hair. Ritva screamed, trying to free herself, kicking his leg. Was that it? Did he have her now?

At that moment Elke barged into the room in her nightdress, pale as flour, with bloodshot eyes and wild hair, pointing a rifle straight at her father. Ritva could see Elke's trembling finger on the trigger.

'Let her go.' Elke's voice was shrill. Larson stared at her and released his grip. 'Sit down.' Larson obeyed. Ritva picked up the knife and uncoiled the rope she had wrapped around her waist.

'Ritva, darling, I am sorry,' Larson said, ignoring Elke. 'I should never have sent you away. I've missed you so.'

'Oh, be quiet,' Ritva hissed. She wound the rope around his torso and the chair several times, then pulled it tight.

'Don't move! Raise your arms and put your hands together.' She cut off a piece of the remaining rope and bound his wrists, then tied his ankles to the legs of the heavy chair. The moment their father was securely bound, Elke let herself slump into a chair.

'Now we can talk.' Ritva's voice was fierce. 'I'm asking you again: what have you got to say for yourself? Will you admit what you've done to Elke?'

Larson recovered his composure.

'So your little sister here has told you a pack of lies and you've fallen for it? You know of course that Elke has a colourful imagination.'

'Don't you dare speak like that about Elke!' Ritva spat and pushed the blade back onto his throat. 'I know everything you've done to Elke – at least be man enough to admit it.'

'Oh, you poor thing, I can see Seili has done you no good, you're still mad. The doctors called your fantasies delusions, but I think you were simply making up lies to get at me.' Ritva clenched her jaw, feeling the wolf stir.

'I've trusted you all my life, Father, but it turns out that you're just as disgusting as your brother. Did you know what Uncle was doing to me? I bet you knew all along.'

Larson breathed in sharply but said nothing. Without taking the knife from his throat, Ritva moved in front of the chair to face him. He turned his head away.

'Look at me! Tell me you knew he came to my room at night and touched me.'

She lifted his chin, forced him to look at her. Up close she could see how much he had aged – his face was streaked with wrinkles and there were deep shadows under his bloodshot eyes. She could not read his expression.

'At least admit what you did. Or do you need me to remind you of each and every thing you did to Elke?'

Ritva pulled Elke's diary from her pocket and held it in front of his face. He looked at her blankly. Elke sat with a vacant gaze, still pointing the rifle at their father.

'15 January 1916. Father told me to put on Mama's dress again. It still doesn't fit me. He made me sit on his lap and kissed my ear.' Ritva flicked through the pages. '19 February 1916. He came into my room at night and touched me under my nightdress.'

'Stop it,' Larson said in a hushed voice. Suddenly Elke jumped up and rushed out of the room. Ritva heard the front door slam.

'And why should I stop? Hearing your dirty deeds read back to you, is it too much detail or not enough?' As she raised the knife to his throat again, he caught a glimpse of it and all the colour drained from his face.

'That knife . . . it's Lappish.'

'Yes. What do you care?'

'Ritva, your . . .' He stopped abruptly.

'What, Father, what?'

'Nothing.' A heavy silence settled over them. Something about the knife had bothered him but now he retreated deep into himself. As Ritva gripped Piers's knife, she remembered her life with the herders, her journey north and back south – all her journeys . . .

'Your uncle never touched you.' Her father's voice startled her.

'What do you mean?' Ritva glared at him. He held her gaze for a long time but she could read nothing in his eyes and the silence unnerved her. 'I know exactly what happened to me. It went on for weeks, months.'

'Your uncle loved you, he just wasn't very good at showing it.' His voice was strained, thin.

'You call that love? Coming into my room, using me? And you knew about it, didn't you?' She grabbed his chin, her hand trembling. 'Look at me!' His pupils were small, his mouth pressed shut. Before she could stop herself, Ritva slapped him hard on the cheek. He flinched, but said nothing. Ritva watched the red mark spread across his face; his stony refusal to talk made her want to hit him again.

'Admit it!' She spat the words in his face, grabbed him by the collar and shook him with such force she nearly lifted him out of the chair. Her heart hammered with the power of what she felt herself capable of.

'He never touched you, Ritva. Most nights, your uncle was passed out in his room, blind drunk.'

'You're saying I made it up? I know what happened to me!' She was shouting now.

She paced around the armchair, Greyheart's feral presence stirring in her, a tense bundle of muscles ready to attack.

'It was me, Ritva,' he said quietly. 'I was the one who came into your room those nights. I put drops in your tea at dinner to make you sleepy.'

Ritva held her breath until she felt dizzy. His words spun in her mind; she could not understand what he was saying.

'I disguised myself with a beard and put on a wool jacket so you would think it was him coming into your room. And yes, I was drinking too, secretly, at night, sometimes even in the day. I had succumbed to the devil I had always raged against. Somehow I didn't believe it was me who did all those things to you . . . and when I took off the beard and jacket in the morning, I despised your uncle even more.'

His voice was flat now, his gaze blank. Ritva's stomach heaved and a sharp pain radiated from the centre of her chest. Her eyes bored into him. Elke had warned her, but she had not listened. Her father, a lying monster? She thought of the knife. It would be so easy . . .

'How could you . . . I don't understand. What you did to me and Elke, we're your own flesh and blood!'

He sat slumped over, ashen-faced.

'My whole damn life nothing was ever truly right, nothing except your mother's beautiful face. And then you came, and Elke, with all your joy and innocence. And I took that away. And Sebastian, my brother, who really cared about me, I betrayed him too.' His voice broke. 'One day your mother found me with one of the neighbour's boys. You were still a little girl then. It was nothing really, I was very gentle with the boy. Your mother was pregnant at the time with Fredo; she was disgusted and would not sleep with me for months. Then Fredo was born and for a while everything was good between us. Your mother was happier than ever and you enjoyed playing with your baby brother. I made a promise to myself to be the best husband and father I could be, but when Fredo died something broke inside me. It was then that I remembered how good it had felt with the boy. I pleaded with God to help me resist, but the temptation was too strong. Only I was more cautious this time. I was a loving father and husband. Ritva, you saw how I cared for your mother when she fell apart after Fredo's death. No one should blame me for seeking solace with a young boy. Do you think I am the only one who ever did this? There are many who do it, believe me.'

Ritva forced herself to say nothing; the magnitude of the story unfolding before her was suffocating.

'But your mother was clever and despite her grief, she found me out. I begged her to forgive me, but this time she withheld herself for so long that I thought she would never take me back. In the end it was only her desire for another child that made her give in. And so your sister Elke was born. I loved our new baby dearly, but your mother did not let me near her after the birth, and fought me off like a lioness. And then your uncle arrived two years later. Sebastian stirred up old memories, bad things that happened to us during our childhood – just seeing him made me angry . . .

'So, when your mother denied me, I turned to boys again. I don't know how your mother knew but this time when she found out, she didn't recover – you know what happened, the screaming, the madness. When she was gone I felt lonely, and you were so like her, Ritva. I noticed your lovely growing body. I tried to hold myself back but then it was as if something I could not control had taken me over. Being with you made me feel alive again, even just for a few moments. I thought you wouldn't notice, that I'd put you to sleep with the drops. I loved you, Ritva, I never meant you any harm . . .'

Ritva's legs felt weak and she had to hold on to the edge of the desk.

'Then one day Sebastian found out. He came to the house late at night to fetch something and bumped into me. He looked as if he'd seen a ghost, a double. I grabbed him and held my hand over his mouth, but he ripped off my false beard. He was so drunk that I got away with it that night and when he accused me in the morning, I held him in front of the mirror and told him to look at himself with his bloodshot eyes. I told him he was just making up stories in his drunken stupor. But he remained suspicious, and one night he caught me coming out of your room. He was sober and had been waiting. I promised I would stop, but I couldn't, it was like the devil was in me!'

'Pah, the devil!' Ritva spat. She circled him like a wolf, but despite her rage she felt nauseous.

'Please forgive me, Ritva!' His voice was a mere whisper now. 'I know I've done wrong.'

'How can I forgive you? My own father molesting his daughters? You should have looked after me, guided me. Instead you drugged me, tricked me, put your hands under my clothes. You *raped* me. You made sure people thought I was crazy . . . and you were happy to leave me to rot in that asylum. That was all part of your plan, wasn't it? First you got rid of Mother when she threatened to tell the truth, then me. Mother tried to warn me, she knew! But I thought she was talking about Uncle. You're a monster!'

'I thought you would be safer in the asylum than here with me.'

'Safer? Do you have any idea about life on Seili? Women die like

253

flies over the winter and the cells are so small you can barely turn around.' Seething, Ritva stepped up close to him and grabbed him by his waistcoat.

'And then you took Elke. All this time you made me think it was Uncle – your own brother. God, how I hate you!' She was trembling all over. 'Where is Uncle now?'

'He rented a room in town. He was drinking even more and then he started gambling. Lost all his sheep. He's in a bad way.'

Exhaustion suddenly gripped her.

'I'm going to lock you in my old bedroom. In the morning we'll decide what to do with you. Elke will have her say too. There will be no sermon for you this Sunday, nor any other Sunday. You can live out your dying days alone in this house, but there will be no more Pastor Larson. And if you ever try to spread your filthy lies again, I'll tell each and every one of your congregation what you did. God, how can you live with yourself?'

As she looked at her father, Ritva's eyes filled with tears.

'Forgive me, Ritva, I've done so much harm . . .' For a moment he stared at her wide-eyed.

'Why are you staring at me?'

'You look just like your mother did when I first met her. And so like your grandmother too. Strong and determined, beautiful. I adored your mother, but deep down I knew I could never possess her. She was as elusive as the Northern Lights and would always belong only to herself. I tried to make her mine, to break her in like a wild mare, but she just laughed at me. I met her in the far North, near Karesuvanto, when I preached amongst the Lapps as my father had done.' He took a deep breath.

'Ritva . . . your mother was a Lapp. She did not want to leave her mother, but I told her that if she came with me she would have a better life in the South. I made her deny her Sami blood, and forbade her from speaking her language – I made her leave everything behind that reminded her of being a Lapp so she could become a proper Finn, like me – and a good pastor's wife. She must have loved me, because she said yes and never saw her mother again. But I know she kept one of her tunics and a photograph of her mother hidden at the back of the wardrobe. She thought I didn't know, but once, when she left the bedroom door open, I glimpsed her wearing the dress. She was swaying in front of the mirror, holding her mother's photograph as if she were dancing with her, and she was smiling. She was the most beautiful I've ever seen her . . . I stole away. I had taught her shame, told her that her people were inferior, that if she made an effort she could be one of us, but that night I realised she would never belong to me.' He cast his eyes down to the ground.

'I have brought only misery to this family. And I could always see the Lapp in you, how at home you were in nature, the way you would sing . . . and then there were your visions.'

Ritva couldn't comprehend her father's words. Her mother, a Sami? Had the fever dreams of her childhood really been visions of the Sami drum? And on the arduous journey north, had it been the calling of her own ancestors that had helped her endure? Her skin was tingling all over. Did she belong to the Sami people after all, not only with her heart but in her blood?

'Show me the dress and the photograph. No, just tell me where they are.'

'They are in a box at the back of the wardrobe.'

Ritva's neck ached, the tension of the last few days gripping her like a vice. Still, she wanted to see the tunic. Would it be safe to leave her father here or would he shout for help? The neighbours lived too far away but she didn't want to take any chances. She pulled out a handkerchief, crumpled it into a ball and ripped a strip of fabric from the seam of her dress.

'Open your mouth.'

'Please, Ritva, don't be cruel.'

'You're calling me cruel after everything you've done? Shame on you. One more time, open your mouth!' Her voice was sharp and this time he obeyed. She stuffed the handkerchief into his mouth. A sense of power surged through her, yet it left a bitter taste.

'I'll be back, don't worry.'

She slid the knife into its sheath, turned her back on her father, and slipped out of the room.

32

Ritva could not find Elke in the house or garden; maybe she was looking for some solace in the birch forest and would return when she had gathered herself. Back inside, Ritva opened the door to her parents' bedroom. She had never been allowed to enter it except during the time of her mother's illness. She lit a lamp – only one side of the bed was made up, the other lay empty. Ritva's heart cramped at the reminder of her mother's absence. She kneeled next to the wardrobe and opened the door. Pushed to the very back was a cardboard box, covered with a layer of fine dust. She pulled it out and placed it on her mother's dressing table. Her stomach fluttered – Mother had often held her on her lap in front of these same mirrors, telling her how beautiful she was. Now, she hardly recognised the woman in the reflection: a pale angular face with strong cheekbones and full but chapped lips, a frowning forehead, and dark brown eyes that would not meet anyone's gaze for too long. She had lived without a mirror for so many years – and now she preferred it that way.

She let her hands glide over the box, then lifted the lid. On top of some dark blue fabric lay a sepia-tinted photograph: a tall woman dressed in a traditional Sami tunic and belt looked back at her, standing straight-backed outside a turf hut holding a swaddled baby in her arms, a girl of about four posing next to her. A slight smile played on the woman's lips while the girl stood with crossed arms, mouth pressed shut, her dark eyes glaring. Ritva stared at the picture; was the tall woman her grandmother, and this feral girl her mother? If only she could reach inside the photograph and ask all the questions that were pushing their way to the surface. Had they been reindeer herders, part of a *siida*? Why had her mother left the North? Had she really loved Father?

She placed the photograph on the dressing table and gently lifted the fabric from the box. She held it by the shoulders – it was a tunic so much like those she had admired on the Sami women; dark blue with colourful patterns around the sleeves and neck, and identical to the one worn by the woman in the photograph. Ritva held it close to her body and moved in front of the mirror. The temptation was too strong – she pulled her rough dress over her head and slipped on the tunic. It smelled musty and was heavier than her dress, but it fitted perfectly.

Tears stung her eyes as she looked in the mirror and saw her mother gazing back at her and, beyond that, the grandmother she had never known. Was she the same age now as Mother had been when Father took her from the North; when he tricked her into thinking she would have a better life here?

She noticed a neatly folded parcel in the box and unwrapped the thin paper – inside was a beautifully decorated headdress of the kind a maiden wore before her wedding night. Ritva had never seen Mother wearing the headdress – she must have taken a risk and brought it with her, disobeying Pastor Larson, her husband-to-be. At the bottom of the box lay a *guksi*, a drinking cup. Ritva stroked the soft shining wood and held it to her lips as if drinking cool, fresh water from a mountain stream. She knew these cups were treasured and no doubt many people had drunk from it: Mother, Grandmother, maybe even her great-grandmother . . .

The last item in the box was a scroll of birch bark, held together with a bright red ribbon. Ritva's hands trembled as she unrolled it – drawn with charcoal on the bark was an oval shape, filled with figures, tents, reindeer, a ladder. Her skin tingled – although the marks were faint, she could see it was a drawing of a drum, and so very similar to the one she had drawn underneath her bed in Seili: the sacred drum of her visions.

'What are you doing?' Elke's voice startled her.

'Elke, are you all right?' Ritva hugged her sister tight. 'I was looking for you everywhere.'

Elke gently pushed Ritva away and looked her up and down.

'What is this?'

'It's Mother's. Elke, Mother came from the North! She was a Sami woman. She left when she married Father and never went back. He forbade her to tell anyone where she was from or to speak her language. She never even told us!' The words tumbled from Ritva's mouth like a waterfall.

'Slow down. Ritva, how do you know all this?'

'Look!' Ritva picked up the photograph.

'Who is this?'

'I think it's our grandmother with Mother as a girl. After you left, Father admitted everything and then he told me about Mother.'

At that moment they heard coughing and then a strangled sound.

'What was that?' Elke said.

'It's Father, pretending to choke on the handkerchief I put in his mouth.'

'You gagged him?'

'Yes, I didn't want him to scream or call out. In case there's a neighbour passing.'

'But what do we do now?'

'I don't know, but I needed to hear the truth from him.'

'You want to leave him all night tied to a chair with a gag in his mouth?'

'I can bring him up here and lock him in my old bedroom. Why don't you go back to your room while I deal with Father? We need to get some rest.' Ritva was raw with tension. Elke said nothing, then nodded and left.

Ritva changed back into her own clothes before going to see her father. She found him hunched over and sweating, his face red and blotchy. There was fear playing in his eyes.

'Promise me you'll be quiet,' Ritva hissed. He nodded and she took off the gag. He took some deep breaths.

'I'll take you upstairs. You can sleep in my old room and then we'll talk in the morning. And don't try anything stupid.'

He shook his head. She untied his legs and the rope around his waist, but kept his hands bound.

'Get up, Papa.'

Ritva shuddered, suddenly flooded with emotion, confused by the intimacy of addressing him like that, the way she used to talk to him as a child. She still couldn't fathom that her papa, a man she had loved, had betrayed them both so cruelly.

'Come now.' Her voice was firm but softer and she did not rush him, but walked behind him holding the lamp as he took one step after another. He dragged himself up the stairs, hunched over, as if carrying a heavy load. He seemed to have aged years since the beginning of the night. They entered Ritva's old room and he sat down on the bed.

'You won't untie me?' He nodded at his bound hands.

'You don't need your hands to sleep, do you?' Ritva's voice had hardened again; she couldn't afford to feel sorry for him.

'Your mother's dress . . . did you find it?'

'Yes.' His question caught her unaware.

'And did it fit you? I do love you, Ritva.' His voice was hoarse. 'And I loved your mother too, and Elke. Please believe me.'

Ritva did not want to hear another word. She pulled the door shut, turned the key and slipped into Elke's room. The moon cast a silvery light across the bed, illuminating Elke's pale face above the white cover. Ritva undressed and slid in beside her sister.

'I'm scared,' Elke whispered. Instead of an answer, Ritva hugged her and kissed her on the forehead. How thin she was, how delicate, how young still . . .

'Shhh, try to sleep, Elke. It's all over – we're safe now.'

Elke laid her head on Ritva's shoulder; she sighed and was asleep in minutes. Ritva listened to her breathing, trying to still her own heart, following the shadows of the curtains on the floor.

The house was quiet – Father must have obeyed and lain down to sleep.

'Wake up! Did you hear that?' Elke nudged Ritva.

'What?' Ritva was barely awake.

'A thump. As if something had fallen to the floor.'

'I didn't hear anything.'

'Maybe Father fell out of bed?'

Ritva sat up, straining to hear, then eventually swung her legs out of the bed.

'I'll have a look.'

'It could be a trick, Ritva. Father is sly. What if he has freed himself and he attacks you?'

'Oh, Elke, I won't let him attack either of us ever again, I promise. You stay here, I'll deal with him.'

Ritva waited a few more minutes then lit the lamp, stepped out onto the landing and stopped outside her old room.

'Are you all right, Father?' she called through the door. Nothing – was it safe to open the door? What if Elke was right and Father threw himself at her and wrestled her to the ground? She put the lamp on the floor and pulled out her knife, then turned the key. When she opened the door a little, it was pitch-black inside as the curtains were drawn. She listened for his breathing but there was only silence. Heart in her mouth, she picked up the lamp and pushed the door fully open.

Two bare feet hovered in the air at the height of her stomach and it took her a moment to understand the whole picture: a kicked-over chair, a rope attached to a beam on the ceiling, the gentle, swaying movement. Only then did her gaze find his face. Even in the dim light she could see her father's features were distorted, his mouth half open, a trail of spittle at the edge, his eyes wide and bulging. She gagged, nausea rising. How had he managed this? Trembling, she put the lamp on her old desk. There was some paper there and on the top sheet she noticed some pencil marks. She pulled out the page and held it to the light. The letters were scrawled as if by a novice and she could only make out a few letters . . . *FO* . . .

FO . . .RGIVE ME . . .
MY DAUGHTERS . . .

As if the effort had been too much, the writing trailed off, leaving only a smear of lead. With a stab Ritva realised Father had been writing in the dark.

'Are you all right, Ritva?' Elke called from the other room.

'Fine,' Ritva replied.

She needed to cut Father down. Elke shouldn't have to see him like this. She closed the door and locked it. She could not recall later how she managed to cut him down, remove the noose from around his neck and to lay his body on her old bed. She must have climbed on the same chair he had kicked over, then the table and used her knife. By the time Elke banged on the door, Ritva had pressed his eyes shut and bound up his mouth. There was nothing she could do about the bluish colour of his skin or the red mark around his neck.

When Ritva opened the door, Elke's legs buckled and only Ritva's quick reaction prevented her from hitting the ground. Elke stared at the corpse.

'What . . . what happened?'

'He hanged himself, Elke. I'm so sorry.' Ritva tried to sound calm.

'What do you mean?' Elke's voice was strained.

'The rope, it was the rope I bound him with. He managed to get it off.'

They stood in silence staring at the body. Ritva felt the same emptiness that had grown in her stomach the day the doctor had taken her mother away, and for a moment she forgot that it was Father who had betrayed them all so terribly.

'What should we do now?' This time it was Elke who found her voice first.

'I'm not sure,' Ritva mumbled. Then suddenly she knew. 'I'll go into town and fetch Uncle, there's no one else we can turn to.'

'Should we not go together? What if someone recognises you?'

'No, you stay. If someone knocks and asks for Father, at least you'll be there to answer. I doubt anyone will recognise me. I'll wear a hat.' Ritva ignored a queasy feeling, remembering how Ulla had recognised her even after all these years.

'I'll be back very soon. Do you know where Uncle lives?'

'Yes, he's renting a room in a house west of the river.' Elke scribbled down the address, put it in Ritva's palm and hugged her.

'Please be careful.'

'I will.'

As dawn broke, Ritva stepped outside and took a deep breath – nothing would ever be the same again.

33

The boarding house was neatly painted with white window frames and a poppy-red door. It stood in an area of town that seemed to have been spared by the civil war. Ritva knocked – an elderly woman opened, her grey hair tucked into a tidy bun, a thin smile playing on her lips. Ritva asked for her uncle.

'He doesn't go out much, old Sebastian, slept right through most of the war. A boy delivers groceries and alcohol to him. Maybe you can persuade him to leave the house more and clean his room? It must be filthy in there.' The landlady leaned forward. 'It's starting to smell, but he gets angry when I bring it up. At least he always pays me on time. Are you family?'

Ritva nodded and the woman showed her upstairs. She knocked at the door – nothing. Her hands were clammy. It had been such a long time since she had seen Uncle, and she had been so very wrong about him then . . . After the third knock she heard someone stir.

'Come in, the door is open,' a deep voice hollered. Ritva entered and gasped as the smell of mould and damp hit her. The room had a single window that was so streaked with grime it hardly let in any light, and a thick layer of dust had settled everywhere as if it had been gathering there for years. A heap of dirty plates and cups stood in the small sink and many open preserve jars were dotted around the room, containing mould at various stages of growth. Newspapers, empty bottles and clothing lay scattered across the floor: single socks, trousers, shirts, a shoe. Ritva could hardly make out the bed amid the general chaos, but when she looked closer she noticed the flushed face of her uncle peering out from under a grey duvet. Seeing Ritva, he bolted upright.

'Ritva, is that you?'

'Yes, Uncle, it's me.' He stared at her as if she were a vision. 'How are you, Uncle?'

'I . . . I am good, oh God, my girl. You . . . I thought I'd never see you again!'

'Oh, Uncle!'

For a moment she was repelled by the rancid smell of his stale sweat mixed with alcohol but then she held her breath and hugged him fiercely, feeling the rough stubble of his beard rub against her cheek. The years of disgust she had harboured for him dissolved in that embrace and she sobbed as all tension of the last few days poured from her like a storm discharging its waters.

'I'm so sorry! I thought you did all those horrible things to me, and you didn't. I know now that it was Father. Please forgive me!'

He held her without a word, stroking her hair as if it were the soft fur of a cat. After a while he looked at her with bleary, red-rimmed eyes.

'I'm so happy to see you, Ritva, I thought I had lost you for ever. Did they finally let you out of that terrible asylum?'

Ritva took a deep breath. 'I ran away, Uncle.'

'You ran away?'

'Yes, it's a long story but I'm just so glad to see you.'

'Your father never wanted you to leave.' He spat out the words. 'I kept telling him to have you released, that it was so wrong . . .' Suddenly his eyes widened. 'Does he know you're here?'

Ritva bit her lip but her eyes had filled with tears.

'Where is he?'

'He's not . . . he's not with us any more.'

'What do you mean?'

'He . . . he killed himself. Hanged himself during the night. I had locked him in my old room with his hands bound but he managed to slip off the rope . . .'

'He hanged himself?' Sebastian's face had lost all its colour.

'Yes. I cut him down. I didn't want to leave him like that.'

'Did you send for the police and the doctor?'

'No, he's still lying on the bed. I didn't know what to do, Uncle – that's why I came looking for you.'

Sebastian said nothing for a long while, then placed his hand on Ritva's shoulder.

'Try not to worry, my girl, you've had to endure more pain than anyone ever should. We'll sort this out. Please, fetch me my old bathrobe from over there by the door, will you?' His voice sounded determined but she could tell he was struggling to keep his emotions at bay. He lifted his legs from under the cover and swung them out of the bed; they were as thin as a bird's legs. How long had he been lying in that grubby bed?

'I haven't been out in a long while, so please forgive the mess,' he said, as if hearing Ritva's thoughts.

'Will you be all right? Do you want to have something to eat?' Ritva looked around for some food and a clean plate to serve him some breakfast. She caught a glimpse of his body before he slipped into his robe – his skin was grey and each rib showed on his torso. It was possible he had not left his den for months.

'Do you ever eat?'

He laughed, a short, rough sound.

'Yes, I do eat. Well enough for a sad old man. Actually I do feel hungry now, it must be your lovely presence.'

'Do you have anything clean to wear?' She picked up one shirt after another with two fingers only to drop them again – how could he live in such squalor?

'Yes, there's a big box. I use up everything I have and then I give it all to the landlady to launder. There should still be a fresh shirt and a pair of trousers.' He shuffled over to the box and rummaged through it. 'It might take me a while to smarten up and get ready. Ritva, why don't you go ahead and I'll see you at the house?'

She nodded; it would be a relief to leave this sad place.

'I really appreciate you coming, Uncle. I know it's not easy for you. Please try not to drink today, we need you to keep your mind sharp.'

'Pah, a sharp mind!' He stabbed his finger at his forehead. 'I used to be sharp up here, before I drank my brains to mush! Anyway, let's get going.'

'I'll see you soon, Uncle.' She hugged him, slipped out of the door and tiptoed down the stairs – the fewer people she met, the better. She sucked in the fresh morning air and made her way back to her old home.

'No one called,' Elke said as she opened the door. She was pale, shoulders drawn up to her ears. Ritva prepared a large pot of coffee and carried it through to the sitting room. Neither of them wanted to sit in Father's armchair. Ritva told Elke about the squalid state she had found their uncle in.

'He's a weak man,' Elke said with a bitter tone. 'He should've stood up for me, but he just crumbled, abandoned the house without a word and then I was left alone with Father . . .' Her head sank to her chest and they sat in silence for a long time.

Two hours later Sebastian knocked. Ritva opened the front door and was taken aback. Uncle had shaved, combed his hair and was dressed in fresh clothes, looking so much like Father before he had grown a beard. She hugged him but recoiled when she smelled his breath, reeking of alcohol.

'Please, show me your father.'

He nodded at Elke, but said nothing more, then followed behind Ritva and Elke as they walked upstairs. Ritva hesitated before she opened the door.

'He doesn't look good, just prepare yourself, Uncle,' she whispered.

In the brutal light of day, the corpse was an even worse sight. Sebastian gasped, then fell to his knees next to the bed and put his hand on his brother's forehead.

'Oh, Stefan, what have you done?'

He wept, his whole body shaking. Ritva put her hand on his shoulder for a moment, then gestured for Elke to follow her out. Uncle needed time alone with his brother.

Back in the sitting room Ritva wanted nothing more than to curl up and sleep, but she was aware that there were so many things to be done and as the eldest daughter she needed to be responsible. Her father's death changed everything.

'We must call the doctor, Ritva,' Elke said, shaking Ritva from her thoughts. 'I'll go and fetch him, then we can explain everything – about you and Father, me, the night he died . . .' At that moment they heard Uncle's heavy footsteps on the stairs. He entered the room, slumped into the armchair and pulled out a small silver flask.

'I know I shouldn't be drinking, but I don't think I can get through this day without it.' He took a large swig and shook himself like a wet dog. He was undone, his eyes bleary, his shoulders collapsed.

'I should've tried to talk some sense into him, supported him rather than hating him – maybe none of this would've happened.' He gulped down another swig and fell into a brooding silence.

'I'm going to get the doctor,' Elke said and got up. 'We can't just sit here and leave Father lying upstairs like that. People will ask questions and we have to deal with it.'

Ritva calculated – it would be nearly an hour's walk to the doctor's surgery at the edge of Turku, but returning in the doctor's carriage would be quick and he and Elke could be back in just over an hour. What if it was the same doctor who had taken her away? And what if he alerted the asylum in Seili?

'No,' Ritva said, standing up. 'We have to think about this – what if they try to put me away again?'

'Ritva is right,' Sebastian said, 'we need to have a plan.'

'And what would you know?' Elke spat. 'Suddenly you show up here, behaving as if you're the wise one, sticking your nose into our affairs as if you've ever cared about any of us.' She glared at him then stormed out of the room. Ritva jumped up but Sebastian held her back.

'Leave her, she's every right to be furious with me. But I want to apologise, if she'll let me. There are things I need to explain to you both.' For the rest of that afternoon and into the evening, they sat together filling in the missed years. Ritva told her uncle of her escape from the asylum and the long journey north, while Sebastian related the horrors of the civil war.

'I only fought for two months – with the Red Guards, of course, the Socialists. I really thought we could win and that I was doing something good – fighting for our workers, for justice. Your father supported the government and the White Troops and ranted against the Reds even from the pulpit, calling us vermin and worse . . . There was so much bloodshed on each side, Ritva. Maybe I'm a coward, but after a couple of months I didn't want to be part of such an ugly war any more and so I holed up in that boarding house. And then one day, in the last few weeks of the war, your father found out about a place where a group of Reds was hiding and he denounced them. They were all shot, all nine of them! I'm amazed he didn't have me killed too, he knew where I was hiding. It was awful, Ritva! They put the Reds into camps and thousands starved to death or died of flu – Finns, ordinary people like you and me, our own flesh and blood!'

He took another swig from his flask. Ritva put her arm around his shoulders; he tensed, eyes welling up.

'I . . . I know how it feels, Ritva.' His voice was deep and slurry.
'How what feels?'
'Him coming to you in the night.' He took a deep breath.
'What do you mean?'
'Our father did it to both of us – to me and Stefan. At night and on Sundays after church. Bent us over, caned us and then . . . He was a big man, and he threatened to kill us if we said anything. Your father and I really believed he would. Even when he died I could never forget what had happened. The only release I found was when I was drunk or in the fields under an open sky with

my sheep. He made me feel like filth and I could never touch a woman without thinking how dirty I was. I put on a front, that I was a hard man, pretended I had an eye on many women, but I never felt I deserved a family.' He held his head in his hands.

'But you had a wife, Uncle, you came to stay with us after she died, didn't you?'

He gazed at Ritva with a vacant look.

'Annetta, yes, I loved her very much. But I couldn't make love with her. I tried, God knows I did. We had no children and when she died I lost all hope.' He wiped his eyes with his fist. 'Your father was different, he stepped right into the same vocation as our father. I was suspicious, but your father had made up his mind: he would become a pastor and swore he would live with integrity. "I'll make amends for what our father did to us," he said. But how could he? He was made from the same wood as him! When he married, I was jealous, I could hardly look at your mother – such a sweet spirit, and what a beauty. How did he deserve a woman like her? Did he not see what a big lie it all was when he looked in the mirror, as I did every day of my life?' He took a deep breath.

'And then you arrived. I couldn't bear it – a baby as well? That's why I didn't come to see you for so many years, it just hurt too much. But time passed and when your little Fredo and then Annetta died, the old jealousy seemed to disappear. I was raw with grief and admired the way your father had turned his life around. But how could I not have seen the danger you were in? One night, I bumped into him outside your room. He looked just like me, Ritva! At first he made me think that I was going insane, that the drink was making me see things . . . but then I waited for him one night and I confronted him as he came out of your room. I ranted and begged him to leave you alone, but he just denied what he was doing. And when you were about to be taken away, I wanted to tell the doctor the truth, what I thought your father had done to you, but I felt so ashamed, I thought I needed to tell him what our father had done to us when we were little . . .

Oh Ritva, I'm such a coward!' He broke off, weeping. 'And then you were gone and I feared for Elke. Your father held it together for six months, but then he started to sneak into Elke's room too. I threatened him with the police, but he just laughed in my face. I thought of taking Elke with me, but how could I care for her? So, after a big row, I left. And not a day has gone by when I haven't blamed myself. Please forgive me, Ritva, I wish I could have protected you and your sister!' His whole body was shaking.

'There is nothing to forgive, Uncle. You've done your best and now you are here.' They sat in silence and after a while Ritva slipped into a light sleep.

She woke to the smell of fresh coffee. She must have slept through the night as when she looked outside dawn had already broken. Elke was dressed in her coat and boots and held out a steaming cup to her.

'I'll go now and fetch the doctor,' she said. Ritva took the cup but said nothing; her head hurt.

'It'll be fine,' Elke said, and Ritva knew that this time she could not stop her from going. Elke hurried out of the house.

'You need to tell them about yourself, Uncle,' Ritva said, finding Uncle still sitting in his brother's armchair.

'Who, the doctor? The police?'

'Both. No one will believe me or Elke – in their eyes, I'm still an escaped lunatic. They need to hear the whole story from you. They might even think we killed Father.'

Sebastian looked panicked.

'Will you tell them?' Ritva pushed.

'Yes . . . of course, for you and Elke's sake. I'm just so . . . ashamed. We never talked about what had happened to us, your father and I. We couldn't even bear to look each other in the eye. The only time was on his wedding day, when he took me aside and whispered: "Don't ever tell Lara or anyone what happened to us. I'm making a different life for this family."'

Ritva realised she had not yet asked her uncle about her mother.

271

'Do you know where my mother came from?'

Sebastian looked startled. 'I thought from somewhere near Helsinki?'

'No, Uncle, she was a Sami! Father met her when he was working up north – he said it was in the place where his father had preached to the Lapps, as he called them – near Karesuvanto. Father brought her to Turku and told her she was never to speak her language again.'

'God, how many more secrets?' Sebastian shook his head. 'I remember our father telling us about his time amongst the Lapps. He spoke about them as if they were children, silly, dirty things that needed saving from the claws of Satan . . . I'm sure he put the fear of God into them.'

'There must be notes and photographs from Father's time up there,' Ritva said. 'All I have is one photograph of Mother as a child, stood with her mother.'

Ritva looked around the room, then went over to her father's desk. She would never have dared even to touch it while he was alive. She pulled at the first, then the second drawer – both were locked. Without a word, she hurried upstairs. She hesitated at the door; Father lay exactly where she had left him, only his skin looked even more waxen now. She did not look at his face as she rummaged through his trouser pockets. Nothing. She shivered as her fingers briefly touched the icy skin on his sinewy hand then rushed out of the room. When she stumbled back into the sitting room, Uncle held up a small brass key, smiling.

'I might be drunk most of the time, but I still have a good nose for finding hidden things. Here, I think you should do the honours.'

Ritva's hands trembled as she put the key into the small hole. The lock of the first drawer sprang open with a click.

'We need to hurry, I don't think you should be here when the doctor or the police arrive.' Sebastian placed his hand on her shoulder. 'You've been through so much, Ritva, I don't want you to take any more risks.'

272

Ritva knew Uncle was right: the risk of staying in the house was far too great and the doctor was not to be trusted.

'The days are not too cold, so you could hide out in the shelter I used to sleep in when I was out with the sheep.'

The first drawer was filled with papers: drafts of sermons, scribbled notes and old bills. As she got to the bottom of the pile, her hands touched a bundle of letters. She pulled them out and breathed in sharply as she recognised her mother's neat handwriting on the faded envelopes. She flicked through the letters, her heart fluttering – they were mainly addressed to her father, but some were to her and Elke. She placed the bundle on the desk. Had the asylum passed the letters on and Father had held them back from her and Elke? Or had they been sent only after her mother had died? Tears stung her eyes but she forced herself to move on. She looked at Sebastian.

'You're right, I should leave. I'm just so tired of running and hiding. And I want to go back north . . .'

'You might not need to hide for long, Ritva, it's just to keep you safe. Please hurry, they'll be back soon. You'll need some food. I'll see what I can find in the kitchen.'

Ritva slipped the letters into her knapsack then put on her coat – it was slightly too warm but she felt better in its embrace. As she walked by the kitchen she saw Sebastian rummaging through the cupboards. How could she have been so wrong about him for all those years? Cursing her father, she was about to walk to the front door when she heard the carriage. She ran back to the kitchen.

'They're here, quick!' Sebastian handed her a parcel of food and helped her leave by the back door.

'I found some old bread, apples and jam. Also some biscuits and a bottle of vodka. Didn't think I'd find any drink in this household, but there it was. And water, three bottles.'

'Thank you, Uncle.' Ritva took the items and stuffed them into her knapsack. Sebastian gave her directions, then pulled her close and planted a kiss on her forehead.

'It's only a simple shelter but it'll keep you dry and no one will look for you there. Be safe!'

Ritva kissed him on his cheek. She waited until Elke had entered the house with the doctor and a policeman, then slipped through the back gate out of the garden.

34

Ritva found the shelter and made herself as comfortable as she could. Three empty vodka bottles and a few scraps of newspaper from January 1918 lay scattered in one corner. She shivered as she recalled Uncle telling her about father's betrayal of the Red Guards – maybe this hut had been one of their hideouts? What cruel madness this war had been, brothers fighting against one another, or even against a sister . . .

She collapsed on the straw bed, bit off a piece of bread and took a large swig of the vodka Uncle had slipped into her hand – today she welcomed its sharp burn in her throat. She reached for the bundle of letters and caressed her mother's delicate handwriting. The letters were unopened – whatever kept Father from reading them had also probably prevented him from throwing them away: was it guilt, or a remaining glimmer of love? She would never know. The last envelope, the only opened letter, was addressed to her father. Ritva pulled it out and smoothed it over her thigh.

Seili asylum, 28 December 1912

Dear Pastor Larson,

It is with the deepest regret that I am writing to inform you that your wife, Lara Larson, died in our care last night. She had developed severe pneumonia after a mild cold and despite our best efforts, she died in the early hours of the morning. Unfortunately a doctor could not be called due to the severe weather, the waterways being frozen solid between Nauvo and Seili.

Please accept our sincere condolences. Your wife was well liked by staff and her fellow patients here. I would be grateful if you could let me know whether you would like Lara to be buried in our small cemetery or have her transferred home.

I will send a parcel with your wife's belongings in due course, together with her letters. As you know, the Board of Trustees recommends that contact between patients and their families should cease while the illness persists, but Lara never tired of writing to you and your daughters and we saved all her letters for you. I will await your response.

With kindest regards

Margaret Oulson, Matron

Ritva's head pounded as she read the lines over and over again. Mother had died only a few months before Ritva was taken to Seili. Ritva recalled the day she had arrived at the asylum, how the matron had stared at her as if she had seen a ghost. And Katarina – was it her mother's features that the old woman had seen in her that had so unnerved her? Ritva's stomach cramped as she thought of her mother's suffering, the unmarked grave . . . Had Katja and Petta been cruel to her too? She clutched the bundle of letters to her heart and curled up on the mattress – maybe tomorrow she would have the strength to read the letters that Father had hidden away like some dark secret. Sleep came quickly and with it, dreams.

She was walking along the echoing corridors of the asylum; an eerie silence engulfed the building and all the doors were shut. As she turned a corner, she glimpsed a woman in a long cobalt-blue dress, hurrying along, her loose hair flowing out behind her. Ritva called after her but the woman vanished and a heavy door fell shut with a clang. Ritva put her ear to each door until she heard a soft moaning sound behind one. She opened it – the woman in the blue dress was sitting on a bare iron bed surrounded by huge piles of letters, her ink-stained fingers gripping a quill. As she lifted her head, Ritva found herself staring into her mother's pale face, her bloodshot eyes streaming with tears.

'Mother!'

'Ritva, my darling! You must get away from this place. They will eat your heart here.'

'Oh, Mother . . .' Ritva rushed towards her and tried to embrace her.

'Go, run!' Ritva could almost see her mother's heart fluttering like a bird. Suddenly, as if blown by a storm, page after page lifted off the bed, spiralling upwards in a wild vortex. As the wind grew, her mother was lifted by an invisible force, higher and higher until she broke through the ceiling, the letters scattering across the night sky like sparks from a giant fire.

'Mother!' Ritva woke to her own scream. When she calmed, she forced herself to eat a piece of bread then opened the first letter.

20 April 1911

My darling Ritva,

Everything is frozen here. The water surrounding the island is thick with ice that moans and creaks at night, just like our bones. One could walk all the way to Sweden if one had the will, the right shoes and, of course, the strength. But I have none of these. And now the water pipes have burst and we cannot even wash and have to melt snow on the stove for our thin coffee. My heart is frozen too – if it weren't for you and little Elke this cold would rob me of my mind. You are the only things that keep a little flame of hope alive inside of me. Are you thinking of me also?

It is nearly May now, but spring still has not come. The birds are ready to build their nests but no leaves have appeared on the trees. Has spring arrived where you are – just across the frozen waters? Turku is so close and yet it seems a world away.

277

How did all this happen? One day, I was at home with you, the next they had spirited me away into the care of the doctors in Turku. For weeks I felt as if I was drowning and then a thick fog settled around me. They took me to another hospital in Helsinki then here, to this wretched island, and still the fog has not lifted.

Some people call Seili 'Seal Island', but these creatures keep their distance – maybe they fear we will steal their skins and slip away? Do you remember the story of Sealskin I often told you?

The world has stopped for me and yet I am hopeful that I will hear from you one day soon.

Many kisses to you and my darling Elke,

your loving mother

Ritva bit her fingernails, then wiped away her tears with the back of her hand. Mother's description of the wretched life on Seili was just as she had endured it; mother and daughter betrayed by the same man, their husband and father. And with a pang Ritva finally understood: it was their wild souls that Father had feared. When he signed the papers and sent them both away to the island he knew that their souls would be trapped there, their souls – their sealskins – taken, just like in the fairy tale . . . Mother was dead now, but her own journey had not ended – she would retrieve of her life and soul what she still could. She fell back on the mattress into a dreamless sleep, the letters surrounding her like a flock of white starlings.

Sometime later, Ritva heard a quiet knock. She unbolted the door and peered through the gap – it was Elke, pale with dark shadows under her eyes as if she hadn't slept since the night Father hanged himself.

'The house was swarming with people, Ritva. The doctor, the police, a detective – all asking questions. Uncle told them everything: how their father had molested them when they were boys, how Father tricked you into thinking it was Uncle when he came to you in the night; how Uncle challenged Father . . . And then they asked me. God, it was awful! I had to tell those men every detail. I felt so dirty and ashamed. All I could do was think that, once this is all over, there will be another life for us.'

'And there will be, Elke.' Ritva put her arms around her sister and held her, stroking her hair.

'They said they need to talk to you and assured us they would not contact the asylum, but I don't trust them, nor does Uncle. We didn't tell them where you are.'

Ritva shivered – she had no reason to trust those men. How could she be sure they wouldn't lock her away again?

'Uncle is organising the funeral,' Elke continued. 'It'll be on Wednesday. After that we can leave . . .'

Yes, there was nothing to keep them here now, Ritva thought. She ached to return to the North and the Sami people, her own blood ancestors after all! Her stomach still fluttered at the thought.

'The whole congregation will gather,' Elke said. 'It disgusts me that they'll never know the truth about Father – not unless we tell them – but I'm so tired, I just want to see his coffin disappear into that hole and know that he's down there once and for all.' She wiped her eyes. 'Maybe it would be safer if you stayed here? I couldn't bear it if anything happened to you. We can meet up the morning after the funeral by the river. I've brought you more food.'

Ritva's head was filled with fog.

'But I won't be able to say goodbye to Uncle.'

Elke shook her head.

'No, but why don't you write to him? I can take the letter.'

Elke was right – if the doctor tricked her, then everything she had struggled for would be lost. The congregation might never know about Father, but at least she and Elke would be free.

That afternoon Ritva scribbled a note for Sebastian thanking him for everything. She noticed how she breathed more easily now, the place around her heart lighter. She would never have to return to that accursed house. For Sebastian, her father's death brought new opportunities – maybe he could buy himself another flock of sheep with his share of the inheritance and start anew. She glanced at Elke, who had fallen asleep on the straw bed, the strain of the past week clearly written on her pale face. She had been freed from Father, seen her long-lost sister again and now she was on the threshold of a new life. Ritva stroked Elke's cheek and gently shook her awake.

'It's time, Elke, you've got to go. I'll meet you by the river the day after tomorrow. Please keep yourself safe.'

The next morning Ritva woke with a knot in her stomach. This was the day they would bury her father and she would not be present. She lay on the mattress, staring at the ceiling, her body tense. Again she had been silenced, was absent. She breathed hard, her hands balled into fists. No, she *would* attend the funeral, despite everything; despite the betrayal, the pain and the danger, or maybe because of it. She too needed to see their father's coffin being lowered into the earth, to bid him farewell in her own way and to end this chapter of her life with her eyes wide open.

Within minutes she had rolled up her blanket, packed her knapsack and left. She hid the bundle near the river then headed towards the cemetery, avoiding the church – she could not bear to hear the parishioners in their ignorance praising her father, those stupid sheep . . . A wave of hot anger surged through her, burning her cheeks. She hid behind a tall spruce in the woodland bordering the cemetery as the congregation arrived, along with five pall-bearers carrying the coffin behind a pastor. What had they been told? That Father had broken his neck falling down the stairs? She could not hear the pastor's words, only a murmur that spread through the congregation as the coffin was lowered into the ground. One by one people stepped forward to throw a handful of earth into the hole. Elke, dressed in black, stood rigid and pale next to Sebastian, receiving everyone's condolences. It was just like Fredo's funeral . . . Tears welled up in Ritva's eyes and her throat felt tight – it was all over.

She turned away and walked deeper into the woodland.

35

The next day Ritva hid near the bridge close to the riverbank. She heard the sound of a large animal before Elke's soft voice called her.

'Ritva, are you there?'

Ritva scrambled up the bank and stood stunned. Her sister was holding the reins of a small, sturdy horse with a light-brown coat and a thick white mane.

'You bought a horse?'

'Yes, a pony, she's Uncle's gift to us. He said he didn't want us to carry our belongings on our delicate backs.' Elke smiled. 'Not that I would call us delicate, but he's right, it's much more convenient.'

Ritva stroked the pony's flank and soft nose; the mare sighed and nibbled her hand, then stretched her neck towards Ritva's bag, eager to find some tasty morsel.

'She's beautiful! Does she have a name?'

'Sebastian called her Sunnika – "gift of the sun".'

Sunnika – so similar to Sunna, Ritva thought; old Sunna who had fed Ritva broth after taking her in, who told the best stories . . .

'Sebastian cried when he read your letter. He also gave us some money to start out with. Look.' Elke fanned out a bundle of notes. 'He'll send us some more money through an old friend in Rovaniemi once he's sold the house – here is the address. He says goodbye and good luck to us.' Elke pulled out a scroll from her coat. 'And he gave me this.'

Ritva unrolled it – it was a finely drawn map of Finland, Sweden, Norway and the Kola Peninsula with Sápmi, the land of the Sami, clearly marked on it. To the far north, still in Finland but close to the Swedish border, he had drawn a red dot – Karesuvanto.

Elke frowned. 'I've never been further north than Turku.'

'It'll be fine, Elke. Let's turn our backs on this godforsaken place and build ourselves a new life.'

Ritva slid her finger over the map until it came to rest on the Swedish side near Nikkaluokta. With a stab she thought of Piers, Arvid and Sofia. Before she could look for her mother's relatives she had to return to Piers's *siida*. Her hand found Piers's knife and his necklace in her pocket; she had not thought of him often, but now that her old world was gone for good, the thought of him and the *siida* warmed her heart more than ever. She sighed and picked up the pony's reins.

'I can't wait for you to meet the people who rescued me and see the North – it's like nothing you've ever known. It's as big and wide as the whole world up there.'

The pony put its muzzle to Elke's neck, nudging her gently.

'She thinks we should be on our way,' Ritva said and rummaged for an apple in her knapsack. They secured the bundles of clothes and provisions and the box with their mother's dress on the pony's back and set out. Neither mentioned their father – Ritva did not tell her sister that she had witnessed the funeral from the shelter of the woodland, nor did Elke tell her that she had caught a flash of Ritva's red scarf amongst the trees.

It was during the long days of trekking through the Finnish forests that Ritva told Elke about the hardships of the asylum, their mother's death, her escape and her original journey north, but she spoke little about Martta and the turmoil in her heart. Elke in turn found the courage to speak about life with Father, the lonely days and devastating nights. It was easier to talk while walking next to each other, and mile by mile they caught up on the lost years. Sunnika carried their belongings and sometimes Elke on her sturdy back, but as the forests thickened and the days grew shorter, it became harder to find fresh grass and one morning at the beginning of October, they awoke to the first frost. Even though Elke and Uncle had told the authorities about Father and why he had put Ritva away, they felt uncomfortable in public and had avoided main roads. But if they wanted to reach Ritva's *siida* before the depths of winter, they would have to take the train to Rovaniemi and travel on from there by sledge. It seemed their only option and, heavy-hearted, they sold Sunnika to a farmer and continued by train. As they arrived in Rovaniemi, the first snow started to fall and when they came across the first reindeer herders near Kittilä, Ritva bought three draught reindeer, a sledge and enough dried meat for their journey. And so they set out westwards, towards Sweden and the *siida*'s winter camp near Nikkaluokta.

The low winter sun cast an otherworldly light on their little group as they sat wrapped in furs and blankets on the sledge, Ritva holding the reins of the reindeer, following the compass, her map and any landmarks she could remember. Hopefully they would reach the *siida* before the sun completely disappeared beneath the horizon in December. Elke adapted quickly to the harsh conditions and despite the biting cold and a three-day blizzard, her spirits were high. She was delighted by the Northern Lights, the tundra and the ever-changing landscape, her former life fading ever further from her consciousness, while Ritva became more nervous the closer they got to the *siida*. It had been months since she had stolen away in the dead of night from those who had shown her so much care and love. Would they forgive her? Often now, her hands gripped the simple necklace Piers had made for her. Would he still be fond of her? And Arvid and Sofia? She longed to be part of the *siida* again, to make herself useful, to feel the comfort of the daily chores and to sit by the fire at night and listen to Sunna's stories. Her heart ached thinking of the old woman – would everyone still be in good health? Had the calf season been good?

Finally, one afternoon in early November, Ritva spotted a group of *lavvus* close to the edge of a forest. Her heart jumped at the sight of the illuminated cones spitting orange sparks from the smoke holes.

'I think that's the *siida*,' she called.

'Oh, it's beautiful,' Elke said. Ritva's stomach fluttered and as if the reindeer pulling their sled could sense the herd in the forest digging for lichen, they raced towards the camp. And then Ritva spotted him: his peat-black hair spilling out from under his cap, he was carrying a bunch of large birch branches towards a tent, dragging his left foot.

'Piers!' Her voice was hoarse from the cold. Her old friend stared at them, then dropped his load and stumbled across the snow towards the sledge, his arms outstretched, mouth cracking into the broadest smile.

'Ritva!'

Seeing him so overjoyed, Ritva's heart filled with warmth. There was no trace of anger or resentment in him, only happiness. She pulled the reins, jumped off the sledge and ran towards him.

'Ritva!' He pulled her close, hugging her tightly. 'God, I missed you so!'

As Ritva stood wrapped in his embrace, all the exhaustion and pain of the past few months dropped away. After a while Piers gently opened his arms and turned towards Elke.

'And you must be Elke. Welcome, welcome.' He threw his arms around them both and walked them towards one of the *lavvus*.

'It's Ritva, she's back!' he called as they approached. Moments later, Arvid shot out of another tent and smothered Ritva with hugs. She buried her face in his hair – she could feel he had grown, but he smelled as good as ever. He slipped something small and cool into her hand.

'You can have it back now,' he whispered. It was Martta's drum hammer.

'Oh thank you, Arvid.' With a pang Ritva thought of the time they had all journeyed together on their raft – Arvid, Greyheart, Martta and her – such a long time ago. Then she spotted Piers unloading the sled, taking their bundles into the tent. She had stolen away in the night without even leaving him a note, but he was welcoming her back with open arms. Perhaps this was where she really belonged.

Soon they were ushered into old Sunna's *lavvu*, which was filling with more and more villagers. Elke tried the bits of North Sami Ritva had taught her during the trek and was met with giggles and smiles. They spent hours sharing news between cups of strong coffee and mouthfuls of reindeer stew while the fire danced wild shadows against the tent cloth.

It was late that night that Ritva finally found the courage to tell everyone that her mother had originally come from the North. As she lifted her mother's tunic from the box, excited murmurs rippled through the *siida*, and everyone threw questions at her.

'How come you didn't know?'

'Was she Sami?'

'Where was she from?'

'What was her name?'

'Oh, put it on, Ritva, please,' Sofia pleaded. As Ritva slipped the tunic over her head, her skin tingled and everyone went silent. Piers was the first to find his voice.

'It's so beautiful!'

Ritva blushed. The dress was similar in style to those worn by the other women, except that there were different patterns around the neck and sleeves.

That night, Ritva lay wide awake, replaying in her mind the moment Piers had run up to her and welcomed her back. Her stomach still fluttered at the thought. Piers had always been a good friend, but now that the past had been dealt with, could there be more between them? She knew he was an honest and good man who would never mistreat her – maybe she could learn to love him after all.

She held his necklace in her hand, her fingers playing with the smooth stone. In his embrace and the warmth of the *siida* she felt secure. Maybe if she married him her long journey would finally end and she could make a new home for herself and Elke.

She fell asleep in the early hours of the morning, but only after securing Piers's necklace firmly around her neck.

PART 4

THE TIME OF THE SACRED DRUM

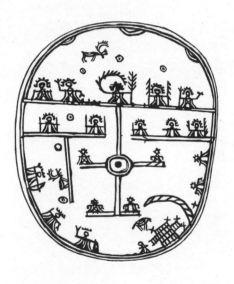

36

Swedish Sápmi, May 1921

Ritva stomped ahead against a fierce spring wind, leading her two pack-reindeer. Her back ached and the straps of her knapsack dug deep into her shoulders. Would she never stop running away? It had all seemed so hopeful . . .

Neither Ritva nor Piers had mentioned his marriage proposal after her return, but in March he had gifted her a silver brooch and two silk scarves and Ritva had happily accepted his new courtship. It had been a promising spring and warm summer; most of the newborn calves had survived and were joyously greeted at the calf marking, and many evenings Piers would whisk Ritva away from the *siida* to sit together in the meadow while he told her stories and taught her *yoiks* about the tundra, even sharing his *luohti*, the unique *yoik* he had been given as a child. They laughed at Ritva's attempts to imitate him and sometimes he would stop mid-song and just look at her. Ritva always blushed – but she had no words for the tangle in her heart. Was this love? The day she had seen Piers again she had felt an excited flutter in her belly, but now, when he looked at her, she almost wanted to hide.

Then one evening in July everything came to a head. They were sitting on the shore of a small lake, chewing strips of dried reindeer meat. Piers lit a fire to deter the swarms of blackflies and mosquitoes and then started to tell Ritva the story of a beautiful woman who had appeared out of nowhere in front of a young herder.

'She simply declared she would be his wife. The whole *siida* warned him that she was one of the *uldas*, an unruly earth spirit, but he ignored them and listened only to his heart.'

'What happened then?' Ritva asked, heart in her throat.

'They got married, had three beautiful children and never suffered any hardship, for whenever they needed it, a silver coin would appear as if by magic in the baby's cradle.'

Piers stared at Ritva, his eyes glistening with an intensity she had never seen in him before. She touched the smooth stone of the necklace he had given her – what would happen now? Suddenly he gripped her shoulders, pulled her close and kissed her on the mouth. Ritva breathed in sharply; she wanted to long to throw herself into his arms and kiss him back, but nothing stirred, only numbness, no pleasure or repulsion. It was in this moment she realised she couldn't go on like this.

'I do . . . want to marry you, Piers, but I can't.'

'But why, Ritva? Don't you like me?'

'Of course I like you, Piers, I couldn't wish for a better friend.'

'But I love you, Ritva. I've loved you ever since you arrived in our *siida*.'

He still held her shoulders and she could smell his strong sweat. She sat rigid, feeling his right hand wander down her back, then up to her neck.

'Please don't do that, Piers.'

'But why? Please, Ritva, I'd do anything for you. You're the most beautiful girl in the *siida*.'

Ritva felt faint. She wanted to get away, but how could she let him down so badly? At that moment Piers kissed her again. His stubbly chin scratched against her skin, his chapped lips pressing on her mouth. She froze and an image flashed before her – Martta kissing her, eyes wide with fear and what she now understood was desire. Martta's kiss had come without warning too and yes, she had pushed her away, yet something about that kiss had felt so different, had stirred her to the core. But not this. She wriggled out of Piers's arms.

'I can't do this, Piers.'

'Please, Ritva, don't run away! I love you.'

But she had stumbled away without another word.

That night as she lay under her sleeping furs, she had been plagued by doubt; she had survived the asylum, braced the cruel elements and walked on wounded feet further than the reindeer migrated each year, yet she could not bring herself to marry the kindest man she had ever known. What was wrong with her? With Piers she could have belonged here once and for all, but instead she had broken his heart. She had untied his necklace and placed it at the bottom of her belongings – she had no right to wear it any longer, nor did she deserve a place in the *siida*.

Trudging in front of her pack-reindeer now, Ritva wept as she recalled that fateful day. They had kept their distance from each other through the rest of the summer and as autumn and then winter drew on, her spirit had darkened and for weeks she had stayed in her sleeping blankets, only venturing out of the *lavvu* when the *siida* followed the reindeer. Elke had tried to encourage her sister to join the life of the *siida*, but even she could not fully comprehend the heaviness that weighed on Ritva's heart.

Finally, in April, Ritva's heart started to lift. Maybe it was the promise of longer days or of the calf marking to come, but one day Ritva peeled herself from her grubby blankets and walked to the river to wash her hair. It was time that things changed, and they would.

Yet, as the snow melted, Ritva had grown restless once more and one morning she awoke, shaken by a dream. She had been back at the asylum and Martta was telling her the story of Sealskin. 'After seven years, the seal woman's skin had started to crack and she nearly went blind . . .' Ritva remembered the tale vividly and even in the dream she had felt Martta's deep voice resounding in her heart. Would her own soul dry up like the Sealwoman's skin? Everyone in the *siida* had always tried to make her feel welcome, even after she had rejected Piers, yet nothing had ever filled the gap that Martta had left behind. Ritva's hands had sought the drum hammer she always carried in her pocket. Curling her fingers around it, memories had come flooding back: the first time she had seen Martta in the garden of the asylum; Martta's embrace as they leaned against the west wing wall; how comforted she had felt by her the first night they huddled together in the earth den under their coffin boat; the day they had seen the first reindeer . . . Maybe their bond had always been more than just companionship. And the way she still ached for Martta – was this love? Was this what the girls teased each other about in the *siida*? Except that when they talked about love it was that of a woman for a man – she had never heard anyone talk about a woman loving another woman, except in whispered rumours. With a stab she realised that although Martta had never talked to her of love, she had shown it in hundreds of small ways: always offering Ritva more food, protecting her from the worst of the cold or rain, keeping her warm when she shivered, holding her gaze always that bit longer . . . And then Martta's desperate kiss – how could she not have understood? Had Martta died alone with Greyheart out in the wilderness that first winter or had she made it to Finland and found her childhood *siida*?

It was that night that Ritva decided she must go to look for her mother's *siida* in Finland. And yes, maybe on the way she would ask if anyone had heard of a woman with broad shoulders travelling alone with a large, grey dog . . .

In the morning she had found Sebastian's map and placed her finger on the red dot: Karesuvanto – the area where Uncle thought Mother's *siida* might have been situated. She had rushed to find Elke. Her sister had taken quickly to the Sami life; as unmarried women, she and Ritva had been invited to join the young herders and Elke spent most of her days with Arvid and the other herders following the reindeer to the grazing pastures and keeping the herd together.

'I want to find Mother's *siida*, Elke. It's not that far away, just two days to the north-east and then across into Finland, which would take another good week, I think, maybe a little more.'

Elke looked as if she had been slapped.

'You want to leave?'

'I need to find out more about Mother, see where she grew up. Maybe we even have relatives there! Please come with me.'

Elke shook her head.

'This is my home now, Ritva. These people have taken us in and shown us more than kindness. And . . .'

'What is it, Elke?'

'Well, I'm getting on so well with Arvid.' She blushed.

Arvid had taught Elke everything he had learned about the herding life since joining the *siida* and he and Elke had become almost inseparable.

'He's so sweet underneath that tough face he shows to the other herders. I think he really is stealing my heart.'

Arvid had been a frightened boy when Ritva had first met him with Martta, but now he was growing into a confident young man. It would be a gift to see Elke with him. And so, a few days later, Ritva had packed kettle, stewing pot, sleeping furs and the box containing Mother's headdress and said her goodbyes, promising to send Elke a message if she found their mother's *siida*.

Ritva had been walking for long hours each day, heading east across the tundra, and though she checked her compass frequently, she felt lost as if cast adrift at sea. She was so tired – tired of running away, of her own company, of not knowing where she belonged. What if she couldn't find the *siida*, or what if no one remembered her mother? Suddenly a sharp pain ripped Ritva from her daydream – her foot had caught on a root, twisting her ankle. She looked up – the fells were still flecked with snow, leaving the hills as if painted with strange white patterns. Often she saw figures in the snow: an angel, a horse, a dancing girl, but today they were only patchy streaks to her.

In the evening her ankle started to swell and that night she had a curious dream. A young woman in a Sami dress appeared out of nowhere, took her hand and silently guided her to a brook; she picked a few leaves that were growing close to the water and placed them around Ritva's ankle. As Ritva looked into the girl's green eyes, something stirred in her – she knew this young woman, but from where? Then, as suddenly as she had appeared, the girl vanished.

The next morning when Ritva was washing herself at a nearby stream, she spotted some plants that looked exactly like those in her dream. Excited, she picked a handful and bound them around her ankle; by midday the swelling had reduced and she could walk without too much pain. Was she still being guided after all?

One week later she spotted the first *lavvus* in Finnish Sápmi. Her heart beat hard as she observed the comings and goings of the village from afar. Would these people know anything about her mother? As she approached the first tents, two black dogs ran up to her barking, and an old man with piercing blue eyes, bent sideways like a gnarled birch, greeted her with a warm handshake. After she had told him about her mission, she made her way from tent to tent, asking everyone whether they recognised her grandmother from the photograph. Her heart sank as one after another pored over the picture and shook their head. Finally, in the last *lavvu*, an old woman with skin as wrinkled as the mountain ravines bent over the photograph for a long time.

'Lara you say your mother was called?' She sucked on a small silver pipe. 'I think your grandmother was Sunna. She was married to Niels and had two girls and a boy. Lara was the eldest. Sunna was from the area near Kilpisjärvi, right next to the Norwegian border. It's difficult to keep the reindeer from straying into Norway or Sweden up there and there were always problems.'

Ritva's heart jumped – her mother had siblings? Were they still alive? She unfolded her crumpled map; Kilpisjärvi lay two days north.

'I remember now,' the old woman continued. 'There was a clergyman up there for a while and then one day Lara was gone – just like that. Broke her mother's heart.'

Ritva shivered – the pastor, her father . . .

'What about the other siblings?' Ritva whispered.

'The boy died of typhoid when he was only nineteen, but Sara should still be alive.'

She might have a living relative, an aunt! Dare she hope . . .?

'Thank you so much,' Ritva said and hugged the old woman.

'You're welcome. Off you go now, and good luck.'

Ritva left the next morning and four days later reached the *siida* near Kilpisjärvi. As she approached the first *lavvu*, a middle-aged woman wearing a blue tunic stepped out of the tent, knives and an axe tucked into her colourful belt. Ritva froze as their eyes locked: the woman was the spitting image of her mother, only older. Ritva's stomach fluttered. The woman said nothing.

'Are you Sara?' Ritva managed to say, her voice hoarse.

'Yes, I am. And who are you?' She looked at Ritva and frowned.

'I am Ritva, Lara's daughter . . . your sister's daughter.'

All colour drained from the woman's face. Then she bolted towards Ritva and hugged her. Ritva sobbed as they stood in a tight embrace; her aunt felt and even smelled like her mother.

After a long while she let go.

'Please, Sara, you must tell me all about Mother, I've so many questions . . .'

'Yes, all in good time, dear, all in good time, but first we must eat. And before that, let me introduce you to Lilja.'

When Sara led Ritva into the *lavvu*, her daughter was baking bread over the fire; the two young women stared at each other – Lilja had the same large eyes and chestnut-coloured hair as Ritva. Suddenly a baby cried.

'I think she wants to greet you,' Lilja said and scooped the child up out of the cradle, holding it towards Ritva so that she could see the baby's round face.

'This is Marit, my youngest. My boy Jacob is seven; he's out with his father, my husband, Olaf.'

That evening, the whole *siida* gathered in Sara's *lavvu*, curious to see lost Lara's daughter. And as if an iron band around her heart had suddenly burst, Ritva was filled with such deep love for these people that it took her breath away. When she looked at Sara's and Lilja's dresses in the firelight, her skin prickled – the patterns and colours on the necks and sleeves of their tunics matched her own completely. This was where her mother's dress had come from, where Mother had been born and spent her childhood. This was where she belonged.

37

Although she missed Elke, Arvid and Sofia, Ritva quickly settled into the new *siida*, spending many rainy days exchanging stories around the fire, absorbing everything Sara could tell her about her mother.

'Lara used to spend all her time with the reindeer.' Sara spoke slowly and with a deep voice. 'Ever since she was a little girl, she was always happiest when the *siida* was on migration with the reindeer. She talked to them, even had her favourites. You remind me so much of her when we were young, you have that same restless spirit.' She smiled and stroked Ritva's cheek. Ritva closed her eyes, feeling her aunt's warm hand; how long it had been since Mother had stroked her like that?

'I adored my big beautiful sister. Lara was so clever and knew a great deal about healing plants. It's a mystery where she got it from, our own mother knew little about herbs.'

A shiver rushed down Ritva's back – the girl in her dream had looked just like Mother, only younger.

'Maybe she got it from her dreams,' Sara continued. 'She had the most vivid imagination. I was quite frightened sometimes when she told me about them, they were so full of strange things: talking bears, journeys to the moon or the sun . . .'

Ritva caught her breath; they sounded so similar to her own visions.

'Our mother did not want to hear about Lara's dreams, and when Pastor Larson arrived – your father – he made a big thing of it. He wanted to see Lara for extra bible study lessons three times a week to cure her of her dreams. He even followed us on migrations. By the time Larson left for the South four years later, Lara had changed so much.' Sara's voice hardened. 'She was only sixteen but she was so serious and hardly ever smiled, and when Larson asked Mother for Lara's hand, both Mother and Lara agreed. I never understood how she could just leave us like that. I never saw her again . . .'

Sara pressed her fist over her mouth as the tears welled up. Ritva hugged her aunt and that night she told her all about Fredo and Elke, the fateful day the doctor had taken their mother away, Ritva's escape from the asylum and the small graveyard behind the wooden church. Sara listened without interrupting. After a while she wrapped her arms around Ritva.

'Please know that you and Elke will always have a place here with us.'

'Thank you, Sara, thank you so much.'

'And Arvid too, of course.'

Enveloped by her aunt's soft embrace, Ritva relaxed – could it be that she had finally found a place where she could settle? If only Elke had come with her. She ached to share all this with her sister. The next day Ritva wrote a letter and handed it to a young Sami man who was making his way south-west to Kiruna and who promised to deliver it to Elke.

Sara shared the herding with her husband, Jan. The week Ritva arrived, he and Olaf were out with the herd. When they found Ritva in their *lavvu* a week later, they looked puzzled, but when Sara and Lilja shared the news about their new relative, they welcomed her with open arms.

Weeks passed and Ritva accompanied Sara and the *siida* on the summer migration into the mountains. While baby Marit slept secured to the side of the pack-reindeer and little Jacob ran back and forth between his father and their little group, Ritva and Lilja chatted. Lilja turned out to be only a year older than

Ritva. Quick-footed and confident around the reindeer, she loved making up stories just as Ritva did and they delighted in each other's company.

As the days grew longer, the midnight sun cast long eerie shadows over the ground and the herders worked around the clock to round up the reindeer that had scattered over a large area, ready for the calf marking. Ritva remembered her first calf marking well, the day she had met Sofia. But nothing had prepared her for the magnificence of this *siida*'s herd: not hundreds but thousands of reindeer galloped counterclockwise around the corral, pounding the ground with their broad hooves, white tail stubs in the air. Ritva's heart thumped like the thundering of the herd – what power and beauty!

When she heard their tendons clicking, Ritva remembered Martta telling her about the sound, the first time they had seen a herd.

By now, all the male herders and many of the women and older children had gathered in the corral, lassos slung over their shoulders. Ritva watched as Sara scanned the herd for her animals, recognising them from the markings in their ears. Through spotting the mothers, she would be able to identify which calves were also hers. Suddenly Sara's lasso swished through the air and looped around a calf's neck. With a tug she wrestled it down, straddled it and held it firmly to the ground; then she pulled a small knife from her belt, cut a pattern into its ear and released it. The calf clambered back onto its legs and ran bleating after its mother. The whole procedure had taken Sara just a minute. Sara laughed, her cheeks glowing. Ritva could feel her aunt's joy and excitement – the cows were healthy and the calves had survived the perils of spring, their only task now was to gain as much muscle and fat as possible before the winter.

As Ritva's eyes followed the herd, she suddenly had the strange sensation of losing herself amongst the animals, becoming, just for a moment, completely at one with their movement, their sound and smell, their wild magnificence. She felt a pressure just behind her breastbone and then she was back, observing the herd, a sea of grey rushing past. Her heart was wide open, aching, longing to be with these animals, to move amongst them, and live with them.

A few moments later the fence in the corral was opened and the herd pounded away into the mountains.

For weeks Ritva buried her secret desire deep inside. How could she even think she'd be able to learn all the skills required of a herder? She could not even distinguish one reindeer from another by its markings – all she had seen in the corral was a mass of grey galloping past. And there were so many other practical things she needed to master: she was still struggling to spin fine sinew thread, could not stand the smell of reindeer blood and even the thought of having to clean out a reindeer carcass during the autumn slaughter made her nauseous. And yet, she could not stop thinking about the reindeer running free in the mountains and the special connection the herders had with them. She had observed their close bond ever since she first found the Sami: the elation and joy during the spring markings and the sombre faces when the day of the autumn slaughter came. The lives of the Sami and their reindeer were utterly intertwined: when the summers were mild and the calves could gorge on the new grass of the pastures, the herders were happy; but when spring was late and icy, and the reindeer suffered, the people suffered too. In harsh winters when the snow crust was too hard for the reindeer to dig for the lichen, they could only survive if the herders fed them.

'The reindeer support and feed us,' Sara told Ritva one day. 'But we need to feed and help them too. That's how it has always been.'

Ritva loved listening to Sara talking about the reindeer, and one evening when she caught her alone in the *lavvu*, she could no longer hold back.

'Aunt Sara, I want to learn everything about the herding life.'

Sara smiled, cutting a piece of smoked reindeer meat into small strips.

'But dear, you're helping us already and that's wonderful. You've learned how to sew boots and bake our bread, prepare stew and collect shoe grass. And soon,' she winked at her, 'you might meet someone special and want to start a family.' Sara's voice became serious. 'You're not too old, Ritva, but it's important you give it some thought.'

Ritva calculated that Lilja had married when she was only sixteen, not an unusual age to marry amongst the Sami. It was the same age that Ritva had been when she was taken off to the asylum. Suddenly she felt cold.

'I'm not sure I even want to marry. In any case I haven't found anyone.' She took a deep breath. 'Sara, I want to become a herder like you. If I could wish for just one thing, it would be that.'

Sara frowned and looked at her for a long time.

'It's a hard and precarious life, Ritva. In a bad winter people sometimes lose nearly their whole herd. And you need a lot of stamina being out there in all weathers with the reindeer, the conditions can be cruel and your body hurts most of the time – look at my hands, ruined from all the rough work.'

Ritva loved her aunt's hands – yes, they were calloused, but they were also strong and warm. They could cut markings in reindeer ears and yet knew such tenderness.

'Besides, there are very few women who are herders after they are married. It's frowned upon for a married woman to be out herding with the men.'

'But you are a herder! You look after the reindeer together with Jan.'

'Yes, but believe me, not everybody likes it.'

'It would mean so much to me if you taught me. God knows why my mother left the herding life to follow my father. Maybe this is her blood stirring in me, but when I saw the reindeer in the corral, it touched me so deeply . . .'

'You've no idea what you're letting yourself in for, Ritva. It's hard for us and we grew up here, knowing only this life – for you it's all new.'

Ritva's heart plummeted.

'Is it because my father was a Finn, not a Sami? Is that why you think I could never be like you?'

'Ritva, my darling, I only want you to have an easier life. After your mother left, I just wanted to be with the reindeer and swore never to marry, but then Jan came along, and of course I did, and I am glad. And when Lilja found Olaf and had Jacob and now Marit, she was happy not to be out in the cold all the time.'

The thought of courtship and marriage felt more alien to Ritva than ever, but she said nothing.

'They steal your heart, Ritva, the reindeer.' Sara looked into the fire for a while.

'Let's wait until September and the autumn slaughter have passed, and when the first snow comes we'll talk about this again.'

'Thank you, Sara.' Ritva did not tell her that it was too late for caution – the reindeer had already stolen her heart.

38

Ritva survived the autumn slaughter, even gutted a carcass and helped scrape the hide clean. Although the smell of the blood still made her feel ill and it was difficult to see the magnificent large-antlered bulls being killed, she had only respect for the herders, who worked with such efficiency: a stab to the neck right behind the head to sever the spine followed by a single stab to the heart. But still, even if death came quickly to the animals and nothing was wasted, it was a day when the sadness was palpable through-out the *siida*.

Then, a few weeks later, at the end of September, the rutting season began.

'We leave them to it and get out of their way,' Sara explained, 'it gives us time to fish and hunt and prepare for the winter.'

Most days Ritva could hear the rutting calls of the bulls across the tundra, wild and eerie, and soon the *luovvi* storehouse was filled with fish from the lakes, ptarmigan, rabbit and hare. Neither Ritva nor Sara mentioned their earlier conversation, but often Ritva felt her aunt's watchful eyes on her. Then, in the second week of October, the first snow fell; Ritva's heart beat hard in contrast to the flakes that settled gently on the ground. Would they speak today? That evening, Sara took her to one side.

'So tell me, Ritva, how do you feel about everything now?'

'I still want to learn from you, Sara. I really *do* want to be a herder.' Ritva lowered her eyes and looked at the floor. 'If you think I'm capable.'

'Well, it's really not up to me. When this life calls you, you need to follow the call, that much I know. And I can feel the herding life stirring in you.' She paused for a moment. 'Maybe you are simply continuing where your mother left off.'

'So you'll teach me?' Ritva said and looked into Sara's large green eyes.

'Yes, Ritva, and I would be happy to.'

'Thank you, Aunt Sara!' She hugged her. 'I won't disappoint you – at least, I'll try my very best not to!'

'Good. Now, let's cut some meat for the stew.'

Ritva was overjoyed, and in the next few weeks she helped Sara and Jan divide the herd into smaller groups for the migration to the winter grounds. All the reindeer that belonged to the *siida* were gathered in one large herd and were only separated out for the spring marking and in winter. Ritva still could not distinguish the reindeer by their ear markings, but she was swift on her feet and managed to separate the animals that Sara pointed out to her. But when two weeks later the winter slaughter of the calves began, it took every ounce of courage Ritva possessed to stop her from running away. Although she knew that calf hide was invaluable for making extra warm clothes for the children and only some of the calves were killed, she could not watch and wished she could close her ears to the animals' cries. And yet there was never any heartlessness involved, only necessity, and Ritva noted every piece of advice and teaching that Sara gave her.

Ritva quickly grew restless when she stayed too long in the *lavvu* and volunteered for any outdoor chores; she was happiest when the *siida* migrated and she could stay close to the herd. Although it was still early days, Ritva often dreamt about having her own herd and one night she woke with a pounding heart – hadn't Sebastian promised to send money to a friend in Rovaniemi once he had sold the house? She searched for the note with the address Elke had given her. She could use the money to buy some reindeer and start her own herd.

And so, after lengthy talks with Sara and Jan, Ritva set out in February with a small group, heading by ski and sledge for the large winter market in Rovaniemi, where each year members of the *siida* would sell furs and handicrafts. She found the home of her uncle's friend. He handed her a thick envelope – it contained more money than she could ever have imagined, together with a letter from Sebastian. Uncle had managed to sell the house for an excellent sum, had bought himself a small flock of sheep and then sent the rest for her to share with Elke. Elated, Ritva returned to Sara and after a few days' rest, she set out to see Elke, unaware that her happiness would soon be tempered by a terrible darkness that had touched her old *siida*.

When Ritva reached the camp near Jukkasjärvi, everyone greeted her with friendly embraces, but she sensed instantly that a shadow had fallen over the *siida*. Elke and Arvid were quick to welcome her, but Elke looked pained. When Ritva had filled everyone in with the news about finding her aunt, she turned to her sister.

'What is it, Elke? Something has happened, I can feel it.'

Elke's eyes filled with tears.

'It's Sofia, and a few of the other women . . .' Elke bit her lip.

'What do you mean?'

'One day a town-dweller from the South arrived and asked if he could take photographs of the families with their reindeer outside their *lavvus*. We didn't think much of it but then he started to photograph only the women. How could anyone have known that those pictures were going to be sent to Uppsala to "prove" that the Swedes are a superior race to the Sami?' Elke's voice was hard now. 'A month later two men showed up and promised five of the unmarried women a lot of money if they would go to Uppsala to an institute that researched the life of the Sami – or that's what they said.'

'Oh God, what happened?'

'They butchered them, Ritva! They told them nothing and then sterilised them. The women were like ghosts when they returned home, their hearts and bodies broken. Why would they do something like this?' Elke dried her tears, then she took Ritva's hand and laid it on her belly.

'I haven't told anyone else yet, only Arvid knows. Feel!' Ritva felt nothing but a very small bump.

'I'm expecting, Ritva. Arvid and I are going to have a baby.'

'But this is wonderful, Elke, please don't feel bad! Sofia wouldn't want you to, nor would the other women, I'm sure.' Warmth flooded Ritva – her little sister was going to have a baby!

'Wouldn't you like to come and meet our Aunt Sara? We could all live together there and share a big herd between us.'

Elke slowly shook her head.

'And leave these good people who've shown us so much kindness? I can't do that. But I would like to meet Sara one day and share some of Sebastian's money with Sofia.'

Ritva felt ashamed that she had not thought of this herself.

'And, I know these are such sad times but . . . we're thinking of getting married in June,' Elke added.

'Oh Elke, I'm so happy for you! I would love to be there.'

The next day Ritva asked Sofia to take a walk with her. Alone in the forest, Sofia opened up and told Ritva what had happened in Uppsala.

'You could come and stay with me and my Aunt Sara,' Ritva said, placing her hand on Sofia's arm. 'No one will know there.'

Sofia shook her head. 'I belong here, Ritva, and besides, Elke has asked me to help her when the baby is born. I've said yes.'

'She told you?'

'Yes, just this morning, and why shouldn't she?' For a moment Sofia's face clouded over, but then she gave a small smile.

'It still hurts a lot, but maybe being with Elke and Arvid will soothe my soul. Time will tell.' Ritva knew that no words could comfort her friend – all she could do was listen and offer her support.

Ritva sent word to her aunt, then made herself useful until

Elke's and Arvid's wedding on a glorious midsummer day in June 1922. The whole *siida* celebrated for three days and nights under the midnight sun and everyone complimented the beautiful bride. Arvid beamed with joy all through the celebrations – he had not stopped smiling since the day Elke agreed to marry him.

When Ritva placed their mother's beautiful headdress on Elke's long hair, a tumble of feelings surged through her: pride at her mother's heritage, sadness that Mother had had to hide this beautiful object under the bed as though she was ashamed, and then, loss – if only Mother could have been here with them. Ritva imagined Mother's hands placing the headdress on Elke like a blessing, and suddenly she sensed her presence next to her like a tingling warmth, a tender caress on the cheek. A wave of happiness rushed through her. All that day she felt her mother's spirit close by and prayed that her soul would be free now, cut loose once and for all from the anguish of the asylum.

Later that afternoon, Ritva stole away to a nearby brook. Suddenly she heard a rustling and when she looked up, Piers was standing in front of her, flushed and out of breath. They had barely spoken since her return and had kept their distance most of the wedding day. Now he held out a little box, carved from antler, a shy smile on his face.

'It might look like an unusual gift, but this has been in my family for a long time.'

'Another gift? But why, Piers? I've brought you only misery!'

'Just take it, please!'

Ritva opened the lid and frowned at the strangely shaped object.

'I heard you are going to join the herding life. I think this will help you. It's a wolf's tooth; you need to hide it somewhere close to the reindeer and it will protect you and your animals. My grandfather told me that this tooth reminds the greylegs of an ancient agreement: they are allowed to take from the herd what they need to survive, but not a single reindeer more. People used to laugh at him, but even in bad winters my family never lost more than a few reindeer to the wolves.'

He looked proud.

'Thank you, Piers. Really, thank you!'

'I wish you well, Ritva. I think you'll make an excellent herder.'

Ritva blushed. That Piers had gifted her something so special despite all that had happened between them – and that he trusted she would be a good herder – meant more than she could say and for a moment she felt a stab of loss. She tucked the small box under her tunic and they parted after a brief embrace.

Ritva ached as she said her goodbyes two weeks later. A part of her wanted to stay with Elke and Arvid and the people who had taken her in, but now that she had found Sara and her mother's *siida*, she felt a strong pull to return. More than anything she yearned to earn her aunt's respect and become a good herder.

39

It wasn't until the next spring during the calf-marking season that Ritva bought a small herd. The reindeer still bore the earmarks of the previous owner and Sara helped Ritva alter them with a small additional cut.

'This will be your marking now,' Sara said, pointing at the ear with the unique pattern.

Ritva thought she could hear pride in her aunt's voice. Life was taking her in a direction she could never have imagined and if she had now tied herself closer to the *siida* by acquiring her own animals, this tie was one of love and a growing sense of belonging.

When Sara had finished marking her own calves, she separated a white reindeer cow and its calf from the herd – they were both *gabba*, completely white.

'I want these to be yours, Ritva. Our ancestors used to say that white reindeer are descendants of the cattle of the earth spirits. In any case, I hope they bring you good fortune.'

Ritva managed to croak a 'thank you'. Yet, as she watched the larger herd gallop around the corral, she was sorely reminded of just how much there was still to learn: discerning a healthy reindeer from one suffering from parasites or anaemia; how to tell whether it was carrying a calf or how old it was; how to milk the cows and make reindeer cheese – never mind how to catch a calf with a lasso and mark it . . . And there were so many labels for the reindeer, distinguishing them by colour, sex and age, how strong they were, even by the shape of their antlers.

'This one's a *saggi*,' Sara said, pointing at a reindeer with only a few antler branches. 'And this we call a *barfi*, one with many branches; but because its skin is peeling from the antlers, it's a *calocoarvi*.' Ritva's head was spinning.

'Don't worry, Ritva, you don't have to learn everything at once.' Sara said and laughed. That afternoon as they sat all together in the *lavvu*, filling up on stew and coffee, Sara put her hand on Ritva's shoulder.

'Listen, Ritva, it'll get easier, but reindeer herding is no game – it takes everything you've got and then some more. But you've done well today.'

'Thank you, Sara. And thank you again for the beautiful *gabba* . . .'

'You're very welcome.' Sara smiled and tossed a bone to the dog. 'And you should always give the dog the marrow of one jawbone; that way you'll be sure he'll help you if you're ever in danger. That's what the ancients used to say.'

'Do you really have to teach Ritva those old tales?' Lilja said as she sipped her coffee. 'Who still believes in them anyway?'

Sara said nothing, but Ritva smiled, remembering the wolf's tooth she carried under her tunic that Piers had given her.

In late November when the herd was grazing closer to their camp, Ritva hid the tooth in a rock cleft nearby, and although on many nights throughout the icy winter they could hear the wolves howling nearby, Ritva only lost two of her reindeer: a yearling and an older reindeer that had injured its leg and always limped behind the others. Everyone worked hard to keep the greylegs away, but some of the herders lost four or five animals. Whether it was good fortune or the wolf's tooth that had protected her animals, Ritva quietly thanked Piers.

Ritva treasured being under the wide skies and how the most magnificent landscapes now formed the backdrop to her life – the tundra and the snow-covered peaks, the fells and the ever-changing light that lent the landscape its magic: rich and golden in the summer; the Northern Lights sweeping across the night skies with their silent spectacle; the first light in spring, setting the snow ablaze with bright orange . . . And yet, being outdoors in all weathers and on her feet for days also challenged Ritva's every strength. Huddling with the other herders around a small fire, she put on a brave face, but on many nights, lying on a reindeer fur on the icy ground, she barely slept. She felt as if the very marrow in her bones was freezing and even when the temperature began to rise, the following weeks of rain and wild spring weather rattled her body and spirit. Despite wearing clothes made from sturdy reindeer hide, as all the other herders did, Ritva felt the damp creeping in – it lay heavy on her lungs and her limbs continually ached with a dull pain. Never had she felt such relief as when, after days outdoors, she returned to Sara's *lavvu* and warmed herself by the fire. Seeing Lilja's and the children's eager faces as they pressed her for news about the herd filled her with pride and she savoured telling them every detail of what had occurred: the day she woke to find that the herd had disappeared in the fog and it took three days to locate the animals again; how Sculfi, their largest herd dog, had chased away a wolf; and how Ritva had dressed the leg of an injured reindeer with a bunch of herbs and its leg had healed within a few days.

Sara said nothing, but listened with sparkling eyes and a big smile.

In early spring the herders followed the reindeer from the forests to the low mountains where the calves were born in the same calving grounds each year.

'The cows are clever and choose the southern slopes where the first spring flowers appear,' Jan told Ritva one morning. 'But it's a sensitive time and we must be very careful not to disturb them – any intrusion and the cow might abandon her new calf.' Each season brought its own dangers, Ritva thought. Indeed the more she learned, the more miraculous it seemed that they ever succeeded in keeping a thriving, growing herd.

*

In early June Ritva caught flu and was still recovering in Sara's *lavvu* when the herders brought the reindeer down from the mountains for the spring marking.

'The herd is here!' Lilja's head burst through the entrance flap. 'Come quick, here.' She dropped a curled-up lasso next to Ritva and disappeared. Ritva, though still unsteady on her legs, scrambled up and put on her coat – the new calves were here! Heart in her throat, she rushed to the corral – a few of her cows had been pregnant, but would the calves have made it through the cold spring? The rest of the herders were with the herd, lassos ready. Ritva tried to make out her reindeer, but, as in years past, all she could see was a blur of grey. Tears stung her eyes – would she ever be able to identify her own animals?

'There, look!' Sara's voice startled her. She was pointing to a white reindeer with a brown, white-flanked calf by its side.

'Look at the *gabba*'s ear. Can you see the marking?'

Ritva strained to make out the marks as the cow trotted past: two cuts and a half-circle – it was hers!

Sara grinned. 'Yes, it's yours! Let's go and get the little one.'

During the winter Ritva had practised throwing a lasso again and again over a pair of antlers stuck in the snow, just like the children did; now she ran next to the *gabba* and the calf and let her lasso fly – it missed, whipping close to the calf's head, but when the herd came round again, she hit her mark and the lasso caught around its neck. She pulled the calf to its knees, straddled it and held its head still, then pulled out her knife and swiftly cut the marks into its ear. She touched its soft white flank and marvelled at its beautiful eyes, framed by long, black lashes; then she let it go. The calf bucked then ran off after the *gabba*.

Happiness overwhelmed her – Sara's gift had given her her first calf! And the moment she had cut the calf's ear, she had felt such closeness to the animal, a curious intimacy, a bond, as if some promise had been made.

'Well done!' Lilja shouted. She had observed everything and her face shone.

Everyone worked in the corral for the rest of the day and with Sara's help Ritva managed to mark all four of her new calves. That evening as the family gathered in the *lavvu*, Ritva felt more content than she ever remembered being and everyone seemed to look at her differently, especially Olaf and Jan, who urged her to eat an extra portion of the stew.

Ritva had already received the joyful message of Elke's son's birth in March, but it was only two weeks after the calf marking that she finally got to meet her little nephew.

'Visitors for you!' Lilja's son Jacob spluttered, then collapsed in a heap. He had volunteered to fetch Ritva who was out with the herd, several hours away from the *siida*. Ritva rushed back and when she couldn't see Elke outside, she dived into Sara's *lavvu*. Elke sat, red-cheeked and plumper than Ritva remembered, drinking coffee and chatting with their aunt while nursing the baby. Arvid and Sofia were by her side. It was Sofia who jumped up first, hugging Ritva. After much laughter and many embraces, Ritva held baby Sammuel for the first time; he was light, yet as precious as gold, Ritva thought. She kissed the top of his tiny head and the soft plume of his light brown hair, revelling in his smell – a scent so unique and special, of newness and milk and home, more delicious than fresh bread. He was very quiet and gazed at her from large blue eyes, then broke into a gurgling laugh. Ritva's eyes brimmed with tears – he looked and smelled so much like Fredo! She kissed him again, then handed him back to Elke and went in search of some silver coins.

'So that the *uldas* won't come and change you for one of theirs,' she said, placing the coins inside his cradle, a custom she had often observed amongst the Sami. Although she was secretly fond of the earth spirits, she certainly did not want little Sammuel to disappear.

Ritva made the most of her time with them all and the two sisters promised to see each other as often as they could.

*

Over the next few seasons Ritva learned more than she had ever thought possible. The following spring Ritva began to recognise the different combinations of colour, fur and antlers of her animals; she was less squeamish during the autumn slaughter and even enjoyed the blood pancakes that Sara showed her how to make from fresh reindeer blood, flour and salt. As she worked with the herders through rain and storms, mild summer nights and blizzards, Ritva learned to read the reindeer's moods, to recognise signs of comfort or distress and even to see changes in the weather before they manifested. And still there was always more to learn.

'You must be as quick as lightning around the herd,' Sara said. 'When a predator is near, the reindeer sense it – you can see it in the twitching of their ears, their nostrils, their eyes, their whole body.' And there were many enemies: lynxes, eagles and of course greylegs. On many winter nights Ritva went out on skis with the other herders, shouting until her voice was hoarse to keep them away from the herd. But despite the threat they posed, on such nights her thoughts often wandered to Greyheart, wondering what had happened to the companion who had put so much trust in her.

All through her apprenticeship Sara supported Ritva's choice to become a herder, but she remained adamant that Ritva should also find a husband. Whenever the conversation turned in that direction Ritva's heart sank – by now many of the young men in the *siida* had tried to court her, but as much as she enjoyed their companionship, she never felt moved to take it any further. Something was always missing – whether it was something in herself or in the men she could not say, but their advances did not stir her heart. After a while she stopped accepting such advances, and when one evening Lilja started to nag her again about the importance of children, Ritva snapped at her.

'Look, I just don't think I'm very motherly. And besides, I really wouldn't know who I would marry.'

'Don't be silly, Ritva, there are plenty of young men who would be happy to be your husband. But you're not getting younger. It's what we're meant to do.' Lilja was nursing her third baby, a girl called Jaana. 'Wouldn't you like to be someone's wife and bring such cherished sweetness into the world?'

Ritva shook her head. 'I don't know, Lilja. I don't think so.'

She adored Lilja's children and whenever Elke and Arvid visited with Sammuel, Ritva was besotted for days, but she rarely pined for children of her own and only sometimes at night did her childlessness suddenly sting her. The feeling quickly passed, however, and despite the hardships of the herding life, Ritva relished not being bound to anyone and the freedom she felt under the open sky. Maybe it was her wild soul, the soulskin she was slowly reclaiming. For the first time in her life she had found contentment and a quiet peace within herself.

Eventually Sara and Lilja stopped nagging her about marriage and on the dark winter days in the *lavvu*, Sara taught Ritva the *yoiks* of her family. The rhythmic melodies rose and fell, simple words strung together like poems, touching Ritva deeply. As Sara sang, Ritva could see the flight of the rough-legged buzzard, feel the rivers break open after the grip of winter, the tent cloth fluttering in the spring breeze. Yet she couldn't listen to Sara's deep, resonant voice without thinking of Martta. Martta humming songs on their journey, *yoiking* on a boulder as she looked out for the reindeer. Ritva tried hard to forget Martta, but with each month and year that passed, instead of Martta's memory fading, it stayed crisp and clear in her mind. Often in the midst of mending clothes, braiding shoe grass or gathering firewood, a memory would jump at her, sudden as a rabbit crossing her path, as vivid as if it had occurred only yesterday; and every spring as she watched the migration of the geese, Ritva's heart ached for her lost companion – a wound opening in the same place each year, never healing.

Ritva lived year after year with her herd and the *siida*. Some years the herd thrived and grew; in others, the spring arrived so late that many of the calves froze to death and the reindeer hungered or died for lack of lichen. Then it was quiet in the tents, herders mourning their lost reindeer for weeks. Their daily routine followed the seasons and Ritva could hardly imagine how once she had known only four. Now the eight seasons of the herding life and the migrations had become the rhythm of her own. Months of winter darkness gave way to an exuberant spring, melting the ice into thousands of roaring streams before a short brilliant summer burst forth, allowing the herd to gorge on the fat grass of the summer pastures. September brought rich autumn colours, glistening golds and reds, before, once again, snow covered the tundra and the sun disappeared beneath the horizon.

And so one year rolled into another; the *siida* following the path of the reindeer just as their ancestors had done for millennia, undisturbed by the currents of history, until a brutal war that had broken out in Europe began to stretch its bloody claws towards even the furthest corners of Sápmi.

40

Occupied with her daily chores and the many challenges of the herding life, Ritva paid little attention to the news that began to trickle into the community. While her *siida* had followed the migrations of the reindeer, the Finnish part of Sápmi had come under Soviet control and Norway had been occupied by Germany. So far there had been no fighting in the area near Kilpisjärvi and as she went about her daily routine, Ritva found it hard to imagine that fighting was happening so close by. Yet she felt unsettled, remembering the terrible scars the civil war had left on Finland, the stories of torture and killing and the burnt city of Tampere. Wouldn't it be wiser for them to leave for Sweden, which had stayed neutral? They could seek shelter with Ritva's old *siida*.

'We're herders, not soldiers,' Aslak, one of the elders, said one evening when the *siida* was gathered in his *lavvu*. 'We are all Sami, we've never made the borders, nor asked for them. Our paths are determined by the reindeer, not by countries. Borders have brought us only grief and double taxes. Imagine one Sami fighting against another because they live on different sides of the border – it's ludicrous! This is not our war.'

Everyone agreed and for some time their life continued undisturbed, but in the autumn of 1941 the news reached the *siida* that the Germans had started to aid the Finnish war against the Russians, and some of the Finnish Sami were fighting with the Finnish army against Sami on the Russian Kola Peninsula, trying to push the Soviets out of Finland. There was much debate amongst the herders, but Ritva tried to ignore the ever-changing announcements – they had enough to deal with, ensuring their animals survived the harsh winter, and now that Sara and Jan were too old to look after their own herd, Ritva's responsibilities were larger than ever.

One December morning in 1943 Ritva went out to feed the reindeer. The ground was so hard the herd could hardly dig beneath the surface and Ritva's eyelashes froze together in the cold. She called the animals with a special *yoik* Lilja had taught her, and soon she was surrounded by reindeer, white steam rising from their nostrils. Her favourite, a five-year-old white cow, a descendant of the *gabba* Sara had gifted her a long time ago, licked her glove, keen for lichen and salt, and Ritva let her hand glide through the animal's thick winter coat. As the reindeer nibbled at the lichen, Ritva gazed into its large dark eyes, sensing a gentleness and kinship that still warmed her heart. Suddenly the animal stopped chewing and stood completely still; when Ritva looked closely, the dark surface of its eye had transformed into an eerie orange glow. Ritva could not grasp what she was seeing: cone-shaped fires flickered in the reflection, first one, then two, then more and more flames, licking, spreading . . . Her skin prickled – it was her *siida*! *Lavvus*, the storehouse and many of the turf huts were on fire, people fleeing from the blaze.

Dizzy, Ritva steadied herself against the reindeer's flank, still staring into its eye. She could hear screams, shrill and desperate, the crackling of the fires now a roar, the acrid stench of burnt tent cloth and smoke clogging her nose. Then, all of a sudden the vision vanished and the cow stood calmly nibbling at her hand, its eye an impenetrable mirror once more. Her heart pounding, Ritva rushed back to her *siida*, but the tents stood peaceful, like glowing lanterns amongst the snow-laden trees. Shaken, Ritva buried the vision deep in her heart, yet that night she remembered the evening long ago when Sofia had told her that some Sami claimed you could see omens in a reindeer's eye.

*

That spring was the coldest Ritva had ever known: even in May, the calving grounds were still covered in snow and many newborns died as the cows could not lick their calves dry quickly enough. Then, one day, Ritva watched in horror as a sea eagle swooped down on a newborn calf and snatched it from its mother. Ritva had heard of eagles hunting calves, even in formation, but she had never seen it before. As the huge bird flew off with the bleating calf in its talons, she could not help but feel it was another bad omen for Sápmi. And indeed, in the autumn of 1944, Sápmi was pulled deeper into the war when Finland agreed a ceasefire with the Soviet Union. Soon no one would escape Germany's reckoning, the brutal revenge for the 'Lapland War'.

The first messengers arrived in the *siida* one grey October day. Ritva could not have known that this day would change her life for ever, but that morning as she lit the fire and the kindling caught the first sparks, her neck tingled and she felt a strange stillness in the air like the eerie silence that often precedes a large storm.

Cucu, Ritva's dog, heard them first. He yapped, then rushed out of the tent, barking wildly. Ritva followed him, but seeing the pitiful group approaching the *siida*, she stopped in her tracks. They were Sami, wrapped in thick overcoats, even the children carrying a knapsack or bundle, blackened stew pots and kettles dangling from their sides, backs bent under the heavy load. The lack of sledges and pack-reindeer unnerved Ritva, and as the group came closer she saw the distress in their eyes. This was no ordinary migration – these people were carrying a heavier load than they would ever impose on a reindeer and they seemed to have been walking for a very long time. Had they lost everything? Her eyes fixed on an old woman, walking with a small family. Her face was grey and she looked as if she was about to collapse, gripping the hand of a young girl who was not much older than four. Ritva was struck to see that she was carrying a *giettka*, a Sami cradle, strapped to her back. Without thinking, Ritva rushed over to the group and invited the old woman and the small family into their tent; everyone would be given shelter by the *siida*, but there was something about the old woman that moved Ritva immensely.

'Come, come.'

The little girl clutched the old woman's dress and stared at Ritva with large brown eyes; her nose was running and her face was dirty, as if she hadn't washed it for days. Once inside the tent, the woman put the cradle down next to the fire and collapsed onto the furs while the rest of the group – a young woman who was carrying her own baby and her husband – settled next to her.

'Thank you, I couldn't walk another step,' the old woman said. Close up, she looked even greyer and older than before and when she took off her shoes and removed the shoe grass, her toes were bloody. Her name was Ulla and once she, the girl and the family had stilled their hunger, she told everyone about their *siida*'s trials. They had come from near Inari, further east; the girls' father had volunteered to fight with the Finns against the Soviets and was killed just two weeks before the Soviet-Finnish ceasefire was declared in September that year. Now Finland was being forced to drive all German troops from its soil and the Germans' revenge for this change in alliance was brutal.

'They call it scorched earth,' Ulla said. 'The Germans are burning everything they pass as they retreat towards Norway. They've blown up bridges and planted mines on most of the roads . . . and then two weeks ago in broad daylight they arrived at our *siida*. They only gave us an hour to pack and leave and the worst thing was that they took all our reindeer. They slaughtered some of the animals right in front of us and didn't even leave us the pack-reindeer or our sledges.'

Ritva shuddered, imagining the burning *siida*, the pitiful caravan leaving without their animals.

'My daughter, Lyddy, the girls' mother, was still raw with grief for Matti, and furious that her husband had volunteered to fight in this stupid war. She was battling against flu when the Germans came.' The little girl stopped chewing and stared at her grand-mother. Ulla handed her a cup of coffee.

'Eat up, Zusa, and here, drink this.' She added some reindeer milk to the thin coffee then lowered her voice to a whisper.

'I think Lyddy died of a broken heart rather than the flu, but the fever was burning her up and we couldn't stop and rest . . .' Ulla's voice was breaking. 'Three days into the trek she died.'

'Please, stay and be our guest, Ulla, it's the least we can do,' Sara said.

Ritva could find no words, but she fetched some sleeping furs and blankets and fed the fire some extra logs, aware of Zusa's large eyes following her every move. When the baby began to cry, Ulla took her out of the *giettka* and handed her to the young woman.

'The baby's called Arla. She's nearly eight months old, but tiny. Poor thing will never know her mother. Thank God for Rauna here, who's nursing her.' Rauna placed her own baby in a cradle, then put little Arla to her breast while chatting with Lilja's daughter Marit who was nursing her firstborn.

That night Ritva dreamt of Zusa riding on a pack-reindeer, baby Arla's cradle fastened to the side. Zusa giggled, waving wildly at Ritva. Ritva searched for Ulla but she could not see the old woman anywhere. Then all of a sudden she heard a quiet beat, steady and low like that of a drum – it was coming from inside the cradle; but when Ritva looked inside, there was only little Arla, fast asleep, a sweet smile playing on her lips.

When Ritva woke, she found Zusa snuggled next to her under-neath the sleeping fur, her thin arm reaching around Ritva – she must have crawled underneath the furs during the night without Ritva noticing. Feeling the girl's warm, steady breathing, a ripple of joy rushed through Ritva and she remembered the dream, Zusa waving and the sound of the drum from the cradle. Was this a sign? She had not dreamt of the drum since Martta had left her . . . Suddenly Ulla started coughing violently. Zusa woke, looked at Ritva with sleepy eyes, then searched for her grandmother.

321

'I'm aching all over,' Ulla croaked. 'I can hardly move my arms.' It was as if, now that she had found a resting place, Ulla's body had finally given up; she couldn't sit up, and when Ritva felt her forehead it burned with a high fever. Ulla's *siida* decided to stay until the old woman recovered, but two days later Ritva awoke to hear Zusa's pleading voice: 'Wake up, Grandma, wake up!'

Ulla had died quietly in the night. Zusa kneeled next to her grandmother, large tears rolling down her cheeks. Ritva stroked Zusa's fine hair and quietly hummed a *yoik* into her ear, struggling to fathom what was happening. The news soon spread across the *siida* and people arrived at the tent. Zusa sought refuge with Ritva, curling up in her lap. Ritva stroked her until she became calm and fell asleep.

Ritva listened to the quiet hum of conversation drifting around the tent; she could not hear what Rauna was discussing with her husband and Marit, but the young woman looked troubled. Was she worried that she was expected to care for the baby, or even for both girls, now that they were orphans? When baby Arla cried, Rauna picked her up and nursed her.

'What will happen to the girls now?' Though Aslak only whispered this to Sara, Ritva overheard the old man. There was a pause; then, like a bird flying out of her mouth, Ritva spoke a truth she had not yet fully understood herself.

'I will take on their care, I can look after them.' Silence spread in the tent and everybody stared at her. Zusa, aware of a change, lifted her head.

'I actually *want* to look after them.' Ritva's voice was strong, though she was trembling inside.

'But how could you?' Sara said, frowning. 'You are forty-seven.'

'Marit would need to help me with the baby for another month or so, then Arla could have reindeer milk and broth, and Zusa . . . well, it seems she likes me.'

Zusa looked at Ritva and smiled, but said nothing.

'I'd be happy to nurse Arla,' Marit said, 'but shouldn't the girls stay with Ulla's *siida*? What do you think, Rauna?' Rauna looked at Zusa who still lay in Ritva's lap.

'Of course I would happily look after the girls,' Rauna said, 'but Zusa seems to have chosen differently.'

Everyone had something to say, until Osku, an elder from Ulla's *siida*, addressed Ritva directly.

'But why, Ritva? You are older and you have your own herd. Why would you want two little girls to look after now?'

Ritva chose her words carefully.

'Maybe it's exactly because of that – I am older now, more mature. I've been shown so much love and care by the people of my *siida*, so now it is my time to give something back.

'Becoming the girls' guardian would mean so much to me,' she added, realising the magnitude of her request. 'I will do everything in my power to look after them well.'

'Well, if you feel you can manage, and Marit is supporting you, I've no objections as long as little Zusa agrees.' The elder looked intently at the girl, his bushy eyebrows curved down into a frown.

'Would you like to stay with Aunt Ritva here?'

Zusa nodded, five vigorous nods. 'Yes, and baby Arla, she wants to stay too.'

'Oh, how do you know that?' Osku asked.

'She told me in a dream,' Zusa said.

'Ah, I see.' He was smiling now. 'Well then, I wish you all the best of luck and Beaivi's blessings.'

There were still many things to discuss, but from one day to the next Ritva had become a guardian to the two little girls.

The next morning the elders laid Ulla gently on a sledge. Ritva, shaken and sad about the old woman's passing and yet filled with a wild happiness, held Zusa's hand and carried baby Arla strapped on her back as both *siida*s followed the sledge until they found a place to bury the girls' grandmother. Two days later, Ulla's *siida* made its way towards Sweden.

41

Ritva's *siida* followed the herd to the lower feeding grounds near Hetta. Olaf and Mikko, Marit's husband, offered to look after Ritva's herd for the time being so that Ritva was able to spend time with the girls. She cradled Arla, sang to them both and told Zusa all the stories that Sara had shared with her over the years, as well as passing on the ones she remembered from her mother. As Ulla had pointed out, Arla was small for her age with big blue eyes and a tuft of dark brown hair, but she and Zusa thrived under Ritva's and Marit's care.

Life became even busier than usual and Ritva held her worries about the war at bay, until one afternoon in December 1944 a Sami man from a neighbouring *siida* arrived looking pale and out of breath.

'The Germans have burnt down Rovaniemi! All of it!' he panted, holding on to a stitch in his side. 'They're burning everything – settlements, whole villages. Everywhere people are fleeing. It's the same in Finnmark – you need to make your way into Sweden.'

What Ulla's *siida* had endured was no longer a random occurrence; it was happening all over Sápmi, and much closer to home than before. That night, the whole *siida* squeezed into one tent to debate the messenger's news and advice. Maybe it was defiance or sheer stubbornness on the part of the elders, but in the end they decided to risk staying in the area for the next few weeks – the conditions were much better here for the reindeer than further west and the winter was harsh. Without the reindeer they would not survive. If they heard of any attacks nearby, they could move quickly, the elders said, and maybe the Germans would spare an area so close to the border with neutral Sweden.

Ritva was not convinced; she now had Arla and Zusa to protect and care for, and she could not forget the vision of the burning *siida* she had seen in the reindeer's eye. Speaking up in the meeting she urged the *siida* to leave, but the elders would not change their mind.

After that night Ritva hardly slept and when the herders were out on their skis guarding the reindeer, they were vigilant and jumpy. Yet nothing could have prepared the *siida* for the ambush that would follow a month later.

The Germans appeared out of nowhere on skis and sledges on a moonless January night; silent, wrapped in white snow suits, rifles slung over their shoulders. The first thing Ritva heard was Cucu's frantic barking and the reindeer bulls' calls from the forest; next came the sound of soldiers' boots kicking open the wooden doors of the turf huts and tearing the tent cloths from the *lavvus*.

'*Raus, schnell, schnell!*'

Ritva picked up Arla, heavy with sleep, and bundled her into the *giettka*. Then she grabbed whatever lay closest: coats, gloves and caps, as many blankets as she could find, sleeping furs, the stew pot, the kettle, cups and food supplies. She threw all the belongings out into the snow, strapped the *giettka* to her back and took Zusa by the hand. Olaf was out with the herd, so Marit and Lilja helped Sara and Jan and the children – within minutes they were all standing outside in the freezing cold, while the soldiers surrounded the *siida* like a pack of growling wolves ready to attack. Ritva watched with horror as the soldiers poured canisters of kerosene over the huts and the storehouse, drenching everything. The soldiers must have carried out many such attacks throughout Sápmi, Ritva thought – they did not hurry but executed the torching with a cruel, efficient calm. A single match was used to light a soldier's torch and once unleashed, the fire took hold with savage speed.

As she stood frozen, her eyes fixed on the fire that was devouring their homes, Ritva saw the burning workshop on Seili, herself stumbling towards the shore, looking for Martta. She could still taste the fear and elation of that night in her mouth; but those flames had brought her freedom, while the senseless fires of this war were an attempt to destroy everything she had worked for: a place she could live without fear and a community she called home.

Ritva turned away. She prayed that the herd was safe – if the Germans found and slaughtered their animals, everything would be lost. When all the huts and *lavvus* were in flames, the Germans packed up the sledges. Some soldiers looked grey and tired, others carried the satisfaction of a job well done on their faces. Within minutes they disappeared into the forest, not once looking back.

The *siida* gathered at the edge of the burning village. Shouts and cries of relief cut through the night as loved ones and neighbours were reunited; everyone had made it out of the huts and *lavvus* alive, but the *siida* lay in ashes.

'Let's find shelter deeper in the forest,' one of the elders said. 'But we need to stay together – the greylegs are close.' Would anywhere be safe from the Germans now? It was doubly cruel that they had come in the depths of winter. Yes, the reindeer could be herded to another area, but to have even the poles of their *lavvus* burnt and the turf huts destroyed left them all exposed to the brutal cold. Baby Arla cried for hours, coughing and spluttering before she finally fell asleep. Ritva's bones ached as she trudged through the forest next to Sara, Lilja and Marit, hugging baby Arla close, despair clouding her thoughts. Suddenly she sensed Zusa's little hand, stuck in fur mittens, slip into hers. She had not even noticed that Zusa was walking next to her.

'It'll be all right, Aunt Ritva,' Zusa whispered suddenly. The weight of Zusa's little mittened hand in hers, no heavier than a bird, touched her heart.

'Yes, I know, darling,' Ritva said, giving her a quick hug. Having this child beside her gave her more comfort than she ever could have imagined.

The first night after the torching, the *siida* set up camp around a large fire, wrapping themselves in anything they had managed to salvage. Ritva knew that Martta's drum hammer lay safely in the pocket of her overcoat, but as much as she would have liked to run her fingers over the reindeer carvings, she could not risk taking off her gloves – the frost would burn her fingers in minutes.

It was early morning when Ritva heard the bell of the lead reindeer – the herd was safe! Soon Olaf and the other herders arrived – they had smelled the smoke and, fearing an attack, had herded the animals deeper into the forest. Everyone peeled their aching bodies out of their blankets and an hour later a silent line of figures headed south, bent by sorrow and with an icy north wind at their backs. Theirs had been a small encampment, but as they approached the village of Savukoski, they saw the cruel extent of the destruction: at least thirty burnt-out dwellings sat like injured crows amid the snow and ice; all that was left were black, charred ruins, the bare windows like the eyes of the dead. Ritva shivered – it had been difficult to imagine how Sápmi could be part of this war, but now she understood that nowhere was safe.

The group travelled on for days, driving their reindeer ahead, sharing whatever provisions they had left. The plan was to move south and then west towards Sweden. Every so often they passed other *siidas* whose dwellings had been scorched too; some villages had been burnt to the ground, and they heard that in Sodankylä and Pello only a few buildings remained standing. Rovaniemi, their largest town, had burnt for three days and nights and its mighty bridge lay mangled in the river. Ritva remembered the jolly market and the beautiful wooden houses, all ashes now. And Uncle's friend, was he safe?

*

One afternoon they stopped by a riverbank to rest. Ritva raised her head to the sky. How she craved light and warmth, but spring was still a long way away and the sky hung heavy with grey clouds that would soon bring more snow. She was about to gather firewood when she caught a movement out of the corner of her eye: two geese, flying low above her head, were starting their descent towards the frozen river, wings outstretched, legs pointing forward to brace against the impact. They stumbled as they touched the ice, then glided and came to a halt a few metres away. Something about their clumsy movement made Ritva smile and for a moment some of her sorrow lifted.

A week after the Germans burnt their settlement, the *siida* reached the village of Muonio. The reindeer grew restless and even from afar Ritva could see the columns of smoke and smell the distinct odour of burnt timber. As they approached the village, it was clear that it was as badly damaged as their own: only a few dwellings still stood, forlorn islands in a drowned sea. And yet, despite this, it had not been completely abandoned: a group of Sami moved silently through the ruins, searching for anything that might still be usable. Their defiance moved Ritva – she wouldn't have known where to start searching amid such devastation, and in some ways it had been easier just to abandon their settlement. Both groups waved to each other and after an exchange of greetings, the villagers invited Ritva's *siida* to join them and rest. They gathered around a fire, squeezing next to each other on makeshift benches.

'They came yesterday in the middle of the night,' an old Sami man said with blazing eyes, drawing on his pipe. 'We heard what had happened elsewhere, but we still didn't expect them. Some of our people have moved on further north but a lot have stayed; our reindeer love the land around here.' He stoked the fire with a stick. 'But we're strong, we can rebuild our homes. We won't be defeated by some stupid Germans on skis.' Ritva's heart jumped. She looked in the direction of the voice. An older, broad-shouldered woman in a dark blue tunic and coat sat opposite her. She was holding a small knife, carving away at a little figure. Could it be possible? But there was no doubt; across the fire from her sat Martta. She had aged, yes, but there were the same strong features and the large, confident hands that were doing what Ritva had so often seen them do – carving a piece of wood. Every fibre of Ritva's body wanted to jump up and throw herself into Martta's arms, but instead she turned away, a wave of nausea rising. She leaned over to Zusa.

'I need to go to the toilet, please hold Arla for a moment.' She passed the baby to Zusa and walked across the snow into the forest. She needed to think. Quietly she counted: more than twenty-seven years had passed since the day she had woken without Martta by her side – would Martta even recognise her? Dizzy, she leaned against a tree trunk, breathing in the cold air. Her hand gripped the drum hammer in her pocket, squeezing it hard. She had held on to this little object for all those years, secretly hoping that one day it would guide Martta back to her, but now she did not know what to do.

She gazed through the trees. Martta was sitting by the fire, just as she had seen her do so many times, carving, pondering the plans for the next day of the journey. Had she married, borne children? Ritva had not noticed a man with her.

Ritva walked deeper into the forest, stumbling through the undergrowth. Suddenly she heard heavy steps crunching across the snow. She turned and froze. How had Martta caught up with her so quickly? Martta stopped an arm's length in front of her and looked straight at her, her eyes filling with tears.

'Ritva, is that really you?' Before Ritva could answer, Martta stepped towards her and pulled her into an embrace.

'I am sorry, Ritva. God, I'm so sorry!' Martta smelled of fire, sweat and resin. For a moment Ritva pulled away, but suddenly there were no more words as they held on to each other like survivors of a shipwreck. Blood rushing in her ears, Ritva felt as if she was drowning, but when Martta's mouth found hers, all time dissolved. With the kiss she remembered their first one, that frosty morning, a lifetime ago; how Martta had drawn her close, the despair and urgency in her kiss. And then Martta had abandoned her . . .

Ritva wrenched herself from the embrace and pushed Martta away. Her gaze hardened.

'Why, Martta? Why did you leave me and Arvid? What did I ever do to you that made you think you could just take off like that and leave me behind like an old shirt?' Hot anger surged through her like a lightning bolt.

'Oh Ritva, you didn't do anything wrong! You've been the light of my life, didn't you know that?'

'Is that how you treat the light of your life?' Ritva glared at her.

'I . . . I was a coward, Ritva, a damn fool. I wanted nothing more than to be with you, but I was so scared to tell you! And when you pushed me away I didn't have the heart to come back and talk about it with you. I was scared you'd think me disgusting, that you wouldn't want me, that I'd bring only shame on you. I thought you'd have a better chance on your own with Arvid. I just wasn't strong enough, Ritva . . .' Martta fell silent and dropped her head. 'I've thought about you every single day of my life, Ritva. I loved you!' Her voice broke and she stood, arms hanging limply at her sides. For a long time neither of them spoke.

'I still . . . love you, Ritva.' Martta's voice sounded stronger now and yet it carried a tremor.

'It's too late, Martta. Too much has happened. I . . . we've changed . . .' Before she could say any more, Martta reached for Ritva's arms and pulled her close, then cupped her head with both hands and kissed her on the mouth again. A surge of heat rushed through Ritva's body, yet again she pulled away.

'Please! The baby's crying . . . I've got to get back.'

'You have a baby? Ritva, please, tell me! I want to hear everything.'

'I don't know where to start, so much time has passed. The baby, Arla, yes . . . I'm her guardian.' Ritva suddenly remembered the drum hammer; she searched in her coat pocket and pulled it out.

'Here, this is yours, I've kept it for you.' She stretched out her arm, the smooth, familiar object nestling on her palm.

'You still have it? Oh, Ritva, thank you! Please, can you ever forgive me?'

Ritva did not answer but put the small hammer in Martta's hand. Martta closed her fingers tightly around it. *Just the way I used to hold it*, Ritva thought.

'And where is Arvid? What happened to him? Oh, God, I've missed you both so much!'

'He thought it was his fault that you left.' Ritva's voice became sharp as she thought of Arvid's pain. 'It's a long story . . . but he's fine now; he married Elke, my little sister.'

'Your sister? I thought she lived in Turku?'

'Never mind, Martta, so many things have changed. God, it's been almost thirty years!' Ritva balled her fists, fighting a wave of despair.

'But I want to be with you, Ritva. Fate has brought us together again, how can we part now? I don't want to lose you again!'

'I can't, Martta, don't you see? We're old now, it's too late.' Ritva turned away, sobbing silently. Martta reached once more for Ritva's hand, but Ritva turned and rushed back through the forest towards the fire.

That night, Ritva could not sleep and Arla cried on and off for hours, as if she sensed the turmoil in her guardian's heart. Ritva's mind was racing; how could she just move on with her *siida* now, when she had secretly hoped to find Martta again for so very long? But to see Martta so aged, and her own years reflected in Martta's face . . . The thought of so much time lost stung like a festering wound. And yet, if fate had given them a second chance, should she not grab it with both hands? What would Sara think, Lilja, and her friends in the *siida*? Surely people would sense their special bond? And two women living like man and wife . . . would they be accepted or called names, or maybe even banished?

She sat up and listened in the darkness – everyone was breathing evenly; Zusa and even Arla were fast asleep now and suddenly, like heavy clouds parting to reveal the blazing light of the moon, she saw everything clearly: she belonged with Martta, they had always belonged together. In that instant, all her despair and anger dissolved and the only thing she craved was to be with Martta, wrapped in the tightest embrace. She lay back down and gently stroked Arla's face.

'And you, my little one, will soon have another pair of eyes watching over your sweet self.' As if she understood, Arla sighed and curled her lips into a smile.

When Ritva awoke, she could hear the sound of someone chopping wood. Everybody was already up and the blanket next to her lay empty. Alarmed, she looked for the baby then saw Arla snuggled up in Zusa's arms.

'You were sleeping so well,' Zusa said. 'I didn't want to wake you.'

'Thank you, Zusa.' Ritva smiled and stroked Zusa's head, warmth spreading through her as she recalled the clarity she had found in the night. She crawled out of the sleeping furs and stretched. She had to find Martta – they had not spoken another word after the exchange in the forest.

It was still slightly dark and Ritva lifted her head towards the sky, seeking the square of Orion, then the Great Bear as she had always done since the day Martta had pointed out those constellations to her. In the distance the Northern Lights flickered. She made her way around the *siida* looking for Martta, careful not to stumble over the debris, peering into the few buildings that still stood, asking whomever she met if they had seen Martta. Finally she approached a young woman who was stoking a fire in the ruins of one of the last remaining huts.

'Have you seen Martta?' Ritva's voice was strained.

'I heard she's decided to go further up north.' The woman put a blackened kettle on the stove. 'I don't understand her, only yesterday she was talking about how important it was for us all to stay here so that we can rebuild our village. But then Martta has always done what she wanted. I've never known what to make of her: not marrying, no children, not very womanly, really, if you think about it. Although she's always been kind enough.' She sighed. 'This war breaks us all up.'

Ritva's heart thumped – she clenched her jaw and buried her fists in her pockets.

'She left? Where did she go?'

'Finnmark, near Kautokeino, that's all I know. But why do you want to know?'

Ritva stared into the fire. Kautokeino, Norway.

'We knew each other once . . . a long time ago.' Ritva heard her own voice as if it came from far away. Like an arrow's single aim, Ritva's mind held only one thought, one name: Martta. Suddenly she collapsed into dark oblivion.

She woke with a burning pain in her chest; she longed to return to that dark, nebulous space, but the alarm on Zusa's face kept her from fainting once more. Word had spread and people surrounded her with concerned faces. Ritva's gaze searched the crowd for Martta, though she knew it was futile. One of the elders stepped forward.

'Martta gave me this for you before she left. I tried to persuade her not to go on her own, or at least to wait until spring, but she wouldn't have it. She said she wanted to catch up with some members of our *siida* who have headed north. She is strong, you know . . . and stubborn.' He put the parcel in Ritva's hand. 'You knew her before?'

Ritva nodded.

'I knew her, yes, a long time ago.' It took all Ritva's strength to keep her tears at bay. When everyone had left, she untied the parcel. Martta's small drum hammer lay inside, together with a note. A small brass ring rolled onto the floor; she picked it up then read the words:

Dearest Ritva,

   This ring, this arpa, *is for you. In the old times, the* noaidi *would play the drum with the hammer and put a ring on the skin. It would jump here and there with each beat and the place and picture it landed on when the drumming stopped would tell us a truth. Sometimes there were two rings and the* noaidi *would take one and hide it high up in the mountains in a sacred place so he would always be connected to that place, to the power of it, the magic of it. Ritva, you are this place for me, you are my mountain. I will keep the other ring and pray that it is our fate to be together again and that one day we can hear the sound of the sacred drum.*

   All my love,

   Martta

Ritva turned the ring in her trembling fingers, then held it in front of her eyes, facing north. She strained to see through it, beyond the forest, to reach across time and space for her companion and soulmate. And for the briefest moment she saw a figure, a black smudge, struggling through the white vastness of the tundra.

42

Throughout the long winter Ritva turned her sorrow into an even fiercer love for the two girls in her care. The *siida* kept moving and as Sami families fled towards Sweden or returned to rebuild their settlements, Ritva heard terrible stories of destruction: the Germans had not only burnt the villages and slaughtered many reindeer, but had also scorched parts of the forest so that much of the grazing ground for the remaining reindeer was lost. Finally, a week after the calf marking in June 1945, the *siida* passed a Red Cross convoy and learned that the war had ended at last. Yet despite the celebrations that summer, Ritva was subdued, and only seeing that the girls were happy and thriving kept her spirits up.

One afternoon the following April, Ritva was sitting on a rock outside her *lavvu* in the pale sun, watching Arla waddle over to her old dog, Cucu. The toddler screeched with delight as she patted the dog's fur, then glanced up at Ritva and stumbled back into Ritva's open arms. Ritva kissed her forehead and nuzzled her hair, drawing in her sweet smell. Arla giggled, struggled free and made her way back to the dog. Arla and Zusa had brought her so much joy, and indeed the whole *siida* was fond of the girls. But Ritva's pain over Martta had not lessened and she knew she could not contain her restlessness much longer. Later that day she approached Sara.

'I just can't settle, Sara. I need to find Martta and see what this is between us. But I can't take the children. Please, will you look after them for me? I will come back.' Sara held Ritva's gaze for a long time.

'I can only imagine what has been stirring in you for all these years and I understand that you have to follow your heart – but travelling on your own is still dangerous, Ritva, and the children will miss you.'

'I've travelled further in my life than I ever thought possible. I need to take this risk. I know that the girls will miss me, but I won't have any peace until I find Martta.'

'Oh, they will, Ritva, they adore you. And I will look after them. I just don't want to lose you again.'

'Thank you, Sara! I promise I'll return. If I travel in summer the days are long and I can walk further.'

So Ritva made up her mind and, on a bright June day in 1946, she fastened her bags and sleeping furs onto one of the pack-reindeer. Little Arla was asleep and she did not want to wake her, but she called Zusa.

'I need to make a journey to find an old friend, but Aunt Sara, Marit and Lilja will look after you and Arla while I'm away. Please take care of your little sister for me, won't you? You're such a big girl now, and it won't be long before you can go out with the herders yourself.'

Zusa swallowed her tears but Ritva's eyes filled. Was this the right decision? The girls had been her comfort all through the dark winters and she had made a promise to care for them . . .

Ritva shook herself; she hugged Zusa and planted a kiss on her forehead, then headed north towards Finnmark.

Trekking long days across the tundra, Ritva mulled over the stages of her life, tormented by lost opportunities. She asked everyone she met about Martta, but no one had seen her. Finally, as she passed Kautokeino, an old Sami herder remembered a woman travelling alone the winter before last – she had arrived on skis, hungry and exhausted, rested a few days in his *lavvu*, then had taken off again towards Stuorajavri, a settlement close to a large lake four days' journey north.

Ritva recognised her from afar. Martta was bending over a tree stump, pounding her axe into chunks of wood until they split.

'Martta!'

The woman stretched and squinted into the sun.

'Ritva?' For a moment both stood still, then Martta dropped the axe. They ran forward and fell into each other's arms. Ritva caressed Martta's face, touched her shoulders, her arms, her back. Yes, this was Martta, real and alive – flesh and blood, hair and skin, as real as her own fast breath.

'You came looking for me?' Martta's voice was hoarse.

'Yes. And don't you ever leave me again, understand? I've had enough of you running away!'

'I'll never leave you again,' Martta said gravely, then smiled. 'Unless you forget to kiss me, right now.' She lifted Ritva off her feet, whirled her around and kissed her on the mouth.

'I want to hear about everything that has happened to you,' Ritva said, looking deep into Martta's eyes. Could stories ever fill the gap left by all those lost years?

'I know you said you left me and Arvid because you were worried I would be disgusted by your feelings. But, Martta, I was so young, I didn't even understand my own feelings . . .'

'When you pushed me away I thought you hated me. I didn't know what to do. And I was worried you wouldn't want to be with me once we were living with a *siida*.' Martta blushed and looked away.

'Well, we've both paid for our own stupidity. It's taken me many years, Martta, but now I realise . . . I've always loved you.

'Arvid missed you too, you know,' she added. 'He put on a brave face, but I knew he was hurting inside. We should have found a way to be together . . .' She shook herself and touched Martta's arm. 'I am sorry, Martta. It just . . . hurts to know we've lost so much time.' They sat next to each other, a heavy silence stretching between them. After a while Ritva stirred.

'What happened to you and Greyheart out there in the snow?'

Martta looked up, her eyes red from her tears.

'We survived – just about. It was very tough, but we made it through that winter.' Ritva could see the pain in Martta's face.

'You remember that blizzard? It was impossible to see a single thing. I struggled on for a while, then dug a shelter in the snow, just a deep hole really. I found some lichen and branches and together with the wood from my bag, I lit a small fire; it barely warmed us and without Greyheart I'm sure I would have died. We cowered in that hole, the wind howling around us like a crazy thing. I held Greyheart in my lap or clutched to my chest and we just kept each other's heartbeat going. Sometimes he yapped or whimpered but when he looked at me with his beautiful eyes it was as if he was saying, "Where are Ritva and the boy? What have you done?"

'I was sick with worry about you and Arvid and I tried to convince myself that you would have made it to the settlement before the blizzard started. I hardly ate for a week and fed most of the provisions to Greyheart. You rescued him and I made a promise to myself to keep him alive at all costs. I owed him, and besides, he was my only living connection to you.' Martta stared ahead.

'Once the blizzard was over, we stumbled out of the hole. The snow stretched out around us like an ocean and the only way to know which direction we were headed in was to keep watch for the north star. We walked in the few twilight hours and dug shelters at night. Sometimes the Northern Lights whirled around us like magnificent dancers and Greyheart was frightened; he tried to curl himself into a ball, but he couldn't stop peeping out either. I missed you even more than ever. I was nearly snow-blind and very weak when I spotted a small settlement near a lake – just a few turf huts and a smokehouse, Sami people who lived from fishing. A couple with two children gave me a space in their hut. I tried to pass Greyheart off as a dog, but I couldn't fool them. I pleaded and at least they gave him a few scraps. They fed me well and gave me the best place at the fire. They weren't big talkers but they were good people and I was grateful they didn't press me about why I was travelling alone. I tried to find out about you but they didn't have much contact with other settlements. They let me stay through the hardest month of winter, but when I had gathered enough strength I set off again with Greyheart. They gave me dried fish for the journey and a reindeer fur – I've kept it all these years. You're sitting on it.'

It had lost some of its thickness but Ritva could imagine its previous splendour as she stroked it.

'And so I carried on, stumbling through the wilderness. I had neither direction nor purpose. I cursed myself each day for having left you. What could have been worse than this emptiness, this regret?' Ritva's eyes welled up, seeing the pain in Martta's face.

'I was hungry all the time and rarely caught a rabbit, but at least Greyheart was a natural hunter – I've him to thank for not letting me starve. We were a small pack – I talked to him all the time and he'd look back at me with pricked ears, as if he understood every word.

'Spring came and then summer. I decided to keep going northeast. Maybe one day I'd make it back to Finland and my *siida*. Greyheart had grown tall despite our meagre diet. Then one day we stumbled across the half-eaten carcass of a baby moose – it had been ripped open, its entrails and most of the meat devoured, but for some reason the hunter had moved on and left some of the flesh still clinging to the bones. As I cut bits off it, Greyheart sniffed around, growling.'

'That night we heard them for the first time: the most haunting sound, so beautiful and terrifying it made my hair stand on end; a large pack of wolves, howling deep inside the forest – first one, then two, then the whole group. Greyheart was trembling all over and gave a few loud barks in the direction of the forest. He listened, sniffed, then broke into a high-pitched howl. I'd never heard him do anything like that before, Ritva: again and again he threw back his head and howled into the night – a proper wolf after all!

'Eventually one of the pack answered, then another and another, until they were all calling to him in a wild chorus. Then, all of a sudden, the howling stopped.

'The next day we heard them closer by. Greyheart yapped and barked, ran to the edge of the forest and back to me, then he howled. As they'd done the previous night, the whole pack answered. Their howls made my blood freeze and I knew then that our time together was coming to an end – I could never compare with such a magnificent pack, I could never be Greyheart's true family.'

Martta sighed and Ritva laid her head on her shoulder.

'On the third day, the wolves moved even closer – I caught a glimpse of a large grey at the edge of the forest. They had come to meet Greyheart. And this time the temptation was too great; Greyheart sprinted towards the forest, but just before he reached it, he stopped and ran back to me. He licked my hand and my face, whimpering, and looked at me. I stroked him one last time, then stood up. He turned away and bolted off into the woods – this time he didn't look back. That night, I heard the wolves again, and maybe I imagined it, but I could hear a different voice amongst them. I swear it was Greyheart's howl.'

Both of them fell silent for a while.

'What happened then?' Ritva asked.

'I went further north to Kiruna. I heard they were hiring people for the mines there. The company owner saw that I was strong and he gave me a job even though I'm a woman. I didn't last long there, but I met some other Sami and one day I decided to try my luck and head back towards Finland to find my old *siida* . . . I also hoped you might make your way to Finland some day . . .'

With a stab Ritva realised that they had always been in each other's thoughts all those years, the connection between them as alive and potent as it had always been. Ritva pulled out the drum hammer from under her tunic, put it in Martta's hand and folded her fingers around it.

'I kept it for you. And the ring you left me too – I've always kept it close to my heart.' She took Martta's other hand and placed it on her chest where the ring lay hidden in a small pouch she'd made especially for it.

There were no more words that night as they made love, lying together near the fire entangled as tree roots. Although they were not the young women who had known each other on Seili and on their long journey north, their bodies still recognised each other as if they had never been parted. Lying in Martta's arms, all the hardship and struggle dissolved and Ritva let herself feel her own desire, knowing it would be received.

She lay awake through the rest of the night, drinking in the blessing of Martta lying next to her as orange sparks flew like fireflies through the smoke hole into the star-studded sky. She was home.

43

A few days later, Ritva sent a message with one of the *siida* members who was travelling south, to tell Sara that she would stay with Martta until the following spring. She missed the girls sorely, but like the woman in the Sealskin tale who had returned to the sea, she knew she had to bear the yearning for her children and nourish her own wild soul in Martta's arms, if only for a short while longer.

Ritva was welcomed by the *siida*, but she made sure never to show too much affection for Martta in public. At first they lived with the women and children in the summer camp, sharing the daily tasks, until Ritva persuaded Martta to ask if they could join the herders. They spent days, sometimes even weeks, out with the herders, helping with the calf marking and the autumn slaughter and, after the first snow, they migrated with the reindeer to the lower forest. As unforgiving as the winter was, with Martta, no challenge seemed too big and each morning Ritva marvelled at finding Martta on the sleeping fur next to her. But being away from her own herd, Ritva worried about her animals: was the snow soft enough for them to be able to dig for lichen? How many reindeer would be killed by wolves that winter? In March, when the first catkins emerged on the willow bushes, Ritva took Martta aside.

'I need to go back, Martta. I promised the girls and Sara I'd be home in time for the June marking. There should be lots of new calves. Will you come with me? I have quite a big a herd now, enough to support us all. We could all live together.' Her heart thumped as she had said it: *we could all live together* . . . Martta's eyes rested on her for a long time.

'Yes . . . If you think the girls and your aunt will accept me?'

'Of course they will!' Ritva threw her arms around Martta; only now did she realise how tired she truly was; tired of running, tired of hiding her love. More than anything she never wanted to lose Martta again.

And so, in May 1947, a few weeks before the herders brought the reindeer back from the mountains, Ritva returned with Martta to her *siida* near Kilpisjärvi. Marit and Zusa nearly knocked Ritva off her feet when they saw her and only little Arla hid behind Sara's tunic, peeping out at Martta with large eyes. It didn't take long before Arla and Zusa grew fond of Martta, who carved little animals and entertained them with new stories.

One day Sara pulled Martta aside.

'Ritva has been through so much – please take good care of her, won't you? I don't mind who she chooses to love, man or woman, but I want her to be happy.'

'I promise, Sara, on my life that I will. I would marry her if I could.'

'Good,' Sara said, 'so it is then.'

From then on, Ritva and Martta lived in their own *lavvu* together with the girls. It was a relief and a great luxury as most tents were shared with a larger family. The following summer, Martta worked with some of the young herders to rebuild the turf huts the Germans had burnt down, and when they had finished she built a hut for Ritva and the girls – at last they had a home of their own.

Despite her happiness, Ritva sensed that there was sometimes talk about her and Martta behind their backs; gossip was frowned upon in the *siida* and yet she had noticed that ever since she returned with Martta, some people seemed to be more reserved. One summer morning when Martta and Ritva stole away into the forest together, they heard giggling and quick steps running back through the woods. When they returned to the *siida* later that afternoon, no one said anything but Ritva sensed disapproval everywhere: in the way that some women looked at Martta or suddenly chided their children if they played with Zusa. Ritva noticed that neither she nor Martta was invited for coffee and the communal sinew-spinning any more.

'Just give it time, Ritva,' Martta said, 'they'll get used to us.' But Ritva was worried through the long winter months about their future. Then, on a bright day in early April 1949, things took a different turn. The streams had started to melt everywhere and the sun glistened off the snow; Martta was out all day with the herders, bringing the reindeer closer to the camp while Ritva stayed behind. On her way back Martta spotted old Aslak with his five-year-old grandson, Joná, fishing on the other side of river. Joná smiled and waved at her; Martta waved back and carried on. A few minutes later, a sudden thought stabbed her – it had been on a day just like this that her little sister had drowned. Martta saw Uma clearly in front of her, waving her arms, her lips uttering a name . . . Martta's heart pounded – Joná!

She sprinted back along the path and moments later she saw them both: Aslak shouting, running along the riverbank, Joná swept away by the current, his head barely above the water. Without a thought Martta threw herself into the rushing river and reached Joná within seconds. She recalled nothing after that, and when she arrived wet and trembling at their tent, she collapsed into Ritva's arms, spitting out words and broken sentences.

The next day little Joná was already up, but Martta was struck down by a high fever and grief over her sister's death resurfaced like a familiar demon. It was only Ritva's calm voice and the boy's daily vigil by her bedside that brought Martta some comfort whenever she emerged from her dreams.

'You were only a child when your sister died,' Ritva whispered one night. 'You couldn't have saved her, but you did save Joná – he would have died without you!'

Martta said nothing, but finally, sobbing in Ritva's arms, she surrendered the guilt she had carried all her life. That night the nightmares finally stopped and she dreamt of Uma as she had been in life: radiant and smiling.

Aslak's gratitude knew no end and when Martta finally recovered, he gifted her a white reindeer fur and a beautiful knife he had carved. Overnight the attitude towards Martta in the village had changed from mistrust to respect, and she and Ritva were invited once more into the *lavvus* of the other families, who were eager to hear about Joná's rescue first-hand.

Aslak was too old to go out with the herders and now he often came to visit their *lavvu* with Joná. Ritva had liked the old man from the first moment she met him, but now her affection grew deeper as she listened to him telling Zusa, Arla and Joná about the old Sami ways.

'Do you know we all came from the sun?' he began. 'We were born from the sun and we'll return there when we die. The midnight sun gives us strength to live through the long winter and we rejoice when we see Father Sun again for the first time in spring.' He took a sip of coffee from his cup, then frowned.

'We've lived through many hard times; the Christians did not believe in our old ways and destroyed many of our *sieidis*, our sacred places. But you see, there are many such places – a rock face, a lone tree, the top of a mountain – and you cannot destroy everything. The clergymen might have discovered and robbed one place but missed the white *sieidi* rock that sat just a little to the left of it. Besides, all of the tundra, the wide skies, the rivers and the mountains receive our prayers and all of nature is our home. Even when they destroyed our magic objects, they could never destroy our roots.

'They've taken our mother tongue and much of our fatherland, but it is we Sami who have lived here with the reindeer for thousands of years. In summer we yearn, just like the reindeer, to be up in the high mountains where we won't be plagued by mosquitoes, and in winter we come down into the shelter of the forests. Our animals have roamed these lands for millennia and don't care about borders or the lawmakers from the South, yet we are fined if our reindeer cross these borders. Ah, what a shambles.' He sighed.

'But come here, Arla.' He sat the girl on his lap, then pulled Joná and Zusa close.

'Let me tell you about more pleasant matters – our trees. Trees have always been our friends: pine, spruce, alder, willow and juniper. Juniper grows high up and is a great helper when nothing else will catch fire. From Grandfather Pine's soft needles we brew tea in early spring and we chew his resin mixed with beeswax as medicine. We can even make bread from his bark.' He winked at Zusa and Arla, who hung on his every word.

'Ah, and Sister Birch with her lovely white bark . . . we make so many beautiful things from her: baskets and shoes, rattles and containers; the fine inner skin makes good paper and in spring she gives us sweet juice. There's no better kindling than birch bark and we weave her fine roots into containers for salt. Even the burls that grow like ugly boils on the trunk can be made into cups or even sacred drums . . .'

Drums . . . Ritva had not heard the elders nor anyone else in the *siida* mention drums, and after the first awkward conversation in her old *siida*, she had hidden the memory of her visions deep inside her heart. Nor had she asked Sara about them. Martta threw Ritva a glance.

'Could you tell us more about the drums, Aslak?' Martta said.

'Ah yes, the drums . . . People are afraid of the drums these days, but there's nothing to fear. The drum reminds us of many things: the sacred heart of the reindeer, a baby's heartbeat and its mother's, the earth's beating heart and our own. Many stories have been woven into the drums and if you listen carefully, they will reveal themselves. Drums are alive, they carry the heartbeat of the world back to us.' He paused and stared ahead as if he were listening to something.

'You see, the drum is like a mirror of our soul. When we beat it, we see deeper and clearer; we travel to those who would support and protect us and sometimes we can even hear the drum calling to us in our dreams.'

Ritva's skin prickled.

'How do you know so much about the drums?' Zusa asked.

'I come from a long line of *noaidi*, the shamans and healers of the village, but I don't talk about it much. Some people frown upon the drums and say that I worship the devil.'

'And . . . do you?' Arla stuttered.

'Of course not!' He smiled. 'I honour our ancestors and our old ways and yes, I don't believe that there is only one God; I believe God wears many skins: he might come to us in a storm, in the golden light of the midnight sun or in the skin of a bear.'

Ritva looked at Martta – a long, long time ago, on Seili, Martta had used almost the same words to tell Ritva about her own beliefs.

Ritva was as hungry for Aslak's wisdom as the children, and when she plucked up the courage to ask him, Aslak agreed to teach them more.

'The drum brings us power,' Aslak began another day when they were gathered in his tent, 'and if you set your mind on something it will support you. We can call upon the drum in times of need and it will bring healing and help. If we are lost, it can guide us – it can even be a compass to help us find the herd. But you must never abuse it, for it is alive and it can hear you.' Aslak pulled a small bundle from his tunic.

'We pray with the drum and give thanks. It opens our hearts and carries our spirit far and wide. Did you know that it can even sing? There are many songs hidden in the drum.'

He unwrapped the bundle – it was a bowl drum, not much bigger than the large palm of his hand.

'The *noaidi* of the North's drum is much smaller than the frame drum of the South. Most of the large drums have been burnt or taken to museums in the South. Those were terrible times. You see, the *noaidi* and the drum are one: you could say the drum is the *noaidi*'s heart and when the drums were taken away, the *noaidi*'s heart broke too. And yet, through all those terrible years the drums lived on in our hearts. Besides, some of our ancestors hid their drums in the mountains where they have remained until this day, watched over by women and men who know the secret places.'

Ritva's heart raced – the drum of her visions . . .

Aslak held the drum in his left hand and warmed it over the fire, then placed a small brass ring on it, similar to the one Martta had given Ritva.

'This is *arpa*, the ring that gives the answer as it travels across the drum. Will the hunt be successful? What weather is coming?'

Aslak started to beat the drum. As Ritva listened, everything around her dissolved and, as if lifted by giant wings, her spirit flew out of the smoke hole, the bird of her visions carrying her higher and higher into the sky. From up there she saw everything as if she were viewing it for the first time: the tundra with its lakes and rivers, the migration of the reindeer and the herders – how everything was connected and held in balance. She flew higher still and glimpsed more of the land, the Baltic, the northern lands, the whole continent and, as more of the world revealed itself, she understood: all of life was connected in one large woven web and she was a part of it, and so were Martta and the girls and Aslak and the *siida* and Elke . . .

Suddenly she found herself back in the *lavvu*. Aslak had stopped drumming and the brass ring lay resting on the sign of the sun.

There were no words; Ritva was empty and full at the same time. She took a deep breath and squeezed Martta's hand.

Ritva was keen to learn how to build a drum, but although Aslak was happy to share his tales, it was Martta he chose to teach. Ritva wondered whether she should share her visions with him, but decided in the end to trust his decision – maybe she was not a creator of new drums but someone who carried the memory of an ancient drum inside her. And it was this drum she still needed to find.

After the calf marking at the end of June, Martta stayed with

Aslak for a whole week while he taught her how to build a drum.

'We carve the drum from a birch burl and stretch reindeer hide over the open mouth,' he explained, 'then we fix it in place and decorate it.'

Used to carving, Martta's hands easily hollowed out the burl and she finished the base in two days. Aslak laid out different hides for Martta to choose from. Some were bleached by the sun and nearly white, others were a rich red-brown.

'I leave the hides to soak for two days with willow bark until they take this colour,' Aslak said. Martta pointed to a white mark stretched across the middle of the hide.

'What's this?'

'Ah, that's the backbone of the reindeer where the colour hasn't taken.'

Martta had found her drum hide; the back bone would run across her drum like the band of the Milky Way. She stretched the skin over the burl and Aslak showed her how to secure it with strips of moistened hide. It took another few days and great care to finish the drum and draw the delicate images on the hide and then it was time to wake the drum's spirit.

'Before you beat the drum, let your hand glide over it to wake it and hold it over the fire to catch the heat; the flames will help it grow firm and find the right sound. Then lift your drum to Father Sun and Mother Moon. Catch the wind in it and let it be blessed by the waters of a stream and the earth.' And Martta did.

Towards the end of the summer, maybe because of Aslak's teachings or the drum that Martta had brought home, Ritva's dreams of the drum returned and she woke each night with a hammering heart, the call of the drum in her ears. She shared her dreams with Martta.

'It must mean we're very close,' Martta said. 'We need to climb the sacred mountain before the first snow arrives.'

Had the time finally come to find the drum of her visions?

44

On a bright morning in late August, Ritva woke early. Maybe it was the smell of freshly brewed coffee or her dreams, but she was instantly awake, excitement rushing through her. This was the day they had decided to climb further up the sacred mountain than they ever had; maybe today they would be lucky . . .

Her eyes searched for Martta and the girls. Martta was stoking the fire underneath the blackened kettle, humming a *yoik*. Her wrinkled face cracked into a broad smile when their eyes met. To wake and see that Martta was there . . .

The girls were still asleep but Ritva's body tingled with anticipation. She got up and wrapped her sleeping blankets around her shoulders, then moved closer to the fire. Martta poured her a cup of coffee; Ritva took a sip and spluttered.

'God, I'm not dead yet, Martta – you could wake a corpse with this coffee!'

'Well, my dearest, we have a long day ahead of us,' Martta said, laughing.

Dearest. Warmth like the gentle morning sun spread through Ritva's body. Even after all these years . . . Then she remembered her dream.

'I saw it all in my dream, Martta. The mountain, the cleft in the rock where someone once hid the drum. It's up there, I know it. I think you can't see it when you walk up, only on the way down. As we climb up there today, we need to look back over our shoulders occasionally.' Ritva's heart fluttered. After all the visions she had had . . .

'We're very close,' Martta said, finishing Ritva's thought. 'Ritva, I've never dreamt about the drum before, I only recognised the description from your visions, but last night I saw the drum too. All the figures were dancing: reindeer, humans, a wolf, circling around the sun. The drumbeat was like the heartbeat of the earth and it grew louder and louder until I could feel it in my bones, as if it was waking long-forgotten memories.'

A deep look passed between them. Then Arla stirred; she opened her eyes and looked at Ritva.

'Ritva, I dreamt we were riding on a wolf up a mountain, all of us – you, Aunt Martta, Zusa and me, all on a huge grey wolf. He had lovely long fur and big yellow eyes, and we were singing and Aunt Martta hit a drum and the wolf was dancing and then a bird came . . .' She sounded out of breath. Then Zusa chipped in.

'I dreamt about a wolf too! He was gigantic but friendly. I just got on his back but then I woke up . . .'

Ritva smiled and looked at Martta, both remembering their former companion. Everything was falling into place.

'Sorry to disappoint you, girls, but we'll need to climb up the mountain using our own feet,' Martta said. 'As for the wolf, he's late. But you never know, he might catch up with us.' She winked and they all giggled.

Within half an hour they were on their way, Arla's hand firmly in Ritva's and Zusa walking next to Martta, who was leading the small group. Ritva smiled. They were an unusual family, but a beautiful one. They hummed without talking too much, Arla constantly looking out for the wolf and for the bird she had seen in her dream, Ritva gazing back every so often for a cleft in a rock. There were no trees this high up, only lichen, rough grass and some late berries.

'Please tell me a story!' Arla said after a while. And so, although her chest was heaving, Ritva reached deep inside for a story she had not yet told the child.

'Once there was a little boy who got lost in a deep forest on a late autumn day. When it was nearly dark, he stumbled over a big brown bear, who, when he stood on its hind legs, was four times the size of the boy. The bear growled and bared its teeth but instead of running away, the boy stayed calm and bowed before the great animal as his mother had once told him to do. The bear, a female, went back onto all fours, approached the boy, sniffed him up and down and then ever so gently put her paw on his shoulder and ushered him towards a burrow and down into a dark hole. The boy could not see a thing in the earthy cavern and so he used his hands, patting the ground around him. Soon he found a ball of the softest fur – which proceeded to lick his hand: it was a tiny bear cub. And so the boy became a sibling and playmate for the little cub for a whole long winter, tucked up in the burrow, the big mother bear suckling not only the cub but also the boy. The thick milk gave him everything he needed and more.'

Arla's eyes widened.

'The boy drank the milk from the bear?'

'Oh yes, dear, and the milk was very sweet. Like reindeer milk with lingonberry syrup.'

'And what did the milk give him?'

'All the strength in the world. And the boy learned to see in the dark and to dream up stories. In spring, when he said goodbye to the bear and the cub, his heart was heavy but also full of love. After only one day alone in the spring forest, he heard a familiar voice calling his name – his dear mother, who had never given up searching for him.'

'What was the boy's name?' Zusa asked.

'His mother called him Mano after the God of the moon. She found it difficult to believe the boy's story, but was happy that he could now see in the dark. Mano became a famous hunter and was well loved and respected by his people.'

'What a beautiful story, Ritva,' Martta said. She had stopped and pointed to a large triangular rock of grey granite speckled with bright orange lichen.

'Look.' A crack ran from top to bottom as if the rock had been struck by lightning.

'This is a sacred rock, I'm sure of it. Nature is always sacred, but we used to worship at places such as this, they were called *sieidis*: large, beautifully shaped rocks that could be seen from far away.' Martta gently patted the rock, then let her hand rest on it. The stone exuded a gentle warmth. 'It's a special rock, I can feel it. Maybe Beaivi, the great Goddess of the sun, was worshipped here.'

They all gathered at the rock and placed their hands near Martta's.

'Or is still worshipped here?' Ritva said and smiled.

'Shall we say a prayer to Beaivi to ask her to help us find the drum?' Zusa asked.

'Yes, let's.' Martta placed her hand gently on Zusa's hair. All four stood and lifted their faces towards the sun.

Arla saw it first, her voice shrill.

'The bird! It's the bird from my dream!'

High above them, an eagle circled over the mountaintop. A shiver ran down Ritva's back, but it was Arla who took the first step, letting her hand slip from the rock so she could run after the bird. All the tiredness vanished as her little five-year-old legs hurried up the mountain and everyone rushed after her. Ritva reckoned it would only take them another hour to reach the summit.

'Calm, calm . . .' An inner voice startled her. Everything was different up here: otherworldly and mysterious, and so much more ancient than a single human's life. Ritva's heart beat hard, blood rushing in her ears. Then she heard it again: a fine voice like she had always imagined the whisper of fairies to be.

'Look behind you.'

Ritva nearly stumbled as she turned, for there was a rock with a deep cleft, exactly like the one in her dream. They had passed it without noticing; only now, looking back, could she see a dark crack. Suddenly a sharp pain flashed through her.

'Stop, stop everyone!' She turned to call after Martta and the girls, but it was as if her vocal chords had been cut, and no sound escaped her lips. Ritva clasped her chest and hurried towards the rock. She could see the little group walking further up the mountain – they had not heard her, and yet she knew that in this moment everything was as it should be. As she grew calm, the pain lessened.

The crack went deep into the rock and as Ritva peered inside, she could see nothing but darkness. A cool draught touched her face, a musty smell. With her right hand she reached inside. The rock was cold and damp, slippery on the sides. What if something were hiding in there and bit her? She pulled her arm back, then breathed deeply until her fear vanished. She steadied herself with her left hand on the rock face and reached in deeper than before, the whole of her arm disappearing into the cleft.

Suddenly her fingers touched stone: a heap of small rocks had been carefully placed there. She grabbed the first stone and pulled. It dislodged easily and a few others tumbled out with it. Her heart hammered as she pulled out one rock after another. The stones had been put there to protect something from the elements, from animals and humans, but could it be . . .?

Suddenly her hand touched something hard and stiff as old leather. It was a small tied-up bundle. She gripped the object and pulled, trying not to lose her balance. The object tumbled into her lap, dislodged from the depths of the rock where it had lain hidden for so many years. She clutched it to her chest. The leather smelled as old as the beginning of the world. How long ago was it that someone had hidden this precious object here, hoping it would survive against the odds, see better times, a world without persecution or fear? A hundred years, two hundred, more?

Ritva sat on a small boulder and untied the brittle leather strips that held the bundle together. They fell apart in her hands like dry sticks. She glanced up the mountain but now she could see neither Martta nor the girls. She alone would be the first to see what lay inside the bundle. She unwrapped the first layer, thick reindeer hide that had lost most of its fur; then a second, a piece of dark blue fabric. As she unfolded the last layer, a thin fleece, she gasped – there it lay, smaller and heavier than she had anticipated: a drum, its base a wooden bowl, carved from a single piece of birch, with two holes for gripping and small marks scratched into the wood. The pale skin of a reindeer was stretched over it, decorated with tiny figures and symbols in a dark red colour. There was no doubt that what she held in her hands was an old *noaidi*'s drum. And not only that – these were the marks from her dreams and visions! The same markings she had seen the day she fainted at her parents' dinner table as a girl of six, then during dark nights in the asylum, and the journey north, and more recently . . .

Ritva sat for a long while holding the oval-shaped drum. She let her fingertips trace the figures on the drum's skin, as if she could reach into a long-distant time that way. Reindeer floated around the edge of the drum, a dancing wolf, people ascending a ladder . . . three lines painted as if to divide the drum into different realms. Suddenly a memory of three worlds that one could move between arose in her like a secret knowledge that had lain dormant in her blood: the lower world, the world of the ancestors, where deep healing occurred; the upper world, reached by a magic ladder, the realm of the spirits and the gods; and a middle world, where people and animals mingled easily with spirits and gods. Ritva shivered. What had happened to the drum's owner? Had he been punished or even burnt at the stake? Had he survived but with a broken heart? She stroked the drum's skin gently as if it were the cheek of a child. Ritva knew the drum was not yet complete. Her heart raced as she thought of Martta's drum hammer and the brass ring.

Suddenly someone called her name. She looked up – Martta and the girls stood further up the mountain beckoning for her to join them. An urge to be with her loved ones and reach the summit rushed through her. To be close to the sky with those she cherished most, to hold the drum up to the sun . . . She jumped up and waved back, then wrapped the drum in its layers and clambered up the hill, clutching the precious object close to her heart. The two girls ran to meet her. Zusa threw her arms around her and squeezed her hard.

'Where have you been? We've been looking for you every-where.' Zusa was out of breath and flustered; Arla arrived behind her, coughing.

'But I've only been gone a few minutes.'

'No, you haven't.' Zusa shot her a cross look and folded her arms across her chest.

'We looked for you for hours. Where were you hiding?'

Ritva looked from Zusa to Arla, then at Martta, who had now joined them.

'No, I wasn't hiding, sweetheart. I . . . how long have I been gone?'

Martta's eyes met Ritva's.

'Long enough . . .' Martta said. 'What's in that bundle?'

'I . . . I found . . .' Suddenly Ritva's chest heaved and her eyes filled with tears. 'Martta, I found the drum!'

'You found the drum?' Martta breathed in sharply. 'Where?'

'A cleft in the rock, just like my dream.'

Ritva sat down to tell them all about her search and what she had found; Arla climbed into her lap, while Zusa and Martta perched close by.

'Show us the drum, Ritva.' Arla's tiny fingers pulled at the bundle.

'Why don't we hike up to the summit, it can't be very far,' Ritva suggested. No one objected and they climbed onwards until they reached a small plateau that overlooked the vast tundra. Ritva's hand found Martta's – there were no words, only wonder and joy.

They put their knapsacks and walking sticks on the ground and gathered around Ritva. She held the bundle in front of her, then removed layer after layer until the drum was revealed in her hands.

'There's animals on it,' Arla shrieked, her tiny finger flitting from one figure to another. 'Reindeer . . . and a man. He's climbing a ladder.'

At that moment the sun broke through the clouds, enveloping everything in its brilliant light. Martta reached into her dress, pulled out the drum hammer and placed it on her open palm.

'Drum and hammer are beautiful on their own, but only when they are together does the drum come to life and share its magic . . .'

Ritva handed the drum to Martta.

'I think you should play it. Your Sami line is unbroken and you have carried the drum hammer for a long time.'

'Thank you.' Martta's voice was hoarse. She gently took the drum from Ritva and slipped her thumb and index finger into the two holes at the bottom of the drum – they fit perfectly. She held the hammer in her right hand and stood up, then walked into the middle of the plateau. Ritva and the girls followed. So many *noaidi* had been mistreated or killed because of a drum such as this – or rather because of the Christian men's hatred for its wisdom and power. The drum weighed so little, yet Martta sensed the weight of her ancestors' suffering pressing on her heart. She took a deep breath, lifted the drum towards the sun and held it there, silently calling to Beaivi, the Goddess of the sun, to lend her power. She pulled the drum close to her chest and started to beat it with the little hammer. The moment the first beat hit the skin, sounds from deep within her flew from her mouth like a flock of birds. And Ritva joined her as if it were the most natural thing, song after song, released from hearts and throats . . . Their bodies moved and swayed, stirred by the beat of the drum, the drum singing through them, ancient *yoiks*, the forbidden songs, soaring wild and proud as if they had never been lost.

Martta's skin prickled and she sensed circle after circle of ancestors gathering around them, drawn in from all directions by the drum, as if in this moment the mountain summit was the very centre of the world.

And suddenly in Ritva's heart the suffering souls of Seili stirred, as if they too had been summoned by the beat of the drum: her mother, Irina and all those who had died on the island, the lepers, the ones declared mad and all those who would never stand on such a mountain in freedom. Tears streamed down Ritva's face as her lips formed a silent prayer: *May no soul still wander lost in that wretched place* . . . She threw back her head and like an answer, a song rose in her, first the words, and then a melody:

Lift your face towards the sun,
lift your bones towards the sun;
lift your souls towards the sun;
you are warm, you are free,
you are warm, you are free

Ritva lost all sense of time as she repeated the words to Martta's drumbeat, praying for each soul that had perished on Seili to follow the invitation, to lift themselves up towards the sun and be received into its eternal embrace.

Suddenly, without a sound, Arla's little body collapsed onto the grass. Zusa shrieked and kneeled down next to her sister, shaking her, but Martta continued to beat the drum. Ritva, startled by Zusa's shriek, saw Arla sprawled on the ground. Her first impulse was to scoop her up and try to wake her, but then she remembered how she herself had fainted at her father's table – her first fever dream, her first vision. This was a sacred time and place and Arla did not need to be pulled from her trance, only protected and held. Maybe it was a sign that it would be Arla who was destined to carry the drum forward one day . . .

Martta finished drumming a short while later. She wrapped the drum up again and hid it beneath her tunic. When she came round, Arla was pale but she smiled.

'I was riding on the wolf! He was so big and furry and then the bird talked to me. I can't remember what he said, but he looked at me and then it was as if I was the bird . . . it was so strange.'

A few moments later Arla fell asleep. Ritva bundled her up and carried her all the way back down the mountain while Zusa held Martta's hand. They had no words but walked easy in the silence. Everyone had been changed by this day on the mountain and by the song of the drum.

EPILOGUE

Laila reached the mountaintop, panting and sweating. From the plateau she could see right across the wide expanse of the tundra – what better place to honour her ancestors and the sacred drum? She remembered her Grandmother Arla's story of the day she had had her first vision here, as a young girl, right on this mountain where Ritva had found the drum. Laila looked around; maybe it had been right on this very spot?

Many of Arla's and old Ritva's visions and premonitions had come true over the years: Ritva had seen the dark cloud of Chernobyl over Sápmi, the slaughter of thousands of reindeer, but also the dawn of a new pride amongst the Sami, as precious and delicate as spring shoots: the birth of the Sami flag, a hymn and the first Sami parliament . . .

Laila took the drum from her bag, unwrapped it and stroked the delicate drawings on the skin. Then she began to beat the drum with the little hammer – quiet and slow at first, then faster and faster. As her spirit lifted and she travelled with the beat of the drum she saw old Ritva's journey as clearly as if she'd been there; Ritva had walked across the northern lands as though she was stepping on a giant drum, each footstep a beat, tracing a large oval across the land.

Goosebumps rose on Laila's arms as she understood with sudden clarity: the drum had always been a map of her ancestors' lives and had guided them all: Ritva, Martta and then Arla, her grandmother. She opened her eyes and held the drum close to her heart. So many of the sacred drums had been left to rot in the museums and archives of the South, like forgotten prisoners; if only they could be released and returned to Sápmi so that they could breathe once more and share their power with their people!

For weeks, Laila had tossed and turned at night, trying to solve the riddle of her future. Could she still be a herder and yet also become a journalist? Rivers had been dammed, mountains drilled into, forests cut down and the sacred *sieidi* places ransacked – and still the herders' bond with their reindeer was unbroken. Her own heart also still lived with the reindeer, but the old ways were threatened by logging and mining, by laws made far away in the South and further still, in the courts of Europe.

'I can't help you, dear,' her grandmother had said, 'you must decide for yourself. I could not live away from the reindeer for long – wherever I go, I carry the tundra and the snow-covered mountains inside me. The sparkling rivers flow through my veins and when I breathe, it's the wind of the pine forests that rushes through my lungs. The grunting of the reindeer cows lives in my ears and when the herd gallops around the corral, pounding the earth with their broad hooves, my heart sings.' Laila ached as she recalled her grandmother's words. Was it possible to be a herder and to write, to beat the drum, mark the calves and still fight with words? And suddenly she understood: she was the drum's guardian now and she would protect it with all her might. And maybe it was not only possible but necessary to firmly hold both the old and the new ways in her hands.

At that moment a hawk's cry pierced the sky above her. As she looked up, the bird drew large circles over the plateau. It was time to go. She wrapped up the drum, placed it under her coat and started her descent from the mountain.

Glossary

duodji: Skilful Sami craftsmanship developed over centuries.

giettka: A Sami cradle.

koftas: Sami tunics.

kota: Sami turf-covered hut, also known as *goathi, goahte, kata, kåhte* and *kåta*.

Laestaedian: Laestaedius was a half-Sami Christian priest who translated the bible into the Sami language, fought alcoholism amongst the Sami and preached a strict puritanical Christian way. Many Sami today still follow the Laestaedian faith.

Lapps: A derogative term – the Sami have been called Lapps or Lapplanders, which comes from 'Lappen', a rag.

lavvu: A traditional Sami tent, made like a tepee from poles and tent cloth with a smoke hole.

lulohti: A personal *yoik* given to a newborn (North Sami).

luovvi: A Sami storehouse built from wood and elevated from the ground.

noaidi: Sami shaman – many shamans were persecuted, forced to renounce their faith and hand over their drums. The *noaidi* would use the drum for divination, healing and orientation.

Sami: The indigenous people of Sápmi.

Sápmi: The land of the Sami, spanning across the northern part of Norway, Sweden, Finland and the Kola Island of Russia. Also known as Lapland.

sieidi: Holy places that have unusual land forms which are different from the surrounding countryside. Sami shamanism considers these places to be spiritual 'focal points' and worships them as gateways to the spirit world. At these *sieidis*, sacrifices were made, of animals and objects.

siida: Sami kinship-based community. Each *siida* made seasonal movements along established trails from winter villages to spring, summer and autumn camps.

suoidni: Long grass that is dried and braided and used inside shoes.

yoik: Traditional Sami chant or song. *Yoiking* was forbidden by the church for many years.

Author's Note

It was in 1991 that I heard the music of Mari Boine for the first time. Her singing and drumming were like nothing I had ever heard before and they moved me deeply. I remember listening to her powerful voice, tears running down my face, a longing cracking open in my heart for the place where such music came from. That place, I learned, was Sápmi – more commonly known as Lapland, it is the land of the Sami, the indigenous people of Northern Europe.

Mari Boine is a North Sami from the Norwegian part of Sápmi; and through her album *Gula Gula* (*Hear Hear*), which includes the traditional Sami *yoiks* of her ancestors and songs inspired by her heritage, the Sami culture and fight for survival became known to a larger audience, perhaps for the first time.

Sápmi stretches across four countries – Norway, Sweden, Finland and the Kola Peninsula of Russia – but the Sami have lived in this area since prehistoric times, long before any such borders existed. Currently the total Sami population is estimated to be around 80,000 people, with approximately 20,000 living in Sweden, 50,000 in Norway, 9,000 in Finland and 2,000 in Russia. Also, some 30,000 people of Sami ancestry live in North America (Báiki, 2006). Most of these are the descendants of Sami people – Norwegians, Swedes and Finns – who emigrated to the United States and Canada, but some are the descendants of Sami herders and Yup'ik (a group of central Alaskan indigenous people).

The Sami language is divided into three groups: Eastern Sami,

Central Sami and Southern Sami. These groups may be further divided into nine variants, including North Sami and Lule Sami. Aggressive assimilation policies have resulted in Sami languages being oppressed and even forbidden for long periods of time. But while some of the languages are critically endangered and have very few speakers left, others have survived and are taught and spoken still.

Elected bodies of people of Sami heritage have existed since 1972. The Sami Parliament of Finland was established in 1972, followed by the Sami Parliament of Norway in 1989 and finally, by the Sami Parliament of Sweden in May 1993. The Sami have had a common Sami flag since 1986. The Sami parliaments give counsel on Sami issues, but they are subordinated to the parliaments of each country – and too often their advice and demands have not been taken into account by law- and policymakers.

The Sami have suffered centuries of discrimination and oppression, particularly regarding their religion, spirituality, language and land rights, yet the plight of the Sami people is not well known, even amongst the populations of Sweden, Norway, Finland and Russia.

The survival of the Sami depends on the protection of their lands, their sacred places and their culture, but the threats are numerous and pervasive. These include oil exploration, mining, logging, the construction of hydropower dams and large windmill projects, military bombing ranges, opencast mines, waste dumping, tourism and commercial development. Some threats are new, while others have existed for decades. The 1986 Chernobyl disaster caused nuclear fallout in the sensitive Arctic ecosystems: fish, berries and meat were poisoned, and Sami herders were forced to slaughter thousands of their reindeer (in Sweden alone 73,000 reindeer had to be killed). Land rights are also an issue. Finland has historically denied land rights to the Sami people, with ninety per cent of Finnish Sami land officially belonging to the government still.

It is estimated that as much as forty per cent of Sami make a living based on the traditional and sustainable use of their territory, including reindeer herding, fishing, hunting, small-scale agriculture and the use of natural products to make handicrafts. Only about ten per cent still practise reindeer herding as a primary occupation, but the land-based way of life still dominates and guides Sami culture (www.sacredland.org).

And it is this way of life that is threatened, as Aslak Eira, a reindeer herder in the mountains close to Tromsø in Norway, explained in a *Guardian* article of 21 February 2016: 'The problem is land grabbing. Government expropriates land for roads and tunnels, wind farms and mines. Our land is being eroded by development. Almost half of our winter lands have gone. I fear that in future there will be nowhere left for the reindeer.'

Mining and blasting for iron ore threaten the Sami's traditional way of life, especially near the town of Jokkmokk on the Arctic Circle, which traditionally has been heartland for Sami reindeer herding. Jakob Nygerd, a Sami herder, spoke about the Kallak mining conflict in a BBC *News* interview on 30 July 2014: 'If you throw a knife in the heart it is only a small cut, but the result is death . . . We take many things from the reindeer into our culture so I think if reindeer herding dies then our culture also dies.' Jenny Wik Karlsson, head lawyer for the Swedish Sami Association, believes that plans should be abandoned for the Kallak mines: 'I would ask them to think – can the world afford to lose another unique culture?'

And this year, in April 2016, a new Forestry Law has been passed in Finland with devastating consequences for the Sami. Before the vote, the president of the Finnish section of the Sami council, Jouni Lukkari, called for urgent help from the international community: 'Sami reindeer herding and the Sami way of life are in danger of disappearing if the new Forestry Act legislation passes in the Finnish Parliament. In this case we will have few opportunities to influence the decision-making over our lands. Rather, our territories will be controlled by market economy values.'

Sami elder and cultural guide from Swedish Sápmi, Laila Spik, who I was privileged to visit and learn from, echoes this: 'We must fight for Sami rights, for the land, we must fight for the animals and also let the people know about our history and our language.'

The Sami face an uncertain future, but I believe that the Sami people – with their knowledge and wisdom about the interconnectedness of nature and the interdependency of all living beings – can teach us invaluable lessons about sustainability and how to respect natural resources and walk lightly on the land. As individuals and as international communities, we need these lessons – more now than ever before.

When I spoke again with Laila Spik before the publication of *The Eye of the Reindeer* she said: 'My hope is that this novel will make people want to know more about the Sami people. The book can be a way to open the door to the North and us Sami people. We are the people who live under the stars and the Arctic light and we have lots of stories that the world has not heard. People can visit the land and the people, they can read further and find a thread they can follow and find something that interests them. The life we have could give them knowledge about nature and how we take care of nature.'

It is my sincere hope that the Sami culture will not only survive but that it will receive the recognition and protection necessary to thrive. And may the sacred drums come home to their people.

Eva Weaver, August 2016

Acknowledgements

This book has been supported by many beautiful souls. Like *The Puppet Boy of Warsaw*, the kernel for *The Eye of the Reindeer* emerged amongst a group of artist friends and writers at the BLANK studios and gallery in Brighton in 2008. Thank you especially to Rosy Martin for telling us about the island of Seili and its grim past, one of the first inspirations for writing this book.

A big thank you to everyone who opened their doors and hearts to me on my first research trip to Turku and Seili in April 2013: Jaana Kouri and her partner Teemu for their great hospitality, welcoming me back after three nights on Seili island; Jutta Ahlbeck PhD, for entrusting me with parts of her research about the women of Seili; Anne Willenius from the National Archives in Turku; and the research staff on the island of Seili, especially Ilppo Vuorinen, who showed me around and answered many questions.

I am extremely grateful to the Sami people I have met, especially Sami elder Laila Spik and her family, who so generously shared knowledge, wisdom and stories from their ancestry and about the Sami way of living, and who invited me to spend time at Saltoluokta, and later to witness the calf marking, an experience that touched me deeply and that I will never forget.

Thank you also to Lilja Takalo, who taught me how to build a Southern Sami drum and shared some beautiful stories with me, and to Mirja Paassovaara who tirelessly translated.

Gratitude to Matti and Kerstin, who not only took me on a fantastic horse-riding trip across the tundra in Swedish Sápmi, but also taught me more about the Sami ways and the herders today; and to Carl Eric Malström and his wife, who so generously opened their house to me during a research trip in May 2014, and who never tired of my questions.

Warmest thanks to my agents Charlotte Robertson and Natasha Fairweather, who encouraged me through the rewrites, and to Clare Alexander and Sally Riley from the Aitken Alexander Agency.

Thank you to my coach and mentor, Eric Maisel, who kept me going through all the challenges with calm and clear guidance; and to the publishing team at Orion, especially my publisher Kirsty Dunseath for her keen eye and thorough edit, and for believing in this book.

I feel privileged to have met so many amazing people during my years of working as an art therapist in mental health services – including patients and staff, especially B.M. and many other brave women in medium secure services who, through their survival and healing journeys, taught me so much about the depth and fierceness of the human heart and spirit.

I am deeply grateful to my dear friends and writing buddies from all over the globe, and particularly to my trusted first readers, Sophie Fletcher, Eva Coleman, Zara Waldebeck and Betsy Witherup, for their invaluable feedback on the first draft; and to Jo Coleman, Jude Wheeley and April Boshard for their most helpful comments on the manuscript during the later stages; and to Jenix Sessions for mulling over some questions.

Thank you to all my friends, especially Dee Leyden, Emmanuelle Waeckerle, Eve Shepherd and Johanna Berger and Mags Mackean for your encouragement; to my writing buddy Mark Rowden for mutual support and many shared writing hours at the Whitecliffs café; to my teacher and mentor Barbara Carrellas, who helped me to hone my intentions and keep perspective on the novel; and particularly to my life partner Maz Michael for sharing the big adventure that life is with me.

Love, trust and ongoing encouragement from all of these fine people helped me to keep believing in myself and the novel – I could not have written *The Eye of the Reindeer* without you.

I am forever grateful to have been given the opportunity to connect with the Sami people and their beautiful homeland, Sápmi. The Sami's dedication to uphold, nourish and adapt their ancient traditions despite today's immense challenges and adversities has deeply touched me. A piece of my heart will always be with the reindeer and their people.

Further Reading

Hans Christian Andersen; Erik Christian Haugaard (trans.), *The Complete Fairy Tales and Stories*: London, Gollancz Children's, 1994.

Emilie Demant Hatt, Barbara Sjoholm (trans.), *With the Lapps in the High Mountains: A Woman among the Sami, 1907–1908*: Madison, University of Wisconsin Press, 2013.

Andrew Eddy, *Revontuli*: Seattle, Booktrope Editions, 2013.

Harald Gaski (ed.), *In the Shadow of the Midnight Sun: Contemporary Sami Prose and Poetry*: Karasjok, Davvi Girji, 1996.

Ulla-Maija Kulonen; Irja Seurujärvi-Kari; Risto Pulkkinen (eds.), *The Saami: A Cultural Encyclopaedia*: Helsinki, Suomalaisen Kirjallisuuden Seura, 2005.

Sunna Kuoljok; John-Erling Utsi; Thomas Rutschman (trans.), *The Saami: People of the Sun and Wind*: Jokkmokk, Svenskt fjäll-och Samemuseum, 1993.

Karin Kvarfordt et al.; Robert Crofts (trans.), *The Sami – An Indigenous People in Sweden*: Kiruna, Sami Parliament, 2005.

L. L. Laestadius; Juha Pentikäinen; K. Börje Vähämäki, *Fragments of Lappish Mythology*: Beaverton, Aspasia Books, 2002.

Veli-Pekka Lehtola, *The Sámi People: Traditions in Transition*: Fairbanks, University of Alaska Press, 2004.

Barbara Sjoholm, *The Palace of the Snow Queen: Winter Travels in Lapland*: Emeryville, Shoemaker & Hoard, 2007.

Nils-Aslak Valkeapää, *Greetings from Lappland: The Sami – Europe's Forgotten People*: London, Zed Press, 1983.

Nils-Aslak Valkeapää, *The Sun, My Father*: Seattle, University of Washington Press, 1997.

Nils-Aslak Valkeapää, *Trekways of the Wind*: Kautokeino, DAT, 1985.

The story of Sealskin/Soulskin is adapted from Clarissa Pinkola Estés's story with the same title from *Women Who Run with Wolves* (New York, Ballantine Books, 1992).

'They are destroying the strength of our souls and bodies here at the end of the world.' (From a letter written by one of the patients incarcerated on Seili, translated by Jutta Ahlbeck PhD).

www.samer.se
Information portal of the Swedish National Sami Information Centre.

www.sametinget.se
Swedish Sami Parliament website: Information about current Sami issues and politics; links to the Sami Parliaments in Norway and Finland, Sami organisations in Sápmi and relevant international organisations.

www.un.org/development/desa/indigenouspeoples
Website of the UN Permanent Forum on Indigenous Issues.

www.laits.utexas.edu/sami/dieda/hist/early.htm
University of Texas extensive history of the Sami.

www.lailaspik.vingar.se
Sami elder Laila Spik's website.